LANDFALL

THOMAS MALLON

LANDFALL

Pantheon Books, New York

Copyright © 2019 by Thomas Mallon

Chart on page 356 courtesy of William Inboden, Clements Center for National Security, The University of Texas at Austin

All rights reserved. Published in the United States by Pantheon Books, a division of Penguin Random House LLC, New York, and distributed in Canada by Random House of Canada, a division of Penguin Random House Canada Limited, Toronto.

Pantheon Books and colophon are registered trademarks of Penguin Random House LLC.

Library of Congress Cataloging-in-Publication Data
Names: Mallon, Thomas, [date] author.
Title: Landfall / Thomas Mallon.
Description: First edition. New York : Pantheon Books, 2019.
Identifiers: LCCN 2018018277. ISBN 9781101871058
(hardcover : alk. paper). ISBN 9781101871065 (ebook).
Subjects: LCSH: Bush, George W. (George Walker), 1946–
—Fiction. Presidents—United States—Fiction. United States—
Politics and government—2001–2009—Fiction. Political fiction.
GSAFD: Historical fiction
Classification: LCC PS3563.A43157 L36 2019 | DDC 813/.54--dc23 |
LC record available at lccn.loc.gov/2018018277

www.pantheonbooks.com

Jacket photograph by Mandel Ngan/AFP/Getty Images
Jacket design by Jenny Carrow

Printed in the United States of America
First Edition
2 4 6 8 9 7 5 3 1

For
John McConnell

. . . war appears
Waged in the troubled sky, and armies rush
To battle in the clouds . . .

—*Paradise Lost*, Book 2

CAST OF CHARACTERS

(Persons with names in quotation marks are entirely fictional.)

Buzz Aldrin: American astronaut; landed on the moon with *Apollo 11*

Mohammed Yusef Asefi: Afghan physician and painter

"Kevin Barden": U.S. embassy staffer in Baghdad

Cherie Blair: prominent barrister; wife of the British prime minister

Tony Blair: prime minister of the United Kingdom

Kathleen Blanco: governor of Louisiana

Lindy Boggs: former member of the House of Representatives (D-LA) and former ambassador to the Holy See

Josh Bolten: director of Office of Management and Budget; White House chief of staff (April 2006–January 2009)

John Bolton: U.S. ambassador to the United Nations

"Emile Bourreau": assistant concierge at the Hotel Monteleone, New Orleans

Stephen Breyer: associate justice of the U.S. Supreme Court

"Bill Bright": builder and political operative from Slaton, Texas

Tom Brokaw: author and former network anchorman

Sherrod Brown: Democratic senator-elect from Ohio

Barbara Bush: former First Lady of the United States

George H. W. Bush: forty-first president of the United States

George W. Bush: forty-third president of the United States

Laura Bush: First Lady of the United States

Neil M. Bush: younger brother of the president of the United States

"Mrs. Randolph Caine": New Orleans realtor and preservationist

Steve Cambone: undersecretary of defense for intelligence

Camilla, Duchess of Cornwall: wife of the Prince of Wales

Andrew Card: White House chief of staff (January 2001–April 2006)

James Carville: Democratic political consultant and commentator

"The Chairman": head of the "National Endowment for the Arts and Humanities"

Charles, Prince of Wales: heir to the British throne

Dick Cheney: vice president of the United States

Liz Cheney: daughter of the vice president; principal deputy assistant secretary of state for Near Eastern Affairs

Lynne Cheney: wife of the vice president

Jacques Chirac: president of France

Bill Clinton: forty-second president of the United States

Hillary Rodham Clinton: Democratic senator from New York; former First Lady of the United States

Stephen Colbert: comedian; host of *The Colbert Report*

Howard Dean: former governor of Vermont; chairman of the Democratic National Committee

Tom DeLay: member of the House of Representatives (R-TX) and majority leader

John Dingell: member of the House of Representatives (D-MI)

Christopher Dodd: Democratic senator from Connecticut

Bob Dole: former Republican senator from Kansas and defeated presidential candidate

Elizabeth Dole: Republican senator from North Carolina; wife of Bob Dole

David Herbert Donald: retired Harvard professor and Lincoln biographer

Matt Drudge: Internet news aggregator; editor of the *Drudge Report*

John Edwards: former Democratic senator from North Carolina and defeated vice-presidential nominee

Betty Ford: former First Lady of the United States

"Gary Fowler": community activist in Holy Cross neighborhood of New Orleans

Bill Frist: U.S. senator from Tennessee; Republican majority leader

Michael Gerson: chief speechwriter to the president

Gabrielle Giffords: U.S. representative-elect (D-AZ)

"Tim Gleeson": Australian contract security officer in Baghdad

Jim Granberry: mayor of Lubbock, Texas (1970–1972)

Merv Griffin: television host and show-business entrepreneur

Stephen J. Hadley: national security advisor

Joe Hagin: deputy White House chief of staff

Kent Hance: member of the House of Representatives (D-TX), 1979–1985

"Fadhil Hasani": interpreter for Allison O'Connor in Baghdad

"Pirnaz Hasani": infant daughter of Fadhil and Rukia Hasani

"Rukia Hasani": wife and widow of Fadhil Hasani

Dennis Hastert: Republican speaker of the House of Representatives

Mary Hatfield: Democratic party activist Lubbock, Texas

Carol Blue Hitchens: journalist; wife of Christopher Hitchens

Christopher Hitchens: journalist

Karen Hughes: former counselor to the president; undersecretary of state for public diplomacy and public affairs

Rielle Hunter: videographer and mistress of former senator John Edwards

John Irving: American novelist

Bobby Jindal: member of the House of Representatives (R-LA), 2005–2008

Frederick W. Kagan: resident scholar, American Enterprise Institute

Hamid Karzai: president of Afghanistan

Brett Kavanaugh: White House staff secretary

Karen Keller: personal secretary to the president

John Kerry: Democratic senator from Massachusetts; defeated 2004 candidate for president

Zalmay Khalilzad: U.S. ambassador to Afghanistan (November 2003–June 2005) and U.S. ambassador to Iraq (June 2005–March 2007)

Larry King: host of CNN's *Larry King Live*

Michael Kinsley: journalist and editor

Henry Kissinger: former secretary of state

Junichiro Koizumi: prime minister of Japan

"Matthew Lang": archivist, George W. Bush Presidential Library and Museum

Trent Lott: Republican senator from Mississippi

John McCain: Republican senator from Arizona

Scott McClellan: White House press secretary (July 2003–May 2006)

Sean McCormack: assistant secretary of state for public affairs

Peter MacKay: Canadian foreign minister

"Anne Macmurray": babysitter and nanny for Holley Weatherall O'Connor

Mary Matalin: book editor; advisor to Vice President Cheney

Harriet Miers: White House legal counsel

"Charles Montoya": Army private wounded in Iraq

"Lucinda Montoya": Private Montoya's aunt and caregiver

"Father Anthony Montrose": New Orleans parish priest

"Mrs. Morris": U.S. embassy staffer in Kabul, Afghanistan

Ray Nagin: mayor of New Orleans

Gordon Novel: New Orleans resident with ties to assassination conspiracy theories

"Allison O'Connor": staff member of the National Security Council

"Holley Weatherall O'Connor": daughter of Ross Weatherall and Allison O'Connor

"Patricia O'Connor": mother of Allison O'Connor

Sandra Day O'Connor: associate justice of the U.S. Supreme Court

Peter Pace: chairman of the Joint Chiefs of Staff

Dina Powell: deputy undersecretary of state for public diplomacy and public affairs

Vladimir Putin: president of Russia

Lyudmila Putina: wife of Vladimir Putin

Nancy Reagan: former First Lady; widow of President Ronald Reagan

William Rehnquist: sixteenth chief justice of the United States

Condoleezza Rice: U.S. secretary of state

Ann Richards: former governor of Texas

John Roberts: seventeenth chief justice of the United States

Karl Rove: White House deputy chief of staff for policy

Donald Rumsfeld: U.S. secretary of defense

Salman Rushdie: Indian novelist

Terri Schiavo: (1963–2005), central figure in protracted right-to-die legal battle

"Rolf Schmidt": German constitutional lawyer working in Baghdad's Green Zone

Brent Scowcroft: national security advisor to President George H. W. Bush

Cindy Sheehan: war protester; mother of soldier killed in Iraq

Mina Sherzoy: founder of the Afghan Women's Business Federation

Tony Snow: White House press secretary (May 2006–September 2007)

Jack Straw: British MP and foreign secretary (June 2001–May 2006)

Andrew Sullivan: political journalist and blogger

Margaret Thatcher: former prime minister of the United Kingdom

Greta Van Susteren: television journalist, Fox News; host of *On the Record*

Donatella Versace: Italian fashion designer

Michael G. Vickers: analyst, Center for Strategic and Budgetary Assessments

John Warner: Republican senator from Virginia

Gene Washington: former professional football player for the San Francisco 49ers

"Carlotta Watson": resident of New Orleans' Holy Cross neighborhood

"Archer Weatherall": son of Ross Weatherall

"Caitlyn Weatherall": daughter of Ross Weatherall

"Darryl Weatherall": attorney in Lubbock, Texas; brother of Ross Weatherall

"Deborah Weatherall": university librarian; wife of Ross Weatherall

"Donna Weatherall": mother of Ross Weatherall

"Ross Weatherall": director, Homeland Heritage Division, National Endowment of the Arts and Humanities

Allen Weinstein: archivist of the United States

Jim Wilkinson: senior advisor to Secretary of State Condoleezza Rice

Tom Wolfe: American novelist and essayist

Paul Wolfowitz: deputy secretary of defense and president of the World Bank

WEST TEXAS, FALL 1978

Monday, September 18

There ain't nothin' 'tween Lubbock and the North Pole 'cept a barbed-wire fence, and it's blowed down.

Pedaling up Nineteenth Street, sixteen-year-old Ross Weatherall recalled the many times he'd heard this stark declaration from his grandfather, who'd given up farming during the Dust Bowl and moved into town to start a hardware store. Grandpa had prospered in Lubbock, though the winds that drove him off the land sometimes even now roared through this city on the South Plains. Ross had seen the scratched windowpanes of the house Grandpa built in the thirties, the tiny striations made by grains of dirt whirled against the glass.

The wind was kicking up now, and there was no collar to turn up on the shirt Ross had recently purchased at Buster Hanks' Men's Store, imagining it to be both fashionable and sort of British-looking. The heat was concerning him even more than the wind: it was 8:15 p.m. and still 88 degrees according to the Texas Bank sign he'd passed a few minutes ago. At one point this afternoon it had hit 96, and all day Ross had been sweating through the shirt, whose checkered pattern, he now realized, didn't live up to its supposedly daring lack of a collar.

He headed west along the southern rim of ever-expanding Texas Tech University, whose new buildings seemed to have sprouted into existence via time-lapse photography or some other sci-fi miracle. *We are not alone*: Ross hummed the signature notes of the theme from *Close Encounters of the Third Kind*, a movie that still seemed to him superior in every way to last year's *Star Wars*.

Across Nineteenth Street sat the city's best and biggest homes, even nicer than the house he lived in on Twenty-first. One of them, a mile or two up, was his destination. Wanting to make sure he had the right address, he switched to no-hands, a risky mode given the wind, and reached into the pocket of his blue jeans for the newspaper ad:

BUSH
BASH
8:00 p.m.
4907 19TH
Free Beer—Music

In smaller type at the bottom, it read:

Pd. Pol. Adv. George Bush
for Congress Committee
Joe I. O'Neill, Treas.

Ross had torn the announcement from today's *University Daily*, which his brother, a politically minded pre-law senior at Tech, had previously circled. Darryl lived in a campus dorm and this afternoon had left the paper behind when making a pit stop at the house to drop off laundry with their mother. Tonight, after finishing his usual early dinner and what little homework he had from Lubbock High, Ross had noticed the ad and thought: Why shouldn't I go? The beer didn't interest him, but music of almost any kind did—not to mention the chance of some company. Everyone was out of the house tonight, as they were on most nights: Darryl at school; their father, an orthopedic surgeon, back at the hospital; their mother off to listen to some unfamous author give a lecture at the Lubbock Women's Club. Ross imagined there'd be a big crowd at a political event like this "Bush Bash," so even if Darryl showed up—unlikely, since he was always doing twenty things at once—he might still escape his big brother's notice.

He knew he'd reached number 4907, a big ranch house with a humongous green lawn and half-moon driveway, by the number of cars parked outside. Music was coming from somewhere on the premises. Ross tucked his bike, more from embarrassment than any concern with its security, between two azaleas on the lawn. The front door stood wide open, and he could see straight through the big house, all the way to the kitchen door, which was open too. Everybody, as well as the music, was out back by the pool.

He walked inside, feeling like a burglar, and noticed a framed GRANBERRY FOR LUBBOCK poster, a souvenir of the spring 1970 election that had made young Jim Granberry mayor just before the tornadoes came through. Since there was no basement in the Weatherall house on Twenty-first, Ross, then about to turn eight, had had to ride out the twisters in the first-floor bathtub with his older brother, while their parents hunkered down in the bathroom upstairs. Ross had brought a book into the tub with him, which Darryl, before flinging it out into the hall, thought was just about the funniest, dumbest thing he'd ever seen.

Now reaching the empty kitchen, Ross could identify the music coming from the pool patio as "Crazy Little Mama at My Front Door," a record by Alvin Crow and the Pleasant Valley Boys, local favorites. Ross thought he might see the former mayor out on the patio, maybe even shake his hand, but Jim Granberry wasn't to be found in the little crowd of maybe twenty people. There was, fortunately, no sign of Darryl, either. TILT ME, I'M EASY read a label fixed to one of two beer kegs.

"Hey, kid, allow me," said a guy who identified himself as "Bill, from Slaton." He poured Ross a large cup of beer with very little foam. Ross would have been satisfied with a Dr Pepper, but the guy seemed so eager for him to have the beer that he accepted it. It was hard to believe that just down the street at Tech the biggest ongoing debate involved whether to allow the sale of alcohol on campus. Darryl was emphatically "pro" on this question, though on another current matter he took the conservative view that a student-drama production of *Equus*, featuring nudity, should not be allowed to proceed. That topic had dominated one recent dinner conversation in the

Weatherall home; Ross himself had taken no position on the naked-ness, because he could scarcely make himself think about a play that featured some crazy kid putting out horses' eyes.

A single big BUSH sign, the "S" shaped in a way that suggested a pair of horseshoes, hung from a pole near the stereo. "Is he coming himself?" Ross asked Bill from Slaton, who told him, "He is indeed! He'll be here in a bit, once he's done shaking hands down at Town & Country," which was the shopping center on the other side of Tech. "In the meantime, drink up!"

Nobody here looked especially stoked to Ross—just a bunch of guys and sorority girls who seemed like they were having a quick drink before heading someplace else. There were, however, two guys manning a card table stacked with flyers and bumper stickers, and one of them held a clipboard, scanning the attendees with a weak hopefulness, searching for ones who might like to sign up as cam-paign volunteers. Ross wondered if he should be doing that himself, if only as a thank-you for the hospitality, but the guy with the clipboard looked a lot more serious than Bill from Slaton and a lot more likely to object to the beer in his obviously underage hand. Ross had last shaved four days ago and wouldn't need to again for another week. He was enjoying the beer—he'd never had more than a few sips at his parents' parties—and could feel himself cooling off, his legs loosen-ing. He went over to a bowl next to the chips and salsa that was full of campaign buttons; he picked one out and put it on.

He knew next to nothing about this election, which had been the subject of a classmate's subpar Current Events presentation last week. All he remembered was that old Mr. George Mahon, who'd been in Congress since Grandpa came to Lubbock, was retiring, and that Bush was one of two young guys competing to replace him. Except for what it said on the posters around town, Ross wouldn't have recalled that Bush was the Republican and the other guy the Democrat, and from what the Current Events kid had said, there wasn't enough dif-ference between them that it mattered.

The Alvin Crow tape finished, and when no one seemed able to find another, somebody shifted the boom box to its radio setting. A string of Japanese lanterns came on along with the outdoor house lights, and several of the guests clapped. It was at this moment that Ross noticed a pretty girl from school with reddish-brown hair, someone new in town whose name he didn't think he'd heard and with whom he shared no classes. Even from a few feet away he could tell that she was wearing makeup to cover freckles. He wanted to say to her: *Why would you do that? You sort of look like Sissy Spacek.* If he got the words out he knew he'd then be fumbling to tell her they were a compliment, but right now, mutely looking at her, he found himself surprised that they had even occurred to him, and at how they *wanted* to be spoken. Was this what people meant when they said "that's the alcohol talking"? When she got closer, he was positively startled to find himself touching her arm and saying, "Hey, didn't I see you out at Reese over the weekend?"

Thousands of people had been out at the Air Force base on Saturday, watching the Thunderbirds and some Navy parachutists perform.

She was drinking her beer less furtively than he was sipping his, and she smiled. "You may have. It was pretty lame—though not as lame as this. Oh," she added suddenly, moving toward the boom box to turn up the volume. "Listen."

In 1961, when Kent Hance graduated from Dimmitt High School in the Nineteenth Congressional District, his opponent George W. Bush was attending Andover Academy in Massachusetts. In 1965, when Kent Hance graduated from Texas Tech, his opponent was at Yale University. And while Kent Hance graduated from University of Texas Law School, his opponent—get this, folks—was attending Harvard Business School. We don't need someone from the Northeast telling us what our problems are.

A few good-natured boos issued from the crowd, but as the girl turned the volume back down and the radio station went back to music, Ross noticed how most of those standing by the pool seemed almost unaware that the commercial they'd just heard had any connection, even an antagonistic one, to the event they were attending.

"I'm Ross," he said to the girl.

"I'm Allie."

That's right, he thought. Allison O'Connor. He *had* heard her name from somebody at school. "Aren't you new here?" he asked.

"Three months. It only *feels* like thirty years." Her father, she explained, worked in computers and had moved the family from Philadelphia to Lubbock to take a job at Texas Instruments.

"What brings you here tonight?" asked Ross, before they both laughed at how adult and stiff he sounded.

Allie waggled her beer cup, annoyed that it was empty. "My parents think I'm studying with some girl whose name I made up."

Bill, the guy from Slaton, was regaling two guys with a joke the Hance people had been telling about this fellow who thought a "cattle guard" was a uniformed officer—and who was clearly supposed to be Bush, unacquainted with West Texas ways. It seemed odd to Ross that a guy wearing two Bush buttons would be telling this joke on his own candidate, but Bill's two-man audience, preoccupied with tilting one of the kegs forward, wasn't paying much attention.

"Isn't Bush's father a big deal?" Ross asked Allie.

"Try number-one spy at the CIA under Ford. And head of the Republican Party, or Committee, or whatever it is, when Watergate was going on."

She was clearly better informed than the kid in Current Events. Finding that he wanted another beer, and wondering if anything might be left in the kegs, Ross laughed. "So does that mean you're for the other guy? Hance?"

Allie rolled her eyes. "They're *both* against giving the Panama Canal back to Panama."

Ross got ready to say *Give it back? Didn't we build it?*, but he was interrupted by some scattered cries of "Bush! Bush!" and some effortful, uneven applause around the pool. The candidate had arrived, in a white Oldsmobile Cutlass that Ross could see through the house's open doors. George W. Bush waved to those who'd come to see him and pointed to the TILT ME, I'M EASY keg: "I usually like to have that *second*, and chasing something stronger, but if it's all you've got . . ."

Amidst laughter, the man who appeared to be his driver went and got Bush a cup of beer, while someone else handed the candidate a microphone he didn't really need. A couple of guys who'd earlier gone into the house weren't even bothering to turn down the *Monday Night Football* game they had on, let alone come out to hear Bush's pitch. As he got ready to make it, he pointed toward the indoor TV with a look of feigned anger that he then erased with a shrug, prompting more ice-breaking laughter.

Allie whispered to Ross: "Don't believe that little gesture. He's actually pissed off. I can see it in his eyes." Ross couldn't tell, but he did observe that Bush was chewing a plug of tobacco.

"I appreciate y'all coming out," the candidate began. "The last time I was here at Tech I was talking to a bunch of you in the Coronado Room." He mispronounced the name of that space within the Student Union Building—made it rhyme with "tornado"—but he certainly *sounded* like a Texan, thought Ross, no matter what the Hance commercial had said. "It's good to see students turn out," Bush continued, "because frankly I think there's too much apathy in today's university. I was on campus maybe twenty times this spring during the primary campaign, and only seventy of y'all voted."

A confused silence ensued. No one had been expecting a scolding, if that's what this was.

"Of course," Bush resumed, with a wink, "most of those seventy voted for me, so I guess I can't complain. There were some rough moments in that campaign, but my opponent was a good man, and I'm now proud to have his endorsement." A brief pause and a glance toward his shoes signaled a change of focus. "Okay," said the candidate, looking back up, "how many of you think things are going well in Washington?"

Some soft requisite boos answered him.

"I didn't think so," Bush replied. "I don't either. I grew up in Midland and I'm in the oil business down there. I'll bet some of your folks are in it too, or are in natural gas. Well, it's the overregulation embodied by Jimmy Carter's Natural Gas Policy Act that got me into politics."

Allie whispered to Ross: "Oh, please, he was *born* into it."

"What about the farm crisis?" asked Bill from Slaton, startling the candidate and pretty much everybody else with the interruption. Bush looked uncomfortable, as if he really *would* like something stronger than beer to drink. He took a long sip and then stared at the questioner, seeming to ask: *Why are you poking at my weak spot?*

"You want to help the farmer?" he finally responded. "Deregulate natural gas and oil. In the end, what that saves him will do more good than any adjustment to the number of set-aside acres the government tells him not to farm."

"Wasn't Earl Butz really the cause of the current price mess?" asked the guy from Slaton.

Bush fixed him with a what-the-hell-is-wrong-with-you look. This wasn't a debate, and he wasn't about to put the blame for anything on a former Republican secretary of agriculture, even one now chiefly remembered for a godawful racist joke involving tight pussy and loose shoes. The guys behind the sign-up table also exchanged perplexed glances about the questioner.

"Anybody else?" asked Bush. Bill from Slaton appeared content to subside, but nobody had another question, so the candidate moved on to something new: "Jesse Jackson says the economic pie has to grow—and that makes sense to me."

Even Allie looked mildly intrigued that Reverend Jackson's name should be uttered with approval.

"In saying no to spending and in saying no to measures that erode free enterprise," Bush continued, "you are actually saying yes to people at the *bottom* of the free enterprise system."

Several people applauded, a few of them, it seemed, out of something beyond politeness.

"So if you'd like to help me, please sign up with those fellows over there and help us to make Texas a real two-party state at last. Thank you." More applause, and then laughter, when Bush pointed to the second keg: "And, yes, I will have another, since my man Mike here is driving the car."

Ross had joined in the clapping while looking around for Allie

O'Connor, who seemed to have gone off somewhere. Heading toward the house, he felt a hard tap on his shoulder, courtesy of Darryl, who'd just arrived and was distinctly displeased to find him here. He grabbed the top rim of Ross's shirt, the place where a real collar should be, and growled: "You'd better not let Anita Bryant see you in this fruity shirt, little brother, or she'll kick your ass. And if you have another one of *these*"—he tossed Ross's empty cup into one of Mayor Granberry's flower beds—"*I'll* kick your ass."

Ross's anger was threaded with the hope that Allie had actually left and wasn't witnessing this humiliation. Still three inches shorter, and much lighter, than Darryl, he was mortified enough to consider taking a swing at his brother. But in the end he just let Darryl smirk and walk away, watching him until he felt a second, much gentler tap on his shoulder—from someone who'd witnessed the fraternal dustup.

"Hey," said George W. Bush, with a consoling smile. "In my family it's the *big* brother—that would be me—who screws up. At least now and then. See that fine, responsible young fellow over there?"

"Your brother?" asked Ross. The blond fellow being pointed to appeared about ten years younger than the candidate.

"Yo, Neil!" cried the elder Bush. "Wave hello to—what's your name, dude?"

"Ross Weatherall."

"Neil! Wave to my man Ross!"

Neil Bush, whom Ross had taken for a Tech student, waved.

"My campaign manager," explained George Bush. "Twenty-three years old. Finished up at Tulane last year."

Ross looked incredulously at the candidate's brother. Could someone so young hold a job that important?

"He's living over the Republican county chairwoman's garage. I guess I can't be all that bad if I inspire such devotion." Bush laughed and handed Ross his beer. "Here, finish this." He patted the boy's arm, winked, and walked away. Darryl was now nowhere to be seen, so Ross took the beer and chugged it down. And while he did, Allie O'Connor's beautiful russet hair came into view, as if it were the Olympic torch.

She told him it was 8:45 p.m. "You have just time enough to take me to the movies." *Hooper*, with Burt Reynolds playing a stuntman, was at the four-plex, several blocks away.

Ross hesitated.

"I *know* you don't have a car," said Allie. "We can walk."

Having her believe he'd come here on foot seemed less shameful than letting her know he'd arrived on a bicycle. He wondered if he could leave his Schwinn between the azaleas, not even come back for it until tomorrow morning. He wavered for another second or two—it was a Monday night—and then said yes. The stars had begun to come out; the strong, hot wind was turning into a cool breeze.

He caught a glimpse of the waving, departing candidate. He felt Allie pushing him in the same direction, toward the street that would lead them to the movies. Experiencing the wonderful, fine buzz of the beer, Ross looked ahead toward George W. Bush and then back toward Allie and vaguely realized that, in totally different ways, he was a little in love with both of them.

———

Thursday, November 2: Home of George W. and Laura Bush, 1405 Golf Course Road, Midland, Texas

Barbara Bush watched her daughter-in-law read *The World According to Garp*. Laura was *not* looking up at the clock the way she herself, flipping through a magazine, had been doing with visible irritation every couple of minutes.

Both women were waiting for their husbands to arrive and join them for a late supper that Laura had already cooked. But it was now 9:30 p.m., and from the elder Mrs. Bush's point of view this was becoming ridiculous. George W. had been scheduled to appear at an early-evening candidates' forum up in Lubbock, an hour and a half away; he'd promised that it would be over by seven-thirty and that he and Neil would drive straight down to Midland. George Sr. had spent the afternoon in Amarillo giving a speech for Bill Clements and John Tower, the gubernatorial and Senate candidates at the top of the ticket; *he* was supposed to fly into Midland in time for this delayed dinner, after which the senior Bushes would spend the five days until the election here at George and Laura's starter house. Bar knew that she and her husband would be stir-crazy, in a variety of ways, by tomorrow night.

"Is that really any good?" she asked Laura, pointing to the novel by this man Irving.

"A little overstuffed," said Laura, after a moment's consideration. "Sort of like a modern, mediocre Dickens."

"Why not read Dickens instead?" asked her mother-in-law.

"I have."

"All of it?"

"Just about." Her eyes had already gone back to the page.

She couldn't be more different from me, thought Bar, who nonetheless doubted that, by the time all four of her sons had wed, she would like any of their wives better than this one. Laura had met young George only sixteen months ago and been married to him for less than a year, but she hadn't been the least bit fazed the time or two she'd been thrown into all of the holiday commotion at the family compound up in Maine. Of course Laura still got to live in the town she'd grown up in, anchored to her own past in a way that Bar herself had never been permitted, not since she was twenty-four and her own George had dragged her to Midland—and then to all the other places, from Houston to Washington to Peking.

She got up to freshen her drink in the kitchen, and in the glass door of a cabinet noticed again how her hair was going from gray to snow white. She was only three years past fifty, and her life had offered plenty of excitement—China, for goodness' sake! not to mention the CIA—and there would be more to come soon, once George began running for president in earnest a few months from now. But she still had the sense that time was washing over her when she ought to be swimming deliberately through it; still had moments when she felt herself falling back into the depression that had overtaken her, quite brutally for a while, when they got back from Asia. She now thought of her own maroon-colored set of Dickens novels back home in Houston and wondered if she herself would ever read another of them. Who was she kidding?

It was so *quiet* here. By the time she was Laura's age—thirty-two this Saturday—she'd had five children and buried one of them. She wasn't about to ask her daughter-in-law and George W. when they might be getting started in that department, but at last year's wedding the two of them had seemed unimaginably old to be getting married. She knew that it had struck the elder George, someone who'd been through a war and a wedding before he was twenty-one, the same way.

A noise at last: the car. A pair of her sons—George W., as always, the more boisterous of the two—soon came through the back door and into the kitchen.

"Were your ears burning?" her eldest boy asked her. "I was talking about you in Lubbock."

"Oh?"

"Hance," Neil interrupted to explain, "made a crack about George's being born in Connecticut."

The candidate added: "I said I would have preferred Texas, but thought I should be close to my mother that day."

She could see him waiting for her look of amusement and approval; even now he was trying to make her laugh the way he had after Robin died of leukemia and, with his father usually away on business, it became just the two of them alone in that little house across town. "Not bad," she replied, with a supposedly grudging smile, as if offering a strictly political appraisal of his retort. "They're here!" she called out to the living room.

Laura Bush came to the kitchen, gave her husband a kiss and her young brother-in-law a hug. Bar took the Saran Wrap off a salad bowl—as much cooking as she would do over the next five days. "Sit," she said. "All of you. We're not going to wait for George."

Laura brought the food to a table, already set, in the small adjacent dining room. Her mother-in-law took a seat between her sons. Returning to Hance's needling, the elder Mrs. Bush asked, à propos of the local voters: "Do they want you to ride around on a tumbleweed? It's not good enough that you moved here at the age of *two*?"

"His real crime," said Neil, "is having gone *back* east, for school."

After a long moment, Bar looked at the candidate. "We haven't come all this way to see you lose, have we?"

"God, Mother," said Neil. "*Harsh*. They're only a few points apart in the polls."

"I can't blame Hance for playing the good ol' boy," said George, avoiding the salad and tossing a chicken enchilada onto his plate. "It makes sense."

Laura sat down beside him. "It wouldn't hurt if you blamed him for the business with the beer."

The brothers shot each other wounded glances. "We went over this last night, no?" George asked Laura, more plaintive than accusing. He got up to get a bottle of Jack Daniels, which he set down on the table between a plastic jug of Coke and a pitcher of iced tea. His wife gave him a look that didn't really criticize but let him know she was watching.

"Would anyone care to fill me in?" asked Barbara Bush, who looked as if she actually, already, knew plenty.

Before anyone could speak, the kitchen's wall telephone rang. Laura went and got it. "Jim Granberry," she told her husband.

"I'll take it in the bedroom."

"All right," said Bar, once he was gone. She turned to her younger son. "*You* tell me."

The campaign manager began his explanation with a sigh: "Six weeks ago we had an event in Lubbock. We've done so many I can hardly remember it, but a bunch of Tech students came and we signed a few of them up to stuff envelopes and things like that. The ad in the school paper had mentioned that there'd be free beer. No one thought anything about it. I *do* remember the event being sort of a dud. Nobody drank too much, and the thing ended early. But just the other day Hance's law partner sent around a letter to all these pastors. What's the big denomination here?" he asked his sister-in-law.

"Church of Christ."

"I can never keep them straight," said Barbara Bush. "Are they the snake-handling type?"

Laura lit a cigarette; she would wait for her husband before starting to eat. "I know they sing a cappella," she calmly informed her mother-in-law. "They're not much for organ music." Though a Methodist, she'd been here her whole life and hardly found them exotic.

"Anyway, Mother," said Neil, "Hance's guys are now making it sound as if George has been corrupting the youth of Texas with free beer."

"Tell her the best part," said Laura.

"Nobody knows that Hance actually has a money interest in a Lubbock bar called Fat Dawg's."

Slicing into an enchilada, Bar asked: "And when will that be pointed out to the electorate?"

"It won't be," said Laura.

"George made a pledge, early on and pretty publicly, not to attack Hance in any way," explained Neil. "He's sort of boxed into that."

"What a ridiculous idea," said Bar, appearing to warm to the subject.

Laura dragged on her cigarette and said nothing, though it was evident she felt the same way.

"Did it come up tonight?" her mother-in-law asked Neil. "At this candidates' forum?"

"Yeah, it did," said Neil, looking as if he wanted to put his head in his hands. "Hance said that spreading alcohol around like that 'may be cool at Harvard or Yale' but not at Texas Tech." Trying to cheer up everyone, including himself, Neil added: "God, did George have to go to *both* of them—on top of Andover?" Once the campaign was over, Neil would be finishing his own MBA, again at Tulane.

Laura Bush, whose father had gone to Tech, said, "You're back," when her husband entered the little dining room.

"Who's Granberry?" the elder Mrs. Bush asked her son.

"The mayor of Lubbock. Or at least he used to be."

"The 'Bush Bash'—this beer thing," Neil elaborated for their mother, "was at Granberry's house. He was out of town, but I understand he approved it."

"We've been talking about it," Laura explained to George.

"So what did he want?" asked Bar. "Granberry."

Her son refilled the glass he'd taken with him to the phone. "He's asking me to let him hold a press conference. So he can talk about Hance's hypocrisy, on account of Bull Dog's or whatever it is."

"Fat Dawg's," corrected Laura. "Spelled with a 'w.'"

"What did you tell him?" asked Barbara Bush.

"Same as I've been telling everybody for the past two days: No. I'm not going to get into a food fight with Hance over this."

"Anybody home?" The man coming through the front door sounded more boyish than either of his sons, who stood up when George Herbert Walker Bush entered the dining room. "Hello, beautiful," he said, kissing his daughter-in-law. Laura smiled, but cast a look of displeasure at the fair-haired, slightly plump young man traveling in the elder George Bush's wake. Was *he* supposed to stay here too? There wasn't enough room in this house for even her in-laws. Neil would be sleeping on the living-room couch.

"I'm Karl," he said, shaking Laura's hand. "Don't let me disturb you. I have a few calls to make, and then I'll be going. Is there another room with a phone?"

"Straight back and to the right," said George W. Bush. "Hope you've got a credit card!"

Karl Rove, clearly already acquainted with the younger George Bush, laughed, but just to be safe he looked at Laura and reassured her: "Yes, I do."

"Heckuva smart kid," said the senior Bush as Rove walked off. "Done a lot of work for me in Houston. Already has his own consulting firm—not yet thirty. He may bring this thing home for Bill Clements," he added, referring to the candidate who on Tuesday had a chance of being elected Texas's first Republican governor since Reconstruction.

"Where is Karl staying tonight?" asked Laura.

"He's got himself a room in town," Bush explained to his daughter-in-law. "We were up in Amarillo together and he couldn't get a flight back to Houston, so he came down here with me. Now he can do some business with Clements' Midland operation and head home tomorrow night. *Efficient*, you know? I just wanted to keep picking his brain after we got off the flight from Amarillo, so I put him in the cab with me."

"Maybe you should pick Karl's brain about George W.'s dilemma," Barbara Bush suggested.

"What dilemma's that?" asked her husband.

Their eldest son shook his head wearily, leaving explanation of the Bush Bash, once more, to Neil. When the story had again been told, the senior George Bush said, "Heckuva thing. This Ivy League stuff cuts both ways in life, ya know."

"Your father is co-chairman of the Yale fundraising drive this year," Bar informed her sons. "Don't allow this person you're running against to make Yale a dirty word."

"And where is Dad getting the time to do *that*?" asked George W., as he tore his enchilada in two. Since leaving the CIA, the old man had gone back into business in Houston, taught a class at Rice, and begun running for president. It was true, of course, that he could hardly go out campaigning for his eldest son—not with Hance talking like George W. was some trust-fund baby. The Democrat was also coaching farmers at local Bush rallies to ask if it was true that the candidate's father served on the Trilateral Commission, a name they sounded out with sinister slowness, as if it were an instrument of Beelzebub. Even so, it still hurt George W., in some small way, that Dad should be finding the time to campaign for Clements and Tower and just about every Republican congressional candidate in the country except his own son.

"I don't want to interfere," said the elder Bush, "but when it comes to this beer thing: You're not going to counterpunch?"

"No, sir."

The father gave the son a you're-the-boss look, though it was clear he agreed with his wife and daughter-in-law. "You know, a year from now I'm going to be hearing this Yale stuff from Reagan and Dole. And if I get past them, I'll be hearing it from Carter."

"Well," said his son, "we're going to have an election here in five days, not two years. And I'm not going to do anything different. You know, I did win a primary a few months back. Not that even *that* was all about me." His opponent, Jim Reese, the former mayor of Odessa, had called him "Shrub" and gotten an endorsement from Reagan, whose people wanted to have a little proxy preview of the 1980 race, one that ended with a Reagan surrogate beating a Bush scion.

"Don't go getting ticked off now," said the old man.

"Should we find out what Nixon's boy thinks?" George W. pointed toward the bedroom. Laura looked perplexed.

"Karl was head of the College Republicans when Dad was at the RNC," he explained. "Rove! Get out here!"

The consultant emerged from the bedroom, telephone credit card in hand.

"Talked to Nixon just the other day," said the elder Bush, a bit disconsolately. "I think he still likes Connally for '80."

"You *want* Nixon's endorsement?" asked Neil Bush.

"Believe me," said Rove, now standing near the dining-room table, "there's a way it could be spun into a positive." He wasn't asked to sit down. "I'm going to be taking off. There's a cab coming to bring me to my hotel."

Bush senior, after saying "while we've still got you here," proceeded to tell the young consultant about the Hance situation, as his candidate son, still doing a slow burn, poured himself another inch of whiskey. Rove engaged in a moment or two of almost visible thinking about the political problem just put before him, until George W. gave him the needle. "Rove, didn't you run the Dirty Tricks Department—JV division—of Nixon's last campaign?"

The young man responded, "Are you sure this Bush Bash wasn't a dirty trick?"

Neil Bush looked up, surprised.

"Who organized it?" asked Rove. "You sure it was one of your own people?"

"We don't have a lot of 'people,' Rove," the candidate answered. "Yes, I'm *sure*," he added, though he wasn't.

Everyone heard the taxi driver honk his horn. "If you let Hance *define* you," said the departing Rove, "he'll *beat* you."

"You know," said George W., once he was gone, "Caracas seems like a better and better idea." They all knew he was referring to Jeb, down in South America working for Jim Baker's bank, out from under the contrail of Dad's sometimes sputtering but still rising rocket. Barbara Bush gave her eldest son a look that instructed him to keep the temper he'd inherited, from her, in check.

"I'm going for a run," George W. announced, pushing away the second half of his enchilada.

"After three?" Laura asked, meaning whiskeys.

Her husband pointed to his glass. "This one's only half drunk. Set it out in the living room so I can finish it later, okay, darling?" There was more affection than peevishness in his teasing, but both qualities were discernible. He went off to change clothes while his wife wondered how long it would be before the quick, constant movements between overindulgence and athletic self-punishment broke the spring of her husband's metronome.

"Heard you gave a good speech over in Muleshoe!" her father-in-law said admiringly, touching Laura's arm.

"There's a last time for everything," she replied, lighting a cigarette.

———

Tuesday, November 7: Bush for Congress Headquarters, 2414 Broadway, Lubbock, Texas

The polls closed at 7:00 p.m., and Ross Weatherall spent the next hour pacing in front of the tables he had manned, late each afternoon, for the past seven weeks. He had also hung signs, made phone calls, and passed out flyers on University Avenue; he'd even rung the doorbells of beat little houses in the Mexican part of town. His efforts on behalf of George W. Bush had been so sustained that his brother Darryl, too preoccupied with law-school applications to have much time for politics this term, had actually spoken a few grudging words of approval about him at dinner one night.

Ross had awakened at six a.m. today and been too excited to get back to sleep. He'd turned on *Praise the Lord* and watched the lady with the explosive hairdo and magic-carpet eyelashes talk about the agreement Jimmy Carter had worked out at Camp David between Israel and Egypt. She was convinced that the pact would speed up certain biblical prophecies.

There was no beer available here tonight; someone had explained to Ross that since the Bush Bash they had to be extra cautious around any press photographers who might be coming by. The long tables held only bottles of Coke and a nasty mess of beef Stroganoff, barely warm, that had been ordered in from Furr's Cafeteria.

The radio and TV stations kept saying that turnout had been heavier than expected, but the optimism that had been here at seven o'clock was beginning to fade. Ross's pacing was now less a matter of excitement than nerves. Bush's big winning margin in Midland didn't look as if it could offset the wins Hance was piling up in all the rural counties, as well as in Lubbock. "Fuck Floydada," Ross whispered. "Fuck Dimmitt." His agitation had just been increased by the presence of that weird guy from Slaton, whom he hadn't seen since the night of the now-famous and maybe fatal Bash. He recalled the guy's hostile-sounding questions: *What about the farm crisis? Wasn't Earl Butz really the cause of the current price mess?* And here he was now, the corners of his mouth turning up as everybody else's went down.

A voice behind him whispered, "Ross meets Loss."

"That's real nice, that's real sympathetic," he said, after turning around and discovering Allie. He was thrilled to see her.

"There's better food at Hance's place down the street," she informed him.

The two of them had been to four movies since *Hooper* and had recently crashed Delta Tau Delta's toga party, an event once more in style thanks to *Animal House*. A week ago he'd asked Allie if she was now his girlfriend. *Don't be ridiculous*, she'd replied.

She pointed to a town on the blackboard showing the vote breakdown. "Do you know how I pronounced that, the first time I saw it, last summer?"

"No."

"Le-*vel*-land, like McClellan. Then someone explained: Level-*land*. Like everything around us."

"So?"

"I'd rather have kept my innocence," Allie declared.

Channel 28, KMCC, was updating the state and national results. Clements and Tower were in the lead for the governorship and Senate seat, and across the country the GOP was expected to pick up anywhere between a dozen and twenty House seats. Photos of the new congressional faces appeared onscreen, as the news anchors made guesses as to the pronunciation of some of their names. "College professor Newt Gingrich has taken Georgia's Sixth District, and State Senator Carroll Campbell is the new Republican congressman from South Carolina's Fourth. Richard Cheney, once chief of staff to former president Ford, is the new at-large House representative for Wyoming; and closer to home, Dr. Ron Paul will be representing the Texas Twenty-second."

To give viewers a break, the station cut away to some news besides politics: the King Tut exhibit was being installed in New York, weeks after people had lined up to buy tickets. It would finally open next month.

"I'm determined to go," said Allie. "If I can convince my father I'm even more miserable than I am, I can get him to send me up to New York for a long weekend with my aunt."

Kent Hance's toothy, beaming face suddenly filled the screen. It was sickening to realize that the cheers and the happy blasts of plastic horns were coming from inside the television, not the storefront space in which all the Bush volunteers now stood silently. It was barely ten o'clock, Ross thought. There still *had* to be a chance. But the smartest people here had been the first ones to start looking downcast.

"George W. Bush just called me to concede the race," said Hance, to the loudest burst of cheering yet, "and he couldn't have been nicer." He was already sounding less like a farmer—there was no more need for the aw-shucks act—and more like the lawyer he actually was. The TV analyst said that he would probably end up with fifty-three percent of the vote and declared that the newcomer Bush had run a "respectable" race. Mike Childers—the losing candidate's Lubbock driver, whom Ross had gotten to know a little—was actually crying. And the creepy guy from Slaton was now nowhere to be found. Ross waited for the TV to switch over to Bush's main headquarters in Midland, but wasn't sure he could stand the misery of a concession speech.

A local GOP lawyer stubbed out a cigarette on the floor and muttered, "Jesus Christ, all those Italian cardinals just elected a Polish guy pope, and we can't elect a guy who went to school out of *state*." With no alcohol-related scandal left to fear, somebody brought out two cases of beer from a refrigerator in the back.

"Do you still have that pathetic bicycle?" Allie asked Ross. "The one you tried to hide from me?"

"Yes."

"Good, I have mine, too. Come with me." She slipped three of the beers into her backpack.

"Where are we going?" asked Ross.

Once on his Schwinn, he followed her through the starry night, over the flat streets, neither of them ever needing to change out of tenth gear. As if to make up for tonight's bad political fortune, the wind was at their backs. They had nearly reached Thirty-first Street when Allie turned into the City of Lubbock Cemetery and instructed Ross to dismount. The two of them climbed over a shoulder-high chain-link fence. She led the way to Section 44 of the graveyard:

IN LOVING MEMORY
OF OUR OWN
BUDDY HOLLEY
September 7, 1936
February 3, 1959

Two beer bottles rested near the marker, which was flush with the ground. Allie shook them to see if they were truly empty, then took two cans of Lone Star from her backpack. She handed one to Ross and pointed to the gravestone. "You know the greatest thing he ever accomplished?"

Ross looked at the marker. Like most Lubbockites he knew that the musician's family had always spelled their name with an "e." His father, once or twice, had even met the town's favorite son.

"No," he said, trying to sound impatient instead of heartbroken. "What was the greatest thing he ever accomplished?"

"He didn't die *here*," said Allie.

Ross took a gulp from what would be the third full beer of his life, before Allie pushed him down so that he was lying, flat on his back, atop the grave marker. It was here that she gave him his first kiss, and began singing, with surprising sweetness: *Just you and I* . . .

Part One

JANUARY 20–AUGUST 28, 2005

JANUARY 20, 2005

He felt uneasy, creeped out, when he noticed that Rehnquist, who'd looked like death swearing him in, had already disappeared from the platform. But the words continued to float up the teleprompter, and he wasn't going to lose his momentum. He was about to banish anybody's notion that this second administration of his would be going in for small ball:

> *It is the policy of the United States to seek and support the growth of democratic movements and institutions in every nation and culture, with the ultimate goal of ending tyranny in our world.*

He'd said it. Freedom and security were one and the same, and you couldn't have too much of either.

The applause seemed somehow to drift away instead of toward him, as if riding an easterly breeze from here at the Capitol to the Lincoln Memorial. He wondered who on the dais or out in the crowd knew that he'd been playing on Lincoln's words when he just said "no one is fit to be a master and no one deserves to be a slave," let alone knew that he'd read fully five biographies of The Linc (even *he* got a nickname) in the four years he and Laura had lived in the house halfway up the Mall and over to the right.

He caught a glimpse of Kerry at the end of the platform, his face looking weirdly puffed out, as if it had stolen whatever flesh was disappearing from Rehnquist's. Too far away to see it in detail, he could well enough envision the *disappointed*, more-in-sorrow-than-in-anger look his vanquished opponent would be exhibiting in reaction to the words just uttered—that *pained* expression of his, sort of a sigh that always meant to say *it's more complicated than that.*

He knew Dick's pretty opponent wouldn't be here—the protocol never required the defeated VP candidate to show up—but he'd heard that Edwards, now out of the Senate, was still in the city, over at the Georgetown mansion he'd bought with all those trial-lawyer fees that would finally start shrinking if they got tort reform through this session.

> *America's influence is not unlimited, but fortunately for the oppressed, America's influence is considerable and we will use it confidently in freedom's cause.*

And he would use his political capital, what he'd accumulated in November by kicking Kerry's rear in both Ohio and Florida. He would go beyond tort reform and throw himself into Social Security and immigration.

A light covering of snow stretched across the Mall like a tarp on the field at the Arlington Ballpark. Gazing upon it, and thinking for a second of the team he'd owned fifteen years ago, he felt his resentment toward last year's foes fall away and be replaced by a surge of confidence, a sense that all things great and small were being given to him. He could hear that his delivery was smooth, the one word that had made him stumble in the rehearsals, "susceptible," having been replaced by "prone."

> *Democratic reformers facing repression, prison, or exile can know: America sees you for who you are, the future leaders of your free country.*

The last shall be first. The Bible is everywhere in this speech, directly or just beneath the surface. And if the upcoming nod to the Koran seems obligatory, it also has what Kissinger—had he just seen *his* wheezing, shrinking hulk here?—would call "the additional advantage of being true." He was going to re-win this war he'd already won once, because when you came down to it he had more in common with, and more insight into, the most radical Muslim who read his Koran than the unbeliever who never opened his Bible. He would wager that when everybody on this platform had bowed their heads a few minutes ago, not more than one person in ten actually started praying. The rest had just kept thinking about who they'd been able to sit a row in front of and who they'd had to sit a row behind.

He could feel it again, had to fight it, the sudden shift from merriment to irritability, from runner's high to cramp, the flight and crash he experienced a dozen times an hour; the fast, exhausting alternation he knew he had to battle and often didn't want to. He'd fight it now, with words that had been written for him, but words that he could also utter from the heart, the same way he had prayed, for real, during the invocation.

Head up, he speaks: *America, in this young century, proclaims liberty throughout all the world and to all the inhabitants thereof!*

———

Back inside the Capitol, Barbara Bush got rid of the large red cape and heavy coat she'd worn against the cold out on the platform. Even ten years ago she would never have allowed herself to sport something powder blue underneath them, but she was only five months from eighty now, and had come to recognize the slimming effect of *advanced* old age as one of the condition's few compensations. She could finally get away with lighter colors.

The president's mother blew a kiss to acknowledge some applause a few tables away before sitting down next to the Bill Frists, the majority leader and his wife, as well as Condi Rice. As she shook hands with the man escorting the secretary of state–designate, Mrs. Bush gave Gene Washington—a TV-star-handsome ex-football player, nearly sixty—her smiling appraisal. He was, like most things in Condi's life, a grade-A choice and achievement, at one with the childhood French lessons, the competitive ice-skating, the master's-degree program begun at the age of twenty. More a credential, Mrs. Bush imagined, than a passionate swain.

God, *another* invocation. The former First Lady stood up with everyone else and bowed her head, but as others prayed she performed, through eyes still narrowly open, an inspection of the dais. She could see George and Laura to the left of Cheney and his wife and Senator Chris Dodd, who now looked as sleek and silver as his corrupt old father, Tom, whom she remembered from the days just before his fall, almost forty years ago, during her brief time as a congressional wife. Her eyes moved surreptitiously leftwards to see, at her son's right, Trent Lott and—well, Lott's wife; she could never remember her name. Chris Dodd and Trent headed the congressional committee in charge of organizing this enormous bipartisan luncheon, half of whose guests cordially loathed the other half. All around Bar sat not only senators and congressmen but cabinet members and Supreme Court justices, including Souter, that elfin little Earl Warren, her husband's biggest appointive mistake, who four years ago had gone so far as to vote with the minority in *Bush v. Gore*. Word was he felt uncomfortable after fifteen years in Washington, as well he should: let him go back to New Hampshire and live in that barn with his mother, so that young George got the chance to appoint two justices instead of one. Rehnquist, of whom there was no sign, surely couldn't last much longer.

The first course, a lobster salad, arrived on the tables as soon as the chaplain was through.

"I remember you telling me you don't like to travel," Mrs. Bush said to Condi, who had just picked up exactly the right fork.

"That's more or less true," the secretary-designate replied, with a smile that tried to look amused instead of cautious. "I hate being away from my own stuff." She felt the need—Bar could hear it—to put imaginary little quotes around "stuff," as if she might otherwise be scolded for a crude choice of word. Mrs. Bush, who had been to Condi's apartment, could still picture the piano and the elliptical trainer and the teak-topped desk, every item seeming to seek a neat perpendicularity that the curvature of the Watergate's walls made impossible.

"How are you going to do your job?" Mrs. Bush asked. "Without liking to travel, I mean."

"I don't have the job yet," Rice reminded her, adding demureness to the smile. The president had asked her, at Camp David the weekend after his reelection, to switch from being national security advisor to secretary of state, and with a sore loser's reflex, John Kerry had given her a prolonged, nasty grilling at the confirmation hearing. Just yesterday he'd voted against her in the Foreign Relations Committee, and despite that group's 16–2 margin in her favor, the nomination had yet to get full Senate approval.

Returning to Mrs. Bush's question, the still-unconfirmed secretary remarked upon the man who by now should be her predecessor. "Colin didn't like traveling either. But he did what he had to. If things go the way they're supposed to, next month I'll be in Paris—and two weeks later in Brussels—with the president. Anyone would look forward to that!"

Bar noticed a genuine girlish gush, however momentary, beneath the test-marketed Muzak of Condi's conversation. A part of the younger woman *wanted* her real personality to break through; she was merely afraid of it—as opposed to Hillary, several tables to their left, who despised her own real self and could scarcely remember what it looked like, having sent so many different versions of it out on so many different combat missions, before having to welcome it home always more shot up and disfigured than when it had left.

Anyway, Bar liked Condi; the whole family did, and took a certain pride in having helped to invent her. "I hear you really wanted the Pentagon, not State," she said, without lowering her voice.

"Oh," replied Condi, startled into loud laughter. "Don Rumsfeld wouldn't be willing to give *that* up!"

George Herbert Walker Bush, having heard the exchange, turned from the Frists toward Rice. Smiling with his small, boyish teeth, he offered her a little solace: "That guy never gives *anything* up." He was recalling how the current defense secretary, as a young White House staffer, had *twice* blocked him from getting the vice presidency: urging Ford not to take him in '74 and then, a year later, maneuvering him into the CIA job so that he couldn't run with Ford in '76. Rumsfeld had always been thick as thieves with Cheney, but it was beyond "41" why his son had had to go and give him the Pentagon. Of course it could have been worse: four years ago, before Dick had settled the vice presidency upon himself, he'd floated Rumsfeld's name for *that* job, a trial balloon both the elder Bushes had had the pleasure of popping.

Guessing her husband's train of thought, Bar looked over at Rumsfeld in one of his old, shiny suits, four tables away—with the Carters. She couldn't have devised a nicer bit of penance for him if she'd drawn up the seating chart herself.

"Who can't *you* forgive?" she asked Rice. The Frists had begun to listen quite eagerly.

Condi pretended that her mouth was too full of lobster to speak.

"Trust me," said Mrs. Bush. "You'll come to loathe Don, if you don't already."

"Bar!" said the former president. "For gosh sakes!"

Condi had always been worried that Rumsfeld hated *her*, pointlessly and from the start: the whole Stanford academic world she came out of; the way she tried to mask and gloss over dissension within the National Security Council staff so that, by the time she reported their discussions to the president, one would have thought there'd been agreement all along. Don had once even reminded her, after she'd supposedly overstepped, that the NSA "wasn't in the chain of command."

"Well," said Mrs. Bush, "if you don't hate Don, there must be *someone*."

Condi laughed and looked around Statuary Hall. "Well, I don't see her. My *senator*." She and Barbara Boxer had despised each other for ages, and Condi had long since been supporting Boxer's opponents in California. The senator's fear—acted out yesterday in casting the other "nay" vote in the Foreign Relations Committee—was that Condoleezza Rice would *herself* become an opponent, a few years from now, by running for Boxer's Senate seat.

"She's crazy," said the secretary-designate.

Seeing Mrs. Bush light up, Condi warmed to the topic. "She's got a real conspiracist streak, too." Frist nodded agreement, and Condi elaborated. "She actually thinks we stole Ohio two months ago."

"No kidding?" asked the former president.

Deciding she'd gone farther than she should, Rice now just shook her head and made a rueful little face. "Well, if I do get this job, I'm afraid I'll be seeing a lot of her. The best part of being NSA was never having to come up here and testify—well, except to the 9/11 Commission." As secretary of state, she would no longer be routinely covered by the president's executive privilege.

"When will they wrap things up?" asked Mrs. Bush.

"I'm not sure. It could take another week—I just hope it will be over before the election." The president's mother, she realized, might not know that she was referring to the *Iraqi* election, of a National Assembly, set to take place ten days from now. When not preoccupied with Kerry and Barbara Boxer, Condi had been worrying about the twenty-six people killed in bombings the other day, and whether the ninety thousand cardboard voting booths to be used by the Iraqis would be distributed in time.

The former president saved her from having to explain to Bar that it was Iraq she had meant. "Sunnis gonna show up and vote?" he asked.

"I hope so, sir."

"Be terrific if they do." He flashed Condi the smile that age was turning into a bit of a grimace.

"We won't be here if it takes another week," said Mrs. Bush, referring to Rice's confirmation. "Otherwise we'd love to come to the swearing-in."

"My Watergate neighbor, Ruth Ginsburg, has promised to do the honors," said Condi.

"Better than Souter," said Bush. His appointee also lived in the Watergate. "*Bad* mistake. Bad."

"Glad you finally admit it," said his wife.

Frist picked up Rice's place card and with his pen scratched out the words "National Security Advisor" beneath her name. In their place, with surprisingly neat penmanship for a medical doctor, he wrote *Secretary of State*. "Condi was the best campaigner we had out there last fall," the majority leader added.

Rice smiled. "It *was* a little unorthodox," she admitted. No national security advisor had ever before hit the political trail for a presidential boss. "But with so much at stake . . ." Ambivalence denied the sentence its completion; her voice trailed off. The pre-election politicking had only sharpened Kerry's spite during the confirmation hearings.

Barbara Bush noticed Condi's squeamishness. She was also noticing a picky eater. The secretary-designate, who'd just turned fifty and exercised fanatically, had barely dented her salad.

"Well," said the former president, "nobody gets any do-overs. You did what you did in the fall, and we were grateful, and now you move on." He made a little onward-and-upward gesture with his lobster fork.

"Don't listen to him," said Mrs. Bush. "There are *plenty* of do-overs in life." Two weeks ago she and George had celebrated their sixtieth anniversary with a dinner at the White House that included the unveiling of a flattering replacement for her original official portrait—that lumpy, frumpy monstrosity! She thought about the switch now, but decided not to offer this rarefied example of second chances, so the subject died out in a kind of cryptic abstraction. Mrs. Bush allowed Condi to be captured into a little side conversation with the Frists while she made some last healthy work of her own lobster and allowed herself a bit of solitary rumination amidst the luncheon's echoing din. Hundreds of insincere pleasantries were bouncing off the marble dome all at once, creating a roar to rival the waters off Kennebunkport in the middle of a storm.

They'd been down here too much, Bar decided; the whole family was overdoing it. A hundred and forty relatives in town! Blair House might as well be George W.'s old fraternity, and the White House was little better. This morning, trying to get some peace over a few minutes of needlepoint, she'd had to wear her books-on-tape headphones to drown out the commotion.

They were too old for all the hoopla. Her own George still looked chilled from having been out on the platform. She hoped he would skip the parade in favor of a hot bath and reconsider this absurd Hope-and-Crosby show with Clinton. Young George was sending the two ex-presidents off to Indonesia in a few weeks, even though half the bodies from the Christmas tsunami were still unburied and rotting in the sun. When had it become normal for eighty-year-olds to keep running around as if they were forty? She was getting past it herself: last night she'd twice referred to Barney, George and Laura's Scotch terrier, as Millie, her own briefly famous and now long-dead spaniel.

She looked at Laura on the dais, self-contained and inwardly amused, giving no signs of the impatience with this overproduced luncheon that Lynne Cheney, tightly wrapped in her fur collar, seemed, like herself, to be experiencing. There were actually *gift* bags stacked against the wall, ready to be distributed by Marines, as if they were all guests at an awards show. She waved to Al Simpson. Seated back-to-back against him was Hillary, who also looked impatient, four years gone from the White House and four years away from returning. The junior senator from New York was looking at the just-arrived quail entrée as if it were one of a thousand campaign chicken breasts lying between the present moment and her heart's desire.

———

Trent Lott hadn't done much toast-mastering since Strom Thurmond's hundredth birthday party a few years back, when he'd accidentally waxed a little too enthusiastic about the good old days of segregation; but "43" had to hand it to him. From his smooth good mood and patter you'd never know that he'd lost the leader's job for slipping up so badly.

"Mr. President, I hope you won't mind that we had to go find Missouri quail for today's main course," Lott told the audience, getting the little luncheon program started at last. "The Texas ones we got hold of first turned out to be so *skinny*."

The audience laughed, with half-comprehending heartiness—

Missouri? Trent was from Mississippi—and the president made himself join in with a little shake of the shoulders and unparted lips. He peeked at Laura, knowing that, despite her grin and evident pleasure, she was scarcely hearing the joke. Her attention was absorbed by the landscape painting—a Wyoming scene, Lynne Cheney had informed them—that hung behind the dais; they were all now half-facing it, their chairs having been turned toward the little lectern. Chris Dodd was getting ready to present him and Cheney with official photos of the inaugural ceremony, huge panoramic shots barely an hour old and already framed, a digital advance over what Dad and Dan Quayle had been gifted with sixteen years ago.

Hastert, the speaker, who was starting to look like the Hunchback of Notre Dame, now proffered two flags that had flown over the Capitol during the swearing-in, prompting Lott to reminisce about Cheney's early days of service in the lower chamber, and to declare how Dick had at heart always been "a House guy." Really? thought Bush. Dick had less regard for Congress than *he* had; if the plane aiming for the Capitol dome on September 11 had actually hit it, he could imagine his vice president muttering "No loss" through that sly slit of a mouth.

His own attention was starting to glaze over. Trent seemed to be quoting one of those "in the arena" passages that belonged to either Teddy Roosevelt or Nixon, but you couldn't *hear* enough in this place to figure out which. So he allowed himself to look around for the spot where Lincoln's House desk had once stood, and then he let his eyes scan the statues, two per state, that ringed this huge interior space like some gathering of Dad's buddies pissing on the redwoods at Bohemian Grove. He located the marble form of Sam Houston—his own second, distant father, ever since years ago Laura had given him a copy of that biography to read and he'd discovered a reformed alcoholic whose Cherokee friends called him Oo-tse-tee Ar-dee-tah-skee, "Big Drunk"; a man who'd gone *mano a mano* with his foster father; whose wife had made him give up booze; and who was well into adulthood before undergoing a full-immersion baptism. When somebody told Houston they'd heard his sins had been washed away, the fantastic old s.o.b. had said "Lord help the fish down below."

Laura was reaching for her glass of sauvignon blanc; the toasts had started. So he took hold of his water and stood up with everybody else, the scrape of the chairs on the stone floor making it sound as if a hundred elephants had begun trumpeting all at once.

"To the forty-third president of the United States," said Lott, as merrily as if he were saluting old Strom.

He finally spotted Neil, a few tables deep, and winked, giving him the look they'd often exchanged in the last decade, a can-you-believe-it glance that acknowledged how far he'd come in the past ten years, or the almost thirty since that fall when they'd beaten their heads against the church walls of Lubbock County. It made him sad that Neil, there on his feet next to his second wife, had had a rough ride of it, messing up with women and money, riding Dad's coattails into places he shouldn't have gone.

He looked at his watch—2:19 p.m., which meant the parade was nineteen minutes behind its scheduled start time. A terrible wave of annoyance washed over him—anyone's lack of punctuality offended him like a blast of bad breath—but he emerged from it by summoning the pleasant feeling that the delay was one more thing he could blame Congress for. He didn't give a damn that both houses were under Republican control; this lunch was their show and thus their fault.

Even so, behind the lectern at last, he began speeding through his own remarks: "I want to thank General Myers, who is here. And I want to thank all my friends from Texas who have come. I'm surprised that some were able to penetrate the security."

Everybody laughed. He was winging it, without a note card, and he was sure to forget somebody. Before he got to the Carters and Clintons he'd better say something about Dick, whom he now heard himself describing as "a fabulous man, a man of sound judgment and great character." And, with increasing frequency, a pain in the ass: the vice president had gone on the radio this morning—Imus, no less—to say that the U.S. just might have to let Israel take out the Iranians' nuclear facility.

He made a couple of jokes about Mother and Dad and the twins, and even as people chuckled he felt a sudden free-fall in his mood, a depressed, sentimental swoop that came from thinking how, thanks to him, all five of them, not just Dad, had probably been designated as targets by Saddam Hussein.

By the time he sat down, impatience once more ruled him. He had to keep himself from nodding to the House chaplain, urging him to start the benediction and wind things up. Laura saw him taking another look at his wristwatch and gave him a cautionary tap on the arm, the way she used to do with the drinking. Not so long ago she'd told him: "You only started looking at your watch after you'd *gotten* somewhere." He didn't get it. "It's as if," she explained, "you only got anxious about being late after you'd already arrived." He'd realized, with a tincture of pride, that this was one of those little "ironies" she was always underlining in Dostoevsky or Truman Capote.

They'd be getting out of here after the presentation of one last gift. Trent was going on about "these beautiful, engraved lead crystal objects" while he and Laura and Lynne and Dick were led to two glass cylinders, each a foot tall, that would no doubt wind up in his presidential library four or five years from now. The glassware confused him for a moment, until Laura whispered, "They're hurricane lamps."

———

Ross Weatherall's new office, his fifth-floor perch right above Pennsylvania Avenue, would provide perfect viewing for this afternoon's parade, but right now Ross needed to get outside. The inaugural address had moved him, and at forty-two, he still processed or just *felt* things best by walking or riding his bike, which he'd last week begun using for his new daily commute into Washington from Arlington, across the river in Virginia.

He would have little problem, even with today's tremendous security presence, getting back into the great Romanesque building—once the federal government's main post office—where he worked. Ross's "Senior Executive Service" ID, hanging from the lanyard around his neck, was even now getting him past each checkpoint on the Pennsylvania Avenue sidewalk, all the way down to the corner of

Fourth Street, where he encountered a "designated space" for protesters. He'd heard their chanting all the way from Sixth: RACIST, SEXIST,
ANTIGAY—BUSH AND CHENEY, GO AWAY! He raised his digital camera, which hung from another lanyard around his neck, and snapped
a picture of someone's sign: IRAQ—TOMB OF THE UNKNOWN EXIT
STRATEGERY. Hardy-har. He would send it to his nephew, Ricky,
Darryl's son, a longhaired twenty-two-year-old printmaker who lived
with a girlfriend in Marfa and drove his father, still a Lubbock lawyer,
more or less nuts. But Ross and his nephew got on fine, agreeing to
disagree, teasing each other over the vast political divide.

He'd lately been experiencing an additional family pleasure: Darryl's pride in his little brother's rise was becoming evident and genuine. For the last couple of family Christmases it had been on open
display, a source of contentment to Ross, who had spent a long time
and a lot of effort arriving at the second outermost ring of the Bush
administration. He'd volunteered for both the gubernatorial cam-
paigns, '94 and '98, after Bush came back into politics, like a slightly
impatient cicada, sixteen years after the Hance race, a long stretch
during which all the action had involved his father.

When George W. reached the presidency, Ross himself had been
an associate professor of history at SMU with a fine c.v. (UT undergraduate, Harvard Ph.D.) and a first book, *James Madison and the Arts*,
from the University of Virginia Press. Being a registered-Republican
academic made him enough of a rara avis to get nominated to the
National Council on the Humanities. (Senate confirmation required;
a parchment commission signed by the president!) He'd come up for
his first meeting just after 9/11, and returned four times a year after
that.

The trips were a welcome relief from the p.c. colleagues in his
department—yes, even at SMU—with their theory-ridden view
of American history as a sort of ongoing atrocity. It was delightful,
when traveling to Washington for Council meetings, to be among
a dozen well-credentialed, like-minded conservative scholars: "Mrs.
Cheney's latest unicorns," as a frenemy back home referred to them.
The vice president's wife had headed the NEH under Reagan and

the first George Bush, initiating a spirited pushback against liberal orthodoxy—which had of course sprung back to life at the Endowment during the Clinton era.

Ross had taken the Council's work seriously, serving on a committee that began defunding the usual run of reflexively liberal documentaries on subjects like the Rosenbergs while still saying no to proposals for projects like *Norman Podhoretz: Bearing the Torch.* "Let's not reject their junk just so we can start pushing *our* junk," he told a colleague who'd succumbed to ideological temptation.

An hour past the speech, but still before the parade, Ross finished his walk and reentered the Old Post Office, making his way to the elevators via the food court that filled its huge atrium; the building looked like some sort of Grand Hyatt from the era of McKinley (Karl Rove's favorite president, he had recently noted). He reached the fifth floor and the newly painted lettering across the frosted glass of his office door.

DIRECTOR, HOMELAND HERITAGE DIVISION
MR. WEATHERALL

The government's two cultural endowments, one for the Humanities and another for the Arts—"Great Books" and "Dirty Pictures" in the years after battles over Robert Mapplethorpe and Karen Finley—had only lately, in the interest of efficiency, been combined into one, the National Endowment for the Arts and Humanities (NEAH). It was hoped that the merger would keep the two tiny, flat-funded entities from disappearing into "decimal dust," a term Ross had recently been taught by one of the new amalgam's budget officers. Here in Washington there was a bipartisan lack of appetite for any renewal of the culture wars, not when the real ones in Iraq and Afghanistan had yet to be fully won. The newly fused NEAH was spending its $300 million on a sturdy array of middle-of-the-road efforts, heavy on historical lessons and citizenship-building.

Ross had been offered the directorship of the new Homeland Heritage Division as a reward for his good work on the NEH Council and his longstanding support of the president. He also owed his job to a newfound ambition he'd felt swelling inside himself as soon as he was sworn in on the Council. He might be on the Pluto-like periphery of the administration, but he was part of it, and with that knowledge came a scintilla of the president's own swagger and the unexpected desire to attain an orbit closer in to the solar center that was the White House itself.

The mission of the Homeland Heritage Division would be to showcase local history within the, well, homeland—a word Ross found a trifle Third Reich–ish, no matter that it had been embraced by both parties and the media over the past four years.

An underemployed intern, tasked last week with researching the Old Post Office's original blueprints in the National Archives, had reported to Ross the interesting fact that his fifth-floor office had first been occupied, during the Rove-cherished McKinley administration, by the U.S. Postal Service's Superintendent of Rate Increases. How busy, Ross wondered, could *that* guy have been? Had he racked his brain all morning over whether to raise the price of a stamp from one cent to two—deferring any decision until after lunch?

Hearing a sudden roar of motorcycles, Ross knew he should be joining the rest of the staff in the big reception room down the hall, but he preferred the idea of watching the parade from inside his own big solitary space, its layout untampered with since the superintendent's occupancy a century ago. He took up position at the window near the flag behind his desk.

As the first marching bands made their way down Pennsylvania, he thought about taking a picture of the sharpshooter visible on the roof of the FBI Building, diagonally across the street. His nine-year-old son would surely deem it the coolest thing ever, but Ross decided it might not be wise to start staring through a lens at someone who might be staring at *him*, while armed to the teeth. For all he knew, he wasn't even supposed to e-mail his inaugural pictures—especially the ones he'd taken for his nephew—from his government computer here.

He was still considering all this when the First Lady, clad in the whitest of white coats, like a West Texas cotton princess, entered his field of vision. This picture of wintertime glamour contrasted with his memory of the first televised glimpse he'd had of Laura Bush, back in 1978, when she'd sat in a green sleeveless blouse, beside her new husband on the back of a pickup truck, waving to the voters who would wind up politely deciding to go with Kent Hance instead. And now, here were the two of them again, standing up through the retracted roof of an armored limousine the size of an aircraft carrier. Ross zoomed in on the coat and took a picture, wondering if the outfit would pass muster with his thirteen-year-old *fashionista* daughter back home. Excited by the moment, he went ahead and snapped the sharpshooter after all, and then wondered, having taken care of his two children, what picture he might take for his Bush-hating wife.

He'd come back to his apartment from last night's Black Tie and Boots Ball with two tiny Texanish souvenirs, as politically neutral as possible, but he wasn't sure that he could mail even them home. Deborah had said no-thank-you to the idea of coming up from Dallas to go to the ball with him, and she had been aghast at what he spent to get into it stag. She hadn't complained during the past couple of years when he started spending a day or two extra in the District after the Council meetings, and they'd left open the question of where they were actually going to live, now that he was here full-time on staff. Until they settled it he would be in his efficiency apartment over in Arlington, and she'd be home with the kids, still at her job in the SMU library.

The truth was he didn't much want her to join him here. The Council meetings, those ideological mini-vacations from his university job, had also provided a resurgent sense of bachelorhood, a surprise sexual yearning that was either an unwelcome side effect or marvelous fringe benefit of his newly sparked ambition. He had developed, he needed to admit, an intractable little case of Potomac fever, a condition almost always libidinous as well as political. He was discovering that he might not be the thoroughgoing Dependable Guy he'd always seemed; to his even greater surprise, the discovery didn't displease him.

It occurred to Ross that he might safely send Deborah the pictures he'd taken last night of Lyle Lovett and Van Cliburn, if not the one he'd gotten of the president, who during the five minutes he was there had appeared in Ross's viewfinder as a distant pinprick of gray hair—the same way he looked at this moment, a hundred yards from Ross's waving hand, receding westward on Pennsylvania Avenue. The FBI sharpshooter, Ross supposed, could now relax a little.

A knock on the frosted glass preceded the entrance of NEAH's Chairman, who carried a festive-looking glass of iced apple juice, his secretary having forgotten to file for a two-hour waiver of the no-alcohol-in-federal-offices regulation. A composer of melodic classical music at USC—two years younger than himself—his boss was whistling a tune that Ross could recognize but not name. In the hand not holding the glass, he carried a small stack of old WPA guides to American cities, classics of descriptive Depression-era prose by writers who'd been grateful to get the federal make-work.

"Start looking through these," said the Chairman, setting down the guides, along with the apple juice, beside the stack of crinkled, screened-for-anthrax snail mail on Ross's desk. The terror-thwarting precaution caused so many misroutings and delays that the agency would cease functioning if it couldn't conduct eighty percent of its business electronically.

"I'm giving you the first look at our latest initiative," said the Chairman, "which couldn't be more nonpartisan if it involved the League of Women Voters. We're going to do updated versions of twelve of these, highlighting three-quarters of a century of cultural, racial, and architectural progress that's been made in each one of the cities since the originals appeared. Starting with the one on top. You're going down there next month—lucky you!—to get things started." He shook Ross's hand. "Come join everybody in the lounge before the whole parade is over."

The Chairman exited the office whistling the same song, which Ross now recognized as "Way Down Yonder in New Orleans."

———

The Commander-in-Chief Ball inside the National Building Museum was free to all uniformed active-duty personnel. Even so, among all the dancing corporals and midshipmen one could find plenty of civilian high rollers—"Pioneers" who'd raised one hundred thousand dollars for the Bush campaign, along with younger "Mavericks" who'd bundled fifty grand—because of all nine inaugural balls this was the one that meant the most to its honoree and the one at which it was seemliest to be seen. The president was sure to say he'd saved the best for last when he arrived here after lightning-quick stops at the balls in Union Station, the Washington Hilton, and the city's vast convention center.

Barbara Bush and 41 had already come and gone, but the number of brass, military and otherwise, continued to grow during the wait for 43. Not far from the main platform Condoleezza Rice introduced Gene Washington to Joyce Rumsfeld and Don, who remarked that the sports-loving Condi might someday make a fine commissioner of the National Football League. Washington agreed.

"*I* once tried to hire her, you know," said the defense secretary. "I asked her to join the board of Gilead Sciences!"

"Oh, that," said Rice. Rumsfeld was referring to one of the companies he'd had a hand in during the nineties.

"For a not-bad fee," he reminded her with a grin—and a bit of an edge. "But she was already sweeping up too many other offers."

Condi replied with a wordless smile, though she might have pointed out that Gilead Sciences, like the rest of the boards, would have gotten more than its money's worth in securing a conservative African-American woman, newly prominent from her work under 41. Really, what might Don bring up next? How in late '03 he had accused her of planting stories that the White House was going to transfer decision-making about the Iraqi occupation from the president's defense secretary to his national security advisor? The needling never stopped.

Condi was relieved to notice the approach of some fellow Watergate residents, Bob and Elizabeth Dole.

"My old campaign chairman," Dole grumbled to Rumsfeld, extending his good hand, the one without the pencil that discouraged people from grasping his damaged arm.

Rumsfeld twinkled, as if he actually had happy memories of 1996. "One of my highest honors," he said.

"Would have been higher if we'd won," Dole harrumphed. "I might even have given you the Pentagon. But I suppose knowing Cheney was a good way to get it."

Rice looked to see whether being teased was making Don uncomfortable, before remembering that he didn't *do* uncomfortable, with anyone. She shifted her gaze to Senator Elizabeth Dole, whose cosmetic work was shockingly bad. Pushing seventy, the first-term senator looked neither old nor young; simply indeterminate.

Rumsfeld, with some amusement, told Dole about a secret meeting he and Cheney had had at the Madison Hotel to plan the 2000 transition even before *Bush v. Gore* decided which ticket had won. "Right across Fifteenth Street from the *Post*, whose reporters never thought to look out their windows."

Dole ignored him, but picked up on the last word of his sentence. "Know why there are so many of them in *this* building? Windows?" he asked Gene Washington.

The ex-football star confessed that he didn't.

"When it got built they thought having a lot of fresh air circulate would keep the clerks from coming down with malaria. They didn't know until later that the malaria was coming in with the mosquitoes." Dole paused for a moment's reflection and said, mostly to himself, "The bug was riding the bugs."

"What clerks are we talking about?" asked Washington. He looked around at the Corinthian columns, equal in splendor to those in Statuary Hall.

"The guys who paid out the Civil War pensions. I guess I'm the only one old enough here to still call this place the Pension Building—though Rumsfeld's not far behind."

"How much do you think you would have gotten?" asked the defense secretary. "If you'd been in that one instead of World War Two?"

"A pittance. Probably would have gone to my mother."

"Why her?" asked Rice.

"Because I never would have survived," said Dole, whose tuxedo concealed not only a withered arm but a destroyed shoulder. "Not at the hands of some battlefield sawbones at Chickamauga."

He raised his good arm to wave to Colin Powell, who was working this particular crowd like a fellow military man instead of a just-retired diplomat. He looked flamboyantly relieved to be gone from State, no longer the agonized four-star dove scorned by all the neocons around the table in the Roosevelt Room. He waved back to Dole, but Rice noticed that Colin wasn't about to join a group that included Rumsfeld. Meanwhile the band played "The Way You Look Tonight," as Dick Cheney twirled his wife, in a peach-colored dress, through a little applause-generating turn on the stage.

"You know," Rumsfeld said to Rice, "Colin saw himself as representing the interests of the State Department to George W. Bush. That was a mistake. You should represent the president's interests to State."

Rice had already formulated something of this same notion herself, but coming from Don it sounded like bad advice, a trap.

Having warmed up the crowd for George and Laura Bush, the Cheneys exited the stage. "A downbeat away," muttered Dole, watching them recede before the president and First Lady emerged.

Like Laura Bush, Condi was wearing Oscar de la Renta. Along with Mrs. Dole she purred over the beading on the First Lady's blue-and-silver gown, but her mind remained focused on Rumsfeld's suggestion. She recalled what she'd asked the president at Camp David the weekend he proposed she leave the White House for Foggy Bottom. *How am I going to know what you're thinking if I don't see you every day?* She'd immediately wished she hadn't chosen words so needy, or with such a whisper of intimacy to them.

Today's parade had gone on until 5:40 p.m.; the president and Mrs. Bush had left the White House at seven; this was the ninth ball they'd hit and the clock had yet to strike ten. "What a fabulous day we had today!" the commander-in-chief told the crowd. He recognized someone close to the platform, a soldier with an artificial leg whom he'd twice visited at Walter Reed and who was now out there on the dance floor. Condi knew that even before he could give the guy a thumbs-up, Bush's emotions would have gone from zero-to-sixty.

The president—sure enough, his eyes glistening—acknowledged

the Cheneys and then Rumsfeld ("I'm proud to serve with this fine man") but left out Condoleezza Rice, who had slipped halfway behind one of the pillars, removing herself from his line of sight.

"I meant what I said today," Bush told the soldiers. "We have a duty to free those who are captive and to end the world from tyranny."

From behind the column, Condi could see the president wince over the mangled verb choice. The first couple were both tired, and Laura was surely relieved to know that she'd be reading in bed twenty minutes from now. At a cue from the band, Mrs. Bush accepted the arm of a male soldier and began to dance, just as her husband did with a female marine. The couples soon switched partners and the Bushes danced with each other to the theme from *Laura*, that forties film noir, for what must have been the ninth time this evening.

To her horror, Condi thought that Don was now asking *her* to dance. *Out on the floor* were the words she thought she'd just heard over applause for the first couple. Then she realized that Rumsfeld had only expressed a hope that her nomination would soon get "*to* the floor," of the Senate. "For debate," he added.

Dole, who had once managed countless such matters, gave Rice a reassuring pat with his pencilless hand. "This 'debate' business is a phony. It's just Bobby Byrd wanting to give Bush a hard time for a couple of hours. Has nothing to do with you."

"I'll grin and bear it," the secretary-designate promised, gratefully.

"If you get fed up," Dole suggested, "have a friend drop some remark to the press about the Klan—which back in West Virginia was young Bobby's equivalent of the Elks Club. He doesn't like being reminded."

"Oh, Bob!" said his wife, fresh from air-kissing an army captain. She herself made a point of never crossing the Democratic elder.

But Gene Washington fairly roared. "I'm going to make sure she remembers that!"

The Bushes had left the stage, and Condi saw Dole look at his watch.

"We could run you home," she suggested to her Watergate neighbors. "I've still got the NSA car!"

"We'll take it," said Dole.

For a second Condi worried what Elizabeth might think about her and Gene ("we") running the Doles to what was apparently "home," at least on some nights, for the unmarried Rice and her escort. And then she decided she was too relieved to be getting away from Don Rumsfeld to care. She said goodbye to the secretary of defense and his wife and began making her way out, stopping to pose for pictures with two servicemen.

Rumsfeld called after her: "By the way, I've got something of a protégée joining the NSC staff next week. I think you'll find her an interesting addition."

2

JANUARY 30, 2005

The Green Zone; Baghdad, Iraq

"Thanks," said Allison O'Connor, once she was back inside the blast walls and being driven up the Hotel Rashid's date-palmed driveway.

"A pleasure," said Fadhil Hasani, her driver and translator, as she exited the armored Humvee. For much of the trip back to the embassy compound, Fadhil had been talking happily, about the new baby he and his wife were expecting, to both Allison and Tim Gleeson, the Aussie PSD (personal security detail) she'd had with her today and a couple of times before.

She walked around to the driver's side to say goodbye to both men.

"Safe home," Tim wished her from the backseat. Leaning through the open window, he gave her a kiss.

"You too," said Allie. If he didn't get shot going to places like the ones they'd gone today, Tim would return to Oz after a ten-month employment contract with "gobs of money," he'd assured her; enough to buy a house for the wife and child he had waiting back home.

Fadhil, who'd worked with her regularly, extended his arm through the driver's window for a chaste handshake. "God be with you, Miss Allison." He had tears in his eyes.

She felt an impulse to apologize, for her occasional short temper, for the whole botched war, for the cruelties of fate that would leave Fadhil in this place long after she and Tim had gotten out. She settled for saying, "You'll give my love to Rukia, right? And remember to send me a picture of the baby?"

"Oh, yes, of course," he replied, his eyes still glistening, even while his facial expression seemed suddenly abashed over the "*of course*," as if the effusion of politeness might itself be rude. She had never figured out the degree to which Fadhil was constrained by natural shyness or male religious reserve. At times he could chatter lyrically about things like the date-palm orchards he'd grown up around, but then he would quickly go silent, as if he'd said too much, however inconsequentially, or just remembered the dangers of his unexpected profession, this translator's job that marked him as a collaborator to some and which might, Allie thought, be a source of nonpolitical shame as well, an enforced if lucrative substitute for the architectural work he'd trained for in England and could not find at home.

She reached through the window and gave him a tight farewell hug, and heard him whisper *thank you* even as he flinched.

After a few hours outside it, Allie felt relieved to be back in The Bubble, as she'd learned to call the four-square-mile Green Zone upon arriving six months ago. Even with yesterday's rocket attack—two Americans had been killed inside the perimeter—she generally felt safer here than she had in her old Chicago neighborhood, during law school in the late eighties.

Making a quick stop in her room, she threw on some sweatpants and a University of Pennsylvania T-shirt (her undergraduate alma mater) before going down to the Rashid's gym—past the second-floor disco, which already, at six p.m., was thrumming with noise.

She set the treadmill to 7.5 miles per hour and the television to CNN, which was reporting not on the Iraqi elections but the jury pool for the Michael Jackson trial, scheduled to begin tomorrow in L.A. She decided to hold her nose and switch to Fox, but found no Iraq coverage there either, just a Sunday-morning segment on how the media this past week had covered the death of Johnny Carson. That left Al Arabiya, whose usually jaundiced commentator seemed happily caught up in a report on what looked, at least so far, like a successful election. He pointed to the quarter million exiles from the time of Saddam who'd cast absentee ballots; the full one-third of the candidates who were female; and how participation by the once-powerful Sunni minority, angry at being shoved aside with Saddam, appeared to be "exceeding expectations," giving the Americans a chance to claim success.

Sunni turnout couldn't have exceeded expectations by *much*, thought Allie, judging by what she'd observed this afternoon in Gazalia and Azamiyah, two of the sect's Baghdad neighborhoods. Switching off the TV, she took the treadmill up to eight miles an hour, and noticed a few more strands of gray in her long red ponytail, as its wagging picked up speed and amplitude in the gym's mirrored wall. The sun over here had given her more freckles than she'd had since her high school year in Texas, and she hoped she hadn't already packed up her little tube of concealer.

Back upstairs, after a quick shower, she rejoiced in having the room all to herself on her last night here. Double occupancy remained the norm at the Rashid, but Gloria, the IT woman who'd spent most of the last six months in here with her, had departed last week for home. A strange gal—you had to imagine a chatterbox on the autism spectrum—Gloria had driven her crazy by going on and on each day about all the computer equipment she'd helped to install, oblivious to how the long-term goal here was to *get out*, not to give the Green Zone a permanent American infrastructure.

The concealer was nowhere to be found. Allie threw some scrunchies and socks into the leftover lucite ballot box a colleague had this morning given her as a souvenir. She would be wheels up and out of here at six a.m. tomorrow after a stay that had been interrupted by a few nights in emirates like Dubai ("Islam with hookers," she'd e-mailed her mother) and a quick detailing to Kabul, early in December, for the Karzai inaugural.

It was all catching up with her, the dozen years as a civilian lawyer for the Department of the Army, an adventurous low-paying alternative to the white-shoe law firm she'd started out with in New York. She'd by now seen more of the world than she wanted to, participated in too many projects and romances that had proved equally inconclusive. Among the personal tokens just tossed into the lucite box was a greeting card from her mother that showed a career woman slapping her forehead and exclaiming OMG!! I FORGOT TO HAVE CHILDREN!

Very funny, Mother. It would be funnier if Allie hadn't been carrying the card around since her thirty-fifth birthday, more than six years ago. Here in a country where orphans had become as common as howitzers, she'd found herself prone to adoptive urges, which she tried to repel like "intrusive thoughts," those absurd id whispers telling you that you *could*, you know, jump in front of the subway train.

A knock on the door made her flinch. Even inside the secure Rashid one had to be wary of anything unscheduled. But a look through the peephole revealed a ridiculously unthreatening white boy with a cowlick.

"Ms. O'Connor?" he asked, after she opened up. "My name is Kevin. You have a videoconference request for twenty minutes from now. I'm supposed to take you to a secure hookup. RP Room 214."

"Who is it?"

"They wouldn't tell me. Only that it's Washington."

Somebody wanting her on a Sunday morning back there? She threw on a zippered top, something between a sweatshirt and an actual blouse, and followed the kid down to a Jeep for the quick trip to the Republican Palace. As he drove, she smelled the eucalyptus and discouraged conversation. There seemed to be twice as many helicopters overhead as usual, brought into the sky by today's election and yesterday's rocket attack. The crater made by the latter was now ringed with razor wire, as if it were a piece of ground triumphantly secured instead of gouged out by an explosion. Allison thought of the two people who'd died, glad not to have known either. She wondered if the razor wire wasn't protecting their pulverized World Trade Center–style remains.

She entered the palace where Saddam had never lived, and on her way to the second floor passed a few heroic murals that in twenty months of occupation had yet to be painted over. Kevin led her into a warren of drywalls and partitions that had been thrown up to provide offices for twenty-five-year-old assholes like himself, people whose main credential was having worked for Bush during the Florida recount—a deployment not much shorter than the ninety-day ones they were now "proudly serving" here. She would bet that Kevin went to the Wednesday Bible classes.

"Here we are," he told her. "Room 214."

"Thank you," she replied, settling herself in front of a screen.

"I'll connect you." He went into an adjoining room and closed the door between them.

As she waited for a face to appear on the screen, she had a pretty good idea whose it would be. In fact, it could *only* be him, the unlikely new patron who had chatted her up on a photo-op chow line at Bagram during her recent Afghan visit.

We're not doing so badly with only twenty-five thousand, are we? he'd said, more or less answering his own question about Afghan troop levels.

Better than you're doing with a hundred and fifty thousand back there, she'd replied, gesturing vaguely in the direction of Baghdad.

They'd had only a few minutes of conversation—his half of it probing, her half skeptical—and then two days later she'd received her very own "snowflake," one of Donald H. Rumsfeld's legendary, compulsive memoranda. He *liked* the skepticism, he told her, and believed they could use it in an open slot on the National Security Council staff. Really? she thought. When she'd spent most of her stretch here just settling arcane issues of authority and jurisdiction between the U.S. Army and the supposedly sovereign government of Iraq?

The screen flowered to life with the Department of Defense seal, which soon gave way to Rumsfeld's smiling, squinting presence. He wore a V-neck sweater in what appeared to be his home library. A little clock on one of the bookshelves showed 10:14 a.m.

"Good morning, Mr. Secretary."

"Good evening, Allison."

His skin was as crinkly as her late father's, but the expression had a boyishness that took her back to Lubbock High.

"You packed?" he asked.

"Just about, sir."

"The reports are good."

"Yes. No polling places routed. Unless you want to count the one in Mosul that got shot up by AK-47s."

Rumsfeld shrugged over this news from a Sunni stronghold, as if to say, *Well, if that's the worst . . .*

Modest goals leading toward modest success. That's what they were getting in Afghanistan, he'd maintained; and it's what he wanted here. She knew that he would have preferred no occupation at all— just defeat Saddam's army, then get the electricity back on and get out. If they'd done it that way, the mission *would* be accomplished. When she'd listened to one of his recent press conferences, something in Rumsfeld's tone made her wonder if he'd wanted his friend Cheney's war in the first place. The thought had given her a moment's sympathy for him, but then she remembered all of her headaches and revulsion over Abu Ghraib—having to set up procedural safeguards for those lowlifes with their leashes and electrodes—as well as Rumsfeld's rumored, theatrical willingness to fall on his sword over it, an offer Bush never took him up on.

She still hadn't responded to his shrug. "Well, I guess the hand *is* coming off the bicycle seat," she finally said, using a favorite analogy of his for pushing the Iraqis toward doing things on their own. "Of course they may decide to ride the bike straight toward a Shiite theocracy."

Rumsfeld laughed. "I'll give you another pithy pronouncement— not mine, but the late Pat Moynihan's: 'In unanimity one often finds a lack of rigorous thinking.'"

"Ah, yes," she said. "That breath of fresh air you say I'll provide the NSC. I'd feel a little more confident about delivering it if I had a little more expertise."

"You'll be surprised. Agility is more helpful to us now than the usual qualifications."

He certainly knew how to pivot. From the way he talked lately you would think he had opposed Bremer's calamitous decision to dissolve Saddam's army after the surrender in '03. (The head of the occupation hadn't imagined that sudden unemployment might add to the soldiers' resentments.)

"Well," said Allison, "as an assistant to a special assistant to the president, I'm sure I'll be changing the world right away." When Rumsfeld said nothing, she added: "Joke."

"The ones on the NSC staff who are connected to State will impress you the least," the secretary told her.

"Noted," said Allison. "I guess we'll see."

"What did you see *today*?" Rumsfeld asked, the twinkle back in his eye.

She proceeded to tell him about Gazalia and the three Sunni women she'd noticed arguing excitedly with one another on the voting line. She'd thought they were debating the wisdom of participating in the election, until her translator revealed it was just prattle about the suitability of somebody's prospective husband.

Rumsfeld laughed. "Tell them that story when you get to the White House."

"You think it's a hopeful one?" Allison asked.

"They can decide that for themselves."

Rumsfeld held up a red ticket. "Think you can get over jet lag by Wednesday evening?" He moved his hand closer to the camera; the ticket said it would admit the bearer to the House gallery for the president's State of the Union message.

"I'd better remember to pick up my dry cleaning before I get out of here," she responded.

"Wave to me down on the House floor," said Rumsfeld, as he now waved goodbye to her onscreen. His head was quickly replaced by the DoD seal.

Allison told Kevin, when he emerged from the other room, that she didn't need him in order to get back to the Rashid. His face fell. He had wanted to hear all about Rumsfeld: how she knew him; how, no doubt, he himself might meet the secretary.

She caught a shuttle bus from the palace to the hotel and was soon again inside her room. *Safe home*: she thought of Tim Gleeson's Aussie-accented words. She wanted to *stay* home, but was already guessing when she'd next have to come back here: for the two votes coming up later this year—the ratification of a new constitution and the election of a permanent government. Looking around the room, she realized how little she had to pack and how few goodbyes she had bothered to say. There hadn't seemed much point in hunting up people when you couldn't recall who'd be rotating in or rotating out from one day to the next.

She thought of Rolf, her German, well, fuck buddy—a married lawyer helping the interim government deal with genocidal issues left over from Saddam's time. They'd clicked when he introduced himself to her and used "Germany" and "genocide" in the same sentence. "Well," she'd responded, "they say experience counts." After two drinks at the Rashid's bar he'd proposed a "coition of the willing," and she was off on the usual race to nowhere.

Should she call him? No: six a.m. would be here before she knew it, and on Tuesday morning she didn't want to arrive among the White House Christians feeling skanky. She packed up a few knick-knacks—a tiny box, empty, marked "WMDs," a present from a construction contractor—and began charging her laptop for the long flight home.

Another knock on the door—if it was cowlicked Kevin, she'd murder him—which she opened, only to find Rolf holding two burritos from the RP cafeteria. He was sporting an OIF T-shirt: the almost-forgotten acronym stood for Operation Iraqi Freedom, the initial military phase of the American adventure here.

"That always looked to me as if it meant 'Oy, fuck,'" said Allison.

"Ancient history," said Rolf, handing her a burrito. "But there are no IECI T-shirts." The Independent Electoral Commission of Iraq had had charge of today's voting.

"From 'Oy, fuck' to 'Icky.'"

Rolf unwrapped his burrito and said, matter-of-factly, about the election: "Thirty-five killed. Not bad, really."

"If it ends up that fifteen percent of the Sunnis turned out, *that* will be 'not bad,'" said Allison.

Rolf had clearly not come here to evaluate the election figures. Taking a bite of his burrito and swaying his hips, he began singing to the tune of "Let's Call the Whole Thing Off": *You say Sistani, and I say Zarqawi*—naming the Shiite cleric who'd urged people to vote and the Sunni terrorist who'd threatened to kill them if they did.

Allison put a last handful of books into the lucite ballot box.

"Want the T-shirt?" asked Rolf. "A keepsake?" He peeled it off his appealingly lean torso and tossed it to her.

"Subtle," she said.

"Effective?" he asked.

"Oy, fuck," she said. "All right. Give me a minute to brush my teeth."

She went into the bathroom and noticed in the mirror that the edge of her palm was still stained with some of the purple ink that had been applied to voters' thumbs today, to keep them from casting more than one ballot. After being marked, a Sunni woman in Azimayah had clasped Allison's hand and said something to her in loud, fervent Arabic. A translator converted the words to English: "It's a great day, isn't it?"

She scrubbed at the ink spot, which was harder to get off than she would have guessed.

3

FEBRUARY 2, 2005

CNN Studio Green Room; 10 Columbus Circle, New York City

Ann Richards, now seventy-one and ten years out of politics, took a sip of iced tea.

"Are you sure you don't want something else?" a pretty young network assistant asked. "We've got some wine coolers in the fridge."

"Oh, honey," replied the former Texas governor, "I'm as dry as Shrub there." She pointed to the TV image of George W. Bush making his way down the aisle of the House chamber to deliver his fourth State of the Union message. "A bit more tangy, I hope, but I've got just as firm a seat on the wagon."

Larry King opened a can of cream soda. "You're not off salt, too, are you? I'm supposed to watch my intake." He took a handful of pretzel nuggets from a little bowl.

Richards had accepted a booking on a special edition of *Larry King Live* to be broadcast late tonight, after the speech was delivered and the network's regular commentators had had their say about it. King occasionally did his show from New York instead of L.A., and had taken advantage of his East Coast presence tonight to schedule Ann, who'd lived over near Lincoln Center for a few years and still did a lot of political consulting for a firm up here. She'd agreed that the two of them would watch the speech together, since viewers would expect it to be a big part of their later conversation.

"Larry, honey, when we're on the air, you're going to ask me some actual *questions*, right? Not just say: 'Ann, your take?' I will strangle you with your suspenders if you don't get at least a little specific."

"Plenty of questions, I promise. Plus your phone calls!" The phrasing he always used at the top of the hour had just popped out. "I mean, you know, the home audience's calls."

Richards looked at the TV screen. "This damned event always seems longer than the Oscars."

"That's good!" King responded. "Say that when we're on!"

She sipped some more tea as Bush mounted the rostrum and shook hands with the rounded forms of Denny Hastert and Dick Cheney. "They look like two of those Russian nesting dolls. Like they're waiting to see which one is going to be asked to encase the other. I do hear that ol' Denny behaves as if Cheney is his boss."

"Interesting," said King, before he and Richards and the assistant fell to listening quietly for a few minutes. The president was soon praising a rise in home ownership and after that the way his administration had "prosecuted corporate criminals."

"I always kind of liked Kenny Lay," said Richards, recalling the disgraced boss of Enron. "He was pretty square with me. So don't ask me about him when we're in the studio, Larry."

"Point taken!" said the host.

Bush proceeded to talk about the success of the No Child Left Behind Act, and after that the wonders of ethanol. King couldn't understand why he was bothering with the latter, since he would never again have to face the voters of Iowa.

"But his brother might," Richards explained. "Or some tiny shrub that's still a seed. Maybe one of 'the little brown ones,'" she added, using 41's awkward term of affection for his half-Mexican grandchildren by Jeb.

"This dynasty business bother you, Ann?" asked King.

She ignored the question, listening to Bush make his pitch for immigration reform. "What's all this *domestic* stuff?" she finally asked. "Wasn't he saddling up for the Crusades just two weeks ago?"

"It does seem like a change of pace."

"*. . . so we must join together to strengthen and save Social Security.*"

"Oh, dear God," said the former governor, almost in a whisper. "Here it comes."

"Is that disgust I'm hearing?" asked King. "Awe?"

"*Awe?*"

"They say Social Security's the third rail of politics. Here he is, not afraid to touch it."

"Oh, Larry, he could *piss* on it and not have enough brain cells to feel himself get electrocuted."

"*By 2033, the trust fund's annual shortfall will be more than $300 billion. By the year 2042 the entire system will be exhausted and bankrupt.*"

"He'll be ninety-six!" Richards hollered. "And still getting a check from his *grandpa's* trust fund!"

"Quick math!" praised King.

The two of them could hear boos coming from the Democratic side of the aisle. "Turn it up, sweetie," Richards commanded the assistant. "I could swear there's hissing too."

"*I will work with members of Congress to find the most effective combination of reforms. I will listen to anyone who has a good idea to offer.*"

"Wasn't that pretty much how he governed in Texas?" asked King.

"He *never* governed. Bob Bullock did." Richards embarked on a fast tutorial about the peculiar legislative power reserved to that state's lieutenant governors, and how it had been Bullock, a Democrat, who succeeded in pushing Bush's programs through "the leg'" in Austin. "Bullock started out as a mean old segregationist and ended up with even more regrets than ex-wives. By the time Georgie came to town, Bob was a self-pitying wreck who hit on the idea that respectability would descend on him if he made this boy a statewide success and then helped him become president. He could imagine the Medal of Freedom hanging from his neck as easily as I can feel this thing around mine." She raised and let go of the silver-and-turquoise lavalier she was wearing. "Of course, he up and died a year before Shrub made it to Washington." Her voice began to trail off. "Bullock was all right to me when I was coming up, but . . ."

The president was now setting forth the intricacies of personal retirement accounts, which he promised would take the pressure off Social Security.

"Put this damned thing on *mute*," said the former governor. The assistant obeyed.

"How're we gonna do our prep?" King wondered.

"Just a little break," said Richards, who swallowed some more tea in the now-silent green room. She regarded the televised image of the president, who seemed somehow cut in half, separated from himself, by his dark-red tie.

"How's Molly?" asked King, softly.

"Not good," Richards informed him. "The cancer's back." The Texas columnist, another of Larry's prize guests, had a tongue as sharp as Richards' own. "Rough," said King. "She's been battling it for years."

"Still smoking. Drinking, too."

Richards looked away from the screen, shifting her gaze to an unwatered plant not far from the TV. "She and Bullock liked each other, even though he called her 'a hairy-legged liberal.'" Her expression had turned wistful; she extracted a compact from her purse and looked at her own still beautiful, deeply lined face in the little mirror, which was too small to include her formidably beehived white hair.

"Did *you* ever think he'd get so far?" asked King, eager to change the subject back to Bush. "Was it mostly 'cause of Rove?"

"You mean Turd Blossom. That's what Bush calls him, you know." Richards thought of how the two men, callow candidate and soul-less consultant, had quite to her astonishment maneuvered her out of the governor's mansion ten years before. She had never succeeded in rattling Shrub, who had no more to offer than ownership of a base-ball team as his outstanding qualification for the state's top job. She'd pummeled him by the hour, even taunted him in the elevator on the way up to their one debate, sure she could break his drugstore-cowboy stride. But nothing had worked.

"You know the reason Rove's office in Austin had no windows?" she asked King.

"So he could concentrate?"

"It was an environmental measure for the protection of the public. So they wouldn't be downwind of him."

King laughed. "Remind me who it was you beat the first time."

"In '90? Clayton Williams, the richest rancher and most ridiculous fool you ever met. He won his primary by out-good-ol'-boying his opponent. And you know who that was? Little Kent Hance, the only man who ever beat Georgie, way back when he ran for Congress. Needless to say, Hance had turned Republican—all that part of the state did during Reagan's time. Shrub even moderated a GOP debate between Hance and Claytie. You know, Larry, Texas is really just a small town that happens to be the size of France."

"I gotta bring us back to the present, Ann." King unmuted the TV: *"For the good of families, children, and society, I support a constitutional amendment to protect the institution of marriage."*

Richards remained silent. How was she supposed to listen to this antigay guff without remembering the dyke rumor that Rove had floated past the electorate and her four grown kids when he was running young George against her in '94? He'd knocked her so badly off balance that even tonight, ten years later, she thought it better not to tell Larry she had plans for a ginger-ale nightcap with half-in, half-out-of-the-closet Liz Smith, the *New York Post*'s gossip columnist.

"Taking on gang life will be one part of a broader outreach to at-risk youth. . . . And I am proud that the leader of this nationwide effort will be our First Lady, Laura Bush."

"Oh, that'll stop 'em!" Richards cried. "Those Crips are going to be *clamoring* for library cards from Watts to the South Side of Chicago!" In a lower, more peevish tone, she told King, "You know, I executed forty-eight people, and had two times as many folks in prison when I left Austin as when I got there. But Shrub made me out to be soft on crime and the voters bought it."

The president seemed ready to switch back to foreign affairs: *"There are still regimes seeking weapons of mass destruction, but no longer without attention and without consequence."*

Richards lifted her seat cushion.

"Did you lose something?" the assistant asked.

"Just checkin' for WMDs. Any in your chair, hon'?"

King noticed how a pin she wore glinted when she shifted. Richards could see him peering at it. "Yeah, it's a silver foot"—a commemoration, she explained, of the jibe at Bush's father that had made her famous back in '88. *Poor George. He can't help it. He was born with a silver foot in his mouth!*

"Did you have it made?" asked King.

"Hell, no—it was a present. From George Herbert Walker himself."

"Classy guy," said King.

Richards dismissively flicked her wrist. "Up to a point. You can bet that the missus didn't sign the card. She's meaner than Bullock was with a quart of booze inside him. Look around *her* neck and you'll find all the pearls of wisdom that didn't go to her son."

"Funny stuff," said King.

"But believe me, he *is* his mother's son."

"She did yell at me once," King remembered. "For not wearing a tie to some White House event. I thought it was informal."

Richards gave him an are-you-out-of-your-mind look.

"*. . . the victory of freedom in Iraq will strengthen a new ally in the war on terror, inspire democratic reformers from Damascus to Tehran, bring more hope and progress to a troubled region, and thereby lift a terrible threat from the lives of our children and grandchildren.*"

"That inaugural speech of his managed to repel both Jim Baker and Pat Buchanan," Richards noted, referencing endpoints on the Republican spectrum, from multilateralist to America First.

In the House gallery, after being mentioned by the president, Safia Taleb al-Suhail, an Iraqi woman whose father had been murdered by Saddam Hussein, embraced Mrs. Janet Norwood, the mother of a U.S. Marine Corps sergeant killed in Fallujah. Even the Democrats were soon on their feet and cheering, though it was mostly Republicans waggling ink-stained thumbs, a gesture of support for the Iraqi elections the administration had just helped to run.

"Well, he's good at Skutniks," said Richards. "I'll give him that."

"Sputniks?" asked King.

"*Skutniks*," corrected Richards, who told King that these were the "ordinary heroes" introduced at State of the Union addresses ever since '82, when Reagan had brought along Lenny Skutnik, a schlubby white-collar drone, two weeks after he dove into the freezing Potomac to rescue a woman from the crash of that Air Florida plane.

"Use that on the air!" King enthused. "Our viewers will learn something!" After a pause he added: "I wonder if he'll tune us in later."

"Skutnik?" asked Richards.

"No, Bush."

"You *are* out of your mind, Larry. He'll be in bed twenty minutes from now. Maybe even sooner. He's got to get up *extra* early tomorrow for the goddamned National Prayer Breakfast."

King reached for some pretzels. As the cheering subsided and the lawmakers resumed their seats, Richards took advantage of the momentary silence to tell him, in a near-whisper: "Call Molly sometime. Or send her an e-mail. She's up half the night at her computer."

———

The Chart Room; 300 Chartres Street, New Orleans, Louisiana

Harry Connick, Jr.'s, rendition of "On the Street Where You Live" was emerging from the jukebox while a mute, closed-captioned George W. Bush neared the end of his speech on the television above the bar.

Ross Weatherall sat at a small table near a window, addressed every so often by a man who would swivel around on his barstool. Gordon, a native of the city who'd introduced himself, appeared to be about seventy; his pronouncements tended toward the quick, startling, and less than fully coherent, though this next one was straightforward: "You know," he told Ross, pointing to the jukebox. "His daddy was the district attorney down here."

"Yes, I've heard that."

"Goes to show you," Gordon added, without saying just what it went to show. He turned back to face the bar once more, having earlier informed Ross that, as a young man, he had stolen a cache of weapons for the CIA to pass on to anti-Castro rebels, and done investigative work for one of Harry Connick, Sr.'s, most notorious predecessors, Jim Garrison, whose long-ago probe of JFK's murder—from what little Ross knew, and despite Oliver Stone's movie—had been a mad, improvisational weaving of conspiracy where none existed.

Ross's own multitasking didn't make all this any easier to follow. In addition to half-regarding the president's speech and half-listening to both Gordon and Harry Connick, Jr., he was composing offline e-mails on his laptop. Flipping it open at the table had earned him an indulgent smirk from the waitress, as if he were some sort of Mardi Gras exotic who'd come in wearing a Viking helmet.

"Am I being a buzzkill?" he'd asked, with a smile, when she took his beer order.

"Honey, down here there's no such thing as a killable buzz."

After two days in New Orleans he was enough in love with the city to be disappointed that she hadn't taken him for a local. He was staying on his per diem at the fine old Hotel Monteleone and having some success with the nascent guidebook project: he'd been out at Tulane today to meet with the American Studies professor through whom the NEAH was running the project grant, and he'd gotten a biographer of Walker Percy to agree to do the section on the Garden District. A local bookstore was even making space for the project in some rooms above their shop in Pirates Alley.

Ross had started to feel a little like Lyle Saxon, the all-around man of letters who had produced the original WPA guide, which Ross had carried with him up and down Canal Street this afternoon. For each place that had disappeared over the past sixty years, he'd found three or four others still just where they'd always been, stores and restaurants and ancient offices whose sudden sighting made the guide's black-and-white plates spring to colorized life, like a movie on TNT. There were, he realized, a hundred layers to everything here, all of them ready to be peeled back, repainted, redescribed, and made sense of. The office of Senator Vitter, a Republican just elected to the upper body after three terms in the House, had expressed enthusiasm for the project and promised that Ross would get introduced to some of the city's important figures on his upcoming trips. Indeed, the Chairman told him he could expect to be meeting not just guys like the Percy biographer, but Governor Blanco, Mayor Nagin, and all the rest. More Democrats than Republicans, in fact: *our latest initiative couldn't be more bipartisan if it involved the League of Women Voters.*

"You're from D.C., right?" asked Gordon, turning back around. "Up there you need to get ready for a terrorist attack that will only *look* like one. In fact, nothing will really have happened, but the UN will want you to *think* something has."

"You may be right," said Ross, taking a sip of beer without looking up from his laptop. He finished off an e-mail to his son. An hour ago, from the Monteleone, he'd talked to his daughter on the Black-Berry the agency now had him carry. When he asked Caitlyn to put her mother "on the line," she'd told him, with an audible eye roll, "Dad, there *is* no line, at least not on *your* end," before instructing him to download something called Skype so they could converse face-to-face, screen-to-screen, like characters in *The Jetsons.* Deborah had claimed to be too busy to come to the phone, and he was only now beginning to realize how bad things were between them.

"The road of providence is uneven and unpredictable, yet we know where it leads: it leads to freedom."

"It leads to *where?*" asked Gordon, responding to the president. "No, it doesn't!"

Ross closed his laptop—he had to get away from this guy—but made the mistake of asking, "Why shouldn't it?"

"Because all roads run in a circle!"

"Ah."

"Everything is connected," said Gordon. "Garrison was right about more than you think."

Ross nodded and put down a tip, determined to leave before having to hear about six shooters, half Mafia and half CIA, looking up from storm drains in Dealey Plaza. When he stood up, he pointed his nearly empty bottle of Bud Light toward the TV screen, a plea that he be allowed to attend to the closing moments of the State of the Union.

"Sure, suit yourself," said Gordon, turning around to the bar.

W. was handshaking his way back up the aisle of the House chamber; the Democrats were emptying out fast. Ross wondered if the important people down front—the Cabinet, the Supreme Court sans Rehnquist—were now trapped, like first-class airline passengers unexpectedly ordered to exit through the rear door. He could see Condi Rice having a businesslike chat with Elaine Chao, the Labor secretary who was also the majority whip's wife. And there was Rumsfeld, not displaying an inked thumb but waving to someone up in the gallery: the First Lady? the dead soldier's mother who'd gotten a hug? No, at the top of the screen he could see someone waving back, a lean, athletic-looking woman with long red hair and what was, he could tell, small as her image might be, a playfully sarcastic expression.

He brought the beer bottle—suddenly, involuntarily—to his lips. After twenty-six years without seeing or hearing from her, of knowing no more about her than what some ashamed and inconclusive Googling had produced, the sight of her seemed less believable than anything Gordon had said. But there she stood, coming to life like one of the old guidebook photos, time-traveling toward him on some cosmic ripple, as if to bring him, once more, his first kiss.

4

FEBRUARY 23, 2005

U.S. Ambassador's Residence; Brussels, Belgium

"No, sir, you go ahead," said Condi Rice. "I insist."

The basement exercise room contained only one elliptical, the preferred machine of both the president and his secretary of state. "I'll take this," Condi said, getting on the stationary bike.

Bush gave her a wink and a suit-yourself shrug. Where he'd really like to be was out in the Maryland woods on his own mountain bike, leaving the Secret Service in the dust. But the elliptical would do. He was feeling pretty good, almost back to his precampaign weight; for the last couple of weeks Laura had been telling him to dial back the workouts, which had started seeming a little fanatical to her, like his devotion to being on time.

Maybe she was right, but if truth be told, however un-Christian it might be, he couldn't stand being around the unfit. Unless they were lost in political conversation, Rove repelled him, and he couldn't say he'd been surprised when Gerson, that doughy version of Dilton Doiley from the Archie comics, had had his heart attack a week before Christmas. He wished Mike the best, but wouldn't mind having him, silver tongue and all, stepping back a bit. For a ghostwriter he was awfully, what would you call it, *corporeal*: never missed a chance to talk to the press about what a deep and tortured wordsmith he was.

"You think we're overstaying our welcome here?" the president asked Condi. "Three nights seems like a lot."

"Not at all," she assured him, while noticing that his arm and leg movements on the elliptical appeared to cancel each other out—as if drawing X's on the air. "You're saving the taxpayers a big hotel bill!"

Bush cocked his head into the nod-smirk combination that said "I suppose." Tom Korologos, the ambassador upstairs, was a fine guy who went way back with Dad; a blunt, no-b.s. fixer and smoother who'd made a fortune lobbying but had gotten off his seventy-year-old ass to spend four months working under Bremer in Iraq at the start of the occupation. *That's* what had earned him his perch here, not all the years shuffling between K Street and the White House and the Hill.

"Okay," he said at last, agreeing with Condi on the matter of hospitality. "But some of our staff guys are eating Mormon the Greek out of house and home." Korologos, improbably enough, had started life in Utah.

Condi put the pedals of her bike through another ten rotations before asking, "So now that three days have passed, how do you think 'Old Europe' is treating you?"

This was a crack against Rumsfeld, who was never afraid to point out that within the "coalition of the willing," the newer NATO countries, the ones from Eastern Europe, had been a lot *more* willing than the slack, half-socialist originators of the Western alliance. Blair had had to drag the Brits to Baghdad kicking and screaming. And the rest, of course, were even worse. But Rumsfeld's comments made things harder; Bush had had to sit there yesterday and smile at the EU representative Don had pronounced irrelevant.

"Well, I enjoyed my breakfast with Tony," the president told Condi, and it was true. Unlikely as it might be, he was sure Blair preferred him to Clinton, even if those two had all that "third way" stuff in common.

"You know, sir," explained Condi, going into her schoolmarm mode, "there's one way in which the U.K. can be considered *new* Europe instead of old. They didn't join the EU with the first 'Inner Six' members; some years passed before they came in."

He tried to look appreciative above the crablike grindings of the elliptical. "Well, it was a lot more fun having breakfast with Tony than having dinner with Pepé Le Pew." He'd had to host Chirac right here, upstairs, on Monday night, a nauseating couple of hours. They'd pretended to be friends, behaving as if the Axis of Weasel days were actually behind them. He'd found himself wishing he were across a table from Berlusconi, that crude and crazy Italian version of Claytie Williams. "Still, I did my best to behave. I hope you noticed I called the potatoes 'French fries' and not 'freedom' ones. Even though they looked like hash browns to me."

Condi smiled, gratefully, over this bit of conciliation. "*Frites*," she said. "Or *aiguillettes*."

"Aggie-what?"

"What the French call French fries."

"Well, let 'em eat aiguillettes. It was pretty damned diplomatic of me, I thought."

Over on the bike, Condi was finally breathing through her mouth instead of her nose. "I *am* glad you told Chirac no," she said, puffing just a little, "when he proposed that Israeli-Palestinian conference."

"*Hell* no is more like it. That's one mess I leave to *you*. I once told Clinton, 'You taught yourself the name of every damned street in Jerusalem. Fat lot of good it did you—or anybody over there.'"

He took the elliptical up two notches, and Condi added another full mph to the stationary bike.

"The worst is yet to come," he told her, getting back to the present trip.

"You mean Schröder?"

"Gerhard the Godawful." The German chancellor had gotten himself elected to a second term more or less by running against *him*. The two of them had a meeting and, even worse, a presser scheduled for this afternoon, all of it down in Mainz, where Dad and Kohl had wowed the locals back in '89. "I'd rather spend an hour with Qadaffi. Or thirty minutes with Gore."

As always, he was pleased when he got a laugh—a matter of the deepest satisfaction to him ever since he'd taken it upon himself, at the age of seven, to cheer up Mother, despairing over the death of his little sister in that hotbox of a house in Midland.

"As it is," he now added, "my time with Gerhard will break Dick's speed record in Afghanistan." Back in December, having gone to Kabul for Karzai's inauguration, Cheney had remained on the ground for less than seven hours.

After a few more scuttlings on the elliptical, he noticed that Condi wasn't saying anything. When it came to Dick, she tended to tread even more cautiously than she did with Rumsfeld.

"What Schröder will hit you hardest on is Vienna," she finally said. The Germans and most of the rest of the Europeans wanted the U.S. to join their talks with the Iranians, as if that were all it would take to get the mullahs to stop a nuclear-weapons program whose existence they didn't even admit.

"Yeah, well, I'll tell Gerhard I'll pencil Vienna in for right after that Israeli-Palestinian conference. Which should be about the twelfth of never." He shot Condi a smile. "You old enough to remember that one?"

"Oh, we listened to a *lot* of Johnny Mathis in Birmingham, sir. I guarantee you it came over the radio when I was strapped in my car seat."

The two of them went at a fast, even pace for a while, until he signaled he was ready for a cool-down. He loved the way this machine was saving his knees.

"I'll get through today, but I wish we were flying back to Fargo instead of Frankfurt." He'd been enjoying all the day trips for the Social Security proposal, the town halls and pep rallies from Omaha to Tampa. For half a day at a time he could trick himself into thinking he was having the sort of domestic-focused presidency he once expected to have.

"How's that going?" asked Condi.

"Social Security?"

"Yes."

He shrugged. So far there'd been mostly bad news. He explained to her how he'd pissed off Max Baucus, who'd been crucial to tax reform, by barging into Montana without letting the senator know he was descending on his home state. It had been a staff fuckup, but so far there'd been no sign of forgiveness. He could hear a faraway sound creeping into his voice as he talked about it all to Condi. "You know, I've been pushing Social Security reform since I ran against Hance."

She nodded supportively, and he told himself this was no time to get into some all-Kraut funk over Mad Max and Grim Gerhard. He stopped the elliptical and mopped his face with the hand towel. All the white noise vanished from the basement when Condi stopped the stationary bike.

"You're the one that got me into *this* trip," he teased. They both remembered the memo she'd sent, just after agreeing to take State, telling him that he needed to get serious about making up with the Europeans, no matter how childish they'd been.

"Yes, I was," replied Condi, trying to imitate one of Laura's it's-good-for-you-and-you'll-thank-me smiles.

"What's that phrase you've been using?"

" 'Transformational diplomacy.' But I've also been saying 'freedom' to the Europeans every chance I get."

He had to resist saying "good girl," though it wouldn't be a catastrophe if the words slipped out. He liked being with Condi because she didn't make him walk any feminist or racial minefield. He was sorry to be seeing less of her these days than when she'd been his NSA, but that was the price to pay for being rid of Powell, who had spent most of the first term looking annoyed, even *pained*, trying to convince everybody he was doing them a favor just by being there.

"Tell me what you used to say back at the start?" he asked her. There was no need to explain that "the start" meant the beginning of Iraq, in '03. "About the best way to handle the Euros?"

Condi lowered her eyes with a sort of faux bashfulness, as if embarrassed instead of delighted to be repeating a bit of mischief that had pleased him: " 'Punish France; ignore Germany; forgive Russia.' "

"Love it!" he replied, wiping his face again. "And look forward to China."

There was no need to explain this, either. He mentioned the 2008 Olympics in Beijing as often as a high school teacher motivatingly invoked the coming senior class trip. As the administration's top sports fans, he and Condi would revel in that farewell junket more than anyone else. In fact, he was almost alarmed by the intensity of his yearning for it. He'd enjoyed his new sense of legitimacy for about two weeks after last fall's clear-cut reelection, before realizing how much he already wanted the whole thing to be over.

———

U.S. Army Airfield, Wiesbaden, Germany; later that day

The armored limo pulled away from the Electoral Palace in Mainz, and Condi, whose devotion to punctuality rivaled her boss's, made a welcome calculation: they would be getting to the base a little ahead of schedule. A greeting from the First Armored Division, Old Ironsides, was sure to lift the president's spirits after his gloomy chat and press conference with Schröder; there hadn't been so much as a freedom fry to joke about. Wiesbaden would be different. No harrowing hospital visit to wounded soldiers was on the schedule. The whole thing would be quick and peppy, a chug-a-lug cocktail before they were airborne for Bratislava and a visit with Putin.

Even so, Condi wished she had some genuinely good news to bring the boss. There'd been almost none since January 30th, that Sunday night she'd called to tell him to turn on the television and see how well the Iraqi elections were going. Today she'd had to update him on a suicide bombing that killed forty people in Baghdad during the Ashura holidays. Reading from the background memo sent over by State, she'd explained that during this particular holiday the Shia tended to go in for self-flagellation (pictures of little boys with bloodied crew cuts!) while the Sunnis just fasted and atoned.

"Sounds like Yom Kippur," the president had remarked.

"More than you know," she'd replied. "Ashura commemorates how Allah parted the Red Sea for Moses."

"*Allah*? And *Moses*?" Bush had asked, seeming to find something hopeful in this surprising piece of ecumenical information.

But right now, here in the limousine, there were only more bad tidings she had to impart. "You're at seventy-seven percent disapproval."

"*What?*"

"Well, specifically, that's the proportion of Germans who believe your reelection makes the world less safe." She offered him the paper that summarized some polling the embassy over here had commissioned.

The president laughed, declining a look at the document. "I thought you were giving me my numbers from *home!*" He pointed to the limo's secure phone. "I was about to pick that up and call Rove to fire him. If it's just the Germans, I can live with it."

Condi couldn't shake off her own dismay. She'd been here in Mainz with 41, back in 1989, and could still remember the cheers—months before the Berlin Wall had even come down. Today the security people, fearing the worst, had shut not only portions of the highway but stretches of the Rhine.

Seated beside her, Laura was reading pamphlets she'd been given at the Gutenberg Museum during a tour of it with Schröder's wife—the only festive item on the itinerary. The First Lady calmly looked up for a glimpse of the "red zone": an area reserved for demonstrators, like that corral off Pennsylvania Avenue during last month's inaugural.

As the car purred onward, Condi felt renewed disappointment over how, at lunchtime today, the president had met with a "pre-selected Round Table" of Americans and Germans, not a regular town-hall audience. It had been the same for her in Paris a couple of weeks ago: the ticket-holders for her speech at the Institute of Political Sciences had been chosen via algorithms worthy of Amazon.com, the process designed to assure at least a neutral reception for "Madame Hawk." If all this bothered *her*, a control freak par excellence, shouldn't others be seeing the problem? It was as if the administration had decided that crowds needed to be quarantined from *them*, as if the White House were conceding the toxicity ascribed to it by its enemies.

But suddenly, just now, she could hear cheering. The limo had gone through the gates of the airbase and was gliding toward a platform set up for the welcoming ceremony. Her spirits rose: if she didn't have good news for the president, she certainly had a surprise in store for him.

"Ma'am," said General Dempsey, shaking her hand after the president's. He presented her to an aide who would take her to the spot from which she'd introduce the commander-in-chief.

"Okay, give me just one second," she told the junior officer, turning around as if to check her makeup in the limousine's tinted windows. In fact she was unfastening four large buttons that ran up the inside of her long winter coat.

"I'm ready," she said, stepping off in front of the president and Dempsey, hitting her stride on the way to the microphone. Snowflakes were landing on her hair, as if to give it the thinnest of veils. And then, as she knew would happen, the breeze caught the bottom flaps of the coat, flinging them open to reveal a pair of knee-high boots tightly encasing two legs whose several inches of exposed thigh had been made shapely by uncountable hours on the elliptical and bike. The thousand soldiers could see it all on the jumbotron. "*We love you!*" they screamed, between wolf whistles.

She waved at them, and smiled, and allowed herself to think: *Fuck you, Barbara Boxer.*

The president would love this. He knew that she was the least grandstanding appointee imaginable; he was always urging her to raise her profile, and this—Our Miss Brooks morphing into Lucy Lawless—would take him out of his funk for the rest of the day. *Dominatrix? Who, me?* It would be the lead clip on the evening news, the picture on everyone's computer screen for the next twelve hours. He wouldn't care that he'd been elbowed out of the story; all that would matter was that Schröder had been elbowed out of it too.

She spoke without notes, because Lucy Lawless would not have tucked any into *her* breastplates. She was *winging it*: "America has the greatest soldiers, airmen, and seamen in the history of the world!"

We love you! More wolf whistles. More screams. This would fuel rumors about her and 2008, and what was wrong with that? The president knew she would never run for office—the thought of it made her want to slather on three applications of Purell—but the talk would build her up against Don and Cheney, since nobody would be urging those two Ford administration fossils to run for anything.

She looked out over her camouflage-clad audience and wondered whether she should make reference to the New England Patriots, or if mentioning them was too dated, their Super Bowl win being now more than two weeks in the past. No, she would quit while she was ahead and relinquish the lectern to the president, who rewarded her with a wink.

She could feel the boost in his mood as he read from his text: *"They tell me the quality of life here is really good. . . ."* The guys and their families roared with laughter, and he laughed with them. *"You have served with honor and distinction—and a little longer than some of you expected."* The troops were even laughing at stop-losses, those horrible surprise extended deployments that Don unaccountably preferred to expanding the size of the army. If George W. Bush could laugh them off, then they would too!

Don didn't believe in the Freedom Agenda, and Dick only subscribed to it strategically, for the way it justified their striking anywhere they liked or needed to. But she *did* believe in it. Yes, she had moved rightwards with the president, but not *because* of him; circumstances, ones that some people were already forgetting, had changed her. And if that disappointed Madeleine Albright, her first female predecessor and the daughter of her academic mentor, so be it: Madeleine could stop with the sorrowful looks and crocodile tears. She was now just part of the opposition, in these days when no divide was any longer bridgeable, when the aisle that ran down each chamber of Congress was a Red Sea that would never be parted.

> *. . . the only force powerful enough to stop the rise of tyranny and terror and replace hatred with hope is the force of human freedom.*
>
> *You are serving in a critical period in freedom's history, and there will be more difficult work ahead. Yet I'm optimistic about our future because I know the character of freedom's defenders. I know the history of those who have defended our freedom.*

There was more to come in the paragraph remaining: a *free* Berlin; *freedom's* "triumph in the Cold War"; the defense of *freedom*; the cause of *freedom*.

As she heard it over and over, she struggled to keep the word meaningful and distinct, but she remembered a little recess game they used to play at the Brunetta C. Hill Elementary School in Birmingham: when you said *toy boat* five times fast, you no longer knew what you were saying.

———

A half hour later, on their way to Bratislava for the meeting with Putin, she was briefing a president whose good humor had already dissipated and whose attention was shifting toward the clouds beneath the plane.

Condi tapped a biography of the Russian leader that rested on the table between them. "You're going to be seeing an awful lot of him," she said. Less than three months from now the president would be in Moscow for the sixtieth-anniversary V-E celebrations, and she would again be wishing he had never said, back in 2001, that he'd "looked the man in the eye" and "found him very straightforward and trustworthy," had even gotten "a sense of his soul."

She knew that in public George W. Bush tended to compliment the character of anyone not actually beating a dog. But the remark about the Russian strongman still made his secretary of state wince.

"Your friend Dick doesn't want me trusting him," Bush now said.

"It's not so much a matter of your trusting him as—"

"I'm only looking to trust him on one big thing."

"Oh?" said Condi. "What's that?"

"I'm not ready to tell even you about it."

She felt startled, even rebuked, though his reply had come with the third wink she'd had from him today. What had he meant? He immediately veered away from the subject and resumed looking out the window.

"Condi," he asked after a full two minutes. "Are we heading for Slovakia or Slovenia?"

"Slovakia, sir."

"Relax," he said, closing his eyes with a smile. "Just kidding you."

Yes, he was, she thought; about his sometimes shaky geography. But whatever it was, he wasn't kidding about Putin.

5

MARCH 14, 2005

Benjamin Franklin State Dining Room; Department of State; Washington, D.C.

Allie looked up at the ceiling's ornamental plasterwork, a huge rendition of the Great Seal of the United States, and wondered if there would be lunch. Or at least some hors d'oeuvred approximation of it. She could find no encouraging sign of either in the enormous reception area—an oddly grandiose venue, she thought, for what was only an announcement, not a swearing-in.

Of course, true-believing Bushies regarded the impending return of Karen Hughes—the president's Amazonian spinmeister from his gubernatorial and campaign days—as worthy of the eight chandeliers above everyone's head. The former TV newswoman, who had managed Bush's "message" through 9/11 and for some months beyond, had left Washington three years ago, famously declaring, once back in Texas, that even her family dog didn't like living inside the Beltway.

Waiting for her to enter this baronial space, Allie wondered about this woman who had always proclaimed George W. Bush to be indispensable, and then decided that serving him was less important than attendance at her son's baseball games. Was it the second term's Freedom Agenda that had lured her back? No, from what Allie understood, the son's getting ready to go off to college had convinced his mother she could rejoin the administration and start selling the Bush message to the whole world as Undersecretary of State for Public Diplomacy, the appointment set to be announced with such fanfare any minute from now.

Allie again glanced upward. The gold leaf adorning the Great Seal appeared heavier than the plaster it clung to. The gilding looked as if it could bring down the lily, and everything she knew about Mrs. Hughes, this heavy-handed and underinformed crony, made her think that with such a messenger to the restive Arab world, one could expect to see, any time now, more mobs ripping more Great Seals from their place above U.S. embassy doorways.

As one of the three NSC staffers asked to attend this event, Allie surmised that her name had been put on the list by Rumsfeld. Why, she didn't know—any more than she could yet answer the larger question of what the defense secretary wanted from her own presence in Washington. The only matter about which she could now hazard a guess was the reason for no reception or lunch today. Having one would force the nominee, as well as the secretary of state soon to be her boss, to hang around for a bit, while the press, bent on turning an announcement into an "availability," started shouting the sort of inconvenient questions that the president, who had a televised press conference the day after tomorrow, was no doubt getting ready for over in the Residence.

The two women—Bush favorites—at last strode in: Hughes in a big blue blazer, unbuttoned and comfort-designed; Rice in a much more expensive jacket, off-white and smartly snapped into place over her trim figure. Its high collar almost suggested the ruff around Queen Elizabeth I's neck. In its way the outfit was as assertive as last month's pain-mistress boots in Wiesbaden. Allie also noticed the hugeness of Hughes's shoes—they must be size twelves—their low heels now planted in the deep pile of a carpet that depicted the crops and seasons of the North American continent.

"Today," said the secretary, as the still cameras whirred and clicked, "I am pleased to announce that President Bush intends to nominate Karen P. Hughes as the State Department's new undersecretary for public diplomacy. Karen will have the rank of ambassador and, if confirmed, will undertake a broad review and restructuring of our public diplomacy efforts. I can think of no individual more suited to this task of telling America's story to the world than my good friend Karen."

The idea that this "good friend" was Rice's first choice for the post sounded as laughable to Allie as the locution "intends to nominate" seemed peculiar. Why the note of hesitation or delay?

"This is a job for a communicator," said Rice, "and Karen Hughes is a communicator *par excellence.*"

En français. Did Condi believe she was still in Paris? *Meow,* Allie scolded herself, after having the thought. She usually found herself liking the secretary of state. The self-discipline; the cinched waist; the clear and compulsive self-censorship: all of it seemed to make a statement—and maybe a more effective one than her own decades of funky, feckless rebellion.

Rice now introduced Dina Powell, the lacquered young Egyptian-American woman with whom Allie had had a few quick dealings in Presidential Personnel, the office Powell would now be leaving in order to work under Hughes. The secretary extolled Dina's ability to speak Arabic as if it put the girl on the level of Madame Curie, before she lightheartedly returned to Hughes: "You know, Karen used to get me ready for the Sunday interview shows when I was national security advisor, so I have no doubt of her ability to alter people's perspectives and make them see what's really important."

Yeah, her ability to turn the truth into treacle. This whole little rollout was too dull for words; Allie soon couldn't keep her mind from wandering and her eyes from being drawn back to the nominee's Brobdingnagian shoes. She thought of what Rolf had said, with a don't-be-disappointed smile, the first time he tossed his clothes onto the floor of her room in the Rashid: *You know what they say: big shoes, big feet.*

Hughes herself now stepped forward to thank her "gracious" friend. She had chosen, Allie thought, just the right word for poor Condi, who seemed to have spent a lifetime offering graciousness as a kind of microwaved substitute for actual warmth. From there, however, Hughes went straight downhill rhetorically, even making the observation that international travel was so *broadening*, as if she were about to board a cruise ship or embark on her junior year abroad. In this new job, she promised, she would remain mindful of her identities as a daughter, a friend of the president, and a mother—no, dear God, make that a *mom*.

When she was through, the invited guests, Allie among them, applauded; the press might as well have, too, for all they had to do. Jim Wilkinson, Condi's young media man, brought the nominee over to shake hands with her fellow administration appointees. "This is Allison O'Connor of the NSC," he said, reading the name off Allie's lanyard. The undersecretary-designate greeted her with the suspicious look one reserves for someone *new*, as if Allie's Johnny-come-lateness were unpardonable, while Hughes's own prolonged sabbatical was just another form of fealty to George W. Bush.

"Ms. O'Connor has until recently been in Iraq," said Wilkinson, surprising Allie with this bit of homework. "She was performing legal work for the Department of the Army."

"Thank you for your service," said Hughes.

I was a civilian, lady. She couldn't grasp the distinction? Even when, according to the printed bio they'd distributed, Hughes had been an army brat who spent some of her childhood in the Canal Zone?

"What *exactly* were you doing over there?" the nominee asked. She sounded almost accusatory.

"Assisting with the elections just before I left."

"A great success!" said Hughes, showing some sparkle for the rubbernecking press. "It's a story we need to be telling!"

"Well," said Allie, "we'll see."

Hughes's smile faded, as if doubt were being cast on her confirmation.

"I mean," Allie clarified, "we'll see if the elections turn out to be a success—long-term."

"Freedom is *always* a success," said the nominee, moving on to the next person. "Hi, I'm Karen."

———

Several minutes later Condi entered her office, nearly as grand as the Franklin dining room, with the new undersecretary-designate.

"Oh boy!" said Karen, taking a look at the Lincoln Memorial through one of the immense fortified windows. "*That's* something they need to see!"

The Muslims? wondered Condi, while the TV purred in the background. She always kept it tuned to CNN and dared anyone to call her a RINO (Republican in name only) for choosing the internationally minded channel over Fox, which provided the background music for most administration offices. She was determined to grow more and more comfortable in her new domain: she had prevailed over Cheney and acquired Bob Zoellick, a calm globalist, for her number two; John Bolton, the veep's hot-headed choice, had been sent up to the UN instead.

And now she would have Karen, with whom she'd bonded during the 2000 campaign, when her friend helped alliterate them toward their delayed victory with coinages like "compassionate conservatism" and "reformer with results." Condi had learned to let her hair down with the big Texan, even allowing Karen to see the tears come to her eyes when they traveled to Poland in '01 and heard the military band from NATO's newest member play "The Star-Spangled Banner."

Bringing Karen back *had* in fact been Condi's idea, though her overriding motive had been to please him, the president. The way he'd lit up when she took Karen into this morning's working breakfast at the White House! It was as if she'd arranged to have a Tex-Mex meal flown in as a surprise from home. Karen made him feel secure in a way that, Condi realized, she might never quite accomplish herself.

Karen was now exclaiming over every photo and trinket in the office; she'd just picked up an autographed football helmet from Gene Washington.

"Here," said Condi. "Have an atlas."

She handed Karen the same pocket gazetteer, not much bigger

than a passport, that she'd given members of the traveling press corps last month, a sort of advance souvenir of all the places they'd be visiting together over the next four years.

"This will be very useful!" said Karen, apparently *meaning* it, as if, despite the couple of tag-along visits she'd made to Afghanistan, she wasn't the least bit sure of where to find the exotic, message-needing places she'd be going.

Condi poured the two of them some coffee. "You've got some tough hearts and minds to crack."

"Oh, they'll come along," Karen replied, tapping the little atlas.

"I don't mean the people in the Middle East," Condi explained. "I mean the career people downstairs. They still believe that Iraq is the president's war and not the country's. Certainly not *their* war."

Karen nodded, showing confidence that this could be straightened out with some message discipline vis-à-vis the Freedom Agenda. "We need to get the extremists out of the process over *there*, and the liberals out of it over *here*."

"Actually," said Condi, gently putting her small china cup onto its saucer, "we need to get the extremists *into* the process. Over there."

Karen seemed confused.

"The biggest mistake being made by our friends, such as Mubarak, is keeping all the Islamists *out* of politics. I'm not talking about the Muslim Brotherhood, but confining the more moderate opposition to the pulpits just turns the mosques into a parallel political universe, a kind of hothouse waiting to explode. It's the same with the Saudis."

Karen made a note on one of the blank endpapers in the little atlas. "Maybe I should speak to the Muslim Brotherhood when I go over to Saudi Arabia."

"The Muslim Brotherhood is in Egypt," Condi explained.

"Got it," said Karen, who scratched out the note.

Condi didn't want to think too hard about what she was seeing. She switched subjects. "I guess you're going to miss waking up to the sound of doves." The remark gave her a chance to prove she'd read *Ten Minutes from Normal*, the $750,000 memoir Karen had just published, in which she talked about how happy she'd been amidst the birdsong of Austin after her year or two at the White House.

"Oh, I'll still be hearing plenty of that," Karen assured her. "I'll be flying home every Thursday night, more or less commuting."

Condi, who detested even pleasant surprises—and this wasn't one—again changed conversational course. "Confirmation is always tricky these days, but I hope you're in by April 15."

"I've been talking to Dina, while she still has her Presidential Personnel hat on, and I've told her not to hurry. She'll send my papers up to the Hill in June. Robert will be done with school by then. Oh, God, by the way, thank you again for that letter to Stanford! It really did the early-admissions trick: a letter from a former provost who now just happens to be the secretary of state!"

Condi was silent.

"Starting late," Karen continued, "will also give me a chance to go out and give a few last paid speeches before going on the poverty wages here."

Jim Wilkinson had informed Condi that her undersecretary–designate had made a million dollars in the past fourteen months. Ten minutes earlier, Karen had made some chirpy remarks about the Kabul school she'd helped raise money for, and Condi now couldn't help thinking that a million dollars might fund the elementary education systems of three Afghan provinces.

During the secretary's continued silence, Karen's eyes were drawn to the ticking of a grandfather clock.

"It belonged to Jefferson," Condi explained.

"So many beautiful things here," said Karen, pointing to several leather-bound volumes of the French Pléiade.

"A peace offering from Chirac," Condi told her. "Last month."

"Those awful people. I'm proud to say I'm the only member of this administration who ever got to renounce her French citizenship!" This was a story Condi had heard a number of times, and read once more in *Ten Minutes from Normal*—how Karen had been born with dual citizenship during her military father's Parisian posting, and then routinely given up the French portion many years later.

A live shot on CNN caught Condi's eye, and she rose to turn up the volume. A rally was taking place in Beirut, a protest against Syria's having last month instigated the murder of Rafik Hariri, a former prime minister whom Condi had liked. Anger over the assassination had at last pushed the Lebanese into demanding that their Syrian overlords leave the country and take Hezbollah with them. The secretary's staff had inserted a half sentence about this hopeful turn of events into her introduction of Karen, and this enormous onscreen demonstration appeared to be the most encouraging development yet.

The administration's newly designated chief of public diplomacy, checking her phone, paid no attention to the TV. And Condi realized it wouldn't be long before, deep down, she disliked Karen as much as Karl Rove did.

6

AFTER PALM SUNDAY; MARCH 21, 2005

White House Residence

"Bushie, Brett Kavanaugh is at the door."

The president opened his eyes and wondered why Laura had woken him. The clock on the night table said 1:08 a.m.—nearly the halfway mark in his normal night's sleep.

"Kavanaugh?" he asked. The staff secretary?

Still blinking himself awake, he noticed the sheaves of palm atop the dresser, sent over, he'd been told, by some local AME minister. Laura waited for him to get both feet on the floor so that she could go back to bed herself.

By now the president realized what Kavanaugh's presence signified. The first couple had flown back from the ranch in Crawford this afternoon, when it became apparent that the Schiavo bill was coming to a vote. Given its nature, it needed to be signed immediately.

Bush stepped out into the hall, and Kavanaugh, startled by the sight of him in a bathrobe, averted his eyes for a moment.

"Sir, the House passed the legislation at 12:41 a.m." He handed his boss the bill.

The president, putting on his glasses, walked over to a table in the hallway. "DeLay must have hopped on a motorcycle to get it over here. What was the vote?"

"Two hundred and three to fifty-eight, sir."

"How many Republicans against?"

"Only five."

Bush motioned for a pen, and as soon as Kavanaugh handed him one he set the document down on the little table with its premature vase of Easter lilies. He signed the bill quickly, in a single movement, not the ceremonial letter-at-a-time procedure with multiple pens he could then offer as souvenirs to supporters and "stakeholders" in the legislation. Once he'd transformed S. 686 into Public Law 109-3, he handed the paper back to Kavanaugh.

"Is Andy coming back?" the president asked. The chief of staff had been vacationing in Maine.

"Tomorrow morning, sir."

Bush nodded. " 'Night, K-Man."

Back inside the bedroom, the president saw that Laura was already asleep again, her copy of *Losing Battles* resting on the night table.

Even after winning it, this felt like a losing battle too—a costly, brutal skirmish in the war that had been going on for years, in Florida, over poor "persistently vegetative" Terri Schiavo: a fight between her parents, who wanted to keep her alive, feeding tube and all, and her husband, who thought enough was enough. Jeb, the governor, had taken the parents' side, even suggesting there was something fishy about the husband and the circumstances in which his wife had fallen ill. But the Supreme Court had said no to the parents on Thursday, and the following day the feeding tube had been legally removed for the third time in this long struggle. The bill he'd just signed, rammed through by the zealously right-to-life DeLay, would give the parents one more chance to put the tube back in, by allowing other federal courts, besides the Supremes, to supersede the state ones.

There was nothing about this whole medical-ethics clusterfuck that Bush liked—especially the pro-parents demonstrators, out in the hospice parking lot, threatening the life of the state judge. He'd made it clear to his staff as soon as he got back this afternoon that he wouldn't reward those people with a picture of himself signing the bill in his bathrobe. He was sick of hearing about "assisted suicide" and "judicial murder," sick of hearing his own press secretary talk, over and over, about the need to "err on the side of life." Yes, that's what he'd tried to do with stem cells four years ago—the most honest, painstaking, and satisfying work he'd done in his whole presidency. But tomorrow morning he would need a crisp answer for reporters who'd be braying to know how this bill he'd just signed didn't violate his states'-rights inclinations, same as the way they used to ask why signing death warrants down in Texas didn't run counter to the "culture of life" he claimed to promote. In fact, he believed his own shuffle on that one: as a deterrent, the death penalty, like a just war, ultimately saved more lives than it took. And, not that it mattered, he'd bet Ann Richards and Bill Clinton had shed a lot fewer tears over the murderers *they* sent to the needle.

As soon as he got into bed, he knew he couldn't sleep. He was hungry—he'd been trying too hard to lose that last extra pound from the campaign. Terri Schiavo, of course, was starving. She wasn't supposed to be able to feel it, but how did anyone know that for sure? A "persistent vegetative state"; dead but not-dead. Over in Iraq, the dead couldn't even *stay* dead, or at least they couldn't rest in peace. The other day in Mosul a suicide bomber had killed a police official; next thing you knew, the "insurgents" were shooting up the guy's funeral.

On top of the desk across the room sat a memo he'd brought up from the Oval earlier tonight, something that had been caught circulating among Republicans on the Hill: *This legislation ensures that individuals like Terri Schiavo are guaranteed the same legal protections as convicted murderers like Ted Bundy. . . . This is a great political opportunity, because Senator Nelson of Florida has already refused to become a cosponsor and this is a tough issue for Democrats.*

If he found out that Turd Blossom had a hand in this, he'd kick his ass back to Austin.

They were supposed to lift off from the South Lawn at 8:05 a.m. He'd be traveling out to Arizona to push the Social Security bill. After a month of such barnstorming, he was still enjoying it, but tomorrow he had to take McCain on the plane with him; he wasn't about to repeat the home-state mistake they'd made with Baucus. Even so, John would be up his ass about torture and rendition, threatening to introduce this Detainees Treatment Act if they didn't change the rules. And how was he supposed to debate torture with Mr. Hanoi Hilton?

He honestly believed that, like the death penalty, torture could save lives. But every so often he needed to talk it through, receive some assurance that he was correct. Laura wasn't the right person for this: any talk of physical pain sent her mind straight back to the skidding and screech in that Midland intersection thirty-seven years ago; the sudden, sickening death of the guy in the car she hit. As soon as the thought would come to her, you'd see her eyes darken, as if a pair of black contact lenses had been put over the pupils. Until the memory clicked off she was just *gone*, her mind having been rushed to a secure location that nobody could find.

Still, it was Laura he wanted to talk to now; so he sighed, loudly and childishly, in order to wake her.

"You know, you could just say 'Honey?' and maybe shake me," she pointed out, once she'd opened her eyes.

"I think I'm hungry."

"Call down to the kitchen for the piece of cake you didn't eat tonight. It's still in the refrigerator, I'm sure."

"It'll keep me awake."

She reclosed her eyes and rolled over. "Just please don't start playing your iPod with those tinny earphones."

He grunted his assent, and then she remembered something she'd forgotten to tell him. "Your mother called. Just before we left the ranch. Not urgent. But if you can't sleep, why don't you call her back? It's only just past midnight in Houston. She'll be up watching TCM while Gampy snores."

He'd seen his mother in Pensacola on Friday, when he'd gone down there to tout the Social Security reforms with Jeb. Mother had been brought along as a prop, sitting there like a wary senior making sure her boys weren't about to do something shady with her benefits. The crowd had eaten it up, though the reporters couldn't stay interested in anything but the Schiavo case.

He decided to take Laura's suggestion, because he couldn't think of anything else to do. He put his bathrobe back on, kissed his wife, and softly closed the door, before walking across the hallway to a sitting room. Within fifteen seconds the White House operators—who'd once, during his father's VP days, tracked him down in a bar he was amazed to discover even *had* a phone—were putting Barbara Bush on the line.

"Mother, I signed the bill."

The lateness of the call didn't faze her, but realizing the hour at which the bill must have passed *did* provoke her. "With all the fuss, you'd think she was a fetus," said the former First Lady. She was, he knew, secretly pro-choice, the only thing she had in common with Nancy Reagan, something they might have shared like a girlish secret if they didn't detest each other.

"It basically just means that they'll be giving her food and water, Mother."

"Forever."

"Well, the parents say they're willing to *do* it forever."

"That sometimes seems to be what *we* signed up for, though we won't *be* here forever."

She was talking about Jeb, and the family goal of eventually putting him here. Sometimes she made him feel that his own presidency was entirely about not fucking it up for his brother later on. He never brought up the gubernatorial races of '94, but he never forgot them, either; how, the night he'd won and Jeb had lost, two unexpected results, his own parents had told the press: "The joy is in Texas, but our hearts are in Florida."

"Maybe," said Barbara Bush, "you should call your brother tomorrow."

He gave her a version of the same grunt he'd given Laura a couple of minutes ago. The Schiavo mess was something Jeb had gotten *him* into, by signing that Florida law on behalf of the parents a couple of years ago. Mother had vigorously defended that in small talk on Friday, not much caring whether the seniors who'd come out to cheer her paid attention to his own Social Security pitch. And now she wanted him to—what? Strategize with his brother about any trouble this just-signed bill might cause *Jeb*?

"Mother," said the president, trying to laugh, "it's more than fifty years since you overthrew me for another man." He disliked himself for making the joke, but it was true: he was still trying to win back what he'd had with her during their days of prankish, grieving intimacy over Robin, days that ended when the infant Jeb began to speak.

He suddenly heard his father snoring in Houston; Mother had muted the television.

"I needed you too much," Barbara Bush said to her son. "And there's only so long one can put up with that."

7

MARCH 29–31, 2005

623 Bourbon Street, New Orleans

"Young sir," said Mrs. Randolph Caine, a widowed realtor and local preservationist, "we haven't really heard *anythin'* about this guidebook project. The rest of us were all too busy talking during supper to let you get a word in!"

Mrs. Lindy Boggs, the dinner party's eighty-nine-year-old hostess, had moved her seven guests up to the second-floor solarium, confessing that she'd "begun to fade" but was having too much fun to say good night just yet. She agreed it was a grand idea for Mr. Weatherall to tell them more about the guidebook.

From under his chair Ross pulled out a copy of the 1938 version. He'd carried it with him from his room at the Monteleone and kept it by his side all through the meal. He owed his presence here in some roundabout way to Senator Vitter's office, and he'd not minded the lack of opportunity to hold forth in the red-walled dining room. Not, by his own estimation, the cleverest of talkers, he'd been at a table where everybody else seemed a natural one, all of them spinning stories instead of argument and prediction, the two chief conversational modes of Washington.

He opened the guide to a Post-it and told Mrs. Boggs's guests that he'd been "hoping to find something about number 623." Alas, the only thing the WPA authors had noted about this 600 block of Bourbon Street was a house near the corner of Toulouse where a historian named Gayarré, who wrote in French, had once lived.

Mrs. Caine expressed disappointment. "Really? Mangin the blacksmith had his anvil right in Lindy's downstairs sitting room. You sure he's not in the index?"

While Ross looked, Father Anthony Montrose, Mrs. Caine's Jesuit escort, asked if the book had much about Claiborne Avenue. "You know," he said, nodding in Mrs. Boggs's direction, "we have a collateral descendant of old Governor Claiborne sitting right here."

"Early nineteenth century," Mrs. Caine explained to Ross.

"Oh, Marie," said Mrs. Boggs, with a dismissive little hand gesture. "Let's let poor Mr. Weatherall put that *old* book away and tell us what he's doing *now*."

It delighted Ross that Mrs. Boggs—a congresswoman for nearly twenty years; Bill Clinton's ambassador to the Vatican; Cokie Roberts's mother!—had remembered his name. He proceeded to say a few words, no more than a paragraph, about the guidebook project, ending with a lighthearted pledge that he'd do his best to get something about number 623 into the updated edition.

Mrs. Boggs smiled back at him. "It's really just an ordinary brick home in the Quarter. I inherited it in '72 from my Aunt Frosty."

"Just as she was going into the House," Mrs. Caine pointed out. "After Hale died," she added, unnecessarily, in a solemn tone. Even Ross knew that Mrs. Boggs's own political career had begun when her husband was killed in a plane crash and she took over his seat in Congress.

"I'm told they finished building it in 1795," she said. "Just a little before poor John Adams came in as president. Cokie gave me that David McCullough book—oh my. So depressing it was almost *consoling*. As much as we're all at one another's throats today, I think the factions were even worse back then."

"It's always nice to have the lion and the lamb lie down together," said Father Montrose, pointing to Ray Nagin, the city's Democratic mayor, and Bobby Jindal, its new Republican congressman.

"As long as I'm the lion and Jindal's the lamb," said Nagin, with a loud laugh. He picked up a nearby ceremonial gavel—a tabletop souvenir of Mrs. Boggs's chairmanship of the Democrats' '76 convention—and pretended to bean the boyish congressman.

Ross, feeling the effects of three different wines, considered the two men, an unlikely blue-vs.-red (and entirely nonwhite) pair: the black mayor who'd reminded everyone at supper that he'd been born in the city's Charity Hospital; the dark-brown Indian-American congressman whose Southern accent was every bit as pronounced as Mrs. Boggs's. Minutes ago they'd all been sitting on dining-room chairs that had come from the old plantation on which Mrs. Boggs had been born.

But along with the good-natured ribbing, he and the others could detect genuine tension between Nagin and Jindal. Both apparently wanted to be governor after Kathleen Blanco, the incumbent, left office. "It's *cheaper* to be a lamb than a lion," the congressman now said. "We eat less." The implication seemed to be that the self-proclaimed lion might be lapping up more than his share of the public oasis. That was always happening down here, of course; Ross had even heard rumors that one of Jindal's House colleagues kept a horde of cash in his home freezer.

"Father Montrose," said Mrs. Caine, trying to avoid a political fracas, "you look lost in thought."

"I've been contemplating the hour," the priest replied, pointing to the delicate hands of the clock on the mantel. "There are one hundred and twenty-five minutes until midnight, and I am wondering if Mrs. Schiavo will live to see another day."

Palm Sunday's legislation had proved a failure. In the nine days since its passage, all the federal courts approached by Terri Schiavo's parents had declined to order the reinsertion of the feeding tube from which their daughter had now been detached for a week and a half. She was thought to be very near the death that some of her supposed advocates, acknowledging its inevitability, had secretly hoped would occur on Good Friday or Easter Sunday. Ross now noticed solemn nods throughout the room. Did those indicate support for the president's position, which he didn't really support himself? Or were they just a sign of deference to the priest? Ross suspected he was the only non-Catholic here. Down in the dining room, Nagin had spoken affectionately of some fierce nuns from his childhood. Jindal, a young-adult convert, had listened almost enviously.

"Having been blessed with a very long life," said Mrs. Boggs, pressing down on the arms of her chair, "I should probably get up and get ready for bed. I shall say a prayer for both Mrs. Schiavo and the Holy Father." Pope John Paul II, about whom Mrs. Boggs had shared some warm ambassadorial anecdotes, was gravely ill in Rome.

Everybody stood and bade good night to their hostess, who told them, "Oh, don't you all go yet. It's early. Even I'm going to make a quick trip up to the third floor before I settle down for the night."

"That little writing room of yours?" asked Mrs. Caine, scoldingly. "Lindy, there's nothing up there that won't wait until tomorrow."

"Oh, there *is*," Mrs. Boggs protested. "I've got something I want Mr. Weatherall to see." She startled Ross by crooking her finger in a request that he accompany her. He followed her frail form up the stairs, like the spotter for a tiny, ancient gymnast. She led him into a room with a dormer window that overlooked the house's courtyard. Down below, beneath a magnolia tree, stood the small statue of an angel. Ross strained to hear the smallest sign of the round-the-clock din on Bourbon Street, no more than a hundred feet away, but he couldn't. The little room itself, along with its writing table, contained family mementos and trinkets, nothing of politics. Mrs. Boggs went over to a small set of bookshelves and almost immediately found what she was seeking.

"This was Aunt Frosty's." She handed Ross a copy of the 1938 WPA guide. "Would you sign it?"

"I'd be proud to!" Under his signature Ross added the initials N.E.A.H., as if it would be presumptuous to accept such an honor for just himself and not the agency.

Mrs. Boggs looked at the inscription and smiled. "At my age I can't count on seeing any long-term project come to fruition, so you've provided me with a lovely bit of continuity, sort of in advance."

Ross felt his eyes misting. He was embarrassed to be showing more emotion than the moment required, and hoped that she would ascribe it to the wine—not to the inner turmoil escaping the surface of his skin.

"Are you all right, sweetheart?" asked Mrs. Boggs.

Could she tell what Easter weekend at home in Dallas had done to him? How he had absorbed a full day of Deborah's verbal fury followed by another of her stone-cold silence? By Sunday night he'd wanted to suffocate himself with the excelsior inside the Easter baskets of his baffled children.

"I'm okay, Mrs. Boggs. You're so kind to ask."

She patted his hand. "Just keep doing your work—and come see us again when you're further along with it."

"Thank you," he said. At around two o'clock today, after hours of deliberately avoiding all e-mail contact with the office, he'd been oddly pleased to get a BlackBerry message from his assistant: *Have you gone native?* Now he felt he actually knew someone here.

He led Mrs. Boggs downstairs, spotting her this time from the front. She said good night to the rest of her guests, urged them to stay even longer, and retired to her bedroom.

"What was all that about?" asked Nagin.

"Something to do with the guidebook," Ross explained.

"My second cousin's niece knows a ton about this city's history," said the mayor. "She ought to be writing some of your book."

Ross flinched. He'd been rounding up excellent published writers, just as the old WPA had, and fending off academics whose prose was no more exciting than his own. Would he now have to resist the mayor's relatives? He replied to Nagin with a nervous laugh: "Well, we'll see."

"No, really," said the mayor, with the stern absence of a smile.

Ross got out his wallet and handed Nagin his card.

"No," said the mayor. "You call my office tomorrow morning. That's how this works. We'll look forward to hearing from you." He snapped his tremendous vote-getting grin back into place and rose from his chair. His wife, who'd begun conversing with Mrs. Caine in order to avoid this solicitation scene, stood up as well. Mrs. Caine took Ross aside as if nothing had just happened. "So how did you spend the first full day of your visit here, Mr. Weatherall?"

"My first *and* last full day," said Ross. "I go back to D.C. tomorrow afternoon. This morning I was at the State Museum, inside the Cabildo, meeting some researchers."

"Did they show you Napoleon's death mask?"

"Yes, they did, actually."

"There are supposedly three others floating around out there somewhere."

"Is that so?"

"It makes you wonder," said Mrs. Caine. "Does death really cut us down to size? Perhaps it just multiplies us."

"Mrs. Caine!" called Nagin. "May I run you home in the mayor's car? If we leave now it'll still be a few minutes before ten. I don't want Jindal here thinking my driver will be on the double-overtime clock."

The invitation didn't extend to Ross or even to Mrs. Caine's escort, Father Montrose, but neither the realtor nor the priest evinced any surprise, as if it were understood that Father Montrose, no matter the hour, still had his own rounds to make. Once everyone was out the door, Ross fell in on foot with the Jesuit. Still startled by his clash with Nagin, he failed to notice for a moment that he was walking in the opposite direction from his hotel.

"Will you be getting to see other parts of the city?" Father Montrose gently asked.

"I hope so," Ross answered. "So far I've just been in the Quarter and over at Tulane."

The priest nodded. "All the other neighborhoods hoist this one, make the fun and excess possible. And some of those other neighborhoods are terribly poor." He had paused in front of a bar at the corner of St. Ann. "Would you care for a nightcap?"

Ross looked up and saw a rainbow flag flying from the balcony above the entrance. "I really ought to get going, Father. I'm actually back thataway." He pointed in the direction of the Monteleone.

"I understand," said Father Montrose. His smile, partly pastoral, displayed mild disappointment too.

Heading down Bourbon Street toward Canal, Ross passed three beaded, shrieking girls who looked as if they'd been marooned here since spring break. The closer he got, the younger they appeared; scarcely older, in fact, than his just-turned-fourteen-year-old daughter, who'd refused to kiss him goodbye on Sunday.

When he came upon Sammy's, a seafood place, he decided to go in and take a seat at the bar, and before he knew it he'd put two drinks on top of the copious wine served by Mrs. Boggs. He kept his Black-Berry on the bar's zinc surface, as if wanting to signal Sammy's other patrons that he remained tethered to the regular world.

He had for nearly two months, since watching the State of the Union address, resisted the temptation to learn the exact Washington whereabouts of Allie O'Connor, though a few search-tappings of this magic little box atop the bar could probably lead him to her in under two minutes. Luckily, the second drink put an end to his manual dexterity and dissolved his focus into the ambient chatter of Sammy's. He amused himself by imagining what Gordon, his old pal at the Chart House, would have pointed out about Mrs. Boggs's arrival in Congress: her husband, the one *killed in a plane crash*, had been *a member of the Warren Commission.*

All at once the BlackBerry buzzed and gyrated, like the remote-controlled coaster you got at Fuddrucker's to tell you that your table was ready. It was an e-mail from the Chairman, whose work habits, like the French Quarter, more or less eliminated distinctions between night and day.

Ross—

Thought you should see what's below. Seems like some eager beaver in Public Diplomacy is trying to score points with Mrs. Hughes in advance of her arrival.

The forwarded message, shining up from the bar, had itself been sent to the Chairman less than ten minutes ago:

Excited to hear about WPA update project. Feeling here is it wd be excel idea to highlight Muslim-American contribution to each of selected cities.

Gather you're starting with N.O. Especially desirable: pix of Muslim women—headscarves, etc.—in front of relevant landmarks.

He would have to deal not only with Nagin but with this as well when morning brought the hangover he suspected he was inducing deliberately, penitentially, over the way his quixotic foray into government was already endangering what had been, until recently, a happy enough little family.

Stepping into Bourbon Street at 12:10 a.m., Ross felt how the breeze had changed from lukewarm to almost cold. Maybe a prolonged dose of it would minimize his gestating headache. And so he walked a couple of blocks this way and then that, thinking of the Quarter's streets as a kind of game board. He stopped in front of Antoine's and paid a moment's attention to three weary, white-coated kitchen staff waiting for a bus home to those other parts of the city mentioned by Father Montrose. Doubling back on Royal Street, he found a half dozen people kneeling outside the cathedral next to a blown-up picture of Terri Schiavo. Their faces exhibited such intensity that Ross wondered if they were trying to raise her from the dead before she even "passed," as everyone nowadays put it. Standing drunk in this city at this hour, he could only believe that, once she was gone, Mrs. Schiavo might be back at anytime, the hole made by her feeding tube a vampire's bite that she could now transfer to others, sending yet more restless, unmoored spirits, like himself, abroad upon the land. He self-dramatizingly turned himself around and walked to the Montelone, where, back in his room at 1:05 a.m. he shed his clothes, turned down the covers, and, for the first time since he'd been a sophomore at UT-Austin, experienced a wicked case of the bedspins.

———

Eight thousand miles to the east, Allison O'Connor was trying not to throw up as the USAF C-17 wove downward through the sky above Afghanistan's Parwan province. The plane's twisting maneuvers were designed to avoid possible enemy fire. Allie had endured only one corkscrew landing before now, on a flight into Iraq, and had futilely vowed to herself that she would never experience another. There were people who bragged about the ones they'd been through, as if this slender evidence of their importance and bravery was worth the danger and the vomit.

This morning she sat several seats away from the First Lady of the United States, who was traveling with exceptionally heavy security but only three staff members and a handful of press. All had pledged themselves to secrecy in the days before the trip. Allie's name had been added to the passenger manifest only on Monday afternoon, about fifteen hours before their departure from Andrews.

Her presence was Rumsfeld's doing, of course—not that she'd had any contact from his office, let alone an explanation. There had been just a casual-sounding set of e-mail instructions from Steve Hadley, the NSA: her presence on the trip would be "helpful to all concerned." How had not been specified, and now, as the C-17 made a last harrowing evasive loop, Allie decided that she'd had enough mystery. Once she returned—they'd be flying home six hours from now—she would have things out with the secretary of defense.

Touching down, without having lost the contents of her stomach, she reflected that the trip could have been worse. A quick refueling stop in Ramstein beat a layover in Dubai, with those little arrows on the hotel-windowsills pointing toward Mecca for the prayerfully inclined, while downstairs at the bar leggy girls plied their trade amidst velvet paintings of James Dean and Marilyn Monroe.

Their route had avoided the airspace of Iran, let alone Iraq. Had they flown over the latter she would have been glad for the C-17's lack of windows; looking down would have been too much like looking back. But she had not resisted—an hour or so ago, on a video monitor—the picture of Turkmenistan's brown plains giving way to Afghanistan's snowcapped peaks, a sight beautiful enough to override the preposterous memory of a UN charter flight she'd once had to hop from Dubai—or was it Abu Dhabi?—in order to get to Kabul. The passenger cabin had then been like a Graham Greene novel: some saintly Quaker relief workers; an obvious arms dealer; a sprinkling of photojournalists and adventure junkies. Someone, she would still swear, had even been wearing an eye patch.

This morning portraits of Bush and Cheney and Karzai had been slapped up inside the hangar along with a big banner announcing: BAGRAM AIR BASE WELCOMES FIRST LADY LAURA BUSH. Even more coalition commanders seemed to be on hand than had been here to greet Rumsfeld back in December. Otherwise everything was low-key—no band, no music. Mrs. Bush greeted each officer by name. During the two long flights it had taken to get her here, Allie was impressed by the attention the First Lady had paid, under a weak overhead light, to her fat briefing book, with a little time out for *The Kite Runner*, the Afghan-set novel that three different people had given Allie for Christmas.

Aboard the helicopter from the air base into the capital, Mrs. Bush forwent any reading for a study of the landscape below. She'd already put on her headscarf, a detestable item Allie would wait until the last minute to don.

"It looks dustier than Midland," the First Lady said, with more wonder than sarcasm, as she studied the ground through one of the Nighthawk's windows.

They set down at Kabul University on a landing pad constructed just for this visit. The campus was much more patched-up and ship-shape than the Kabul Museum, which Allie had seen in December. That whole place had looked pulverized, damned, with a charred old Soviet tank still visible on a nearby hill. A "keyholder" inside the museum had shown her some of the statues, now undergoing restoration, which several years before he'd had to unlock from their cases so the Taliban might take hammers to their presumptuous human forms.

Reaching the microphone, Mrs. Bush nodded her covered head and smiled warmly. On the flight out of Ramstein, aware that an NSC staffer was aboard, she'd asked Allie to eyeball the text of her anodyne remarks and offer suggestions. *"We are only a few years removed from the rule of the terrorists, when women were denied education and every basic human right. That tyranny has been replaced by a young democracy, and the power of freedom is on display across Afghanistan.*" A seventeen-million-dollar grant would start an American university here, the First Lady promised.

After the speech, Allie sat on the fringes of a circle of Afghan officials and educators sharing tea and almonds with Mrs. Bush. A State Department officer, a woman a little older than Allie named Mrs. Morris, discreetly pointed to a bearded man whom she identified as the deputy minister for tourism. "We're not too sure about him," Mrs. Morris whispered. "In fact we're pretty certain he was Taliban. Maybe still is." Allie showed her the wan little visitors' brochure, from 1978, that the man had handed her a few minutes before. Mrs. Morris shook her head: it was just so sad.

They were all soon taken to an institute for the training of women teachers, where a little bazaar had been set up to showcase some craft businesses now "empowering" Afghan women. Mina Sherzoy, a beautiful creature in a bright-pink *firaq*, had returned to her country after two decades of exile in California, first from the Soviets and then from the Taliban. She spoke of "my ladies" and drew Mrs. Bush's attention to the throw pillows and soccer balls and silk blouses they had made. The First Lady bought two pillowcases for her mother, who had, she explained to the seamstress, recently entered a retirement home in West Texas. Through the translator she told another woman, who'd made some hand towels with a dog's-head design, about Miss Beazley, the new terrier at the White House. While listening, Allie thought of Fadhil and the danger that this translator would be in once the Americans lost interest here, as they always did, and the deputy minister for tourism's former colleagues came back down from the hills. When another Afghan woman presented Mrs. Bush with a crocheted American flag, Allie felt herself unable to decide whether this was a gift from the heart or just the latest shape and color of *baksheesh*, one more transaction in a five-thousand-year-old pay-to-play tradition.

Through a second translator Allie asked the maker of the pillowcases, who had a son, what the boy thought about her working outside the house. The woman looked shyly off in the direction of the helipad before responding, "He didn't like it at first, but now he says it's a good thing."

"Why did he change his mind?" Allie wanted to know.

"The money I make sends him to a better school."

The translator and the woman had their own quick, rapid conversation, after which the man explained to Allie: "The private school, what the boy goes to now, is better than the state school." Allie made a note to herself—why not?—to pass this on to the Christian NSC staffers who were so crazy about vouchers for their kids.

While Mrs. Bush was taken to the palace for a meeting with Karzai, Mrs. Morris brought Allie "to the CAFE," which sounded, upon its initial pronunciation, like another feature out of Graham Greene. But the name soon revealed itself to be an acronym, Compound Across From Embassy, for a piece of in-progress construction, more of the still-expanding American presence—all barbed wire, sandbags, and checkpoints, with the inevitable Australian security guards. Rows of "hooches" resembled the double-wides of an Arizona retirement community.

But their own little delegation wasn't staying overnight. In fact this stop at the CAFE was just a time-killer. The one First Lady staffer who'd not gone to the palace dropped off some White House greetings and "chum"—flag pins and tie clips and paperweights—along with a few packets relating to Mrs. Bush's cultural efforts at home and abroad. Underneath some pamphlets about the U.S. rejoining UNESCO were three copies of *Arts and Humanities*, the quarterly magazine of the NEAH. Allie thumbed through it while they all waited, skimming news of grants for Alabama exhibitions of Georgia O'Keeffe and Montana productions of Tennessee Williams. The inside back page listed the Endowment's various divisions and application deadlines, and on it Allie noticed an e-mail address and office location for *Dr. Ross Weatherall, Director, Homeland Heritage Division*.

She felt a sudden thirst for a cold beer in this half-finished, undercooled office. Surely this was sweet, straitlaced Ross, who she seemed to remember had become a history Ph.D.? Well, good for him, though she somehow didn't like picturing him in Washington; she preferred him forever to remain on the sun-baked South Plains, a shiny sixteen-year-old, the one bright spot in her family's brief Texas exile.

"Ms. O'Connor?" asked Mrs. Morris. "There's someone I'd very much like you to meet. This is Dr. Mohammed Asefi, who's helping us plan a reception for coalition diplomats at the National Gallery here in Kabul." Allie shook hands with a slender, merry-looking man.

"Dr. Asefi is too modest to tell you himself—" Mrs. Morris began.

"Dr. Asefi's English is too modest to tell you *anything*," the man apologized to Allie.

"So *I'm* going to tell you," said Mrs. Morris, in her best winning-friends-abroad manner. "He may be a medical doctor, but he's also a *most* gifted amateur painter—enough to have an office in the National Gallery."

"Which is," interrupted Dr. Asefi, lest Allie imagine something as grand as its name, "a sad little place. Very run-down, catch-as-catch-can—is that how you say?—even before the bad times."

"Well, in the *worst* of times," Mrs. Morris continued, "when the Taliban were coming, Dr. Asefi took it upon himself to bring dozens of paintings from the gallery, ones with human figures, marketplace scenes and so forth, up to his office, a single canvas at a time, so that no one would notice. At night, all alone, using water-based paint, he'd cover the people with flowers, rocks, whatever, before rehanging the paintings on the gallery walls. When the Taliban came, they did a lot of damage to the gallery, but they never went after those paintings. And once the terrorists were routed, Dr. Asefi scraped off the top layer of paint and brought the people beneath back to life!"

Allie, astonished, clasped the doctor's hand.

"Many of the paintings are not very good," said Asefi, with his smile. "I think I improve some of them."

"He risked his life for every one of them," said Mrs. Morris—just as the lights went out in the office. Allie flinched, fearing the worst. Behind their desks, Americans and Afghans looked startled for a moment but remained calm. Though the room was only moderately darker than before, Dr. Asefi, smiling as if they had all been plunged into a romantic twilight, said, just above a whisper, "I want a kiss."

Allie laughed. It was unrepealable human nature she was hearing, mischievous and heroically nonchalant. What blessing of temperament had left him so sprightly? The keyholder she remembered from the Kabul Museum had looked as if all life had been bleached from his eyes forever.

Nothing since 9/11 had moved her as much as Dr. Asefi.

The lights came back on—a routine generator problem—as suddenly as they'd gone out.

"Let me take a picture," said Mrs. Morris. As she went to get a camera, Dr. Asefi extracted a photograph from his wallet. It showed two guards posing next to a canvas he'd doctored. "They loved having their own picture taken," he told Allie. "The Taliban."

"Even though they destroyed statues and paintings of people?"

"Life is funny," said Dr. Asefi.

"Say cheese!" commanded Mrs. Morris.

Twenty minutes later, Allie found herself inside a carful of aides and State employees on its way to link up with Mrs. Bush's armored motorcade for a brief foray into downtown Kabul. Spray-painted numbers on the buildings indicated that minesweepers had cleared the streets they were traveling. Allie's senses became overloaded with the sound of the mad, laneless traffic and—even through the SUV's bulletproof glass—the fecal smell of the air. She watched the insect-shuffle of burqa-clad females and thought that more women might now be wearing the garment than on her first post-Taliban trip here.

The First Lady's car stopped at a bakery, where she bought a bag of cookies and presented an amazed child with a kaleidoscope. Minutes later all the Americans were back on the Nighthawk and heading to Bagram to join the same chow line Allie had met Rumsfeld in four months ago. As Mrs. Bush ate chicken tenders with the buzz-cut boys and ponytailed girls in their fatigues, Allie listened to a guy from the Drug Enforcement Agency who'd been in the country for three weeks. He was "teaching the police how to arrest people" and running into a particular problem: "The provincial governors control the trade, and they'll only let the recruits arrest the competition." He popped a chicken tender into his mouth and shrugged. *Whatever.*

On the flight home Mrs. Bush read *The Road to Oxiana* and wrote thank-you notes. Allie briefly wondered why the First Lady couldn't have Karen Hughes's job—or maybe even her husband's. The thought of Dr. Asefi, that twinkling Ariel of the Freedom Agenda, stayed with her. Before she fell asleep, a Secret Service agent came by with cookies from the Kabul bakery. "The security regulations say she's not supposed to eat them," he said, cocking his head toward Mrs. Bush. "But the rules don't cover us."

He looked a little like Rolf; Allie took one of the cookies, thanked him, and then let *Arts and Humanities* magazine put her to sleep. It was still in her lap when they touched down at Andrews at two a.m. on Thursday. She made it back to her Arlington apartment, where half the boxes were still unpacked, in time enough to catch three hours of sleep before heading in to the EOB by nine-thirty.

Logging on to her computer, she found Terri Schiavo dead at the top of her Google News home page. The Christians she'd planned to tell about the apparent superiority of Afghan private schools were speaking of the Florida woman, in hushed voices, pronouncing her a medical Joan of Arc.

Allie was figuring out who should get the four placemats she'd bought at the bazaar when her phone rang. Rumsfeld's clipped, amused voice came on the line. "Interesting trip?"

She waited a moment before using one of his own most cherished formulations. "Tell me, am I one of your 'known unknowns'? Meaning, is your interest in me known to you but unknown to me?"

"The answer to your second question is yes," said the defense secretary. "But it makes you an 'unknown known' to me."

"But if you control the noun, which always beats the adjective, you have the power."

Rumsfeld laughed: "You do pretty well on what must have been a short night's sleep."

"You should be detecting a certain impatience in my voice."

Rumsfeld was silent for perhaps ten seconds. "When is your birthday, Allison?"

"June fourteenth."

"My interest in you will be a 'known known,' to both of us, before that."

"I'll hold you to it."

Exasperated as she hung up, she decided she might as well send all four placemats to her mother.

8

APRIL 30, 2005

The Wyoming, Apartment #702, 2022 Columbia Road NW, Washington, D.C.

John Edwards and Donatella Versace silently marveled at each other's appearance. Gazing upon her astonishingly enhanced cheekbones, which resembled the flesh-covered halves of a tennis ball, Edwards thought of the small mole he had recently had removed from the space above his upper lip. His wife, Elizabeth, had told him that its excision had taken some of the character from his face; she then had to explain that this was not a compliment.

He now mentioned the mole's debatable elimination to the Italian designer.

"Your hair makes up for much," she responded.

Carol Blue, Mrs. Christopher Hitchens, passed between them and asked Edwards, "Have you met Paul Wolfowitz?" She propelled the ex-senator in the neoconservative's direction, and Edwards decided to evince a certain chilliness. Despite his own Senate vote of approval in '02, he was now, he reminded himself, *against* the war, and had been so throughout his vice-presidential campaign.

Ideological sparks had always been a feature of the Hitchenses' parties, but never more so than these days, when the transplanted British journalist, still a self-designated Marxist, was outdoing his late-1990s heresy (siding against Clinton in the Lewinsky affair) with full-throated support for Bush's Iraq war. It was said that the Hitch had even begun to think about acquiring American citizenship.

This particular party—an annual after-affair for those who'd been at the White House Correspondents' dinner around the block at the Hilton—was now underwritten and salted with nonpolitical celebrities by *Vanity Fair*, whose high-end fees and high-gloss pages allowed Hitchens to continue spending the other part of his time fighting one political fight after another in the impoverished precincts of *The Nation* and *Slate*. In fact, *Slate*'s founding editor, Michael Kinsley, was here tonight, and Carol Hitchens made sure to introduce him to both Edwards and Wolfowitz before making further matchups nearby. Edwards gave the editor the full wattage of his now-moleless smile.

The crush of people made one lose sight of how little furniture the large apartment contained: one found a few chairs and tables and slim, vertiginous pillars of piled-up books. Emptied of people, the place would look almost like the huge, cleaned-out Parisian flat Audrey Hepburn comes home to after the murder of her husband in *Charade*. A painting of the Hitchenses, unframed and unhung, sat on the floor and leaned against one of the walls. The apartment—like the couple's beautiful, almost teenaged daughter, serenely doing her homework in one of the bedrooms—seemed unaware of the party going on inside it.

Edwards felt disappointed that Kinsley didn't appear especially interested in him, a potential next president. The editor was giving his attention to Wolfowitz, who had just yesterday stepped down as Rumsfeld's number-two man at the Pentagon and would soon, thanks to Bush's nomination, be heading up the World Bank.

"Does Mr. Gorman consider his switch a promotion?" Kinsley asked.

Wolfowitz smiled thinly at this reference to a Saul Bellow character often said to be a version of Wolfowitz's youthful self. "Gorman is a composite," he replied, nodding to Kinsley and then walking away.

"I guess this means I don't get zero percent APR?" the editor called after him. Turning back to Edwards, Kinsley extolled "our fine tradition that gives the masterminds of failed, criminal wars the presidency of the World Bank." Edwards, not getting the reference to Robert McNamara, pointed toward a plump, dark-skinned man who was speaking, professorially, to a knife-skinny, blond editorial assistant from *Vanity Fair.* "Who's that?" the ex-senator asked.

"Salman Rushdie."

Edwards looked as if he might duck, but then asked: "Should I meet him?"

"Sure," said Kinsley. "But I'm warning you: he can sound like an almanac. He once told me the square mileage and population of Mumbai—down to single digits. If the mullahs had kidnapped him instead of issuing that fatwa, they'd have had to let him go just to preserve their sanity."

Edwards was distracted by a woman who identified herself as being with the Communication Workers of America. "You're even better-looking in person!" she exclaimed, before telling him he absolutely needed to address the CWA's next big gathering. Edwards offered her a card bearing the name of his lecture agent. "We usually start around fifty-five thousand dollars," he said. She told him how brave he'd been to point out the administration's failures in conducting the war he'd been good enough initially to support. "I'm soon going to state," Edwards told her in a confidential whisper, "that I actually *regret* my vote."

"Amazing!" the woman responded. "You *never* find a politician who's man enough to admit a mistake like that!"

Edwards smiled bashfully. "I'm going to wait a few months, do it in an op-ed that's timed for maximum impact. I'd love to get your thoughts about which would be better, the *Times* or the *Post.*"

Kinsley had drifted away.

Across the room the evening's host was talking to one of Edwards's former competitors for the '04 nomination, Howard Dean, the early front-runner who'd done himself in with an ill-considered caucus-night scream, something that, were he to try it here, would hardly be heard above the conversational din. He posed a question to Hitchens and an enormously fat Iraqi, an adherent of Ahmed Chalabi, the crooked oil minister for whom the Bush administration had once had such hopes: "You've got to ask yourself," said Dean, "at what point does misguidedness turn into evil?"

"Are you talking about the 'insurgents'?" asked Hitchens, with scare quotes as strong as his drink. Yesterday's car-bombing toll had been about forty dead and a hundred injured.

"I'm talking about *us, our* policy," said Dean, who had moved on from being governor of Vermont to chairing the Democratic National Committee.

"Christopher," asked the fat Middle Eastern man, "what would *you* call them? Instead of 'insurgents'?"

Hitchens paused for a second, simulating the thought he'd already given the matter. "'Baathists' would work nicely. These 'insurgents' are nothing more than Sunnis still on the battlefield while their captive chief awaits judgment." Saddam Hussein's trial was expected to take place in the fall. "They cannot be 'insurgents,' despite the *New York Times*'s insistence upon the absurdly enhancing term. They're not rising up—*insurgere*—but hanging on. Actually, I'm working up a piece on this."

"*Their* violence has been caused by *our* policies," insisted Governor Dean.

Hitchens responded in a soft voice. "I'd ignore your point if you had one. Zarqawi, by the way, *asked* bin Laden if he could call his gangsters 'Al-Qaeda in Iraq'—so that they might sound like pilgrim jihadists instead of homegrown thugs."

"That only proves what critics of the war have always said," Dean retorted. "Al-Qaeda was never in Iraq, not any more than WMDs were."

Hitchens looked bored—did he have to make the moral argument yet again?—and Dean took the host's weary expression for defeat. "Do you want to call in reinforcements?" he asked, pointing to Andrew Sullivan, who for a moment stood by himself near one of the book pillars.

"I wouldn't want to interrupt Andrew," said Hitchens. "Not while he must be trying to generate enough instant thoughts to satisfy his blog-reading public past midnight. Besides, he's long since gone soft on the war—Abu Ghraib, etcetera." On Monday, Pfc Lynndie England, who had been photographed tugging a leash placed around the neck of an Iraqi prisoner, would plead guilty to a reduced version of the original charges against her.

Hitchens and Dean and the rotund Chalabi supporter briefly regarded Sullivan. "Andrew's going to be a bit too stout to fit into that Vera Wang if he ever succeeds with his gay-marriage campaign," observed the writer. "Perhaps," he asked Dean, "you could offer him and his man an immediate civil union?" The remark was offered and accepted as a compliment to the progressive governor who'd made such arrangements possible in Vermont.

A young conservative journalist had been hanging on every overheard word from Hitchens. The host now spoke for his benefit, so that the fellow didn't entertain any hopes for further synchronization of the Hitch and George W. Bush. "Apostasy is only good when it's incomplete. The more partial the conversion, the more authentic it tends to be. As it is, deviations always leave a trail of nostalgic breadcrumbs. Just look at Andrew over there: no matter how much he wants to bring two penises to the altar, and no matter how cross he feels about all the diddling going on in the sacristy, he's still, I guarantee you, having troubled thoughts about the speeded-up departure of Mrs. Schiavo and the unduly delayed one of his 'old, mad, blind, despised, and dying'—well, dead—pope."

The young conservative winced. Blasphemous sallies like these were the price for having this unlikely ally—a left-wing British intellectual!—on their side of the Iraq question.

"I might remind you," said Hitchens, noting the young man's discomfited expression, "that the late Holy Father inveighed against both the recent ouster of Saddam Hussein and the Gulf War a dozen years before that. He was quite happy to let the dictator acquire Kuwait's oil, perhaps believing it would be used to anoint the feet of the Virgin Mary."

"Funny stuff!" shouted Larry King, a few feet away—not over what Hitchens had said, but in response to Greta Van Susteren's recap of the comedy routines at the Correspondents' dinner. She was offering the summary to Christiane Amanpour and her husband, who had made it to the Hitchenses' but not the Hilton. "So Bush started to tell this old Texas joke, and Laura walked up to the mic and pushed him away and told him she couldn't stand hearing it one more time, and before you knew it, *she* was doing a monologue, all about being a 'desperate housewife.' She was good, too."

"More than good!" enthused King. "Even better than Cedric the Entertainer!" The volume of King's approbation made Bob Dole flinch, and Wolfowitz, wanting to say hello, gently moved the former Senate leader a foot or two away from the CNN host.

"Thanks," said Dole. "Deafness is the one infirmity I don't have yet. So, how are you going to live without Rumsfeld?"

Wolfowitz smiled. "I received my last 'snowflake' yesterday morning. About ten minutes before I was out the door."

Dole remembered the deluge of memos from his '96 campaign chair. "How long is *Rumsfeld* going to stay there?"

"Can't really say," said Wolfowitz.

"Let me put it another way," Dole suggested. "Which'll occur first? Our leaving Iraq or his leaving the Pentagon?"

"Well, I guess he'd like to speed up the former." Wolfowitz imparted this speculation with a sort of disconsolate caution. He and Rumsfeld had pushed for an invasion of Iraq from the morning of September 12, 2001. Wolfowitz hadn't thought postwar reconstruction would be much of a problem. Rumsfeld wasn't so sanguine, but even then preferred a quick exit to a prolonged occupation.

Hitchens and John Bolton now joined Wolfowitz and Dole. "Jesus," said the Kansan, who wound up standing between the ultimate neocon and the hardline UN ambassador-designate, "I feel as if I'm at the point of origin for World War III."

"I was just congratulating the envoy-to-be," said Hitchens.

"You sure they've got the votes to get him out of committee?" asked Dole. Bolton was having a rough ride before the Senate Foreign Relations Committee—not only from Kerry and Biden, but a couple of Republicans as well. "Colin's men have been saying the damnedest things about you all over town," Dole told the nominee.

"Well," replied Bolton, trying to laugh off any danger from such moderates, "they're all over town because they're no longer at State."

"You sure they're all out of the Pentagon?" asked Dole, who had gotten an increased sense of Rumsfeld's doubtfulness about the war from what little Wolfowitz had permitted himself to say.

"Perhaps we can change the subject," said Hitchens. "To the Democratic People's Republic of Korea?" Five years earlier he had paid a visit to the North, where he'd been treated to a bowl of dog stew while much of the non-apparatchik citizenry tried to subsist on grass. "I've been complimenting the president," he told Bolton, "on his use of understatement." Two nights before, at a press conference, Bush had upped the axis-of-evil ante, referring to North Korea's "huge concentration camps."

"All signs point to their getting ready for a nuclear test," said Bolton. "Their vice foreign minister is going around saying they might have to give nukes to terrorists if they feel they're being 'backed into a corner.' We're trying to get our so-called allies to take this seriously."

Kinsley had assumed a position on the edge of the group, cupping his ear for all four men to see. "Don't mind me. I'm listening for the boy who cried wolf. Yes, I can hear his shout traveling all the way from the Fertile Crescent to the Thirty-eighth Parallel."

Hitchens took up the cudgels against his old friend: "I'm sure that Michael has been terribly reassured to hear the Dear Leader telling us how the Great Leader, his dad—"

"Are we talking about the Bushes?" asked Kinsley.

"—expressed a dying wish that the Korean peninsula remain as free of nukes as its northern half remains free of nourishment. Especially since the Great Leader, despite being dead, remains the legal president of the North—a miraculous arrangement that would no doubt have appealed to the late pope, or to those clustering around the brain-dead Mrs. Schiavo's bedside."

Kinsley sighed, and addressed the rest of the group. "He always has trouble keeping *focused*. In print; in conversation . . ."

"Michael's own particular religion is detachment," replied Hitchens. "I once asked him what cause he'd consider getting shot for, and he couldn't answer. Maybe he's waiting for the Dear Leader to make the question moot by killing *everyone*."

A few feet away, Ann Richards, threading her way through the crush, was stopped in her tracks by the sight of Matt Drudge in his fedora. She deadpanned some Sondheim in his direction: "Does *any-one still* wear a *hat*?"

"Hi, Governor."

"Hi yourself." She warned him against trying to quote her: "I've been off the record since '95."

"Not a problem," Drudge replied. "I don't write news; I just aggregate it."

"You what? Christ, I really have outlived myself."

Richards moved away from him so fast that she collided with John Edwards. "Now how are *you* doing?" she asked the ex-senator. "I hear you're building a house down in North Carolina that's going to rival the pyramids of Egypt."

"Well, we're selling the one in Georgetown," he said, his sheepish expression betraying how it wasn't exactly a zero-sum transaction that he and his Mrs. Edwards had underway.

"I also hear you made a *fortune* with that hedge fund. You going to give me some tips?" When Richards saw how uneasy she was making him—it was curiously mutual—she desisted from teasing. "How's your wife?" she asked, in a softer voice. Elizabeth Edwards had been diagnosed with breast cancer the day her husband and John Kerry had lost the election. "My friend Molly down in Texas has beaten it twice, even if she doesn't have a lick of sense when it comes to taking care of herself."

Edwards seemed incapable of responding, and Richards felt unable to read the reason for it: Sensitivity? Guilt? Disconnection from the whole thing? She changed the subject: "What do you hear from Kerry?"

"Not much. Of course he knows I've been preoccupied—by Elizabeth."

"How about you and '08, darlin'?"

"I have a PAC. We call it the One America Committee."

He spoke the title as if it were something he'd been informed of this afternoon. "You ought to call it Project X," Richards suggested. She paused before explaining: "X is what comes after W." Did he even get it? She couldn't tell. "Okay, honey, I'm on my way to snag myself a second ginger ale and get a look at the Versace woman. I hear that's a sight to see."

Heading to the bar, she ran into Dole and gave him a kiss. "We just did a recount of Texas for '96. You still lost."

Dole harrumphed. "I'm guessing you used the old LBJ method."

"Where's *your* Elizabeth?" asked Richards.

"Back home at the Watergate."

"You two ever miss Monica?" *That woman, Ms. Lewinsky,* had lived in the apartment next to the Doles at the height of Bill Clinton's denials.

"Oh, sure, she just came along a little too late to do me any good. I miss the lot of them," he added, before starting to murmur the names of Capitol Hill's forgotten bombshells. "Elizabeth Ray, Fanne Foxe . . ."

"Why'd you ever leave the Senate?" asked Richards.

Dole harrumphed again. "Some genius advised me it would be a 'bold move' in '96. Just the thing to shake up the race and allow me to get out in front of the incumbent."

Richards looked at this onetime "attack dog" who had in fact spent most of his career barking up the tree of compromise. She realized how much, at eighty-one, he still missed it *all.* "Shrub going to get anywhere with Social Security?" she asked.

"No. Could have told him that, but he didn't ask."

"They should put you out there at those pep rallies with Granny Bush. You'd make a fine team of persuasive pensioners."

Dole dismissed the idea. "The old man doesn't like me," he said, referring to the president's father, a year younger than himself. "Besides, I look too much like an undertaker. Doesn't play well with 'seniors.' "

"I keep looking for that Versace woman. Is that her?" Richards nodded to the back of a very imposing female figure, unaware that this was the just-arrived form of Karen Hughes.

"That's the new undersecretary of state," said Dole. "*That's* Donatella," he explained, pointing at the designer, spray-tanned and reconfigured from head to toe.

"Dear God," Richards said, dumbfounded. "That's not surgery; that's special effects."

Karen Hughes asked one of the *Vanity Fair* assistants to lead her to the party's host.

"Undersecretary–designate," said Hitchens, nodding his head with a contempt visible to everyone but its object. "Or, should I say 'Mom'?"

"It's so nice of you to have me here," Hughes told him. "The administration is thrilled to have your support."

"It doesn't extend very far." The young conservative journalist, still hovering nearby, looked at his shoes. "How long will it be," asked Hitchens, "until the nation has your services, Mrs. Hughes?"

"Confirmation always takes time. Just ask John Bolton over there!"

"Mr. Bolton's problems derive from substance," Hitchens responded. "He has an actual record of informed, if controversial, policies and positions. Do you?"

Hughes looked around for an escape. She saw a cluster of guests watching a C-SPAN replay of their own red-carpet arrival at the Correspondents' dinner. "Oh, that looks like fun!" she exclaimed, excusing herself and walking over to the TV. Even Ann Richards was now in front of it, with Donatella Versace, her just-made friend. "What is it about Washington women?" she asked Donatella, pointing to the screen. "No matter how many gewgaws they put on, no matter how high they slit their skirts, they still always look like the mother of the bride."

"So much help these people need," said Donatella.

Richards noticed Hughes approaching and felt no desire to be cordial or to rehash their awful history from the '94 governor's race, when America's newest diplomat had been Shrub's press woman. She kissed one of Donatella's cheek implants and set off again in pursuit of ginger ale.

The television was showing tape of the president's soon-to-be interrupted moment at the microphone. "*See, there was this city slicker driving around lost, and when he came across this ol' cowboy he stopped to ask directions. The cowboy told him that about a mile further up the road he'd come to a cattle guard. So . . ."*

Just as Ann Richards exited past him, a boyish-looking man about three rows from the screen exclaimed: "Hey, that's a joke Kent Hance used to tell about *him*! The punch line comes when the city slicker says, 'What kind of uniform will this cattle guard be wearing?'"

People had no idea what he was talking about. "But *Bush* was the city slicker when Hance told it," he tried explaining. "You know, Andover and Yale and Connecticut and all that. Nineteen seventy-eight?" Two or three listeners shooshed him so that they could again hear the jokes Laura Bush had successfully told an hour and a half ago.

But Ann Richards turned back around and touched his arm. "You mean somebody here besides me has heard of *Kent Hance*?"

"I'm from Lubbock," Ross Weatherall answered. "I was even at the 'Bush Bash' when I was a kid."

Richards saw John Edwards coming near and knew she couldn't bear any more of him, so she spoke a few quick last words to this slightly lit West Texan. "It's a pleasure to meet you, honey. I'm gonna go say hi to my friend Larry King over there. But if you ever want to know a little more of the *real* story about that Bush Bash, just get hold of my e-mail address from one of those *Vanity Fair* girls in the little black dresses. No, really, I mean it. They can rustle up my card for you."

Ross Weatherall, who had been invited to come along to the party by his Chairman, an old friend of Michael Kinsley's, shook Richards' hand. And before he knew it he was shaking John Edwards's too, explaining what he did at NEAH. Edwards responded that he was starting an antipoverty institute down at the University of North Carolina; he'd been visiting a lot of homeless shelters and reading "several" biographies of Robert Kennedy.

Ross knew that the defeated vice-presidential candidate had experienced a lot more tragedy in his life—the illness of his wife, the death of that teenaged son—than he himself could claim from nothing more than a failing marriage whose failure was his own fault. In the face of Edwards's get-up-and-go good works, he felt a bit ashamed of his own past month's drinking; of some lachrymose phone calls to old friends; and the generally shabby place he was sliding into. He felt an urge to talk to Edwards about the poverty he'd seen the other day, on his third trip to New Orleans, when somebody drove him across Rampart Street into one of those poor places Father Montrose had told him to get out and see. But their conversation came to an end when Donatella Versace touched the politician on the arm and gave him a phone number. Edwards appeared nervous, as if afraid of what people might think.

Donatella explained, reassuringly: "Is an Italian doctor I know in Miami. He can put that mole back for you."

9

MAY 9, 2005

V-E Anniversary Celebration; Moscow, Russia

Condi looked through the bulletproof glass and raindrops as the limousine passed a huge banner hung from a streetlamp. She pointed to it and magically alchemized the Cyrillic lettering into English for the president: SIXTY YEARS ON! THE PEOPLE'S VICTORY IN THE GREAT PATRIOTIC WAR!

"Yeah, sponsored by Samsung," Bush added, after seeing a logo at the bottom of the banner.

Condi, aware of her showoffish effort to please him, pretended she wouldn't have noticed the corporate symbol without his having drawn her attention to it. She gave an amused, rueful shake of her head.

"This trip feeling like a waste of your time, diplomacy-wise?" the president asked. There wasn't so much as a folder, let alone a whole briefing book, on the backseat between them. Today's schedule called for nothing but ceremonial chit-chat.

"A little bit," said Condi, worried that the answer seemed rude, given the magnitude of human sacrifice being commemorated this morning.

"Might be just as well to give things a rest with Pootie-Poot—if he was as frosty as you say last month."

Condi's nonstop travels had taken her to Putin's dacha in April. "'Disappointed' was the word he kept using," she now reminded Bush.

The Russian president was, in fact, irritated and dismayed about a host of topics that wouldn't be discussed today, including the new pro-Western government of Ukraine, which had been receiving, from Putin's point of view, far too much American aid and sympathy.

"The good news," said Condi, making her usual optimistic pivot, "is that he's *not* disappointed with your speech." Over the weekend, in Riga, Bush had recognized the Latvians' concern over the reassertiveness of their Cold War masters, but urged them to be respectful toward the sizable Russian population still living among them, like leftover colonials. "Lavrov says Putin thought you struck a pretty good balance," Condi told the president, referencing her foreign-ministerial counterpart.

"Think we'll hear any apologies today?" asked Bush. "For fifty years of imprisoning Eastern Europe? Wouldn't be a bad occasion for it. If the Germans and Koizumi can show up for this, maybe a few more recent bygones can go bygone too."

"I doubt it, sir."

"So do I," said Bush, who quickly changed the subject. "Tell me again—how many rods?" His mind had gone back to this morning's intel briefing at the hotel, much of it focused on North Korea.

"They're harvesting eight thousand of them from the reactor," Condi answered. "Which is enough for maybe three bombs."

Bush made a disgusted, spitting sound, what once would have been accompanied by a spray of tobacco juice onto the limo's floor. Even so, Condi knew he'd rather ponder the Korean danger than the latest horrifying Iraq statistics, which had also been part of the intel briefing.

"These six-part talks are going nowhere," said the president.

Condi was about to urge that the multilateral negotiations over North Korea be given some more time to bear fruit, when Bush jokingly called out to his wife in the seat ahead. "Hey, Laura, maybe you can nudge Hu Jintao on this. That diagram we saw shows you'll be sitting next to him."

"I'm more concerned about the guest we've got back home, who'll be there without any hosts," the First Lady responded. Hours from now Nancy Reagan would be arriving at the White House for a four-day visit, her first to Washington since her husband's funeral last year. She'd be by herself in the Residence until tomorrow night.

"Remember our North Korea conversation with Steve Hadley?" Condi asked the president. "I liked how you were willing to think big."

"As I recall, you liked the *size* of the thought more than its quality." Bush had actually suggested giving North Korea the peace treaty it said it wanted—along with all the recognition and legitimacy that would bring—if they really gave up nukes.

"Yes," said Condi, with a smile. "I think we were getting a bit ahead of ourselves there."

"Why not?" asked Bush, sharply. "We're getting behind ourselves everywhere else."

Condi knew the sudden change in demeanor stemmed from the Iraq figures. The car entered Red Square. As the driver brought it to a stop, Condi whispered a last little warning, or word of solidarity, to the president, as if the two of them were pulling up to another couple's house for dinner. "Putin's gotten much worse since we saw him in Slovakia in February. He's going after journalists and giving his police freer rein than the KGB used to have. All those disgraced Soviet operatives, the *siloviki*, are being brought back and rehabilitated. In many ways these are signs of weakness—"

"No, they're not," said Bush. "They're signs of strength. He's feeling strong from all the oil money he's got coming in. He's like a guy in Midland suddenly being offered the best seat at the Petroleum Club when a couple of months ago he couldn't even get a membership. Pootie-Poot's at the head of the table today."

"The Chechen problem is getting worse—"

"Condi, you're losing altitude."

She'd made a mistake. What he most hated was not disagreement, but repetition. One assertion of Putin's weakness would have been enough.

"That's not the most polite expression," Laura Bush told her husband.

The president winked, apologetically, at his secretary of state. What wasn't he telling her? Condi wondered.

———

Bush felt a trace of disappointment that Putin had not placed all the leaders atop Lenin's tomb, in the classic Soviet manner, but down in front of it, which felt like a confused and ultimately pointless compromise. Russia still couldn't decide what it wanted to be, its old expanding self or a politely stable member of the European club; couldn't even decide what to do with Lenin—whether to keep fluffing and venerating his rubbery carcass or bury it once and for all.

Moving along the dais to his seat, shaking hands as if this were another G8 meeting, Bush was surprised to find himself grasp, almost tenderly, both of Schröder's forearms. He'd never been told until this morning's quick briefing that Gerhard's father had been killed by the Russians on the Eastern Front. The president tried to imagine an equivalent context for himself: Dad dying instead of being rescued after he got shot down; the Japanese victorious in the war; Tokyo the triumphal setting for today's event. As it was, he just winked at the Elvis-loving Koizumi, who counted himself lucky to have gotten an invitation to Graceland for next summer. As for Chirac? He'd rather be sitting down with the Axis of Evil than with this ingrate ally. Bush didn't offer him a single cheek, let alone two; he gave him a fast, grudging handshake before taking his place between Putin and Laura.

What was up with Pootie's face? He'd noticed at the dinner last night that it was as smooth and puffy as Kerry's, different from what he'd seen in February. Vlad looked weirdly inexpressive but also rested, as if he'd taken the sort of nap Bush always allowed himself before a big speech. The Russian seemed cheerful, too; maybe relieved to be having the break from serious negotiation that Bush had just extolled to Condi back in the limo.

In fact the president had something very different in mind for both of them today.

Bush listened to Putin's speech with a soft, relaxed smile: *Through the liberation of Europe and the Battle of Berlin, the Red Army brought the war to its victorious conclusion.* There'd been a little more credit to go around in Vlad's remarks at last night's dinner; Putin had kept things disarmingly light, referring to Laura's desperate-housewives speech, which had gotten picked up even over here. With some satisfaction Bush now recalled that it had been *his* idea for his wife to do the routine at the Correspondents' dinner, even if the resulting lotsa-laffs press détente had lasted all of forty-eight hours.

Funny that he should be here this morning, under a Moscow rain, feet from Lenin's body, wondering if Kent Hance had tuned in that night and heard George W. Bush being the teller, not the butt, of the old cattle-guard joke.

Bush gave Putin a nice-job nod as he resumed his seat and they began watching the military parade. A translator discreetly crouched behind them in case they found themselves in the mood to chitchat. Well, the atmosphere was conducive to it: the parade had none of yesteryear's missiles going by on flatbed trucks; it was mostly banners, albeit without the Samsung branding. Putin amiably pointed out bunches of schoolkids and gymnasts to Laura, and smiled thinly when contingents of troops from the other countries here today stepped past.

Bush knew the resentful part of Putin's feelings came from the side of him that wanted to be part of all that, the portion of him that had astonished Clinton and Madeleine Albright by proposing NATO membership for Russia, an idea that caught them so off guard they could only brush it aside. Well, maybe it was less farfetched than a peace treaty with North Korea—which he himself hadn't been serious about in any case. That had just been something he threw out to shake up Condi—and Dick, too, who was certain to have gotten wind of it right away.

In fact, where North Korea was concerned, he was thinking of something like the opposite of a peace treaty. Instead of carping about Iraq and the interminable American presence in Afghanistan, Putin could cooperate with the U.S. in a strike against Pyongyang's nuke facilities. If he wanted NATO membership, that was a way for him to get it; help out with North Korea and the U.S. would even cancel the antimissile systems planned for Poland and the Czech Republic. That bold enough for you, Vlad?

It ought to be, given how Pootie may have been bold enough to bomb all those Russian apartment buildings and blame the Chechen terrorists—before jailing the reporters who decided to investigate whether this was his way of scaring people into thinking he was indispensable. Was that suspicion less crazy than the theories that Bush and Cheney had deliberately brought down the World Trade Center? Yes, a lot less crazy, Bush had come to think, after watching Putin these last few years. What he'd said after their meeting in '01—and what he'd had misquoted back to him a dozen times since—was this: *I was able to get a sense of his soul.* He'd never specified the condition it appeared to be in.

Was a joint North Korean venture such a crazy proposition? If Iraq's suspected WMDs needed to be gotten rid of, why not the North Korean nukes that everyone *agrees* are there? Better to wait until Kim Jong-il kills twenty-seven million people? This wouldn't be Wolfowitz's war, or Dick's, or Rumsfeld's. It would be his. And this one *would* be fast. If North Korea needed occupation, the South could do the occupying—permanently.

Everyone rose for a medley of national anthems ending with the new Russian one that nobody seemed to know. No wonder Pootie wanted to go back to the old Soviet version, no matter what they decided to do with Lenin.

A female army officer gave Bush and Laura and everybody else on the dais a single long-stemmed carnation to lay on the tomb of the unknown soldier.

"We met at the Elbe River sixty years ago," Bush said to Putin, through the translator, as they walked down into Red Square. "How about meeting at the Yalu?"

He noticed the Russian's surprised expression.

"Something to think about," Bush added.

10

MAY 11, 2005

"Take my arm," the First Lady said to Nancy Reagan.

Nancy's mind went back to General Jackman, kind and a little courtly, who'd been her escort through the whole ordeal last year—standing behind the caisson with Ronnie's casket; gently guiding her into the Rotunda.

The Secret Service agents clearly wanted her and Laura to hurry. The White House had been on red alert for two minutes, and no one knew where the plane that had entered restricted airspace might be heading, but Laura was trying to make everything feel routine, even a bit of a lark, as they descended (without risking the elevator) to the emergency shelter deep beneath the White House.

"Were you ever down here?" Laura asked.

"Never," said Nancy.

"I think the place we're going has been there since FDR's time. They brought me and George to it on the night of 9/11—a false alarm, as I'm sure this will turn out to be."

Nancy felt perfectly calm. This was, after all, the kind of emergency shared by the whole world—unlike March 30, 1981, when Mike Deaver actually thought she should stay out of the hospital room where Ronnie might be bleeding to death. *You don't understand, Mike. I have to see him, and he has to see me. People don't know how it is with us.* That day the fear had lodged in her chest, ready to explode like the Devastator bullet an inch away from Ronnie's heart.

The two women, preceded and followed by the agents, reached the metal doors lettered PRESIDENTIAL EMERGENCY OPERATIONS CENTER. Nancy emitted her soft, silvery laugh. "I bet they called it something a little less grandiose in Roosevelt's time."

"Like 'the basement,'" said Laura, with a smile, grateful for her predecessor's apparent serenity, which was disturbed only momentarily by the sound of the doors sliding closed behind them, first with a soft thud and then a little *pfft*. Nancy winced. "I just remembered that air lock," said Laura. "I should have warned you."

The women avoided the ratty foldout couch and sat down at the conference table. A soldier opened a bottle of sparkling water, and Nancy felt herself lighting up the way she always did when offered something noncaloric. It was touching, really, how anxious Laura had seemed when looking in on her late last night, just after getting off the plane from Europe—almost as if old Mrs. Reagan were the mother who'd moved to that retirement home. Nancy had surprised her successor with the story of how much time she'd spent in Phoenix visiting *her* mother, in just such a place, during Ronnie's eight years here. "I had no idea," Laura had replied. Almost no one did.

Several agents and military men shuffled nervously at the far end of the room.

"Being by myself was fine," she again reassured Laura. "It felt a little like using the private apartment at the library, which I do more than most people would think." Whenever she's up in Simi Valley, a floor above the researchers and tourists, she dozes off looking at the *High Country* painting, with its docile line of antelope, a canvas Ronnie had himself hung before the fast fade began in '94.

"I watched some of the Michael Jackson trial yesterday afternoon," she told Laura, laughing again. She never would have gotten through '94 and '95 without all the coverage of O.J., whom she once described to Merv Griffin as a "lifesaver." *Oooh,* Merv had replied. *There's irony for you.*

"Should we talk about tomorrow?" she asked Laura, who was looking uncomfortably at the pipes overhead.

"Yes," said Mrs. Bush, brightening. "I'm looking forward to it."

The two women would open a little exhibit of first ladies' dresses, all of them red, at the Kennedy Center, in support of a research effort into women's heart disease.

"I'm glad it'll be just the two of us there," said Nancy. "I like the idea of Hillary being present only as a dressmaker's dummy, unable to speak."

"My mother-in-law will be in the same condition," said Laura, with a cautious smile.

Nancy said nothing more. The years hadn't lessened her dislike of Barbara, who'd been allowed to get away with murder by the press.

"I still feel bad about *tonight*," said Laura.

"Oh, don't. Please."

The current First Lady was talking about a fundraiser for the Reagan Foundation, the main purpose of Nancy's visit to Washington. Six hundred people were expected at the Ronald Reagan Building, a few blocks down Pennsylvania Avenue. "Everyone seemed to think it was best to have just *one* president there," Laura explained, as she pointed to a simply framed eight-by-ten photo of Reagan on the far wall.

It was a sweet thing for her to say, clever *and* genuine. Nancy liked her.

"What'll you be wearing tonight?" Laura asked.

"A de la Renta. Lots of beading. White. You know, I sometimes think I overdid the red." She laughed almost shyly.

"Oh, I don't think so," Laura assured her.

How *nervous* she is around me, thought Nancy: *Was I really that awful? That frightening?* The press, who once would have answered yes, kept talking about this trip as her "first visit back to Washington since Ronald Reagan's funeral." They didn't know she hoped it would be her last.

"Where is the president?" she finally asked Laura. "I think you mentioned it when we were upstairs, but—"

"He's out bike-riding, at a wildlife center over in Maryland. I told him it wasn't a great idea while he's so jet-lagged. I just hope he's been informed of this business." She indicated their emergency location with a little hand gesture. Both women knew there'd be hell to pay in the media if there'd been any delay in telling him about the incident.

"Ronnie once had to say he'd issued an order to wake him whenever something bad happened—even if he was in a meeting." She and Laura laughed, though each understood that George W. Bush was in no political position to charm his way out of any perceived inattentiveness to duty.

The air-locked doors slid open and a Marine entered to tell them that the alert had been lifted. The digital clock on the wall said 12:14 p.m.

"That's great," said Laura, who immediately stood.

Nancy rose more gingerly, feeling a certain sadness: Would it be so terrible if this had been "it," the end? Was she really any less alone than her mother had been—always cold, confused, and wearing mittens—in that nursing home?

Back upstairs in the Residence she and Laura ate a light lunch amidst long, friendly silences, until the president joined them just after one o'clock, his head still wet from a post-exercise shower. He gave Nancy a formal kiss but a warm hug, as if he couldn't make up his mind about her. Or about himself.

She had never liked the father—too many bitter memories from the 1980 primary fight—but Bush Sr. had been all of a piece, predictable. Not this son. One minute he looked like a second lead who ought to be wearing a letter sweater; the next he was turning into John Garfield, ready to take a swing at somebody. Twenty years ago she'd found him an annoying cutup: the vice president's son, intermittently on the scene and interested in all the wrong things, a college boy going early to seed. She remembered Laura, too, a little; had figured she smoked so much because his drinking drove her to it.

"I am *so* sorry, ladies," said the president. "It was a little single-engine Cessna being flown by some student pilot and his friend. They almost died of fright when the F-16s shot flares at them. Didn't know what to do except keep going. But they never got closer to us than four miles."

"That sounds close enough to me, Bushie," said the First Lady.

Nancy, who had never spent ten relaxed minutes in this house—

whose heart would speed up if the napkins in the State Dining Room looked to be the wrong shade of ivory—just smiled.

"That's going to be some dinner tonight," said the president, as they all sat down. "It's fitting that it takes the biggest federal building in the country to hold a tribute to Ronald Reagan. And fitting that the building's named for him."

"I guess Ronnie didn't shrink the government as much as he hoped to," said Nancy, forcing her silvery laugh. She was angry with Bush over stem cells, had found his argument to limit research with them to be like angels dancing on the head of a pin. His decision had seemed a personal insult to Ronnie's memory, but she had shut up about it, more or less—and he owed her for that. Maybe the whole thing was "karma," as her daughter Patti would say, payback for the cavalier way she and Ronnie had always taken the cheers and the votes of the right-to-lifers without delivering them anything in return.

"Not right now," Bush snapped when a military aide entered with further news of the airspace incident. But a moment later, as soon as a White House operator informed him that his mother was on the line, he clicked into a genial obedience. "Have you just finished your swim?" the president asked, after taking the call.

"She does a mile every day," Laura informed Nancy, who feigned being impressed.

"I've got a surprise for you, Mother," said the president. He gave Nancy the receiver.

"Hello, Barbara, it's Nancy Reagan," she managed to say.

"Oh, I'd heard you were going to be in town! Are George and Laura taking care of you?"

"I've been fine. Reading a couple of books from the library down-stairs. Biographies. I remember you like them." Barbara would get the reference. When the hatchet job on her by that awful little blonde across town appeared, during Bush Sr.'s term, the press had caught "Bar" masking the copy she was reading with the dust jacket from another book.

"I hope they don't have my size 14s next to one of your 4s in that exhibit tomorrow!" Barbara cheerily offered from her patio in Hous-ton. This was exactly the sort of good-sport self-deprecation the press had always lapped up—without ever bothering to correct the facts. Barbara was a 16 and Nancy was a 2, and everybody who counted knew it.

"Is yours a Scaasi?" asked Nancy. If she'd been Barbara, she too would have used a designer who got his start dressing Mamie Eisenhower.

"I can't even remember which one we picked," Mrs. Bush answered. "The girl had me look at two of them in some storage closet at the library."

Nancy knew what she was thinking: *Shallow* you *probably spent a day and a half deciding on yours.*

"I should give you back to the president," said Nancy. She handed him the phone while thinking: *You can have her.*

———

"*Oooh,*" said Merv. "Great *evening.*" He gently touched Nancy's beaded shoulder and headed back to his hundred-thousand-dollar table before things got fully under way. A NATION HONORS NANCY REAGAN proclaimed the jpeg gigantically projected onto the far wall of the ballroom, which was even bigger than the pavilion they were raising money for: a space at the Reagan Library that would house the *Air Force One* plane that had flown Ronnie and six other presidents.

They had her seated at a long, long table, the sort she recalled from pictures of her father's old medical-society banquets, the ones held in those big Chicago hotels. Tonight she had Cheney on one side of her and Frist, the majority leader, on the other. Rumsfeld sat far down, and Condi Rice, oddly, had been put at the table's head, as if she were presiding. The big ruffles of her satin blouse were, Nancy thought, a little much—something worthy of Scaasi, in fact.

Cheney was now up on the platform, giving the main talk.

I am very fortunate to know Mrs. Reagan, and to have known her husband.

They'd known *him,* unpleasantly, as Ford's young chief of staff in

'76, when he'd done his best, and with success, to maneuver her and Ronnie into the wilderness. It's true that later, during Iran-Contra, Cheney had been mostly supportive of Ronnie, but that one losing campaign, back in the seventies, remained more indelible than anything else. Having Rumsfeld here, too, made Nancy feel as if she were in Ford's library. In fact, it offended her that there actually *was* such a thing in Michigan. *I didn't know unelected presidents got presidential libraries,* she'd told Richard Norton Smith, with arsenic sweetness, when he'd unimaginably switched from directing Ronnie's to directing Jerry's.

Cheney was laying it on pretty thick: *The woman we honor this evening has appeared on Broadway, performed with touring companies, and starred in motion pictures with Gary Cooper, Ava Gardner, Barbara Stanwyck, Fredric March, Gene Kelly, and Ronald Reagan.* Starred? She'd been with Ava and Barbara in a single picture, all three of them together, and she'd had one decent scene. Well, better listening to this than to Pelosi and Harry Reid, who had already slathered on the bipartisan treacle, complete with "morning in America." It was amazing what a husband's Alzheimer's and then her own widowhood could do for a girl's reputation. And astonishing how an hour in these people's company could stir up so much of the old bile that the last several years had drained out of her.

She caught the eye of Sandra Day O'Connor and decided to talk to her before the night was over. *Her* husband had been diagnosed with Alzheimer's years ago and had only recently, Nancy heard, become unmanageable, to the point where Sandra couldn't take him to work anymore. He couldn't stand being apart from her, and was beyond her clerks' ability to babysit him. So the nursing home was next.

Really, it was ridiculous to be raising all this money to build a glass box for an airplane that could no longer fly. They ought to be teasing the secrets of existence out of those embryos that would be going into the trash no matter what "Bushie" and the right-to-lifers wanted. Those infinitesimal little forms inside the eggs could come to life in a different, eerie way, in the healthy old ages of people alive a hundred years from now. She had never forgotten about the eyes that belonged to one of the men who died in San Quentin when Ronnie was governor. He'd donated them to an eye bank, and for all she knew they were open somewhere right now, almost forty years later, gazing into another living pair.

The lights went down in the ballroom: time for a video with her life story, a sort of highlights reel. She only half-attended to it until she saw a piece of some old home movie in which she was impulsively kissing a very young Patti, to the apparent joy of both mother and child. All anybody here had ever heard about were the slaps and the rage between them, but that had by now spent itself into a strangely affectionate afterglow, something that allowed her to watch these long-forgotten inches of film with actual pleasure. As she'd told Betsy Bloomingdale the other week: when your *daughter* has had her first face lift, you know it's past time to let go of the bad things.

She wanted to go home. But she had to get up and speak. Led to the stage while everyone kept applauding, she delivered her remarks from inside a sort of vapor. The brightness of the lights kept her from seeing even Merv at his table down front. She was scarcely aware of the sound of her voice, which she'd learned, on that handful of movie sets and behind enough lecterns, not to listen to, any more than she had ever listened to Ronnie's when she fixed him with The Gaze.

Dessert, a little mingling, a few numbers by Tony Bennett, and she would be out of here—hoping that the Bushes weren't waiting up for her.

Rumsfeld came and took her hands after she permitted herself a second forkful of the lemon cake. She gave him her medium-sized smile and said, "Your old partner in crime gave such a nice speech up there."

"I was actually Cheney's *boss*, twice," Rumsfeld reminded her with that little twinkle.

"Oh!" she replied. "I guess I never really noticed." She notched her smile up to the large size, gave his hands a little squeeze, and turned back to the table. *Trust me, Don, I noticed everything.*

———

Rumsfeld saw Cheney give his wife, Lynne, a signal to keep Nancy entertained while he had a quick chat with the secretary of defense. The two men walked over to a spot a few feet from the table.

"I'm hearing it was seventeen killed," said Rumsfeld.

"Good," said Cheney. "Better than eighty, which is what I'd been told."

"No," Rumsfeld corrected. "Eighty is the Iraq figure. I'm talking about Afghanistan." Riots were continuing in Kabul and at points east over a report in *Newsweek* that American soldiers at Gitmo had flushed a copy of the Koran down a toilet. Now there were fatalities, at least seventeen of them.

Cheney's face fell. He asked if there'd been any progress in getting the magazine to retract the Koran story.

"No," said Rumsfeld. "Even though we know it isn't true."

"General Myers says the riots are really over something else."

"He told me the same thing. But it's not going to matter, Dick. I feel like I'm back to—I almost said 'in'—Abu Ghraib."

Last year Rumsfeld *had*, twice, offered Bush his resignation; and twice had it refused. So here he was, still in charge of the detainee diaspora, lurching from one atrocity, real or imagined, to another.

"No, Don," said Cheney, simply, as if he were rejecting the resignation for a third time.

Condi, determined not to be left out, had gotten up to join them. Cheney nodded hello to her and said, "I've got to rejoin Mrs. Reagan."

Stung by the rebuff, she pretended it was only Don she'd come over to see. "I heard the Pentagon didn't evacuate this morning."

"No," said Rumsfeld. "That Cessna weighs only fifteen hundred pounds. How much damage could it do?" Compared, say, to the Boeing 757 that came toward them at 530 mph on the morning of 9/11. Hours after it struck he'd been walking among the bodies of employees that had melted along with their filing cabinets in the two-thousand-degree fires.

"Was any thought given to shooting it down?" asked Condi.

"The little Cessna? That's a question best asked of the president." He hoped to make her feel both presumptuous and out of the loop all at once. "Did *you* evacuate?"

"Yes."

"Really?" he asked, as if to say: how extraordinary that anyone might think of the State Department as a significant target.

"We've got to fix this Koran story," said Condi.

"Do you want me to fly up to New York and march into the *Newsweek* offices? Or get Gordon Liddy to firebomb them?"

"The riots are already spreading to Pakistan. And I'm worried about Egypt."

"I'm sure Karen Hughes will take care of that."

Condi gave him a warning look, a signal that she just might have to tattle about that to Bush. Rumsfeld didn't flinch; he just waited until exasperation made her change the subject.

"Who exactly is this Allison O'Connor?" she asked. "I'm seeing her name on half the memos I get, and every time I turn around at a meeting she seems to be right there, taking notes."

"You signed off on her for the NSC staff."

"I *know* that, Don; I did it at your behest. But why have you made her ubiquitous? This is no ordinary NSC appointment."

"I'm hoping she'll also be at the Karzai reception in a couple of weeks. Thanks for the allotment of tickets to DoD. I'll use one of those for her."

He felt Condi's anger, but he wouldn't tell her any more. He was trying something that was still halfway between a thought experiment and an actual scheme. He'd seen the president be emboldened and hoodwinked by Karen Hughes's cheerleading; watched him get unduly impressed by Condi's little-sisterly straight A's. George W. Bush was a man confounded by his mother and steadied by his wife. What Rumsfeld wanted to do, as quickly as he could, was introduce Allison O'Connor into the president's feminine mix; startle him with the force of her personality and argumentative zeal; let her take him outside the mental box that Condi liked to maintain for him as a clean well-lighted place. Allison might shake him into a radical skepticism about the continuing, failing Occupation. She was, just as he'd told her, an unknown known: it was known that Bush could be influenced and redirected by several different types of strong women; what remained unknown was whether Allison in particular could do that trick.

"I hear you've taken to calling the whole war, not just the invasion, a 'catastrophic success,'" Condi said at last. She was back in her tattling mode, threatening to spread this latest intimation of disloyalty. And Rumsfeld was determined to keep annoying her with riddles and hypotheticals, to take his doubts out on her because he couldn't take them out on the president or Dick. His history with the latter was just too complex; too long and too topsy-turvy and too close.

"What if it were a 'successful catastrophe'?" he asked Condi. "Would it be easier to resign oneself to that?"

"I don't know, Don. Which would be easier for you to resign *over*?"

11

MAY 23, 2005

Ross Weatherall looked out into the late-afternoon light through the big half-moon window of his office. Down on the sidewalk of Pennsylvania Avenue, a group of tourists who could use some exercise were riding Segways between the White House and the Capitol. He turned his gaze from them back to an invitation he held in his hand: A RECEPTION HONORING PRESIDENT HAMID KARZAI—tonight, at the Freer Gallery of Art, a couple of blocks away. NEAH had a small hand in Afghanistan's reconstruction, and the agency hoped to play a part in bringing some of the country's artistic treasures over to the U.S. for exhibition.

He should of course go. Even Cheney was expected to be there, however briefly. And aside from all else, anything to do with Afghanistan tended to feel like a political and moral tonic. When they remembered it amidst their denunciations of Iraq, even the Democrats liked to say that the Afghan war was the "necessary" one.

And yet, a part of Ross wished he could retract the affirmative RSVP he'd sent in last week. It had been a long Monday, starting with a call from the guidebook office in New Orleans: Mayor Nagin's second cousin's niece, who'd started work there, had no computer skills and did not know that the city had once been under Spanish control. The day had presented one vexation after another and only a single piece of good news. It turned out that a lot of Syrian peddlers and Arab seamen had passed through New Orleans and even settled there late in the nineteenth century. The guidebook project had found an untenured guy at LSU who thought he could produce a respectable couple of pages about them—and maybe even find some site to photograph. So Ross at last had something to tell the person at State who was so concerned about Muslims, even while Karen Hughes remained out of town and unconfirmed.

The real reason it would be better to go straight home tonight was the small stack of legal-separation papers resting on what Ross somewhat laughably called his dining-room table. His last visit to Dallas had been worse than the one at Easter, and these documents were the result. If he didn't fill them out soon, Deborah, already contemplating the next steps, would pitch a fit.

———

Six blocks away, the top of Allison O'Connor's desk was a shambles. Three different think-tank-produced articles on Iraq—one advocating a three-way partition of the country; another suggesting legally prescribed ethnic percentages for apportioning its legislature; the third discouraging Sunni overtures to Iran—were strewn across it. They seemed to be physically wrestling one another in a contest for Allie's attention, and in their midst also lay an envelope from Fadhil, her old translator. It contained a picture of him holding his infant daughter, who wore the bib Allie had purchased as a new-baby present at an airport shop in Dubai: IT'S A PERSON! proclaimed the Arabic lettering.

Thank you, Miss Allison, said a note affixed to the picture. *You are missed at the embassy,* Fadhil had added, the last word shrinking by the syllable in a dying fall of penmanship, as if it were afraid of presumption or prying eyes. There was no ambiguity in Fadhil's own eyes, however: they were dancing with delight over the baby, whose head was tucked under her father's chin, nestled against his shirt collar. On his jacket lapel Allie could see the same golden pin he always wore, with the digits 289178. She had never asked Fadhil their meaning, not from her own fears of presumption, but because the numerals amounted to only one fact among ten thousand other pieces of political and cultural information that there would never be time to acquire during her forays in and out of the world's current wars. But the father's smile seemed to override all the clutter on her desk; it was for Fadhil's expression, not the generic adorability of the baby, that she decided to have the picture framed.

Beside Fadhil's envelope sat something from Rumsfeld: an unusually long "snowflake" alerting Allie to the Defense Department's custody of twenty-seven crates of Judaica that had been found in the flooded Baghdad headquarters of the Iraqi secret police. The objects and papers ranged from sixteenth-century Haggadahs and Talmuds to a 1950s set of yeshiva report cards; the school that issued them had long since vanished, along with almost all of Iraq's Jewish population. The motives and methods for the police's collection of this material remained unclear, but now that American soldiers had found it, the drenched mass of items had been frozen—literally—and were being safeguarded from further deterioration in several refrigerated trailers on the National Archives campus in Maryland. The last line of Rumsfeld's memo read: "Thoughts?"

Mimicking the geography of America's Near East commitments, the right-most portion of Allie's desktop had been claimed by Afghanistan: it hosted the four placemats she'd brought home and still not given away, as well as a newly framed photograph sent by Mrs. Morris from the embassy in Kabul. "To Mrs. Allison" read Dr. Asefi's Sharpied inscription of the picture they'd had taken together. The heads of two people at desks in the background had been playfully scratched out and replaced with gaily inked pots of flowers.

Allie felt like one of them, engaged as she was in a kind of scratch-off game with Rumsfeld, awaiting his promised mid-June reveal of whatever it was he wanted. In addition to the memo about the Judaica, she had several recent snowflakes *inside* her desk. If she had any of the competitive ambition that people around here generally did, she'd be giving them casually conspicuous display beside her keyboard.

People here would also envy the invitation she now indecisively tapped with her fingers. She ought just to give it to one of them. But with Cheney expected at this reception—no doubt to be hustled through the premises like the nuclear football, or Hannibal Lecter on a dolly—it was decidedly nontransferable.

———

Anticipation of the vice president's attendance had caused Condi Rice and Donald Rumsfeld to decline their own invitations to the Freer Gallery. In Rice's case it was a matter of pique, and in Rumsfeld's an instance of strategic psychology, a personal distancing from Cheney, perhaps only temporary, that would allow for the political distancing he had in mind. But these RSVP regrets turned out to be moot. Cheney had already come and gone, done a quick meet-and-greet with Karzai, and taken a hasty look at some Silk Road artworks assembled by the Freer, before any of the other guests arrived.

Hamid Karzai, slight and dapper in his green cape and lamb's-wool hat, now stood in a corner, wrapped in protocol, attended by low-level officials of both the United States and his own fledgling government. A man from the U.S. Customs Service got ready to hand him two ancient Afghan coins recently seized from shady antiquities dealers. America was happy to "repatriate" the specie, the officer declared, and Karzai good-naturedly accepted the pieces of gold. "Only twenty-nine thousand, nine hundred and ninety-eight still to be found!" said the Afghan president.

The U.S. was intent on showing that the war would not result in any Elgin Marbles sort of plunder. Once the Kabul Museum got back on its feet, Afghanistan would be well compensated for any blockbuster traveling exhibition of its treasures in the United States. Tonight the Freer was full of museum directors, each hoping to secure a spot on the tour.

The Chairman of the NEAH now took the microphone to announce an Afghanistan Initiative designed to encourage grant applications from American scholars hoping to do work in the country's history and literature. "They ought to call it the 'Afghanistan *Suggestion*,'" whispered a *Washington Post* reporter to the man from Chicago's Field Museum. The underfunded NEAH had so little money that one of its council members, the flamboyant archaeologist Iris Love, was footing the bill for this reception; the Chairman hoped she would also secure a mention of the party in the next column written by her old gal pal, Liz Smith.

Christopher Hitchens, aware that he was one of the few people inside the Freer who had the man's identity and résumé straight, conversed with Zalmay Khalilzad. Despite his name, Khalilzad was the *American* ambassador to Afghanistan; in fact, he'd been such a success there that he'd just gotten tapped for the Baghdad embassy instead. As they talked, Hitchens remembered that the NEAH Chairman who'd just spoken was Kinsley's friend and had come to his April party; so he called him over for congratulations on doing "the Lord's work" in Afghanistan. "Let me withdraw the figure of speech," Hitchens quickly added, "but repeat the sentiment."

A man from the Heritage Foundation chatted with a recently retired woman from State who had "such nice memories of King Zahir" from her long-ago days in Kabul. She insisted that the pointless war in Iraq was dooming the effort in Afghanistan; the man from Heritage insisted otherwise. As with most of the conservatives here, his admiration for Karzai stemmed more from his having opposed the Soviets than the Taliban.

The Afghan president was amiably showing the man from Customs the slight facial scar he'd gotten in the period following 9/11, after crossing over the border from Pakistan and secretly reentering his country. During a meeting to go over tactics, a bomb dropped by a B-52 nearly killed both him and a CIA operative. The bomb had landed with entire accuracy; alas, the geographical coordinates of its actual target, some miles away, had been incorrectly programmed into the plane's computer.

A woman from Cheney's staff who'd stayed behind looked enviously at Karzai's cape and hat, and told a colleague she felt underdressed. "God," she said, considering the general *éclat* of the man, "he was the best Skutnik ever, wasn't he?" Karzai had sat beside Laura Bush at the '02 State of the Union Address. The thought of putting Iraq's balding new prime minister in that position next year made no administration spirits soar.

A young woman in a waiter's tuxedo made the rounds with a platter of vegetarian hors d'oeuvres. Even odder than the meatlessness was the absence of country music at a Bush administration entertainment. A small quartet played Western classical selections instead.

"Is that hummus?" asked Allison O'Connor.

"Beats me," said the waitress.

Allie smiled and resumed contemplation of a glass case containing a bronze maple leaf created in the first century a.d.

"There *is* American beer," the waitress told Allie. "At the smaller bar over there." She pointed toward a lean, boyish man, one-quarter of whose profile was visible. A few strands of gray streaked his full head of dark wavy hair. He was drinking a long-necked bottle of Lone Star. Allie noticed him sheepishly trying not to tilt it at too high an angle, as if to avoid the appearance of guzzling at such a high-toned function. He set the bottle down altogether in order to offer his card to the man he'd been speaking with.

"I'm Ross," she heard him say.

"I'm Allie," she whispered, after coming up behind him.

———

Ten hours later, a little after five in the morning, Ross opened one eye. Through the open bedroom door he saw Allison O'Connor wearing an oversized Longhorns jersey he'd been given by his son. She was leafing through the legal papers on his dining-room table.

"You know," she called out, "I could fill these out for you in about three minutes."

Ross rubbed his eyes, wondering if he were hungover or still drunk. "Did I tell you the whole story of me and Deborah?" he asked, fearing that he had.

Allie came back into the bedroom. "You did indeed. Somewhere between telling me how our having captured Saddam Hussein means that getting Osama bin Laden is bound to follow—and my telling *you* that you ought to be ashamed to work for an administration that thinks we need a constitutional amendment to keep Harry Lehman from getting married."

Ross tried to comb his hair with his fingers. "Remind me again who Harry Lehman is."

"The boy who was always singing 'On a Clear Day You Can See Forever' in the halls of Lubbock High."

"We had time to talk about Harry Lehman? Between, you know, both . . . times?" He tried smiling in a manner she would find mischievous and winning.

"I'd say you were good for one and a *half*, if you're interested in precision."

She began looking for her clothes. As Ross struggled not to say *please don't go*, he recalled, from some quarter-century-old speck of memory, that the best way to get her to stay, at least for a while, was to make her argue about something.

"By the way," he asked, "don't *you* work for the administration?"

"Yes, for three and one-half sordid months. After thirteen years of working for the United States Army, an institution that this crowd has abused even more than they've abused Harry Lehman."

"And now you work for the . . . *NSC*?" He pronounced the initials with a slow emphasis, indicating that one could hardly be more all-in than that.

"Yes, thanks to my own lapsed judgment, and to 'Rummy.'" She sighed with self-disgust as she continued to hunt for yesterday's outfit. "God, I even wore heels, didn't I?"

Too fuzzy-headed to sustain debate, Ross hid one of her shoes under the covers, and gave her the neediest, puppy-dog expression he could summon.

"Honey," she said, "I can go barefoot if I need to. My own place is only three blocks from here."

"I know! Isn't that amazing?"

She cocked her head. *Really?* she seemed to say. Wasn't fate doing much stranger things in the world than this?

"You can't go," said Ross. "It's not even light out yet."

"I'm going to be at my desk at seven forty-five. When they hold the war-crimes tribunals, I'll be confessing that I was never late. When do *you* clock in?"

"Closer to nine forty-five," he admitted. He got up and shuffled toward some orange juice. "Even later when I'm in New Orleans!"

"Oh, yes," said Allie. "Your guidebook project. Worthy—but maybe a little less urgent than trying to save the Baghdad Central Library would have been?" Saddam's Baathists had burned and looted it during the American invasion.

Ross tried to say something about the fog of war, but all he could manage at the moment was to rummage for a pair of gym shorts to put on. "You know, if I don't see you for *another* twenty-six years, I'll be hitting seventy."

"That sounds like Rumsfeld: a meaningless 'known known.'"

He put his arm around her and asked, softly, "When can I see you again? Please?"

She ran a noncommittal hand through his hair; gave him a quick kiss, straightened her skirt, and headed for the door. He knew that panic was showing in his face. He didn't—and did—want her to see it.

Near the apartment's threshold, she turned around. "'Preservation.'"

"Yes." He knew he'd talked about his work, at too great length, before they came back here last night.

"Your agency gets involved with it."

"Yes. Everything from digitizing smalltown newspapers to saving and cataloguing quilts from the Ozarks. There's a project now—"

"How about some soggy Jewish artifacts rescued from the headquarters of the Iraqi secret police?"

Ross thought for a moment. "Yes, we could be helpful there. I'm sure."

"You're lying."

"Well, I'm not *sure*, but maybe—"

"Okay, come to my office on Friday afternoon."

"I will!"

She was out the door, waving to him over her shoulder.

He thought his heart would burst with joy. He wanted to thank God for the Jews of Iraq, ignoring the logical imperative that he would then have to thank their tormentors as well.

He needed to calm down, but his mind was racing, already trying to figure out who at the agency might be approached for help with this strange find. He was also thinking of other ways to keep Allie around, to tie down this lissome Gulliver who'd wandered back into the Lilliput of his life. He had to keep her *interested*, entertained, needed to play some gender-bent version of Scheherazade's game.

From the time he was a boy on Twenty-first Street back in Lubbock, making his bed had always soothed him; it would be a good idea to do that now. As he pulled off the top sheet he noticed the plastic case for the Buddy Holly CD they had played—had it been before or after the "half" part of the one and a half times? He couldn't remember, and this bit of housekeeping was failing to relax him. Both pillows remained on the floor when he darted away from the bed with another idea. He found his wallet inside last night's pants and extracted from it a business card he'd been carrying around for nearly a month.

Heading over to the dining-room table, he poured himself some juice and pushed the separation papers to one side of his computer. Logging on to his personal account, he began typing an e-mail:

Dear Governor Richards:

We met briefly at Christopher Hitchens' party, where you told me you would be happy to share some information about the "Bush Bash" in Lubbock, Texas, way back in 1978. I'm wondering what you meant, and if . . .

12

JUNE 7–28, 2005

"Yo, Landslide!"

Tony Blair, chatting with a reporter in the Cross Hall of the White House, turned around when he heard Bush's voice.

"These guys had their chance," the president reminded him. "Let's get upstairs."

The two men, after hours of private talks, had just finished a joint press conference in the East Room. "Landslide" had been Bush's nickname for the British prime minister ever since Blair handily won a second term in 2001. Last month he'd won a third, albeit with a smaller majority and against some fierce resentment, most of it from those within his own Labour Party who believed Iraq had turned the PM into the president's "poodle."

"Who's upstairs apart from Laura and Cherie?" asked Blair, when the two men reached the elevator.

"Dick and Lynne Cheney."

Blair, somewhat surprised, took the opportunity to tell Bush that Cheney's recent remark, made on *Larry King Live*, that the Iraq insurgency was entering its "last throes," had not exactly been helpful.

Bush, who'd begun wondering if his relationship with Dick wasn't nearing *its* last throes, gave an affirming chuckle. Once upstairs he got a surprise of his own: Condi Rice was arriving too, right behind him and the prime minister, to join everyone for drinks.

"I didn't expect to see *you*," Cherie Blair told the secretary of state.

The hint of genuine consternation in her voice was enough to make Bush laugh.

"It was so nice of the First Lady to ask me," said Condi, more to her boss than to Mrs. Blair, who to everyone's surprise wouldn't let the matter go. "I remember that time at Chequers, just before 9/11, when we discovered you'd be staying overnight because *someone* had allowed the household staff to believe that a 'Dr. Rice,' who'd been added to the guest list, must be the president's personal physician!" Cherie Blair laughed lightheartedly, as if to say *you scamp*, but everything in her tone suggested *what cheek*.

Condi, who knew the story to be essentially true, was aghast, and the president, who had no desire to rehash the press conference that Laura and Mrs. Blair had just watched together on TV, piled on with some teasing of his own. "You gonna fall asleep here, too?" he asked Rice. During a get-together in '01, up at Camp David, when everyone here had first gotten acquainted, Condi nodded off during a showing of *Meet the Parents*. Bringing this up about anyone else would be harmless, but bringing it up with Condi, the most mortifiable person in any of their lives, came close to cruelty.

The president, who genuinely loved his secretary of state, wondered why he had snapped the towel. He always got aggressive, if only for a moment, when he was bored or frustrated, and right now he was smoldering with a sense of *repetition*. He liked Blair—it was rare that he got to deal with another leader who was more than nominally Christian—but he got to see and hear quite a lot of him. It wouldn't break his heart if Tony and Cherie, scheduled to fly back to London after dinner, decided to skip the meal and dash home after drinks. As it was, they'd all be seeing one another at next month's G8 in Scotland.

He couldn't very well tell Tony that *he* was losing altitude, the way he'd told Condi back in Moscow, but by now they had talked Iraq and its problems to death. Both longed to move on to other stuff, but whenever they tried, there wasn't a whole hell of a lot for them to agree on. Climate change? They'd papered that over at the press conference by murmuring something about "different perspectives" and Bush's need "to know more about it" before doing anything hasty. This would no doubt excite a feeling in the press that he especially hated—namely, that he *owed* Blair (*such a good guy! willing to stick with a lummox like Bush!*) and that throwing a few thousand coal miners out of work would be a nice thank-you gesture.

There'd been no talk between the two of them about North Korea, and Bush intended to keep it that way. If he had to owe anybody on *that*, it was going to be Pootie-Poot, and it would redound to his own credit as a matter of *realpolitik*. Since V-E Day there'd been no hint of a response to his little trial balloon, but he knew that its launch had registered with Putin. How? He'd looked into his damned eyes again.

"How do you think we did with the Downing Street Memo?" asked Tony Blair. Now that everyone had a drink and was settling back, he directed the question to Laura Bush in particular. The memo remained a big story back in London, showing, as it did, that in July of '02, many months before the invasion, Blair learned that his own spy chief was saying the Americans had cooked the WMD intel to jibe with the decision they'd already made to go to war in Iraq.

Condi answered before Laura could. "It's *ridiculous* that anyone would believe that."

"Politics, period," said the president. "They made that memo news just before your folks voted—same way that Walsh guy indicted Weinberger four days before Dad lost to Clinton." The Blairs looked a bit befuddled. "Ninety-two," said Bush. "Iran-Contra. Not worth a refresher course."

"Well," said Laura. "There's also 2000. Your DUI."

"Thank you, darlin', for that reminder." The president raised his iced root beer in a toast to the First Lady. It still amazed him that his '76 arrest, revealed in the nastiest of all late-October surprises—November, actually! five days before the election!—hadn't cost him the presidency.

"I was about to say—" Blair continued, but Cheney interrupted him: "No one can take that memo seriously. If anything, you *over*proved your reluctance to join in the war." He was talking about the prime minister's insistence on trying to get a *second*, absolutely-posolutely

UN resolution before they all attacked Saddam. Such permission had been neither necessary nor obtainable—the inadvisability of seeking it was the single thing on which Cheney, Rice, Rumsfeld, and Powell had ever achieved unanimity—but the president had given in to its pursuit because Blair was facing a no-confidence vote in the House of Commons. The subsequent objections from Gerhard and Jacques's Axis of Weasel made people forget that the UN had already approved the fucking war, months before, after Colin's show-and-tell with that tube of toxins.

The memory of it all was increasing Bush's annoyance. "How'd you like what we said about Palestine?" he asked his vice president. At the presser he had offered some tepid support for the "Road Map" to a two-state solution, what Blair saw as the key not only to Middle East peace but to the end of terrorism as well—a view that Cheney emphatically did not share. Bush was needling Dick for the same reason he'd overdone teasing Condi: simple irritability. Well, at least she now seemed pleased by Cheney's discomfort.

"If the Palestinians settle with Israel, maybe *they'll* become the targets of terrorism," Cheney suggested to Blair.

"Sounds like a Rumsfeld 'hypothetical,'" replied the president.

Cherie Blair looked impatient. She liked Laura and had developed an odd, reluctant fondness for George. But thanks to him everything got continually worse. As a working barrister, she'd always been as unpopular as the early Hillary, but Tony was still getting used to being disliked at home. If he'd come and gone after a single term, he'd always be a boyish golden memory to the public, a JFK who'd made it out of that plaza in Dallas, smiling and unshot, gracefully aging for decades to come.

She heard him trying to change the subject, telling a story on himself, about how a few years ago he'd taken temporary leave of his political senses and wandered into the weird Colonel Blimp vs. PETA passions surrounding the issue of foxhunting. And he was using the story, a self-deprecating one to begin with, to compliment George's supposedly superior motherwit: "So the president says to me, 'What'd you go get involved in *that* for, man?'" He even did his best Texas accent. "I suppose I could say the same thing to him about these Social Security reforms."

Worry suffused Condi's expression, and the prime minister saw it. "Of course," he added, trying to execute a quick recovery, "that's something George *believes* in passionately, whereas I never cared in the slightest about the foxes or their pursuers."

Bush saw Blair's embarrassment, the genuine desire not to wound, and it prompted a nostalgic moment of fellow feeling, a remembered awareness of how the two of them had ultimately wanted to go after Saddam for the simple, unspeakable reason that he was a *bad guy*. But it had all gone so wrong, become so anguished.

"Hey, Blair, wait until you see me do immigration reform too!"

Everyone laughed with an imitation of relief, and when the sound subsided one could hear a murmur of cool air starting to come through the floor vents. Cherie Blair pointed to one of them. "Are you finding that that kicks on a day or two earlier every summer?" she asked.

Bush, momentarily grateful for some combat, winked at her. "We'll keep studying it."

No one felt sorry when dinner was announced and the evening moved toward its conclusion.

————

June 28; Womack Army Medical Center; Fort Bragg, North Carolina

"Is this Mom?" Bush asked the soldier in the hospital bed.

"That's my Aunt Lucinda," answered Pfc Charlie Montoya, a big guy covered with burns over the left part of his face and neck. God knows what was under the T-shirt. "She raised me after my mother died."

The president hugged the woman standing by the bedside. He'd been here in the Fort Bragg hospital for more than two hours, and tears kept filling his eyes the way his pockets had filled up with dogtags, pictures, unit patches, and everything else the soldiers and their families kept pressing on him.

"So, Carlito," he said to Private Montoya, "how long before your aunt gets to take you home?"

It was the soldier's turn to cry—sudden loud sobs that stunned him and the president. Montoya tried muffling them with the trembling, apologetic hand he brought to his face.

"He's afraid of not being with his buddies," whispered the aunt. "Of being somewhere else. But soon. I hope to bring him home soon."

Bush hugged her again, and with his fingertips brushed the burned portion of Private Montoya's face. Awful though it might be, he'd rather cry with the maimed than talk to the doctors bent on extracting them from their emotional pit. A group of shrinks had earlier been telling him about the dangers of "bypassed shame," about how the feelings that came with being wounded had to be "processed." Otherwise the guys would "act out," start fights and do drugs and spiral down into mayhem. But what exactly did *shame* have to do with it? The president had been glad to move from the psychiatrists to the physical therapists, the girls in scrubs telling the amputees to try taking just one more step on those Edward Scissorhands legs they'd been fitted with.

If you wanted an actual damned shame, you could find one in how the networks had whined about having to televise tonight's speech, even threatened not to do it, saying its live audience of soldiers would turn it into a pep rally for administration policies. Oh yeah, this was a real day back at the ballpark. Andy Card had warned him not to get stressed and depleted before going out in front of the cameras, but that's just what he'd allowed to happen. He had only minutes to pull himself together, no time for his usual quick pre-speech power nap.

There'd been only one part of the headshrinkers' show that he liked: the painting class they'd had him wander through. It had looked soothing and decisive all at once, a chance to freeze in place, forever, your own vision of something, no one else's. Maybe Carlito back there should pick up a paintbrush.

One of Andy's guys now took him to the end of the corridor, where he'd link up with Rumsfeld. Don had been working the rooms and bays on the other side of the hall and looked, Bush thought, none the worse for wear. The defense secretary had encouraged him to make this trip, though he didn't much like the speech that was about to be delivered; he'd seemed lukewarm to a few passages during the dry run on the flight down. It was hard to tell just *what* Don thought these days, unlike Dick, with whom everything was same-old-same-old and very apparent.

"Yeah, I'm ready," the president told Rumsfeld, who hadn't actually asked if he was.

Within minutes the two of them were stepping into the Eighty-Second Airborne's giant fitness center, and Bush was up at the podium in front of 750 soldiers whose faces he couldn't make out, thanks to the lights of the reluctant TV networks.

As freedom takes root in Iraq, it will inspire millions across the Middle East to claim their liberty as well.

This was, he'd come to realize, his own domino theory, a reversal of the LBJ version that had always gotten mocked in the dorms and classrooms at Yale—until, of course it turned out to be true, and there went Cambodia and Laos.

The soldiers weren't applauding, he noticed. Some pep rally! The guys in front of him had no doubt been given a strict little lecture on military-political decorum, and good for them. All he wanted was to get through this thing and imagine this space being turned back into a gym.

The progress in the past year has been significant, and we have a clear path forward.

Rove had gotten what he wanted. His argument had been: if we're going to stay the course, what's the point in admitting any screw-ups? Fine. But saying, as Bush now had to, that the insurgents had *failed to incite an Iraqi civil war?* That was a little rich.

No timetable, no deadline for withdrawal: that would be tomorrow's unspectacular, unsatisfying headline. And it would make his next lunch with the GOP leadership even more restive than the one a week ago. Frist and Boehner and Denny were already seeking ass-coverage for the midterms, and they'd be asking him to provide more and more of it in the months ahead.

Before our coalition liberated Iraq, Libya was secretly pursuing nuclear weapons. Today, the leader of Libya has given up his chemical and nuclear weapons programs.

Well, that much was the goddamned truth. Once Qadaffi saw them go after Saddam, he figured he was next. And what if *those* bombs, the ones Mu-Mo had now gotten rid of, were the ones that would otherwise have been dropped on Rome or London or New York? If it had kept *that* from happening, then Iraq was *already* worth it. But in the three-quarters of a second required to shift his eyes from the left glass of the teleprompter to the right, he lost this feeling of righteous certainty about the war's biggest fringe benefit, recognizing that it would never sound more than a piss-poor weak defense of the war itself.

I thank those of you who have reenlisted in an hour when your country needs you. And to those watching tonight who are considering a military career, there is no higher calling than service in our Armed Forces.

God almighty, if Rove wanted to take the don't-give-an-inch approach, why didn't he insist on cutting this desperate-sounding second-to-last paragraph? It made the president sound like an Uncle Sam "I Want You" poster. The politics of it would be awful, and Boehner and the rest of them would let him know it. What would he have available as a response? Only the sad truth: we're short of troops.

Once he finished and the camera lights were doused, the faces of the guys down in front became visible. With those red berets on top of their green uniforms, they looked like a mass of those crimson-clover wildflowers Mother was always complaining about in the Houston driveway, wondering why the gardener could never get rid of them. Anyway, the soldiers were finally applauding, and now there would be another hundred hands to shake and pictures to take and trinkets to accept, another hundred prayers to receive and prayers to promise.

Why had he let himself give this damned speech? Its supposed occasion—the first anniversary of transferring sovereignty back to Iraq—was the kind of A-student fact only Condi cared about. *Let freedom reign.* She'd never told him that those words he'd scrawled across the note she'd passed him, the one giving news of the transfer, were another slip of his tongue. He'd realized it the minute he slid the note back across the table: for God's sake, *ring*, not *reign*. Not so far off as to cause much embarrassment, but what if that was the best anyone could now hope for from the whole enterprise? Minimal chagrin. Condi had told him about Rumsfeld's "successful catastrophe."

He'd sweated through his suit—as bad as Nixon! And if he wasn't careful he'd throw up in somebody's lap, like Dad.

———

Fifteen minutes later the phone rang in Bob Dole's Watergate South apartment.

"It's the president," said his wife.

"Which one?"

"The current one."

Dole harrumphed. "I suppose I should have watched the speech." Elizabeth handed him the phone.

"Bob?" said the president. "It's George Bush."

Again, Dole thought, he might ask: *Which one?* He truly couldn't stand the old man, could still hear himself snapping at him in '88: *Stop lying about my record.* The son? In some ways Dole disliked him even more, for having the same short fuse and quippiness he'd come to dislike in himself.

"You sound like you're on a plane," he told the president. "Must be that *Air Force One* I heard so much about."

"We just left Fort Bragg," said Bush, making Dole wonder if his wife—now, with the departure of John Edwards, North Carolina's senior senator—ought to have been *at* the speech.

"I got to spend some time with the wounded," Bush continued.

Dole felt himself clamming up. He'd lately been talked into writing a book about the day in '45 when he'd been laid waste by that German shell, and the three years it had then taken to glue his body and mind back into something like working order. He'd been out touring with the book all last month, wishing he'd never written it.

"The hospital down here looked great," said Bush, "but I'm hearing lousy stuff about Walter Reed, all kinds of shortcomings, and I'm hoping to have your help as we look into that."

Dole uttered a short, indefinite sound.

"I need your thoughts more generally, too," Bush added. "I'm worried that we're *missing* something with these vets, the guys with long recoveries ahead of them. I'd like your ideas."

"Okay," said Dole. "I'll think some up for you."

"Tell me what the hardest part was."

He hadn't meant *tell me right now*, but that's what Dole proceeded to do. "The fever. A hundred and eight point seven. The sulfa drugs that saved me started collecting in my kidneys and then *they* nearly did me in. The doctors figured it out just in time. They're a lot better at that stuff today."

"I saw a couple of guys this afternoon who've got nobody, and I mean nobody, there for them."

"I had my mother around," said Dole. "Not sure that was better or worse. The day I got to the hospital in Topeka she picked a bunch of cigarette butts out of my body cast. The guys on the troop train between Florida and Kansas had sort of used it as an ashtray." Even through the airplane noise and his wireless phone, Dole could hear Bush choking up. He was *always* choking up, same as the father; the mother, by far the easiest of them to be around, was the only one who didn't. When the silence had lengthened for several seconds, Dole decided to show the president some mercy. "You should have seen the shape *they* were in."

Bush laughed, gratefully.

"I've got my laptop open," said Dole. "The press is saying you offered nothing new on Iraq."

"That's not exactly—"

"I'm sure it isn't. I've been dealing with these people for forty-five years."

"I'm having a hell of a time with the leadership, our own guys on the Hill," the president confessed. "Any suggestions?"

"I hear you read a lot of Lincoln books," Dole replied, with surprising speed.

"I do," Bush replied. "Even had a Civil War reference in the speech tonight."

"Do what he did," said Dole.

"Something in particular?"

"Find yourself a general."

———

Allison O'Connor, much farther back on *Air Force One*, gave the secretary of defense a skeptical look. "Are you sure?" she asked. "He seemed spent to me, even from a hundred feet away, when he came aboard."

"No," said Rumsfeld, who appeared oddly pleased. "I think it's a good time for you two to meet."

After months in abeyance, Allie felt herself being moved to active duty. Two days following Cheney's last-throes remark, Rumsfeld had revealed to her his plan for shaking up Bush's thinking; and here he was now, a few weeks later, escorting her down the aisle of the president's plane, as if giving away the bride in some secret, experimental marriage.

Bush, wearing an *Air Force One* windbreaker, still had his hand on the phone he'd used to talk to Dole.

"Mr. President," said Rumsfeld, "I want to take this opportunity to introduce Allison O'Connor, one of the newest staffers on your

National Security Council. She returned to the States from Iraq a few months ago."

"Hey there," said Bush, standing up and extending his hand.

"She's been a lawyer with the Army and has tip-top experience in both Afghanistan and Iraq, straight through the January elections."

"Excellent," said the president.

Allie shook his hand and said, "Sir." People invariably attempted to prolong their moment with the president, even in a receiving line that had to keep moving, but Bush's painfully evident exhaustion was repelling her from his presence. She could feel her body trying to retreat from the cabin.

"Ms. O'Connor has a sharp, surprising mind," said Rumsfeld. "She's already adding a lot to the NSC."

"What'd you think of the speech?" Bush asked her.

Allie paused for only a second. "Well, you certainly embraced the suck."

Bush laughed, hard and for real, for the first time since lunch. He'd heard this expression from soldiers in Iraq when he made his Thanksgiving visit to them a year and a half ago.

Allie noticed that Rumsfeld looked pleased.

13

JULY 4, 2005

The South Lawn of the White House

As she dozed, Ross cooled Allie with one of the paper fans they'd been given at the gate. When you had it fully open, the wingspan of a bald eagle filled the little ridges.

The South Lawn contained scores of administration members who had stayed in town for the Fourth of July: a few big fish and many small-fry "politicals," appointees enjoying one of the smaller perks of office with their families. *I'm going to the White House for the fireworks,* Ross had e-mailed his daughter this afternoon. He did not tell Caitlyn that he would be accompanied by Allison O'Connor, who had her own ticket to come onto the grounds.

A soft thump of music could be heard all the way from the Mall, overridden though it was by the selections of a country-music d.j. operating at the edge of the grass near the Mansion. The eighteen presidential acres were a merry armed camp; here and there one could spot the machine guns of Homeland Security.

Ross nibbled an ice-cream sandwich and continued to fan Allie. The blanket she lay on—he could remember Deborah spreading it out for their kids on the beach at Galveston—prompted another moment of guilt.

Today was their six-week anniversary, his and Allie's, though he knew that pointing it out would likely make her ram the ice-cream sandwich down his throat. Even so, she couldn't deny that the two of them had been creating the history and texture of a love affair, one punctuated by peculiar professional moments: she had been to the Endowment to consult a program officer about the Iraqi Judaica, and he had gone out to the Archives annex in Maryland to look inside the metal trunks, where freeze-drying had arrested the mold growing over the Torahs and school pictures.

Ross knew that with Allie he was always on ice as thin as the Saran Wrap encasing the frozen Jewish relics. She might vanish from his life as quickly as she'd disappeared from Lubbock after her family's year there. Finishing the ice-cream sandwich, he lay back down on the blanket, hoping she'd kiss him in the way she once had atop Buddy Holly's grave. If she did, he wouldn't care what the guy from the Office of Faith-Based Initiatives, just a blanket away, thought about it.

For the past month and a half he had been hearing her recent adventures: the meeting with Dr. Asefi; the advice she'd been requested to give about judicial procedures for Saddam Hussein's upcoming war-crimes trial; the way that German guy back in Baghdad had pulled her into his work on genocide. At first he'd thought this Rolf was just a funny former colleague, but now of course he realized that he had been Allie's—well, he didn't even want to use the term. She told him that things with Rolf had been "not even remotely serious," which only made him worry: Was *he* now Rolf? Were his and Allie's under-furnished Arlington apartments just different rooms in the Hotel Rashid?

"What are you doing the week of August thirteenth?" he asked.

"Fan me harder and I'll tell you."

For the next minute or two he complied, before saying, "So?"

"I forgot the question."

"The week of August eighth."

She sat up and asked for the other ice-cream sandwich on the blanket. "I'm going to be at the ranch, for at least some of it."

"Whose ranch?"

"His," said Allie, pointing to the president up on the Truman Balcony.

"Wow, I'm jealous," said Ross.

This confession provoked Allie's laughter. "Jealous that I get to *go* there? Not jealous that it'll keep me from doing whatever you had in mind for *us* that week?"

What really bothered him was her apparent relief that his little case of Potomac fever might act as a check on his ardor for her.

"The one has nothing to do with the other," he said. "I'm jealous of both." He lay back, resuming his onetime posture in the City of Lubbock Cemetery.

Amazingly enough, she proceeded to kiss him exactly as she had in 1978.

"So what'll you be doing there?" he asked. "At 'the ranch'?"

"First tell me what you were proposing for that week."

"I'm supposed to take my next trip to New Orleans then. Maybe you could join me for some of it?"

He missed the city. His occasional presence there might have resulted from the same Potomac fever, but New Orleans had become a place apart from everywhere else. In the Hotel Monteleone he was unsurrounded by any of his old possessions, like this blanket, and being there with Allie would complete his truant happiness. When they were in Arlington, her status as his earliest romantic experience somehow encouraged him to think of *Deborah* as "the other woman" who had long ago displaced a legitimate predecessor. He was trying to regard his marriage as a sixteen-year detour.

"Okay," said Allie. "You want to take me along. But surely even the little NEAH has an Inspector General who'll look askance at your receipts?"

"No," said Ross. "I mean, we do, but you could pay for your plane ticket, and I'm entitled to my hotel room in any case. Two can sleep as cheap as one—at least for a couple of days. Come on," he whispered, "*carpe diem.*"

"You mean carpe your *per* diem."

Rather than press the point, he changed the subject. "So why are you going to the ranch?"

"I'm going to be the new middle-aged Monica Lewinsky."

"God, that's disgusting."

"Jesus, Weatherall, it's a *joke*. And it's not like he can *hear* us." She nodded toward the balcony and threw some sprigs of grass into Ross's face. "They're going to have a sort of internal summit meeting to rethink Iraq yet again. A few lower-downs like me will get mixed in with the higher-ups. All of whom will converge on Crawford, Texas. Needless to say, Rumsfeld thinks I'm perfect for this."

The other night, a few days after the Fort Bragg trip, Ross had learned of the defense secretary's odd plan for Allie. She'd imparted it in the most clandestine terms. *This is way above your pay grade and clearance level. I can have you water-boarded if you tell anyone.* The secret knowledge had left Ross feeling jealous of Rumsfeld, too; wishing he could manipulate Allie as successfully as the cabinet secretary did.

"So there you'll be, down in Texas," he now said. "The dissenting straw that stirs the drink."

"Or at least dilutes the Kool-Aid."

They were quiet for a moment, until Allie remarked: "You've never really told me if you're actually *for* this war. Or are just silently loyal."

"Me?" asked Ross. He decided to deflect this new conversational danger with self-mockery: "I'm just a true-believing rube. The Freedom Agenda is *my* agenda." He made a small salute in the direction of the balcony. In point of fact, though he'd given little sustained thought to its premise, he did believe in the war.

"Well," said Allie. "You're going to have a long wait until the democratic rapture arrives. Have you noticed how your precious W is now out campaigning for a reauthorization of the Patriot Act? As if it were the Social Security thing? He's going to need those powers more or less forever."

Almost enough darkness had gathered for the fireworks to begin. A bright spotlight, suddenly swinging across the grass, seemed to signal their start. But when the beam landed on the Truman Balcony, the d.j. called out: "Ladies and gentlemen, please join me in song as we wish a happy birthday to the president of the United States!"

The crowd rose to its feet and cheered, waving its flags and fans. George W. Bush, in short shirtsleeves, waved back. After a bit of reverb, a countrified "Happy Birthday to You" began to be heard.

"God," said Allie, brushing grass off her skirt as she stood up to face the balcony. "It's like North Korea."

"There's no ice cream in North Korea," said Ross. "*Sing.*"

"It's not even his birthday!" Nearly everyone on the Lawn knew that the president had come into the world on July 6th.

"Close enough for government work," said Ross. "*Sing.*"

"Happy *birth*-day, Mister *Pres*-ident," Allie sang in breathy imitation of Marilyn Monroe's long-ago salute to JFK. "Happy *birth*-day to *you.*" She had her arm around Ross's waist and was grinding her hip against his.

Bush waved again but dispensed with any remarks. Everyone sat back down to await the fireworks.

"Admit it," said Allie. "That made you hard."

"Being waved to by my leader? Or you doing Marilyn?"

"Both."

"I'm ignoring you," said Ross. He rolled over. But within thirty seconds he sat up to ask: "All right, what if I put my trip off for a bit and went down to New Orleans the week of the twenty-second instead? Could you fly down that Friday night?"

Allie checked her BlackBerry and said, "Okay. Friday, August twenty-sixth. I'm sure we'll have solved Iraq by then."

The Truman Balcony

"Karl, *you'd* like this." Barbara Bush sliced off a piece of sheet cake adorned with both Fourth-of-July and birthday lettering. "See?" she said, handing Rove a small plate. "It's *yellow* cake."

"Thank you, ma'am." Amidst general laughter on the balcony, Rove gave Mrs. Bush the same tight smile he so often had for thirty years. He wished the fireworks would start.

The president, in a festive mood since his holiday speech this morning in Morgantown, West Virginia, threw a cherry tomato at his chief policy advisor, hitting his chest dead center. "See, Rove? You *are* a target."

"Son," said George Herbert Walker Bush. "Cut it out."

As the White House itself did, at least in public, Rove insisted that he was *not* a target of the special prosecutor now investigating who had leaked, to the columnist Robert Novak, the fact that administration foe Joe Wilson's wife, Valerie Plame, was a CIA agent. It was Wilson who had very publicly disputed one of the White House's chief arguments for making war in Iraq: namely, that Saddam Hussein, in pursuit of a nuclear bomb, had been shopping for milled uranium— "yellowcake"—in the African country of Niger. If Wilson was correct and the shopping had never occurred, the deception was worse than the kind of intel manipulation attacked in the Brits' Downing Street memo; this was outright fabrication.

Laura Bush cut another slice of the cake. "Will somebody take this down to Harriet?" Only ten minutes ago, Jenna, one of her twins, breezing onto the balcony, had mentioned seeing lights on in the office of Harriet Miers, the White House counsel.

"She's working herself to death," the president said.

"So that you can have those dossiers on the plane tomorrow," replied his wife, who didn't see why the matter couldn't wait a few days, until they'd returned from Denmark and then Scotland, where the Blairs were set to host the G8.

The dossiers would contain profiles of possible Supreme Court nominees. On Friday Brett Kavanaugh, the staff secretary, had been hand-delivered an envelope from the Court. Instead of containing the news everyone had expected for six months—the resignation of Chief Justice Rehnquist—the enclosed letter informed the White House that it was Justice O'Connor who would be stepping down, on account of her husband's illness.

"I'll bring it down to her," said Neil Bush, taking the plate of cake from his sister-in-law. He was up here for the weekend without his new wife.

His mother, Barbara Bush, declared, "I'm sure that Harriet is working overtime because she wants to avoid a *mistake*."

She never missed a chance to harp on her husband's appointment of Souter and, like everyone else here, knew of her son's determination to pick a jurist conservative enough to provoke a confirmation fight from the Senate's Democratic minority.

"You know," said the president, "I just remembered that Dad also appointed Joe Wilson to be an ambassador someplace. Togo?"

"Think it was Gabon," said 41. "Never gave anybody any problems."

Now, thought Bar, would come an acceleration of the teasing she had started; she and her eldest son would both feel compelled to stir its rougher undercurrents. Once past Souter they would be making jokes about "read my lips" and George Sr.'s disastrous breaking of his no-new-taxes pledge. And maybe, with Neil still downstairs, there'd be a crack about his involvement in the long-ago savings-and-loan scandal: Hi-yo, Silverado!

Bar had been slow to accept how her husband's presidency had foundered while succeeding at something big, the Gulf War, and failing at almost everything small. And she was slowly coming to understand how it would be something like the opposite for George W. No child would be left behind, but thousands of their fathers would be left for dead in the desert.

No, she had never wanted any of this, good or bad, for this particular son.

"The Dems are going to filibuster every name in every one of those dossiers," said Rove, making the point as a compliment to Harriet, and asserting it with the "bring-it-on" confidence of two years ago.

"They're scared because we're gonna get *two*," said the president. "Once Rehnquist finally goes. Still," he added, "it'll take forever." Even Karen's confirmation remained stalled. She'd finally gotten her papers up to the Hill, but Biden had put a hold on the nomination attached to it—Dina Powell's—all because they weren't reappointing some big Biden contributor to whatever chickenshit board he served on. Bush sometimes wished that instead of having Dick for a vice president he had a Democrat in the job, the way he'd had crazy old Bullock as his lieutenant governor back in Austin. Bullock would have cut through these small annoyances for him; maybe even moved some of the bigger mountains too.

"Hey, Redhead!" exclaimed George H. W. Bush after flipping open his ringing cell phone. "Happy Fourth!"

"Reba McEntire," Barbara Bush explained to everyone. "I allow it." The former president and the country singer often exchanged jokes, she explained, "though usually it's by e-mail."

All now listened to 41's side of the conversation. "Nope, Red, I *don't* know what you get when you cross a gopher with an elephant."

The family waited. The former president then shook with laughter. "Okay, you get 'a lot of *really* big holes in your backyard'! I'll tell everyone here! Say hi to Narvel!"

"You know," said Bar, after he'd hung up, "I really don't know how you ever lost. Between that sort of thing, and those"—she pointed to the bowl of pork rinds by her husband—"it amazes me that *anything* Yale was still able to show through the cornball surface you acquired."

"Look who I brought with me," said Neil, returning to the big half-moon balcony with Harriet Miers in tow. The current president rose from his patio chair to give his counsel a peck on the cheek. "The hardest-working woman in show business," he declared to everyone. "Shouldn't it be Kavanaugh lugging those things up to me?" He took from her a heavy stack of file folders.

"Who's on top, Bushie?" asked the First Lady.

The president put on his glasses to look at the first label. "The CBS News guy?" he asked Harriet, sounding baffled.

"*Another* John Roberts," she explained. "You put him on the Court of Appeals?"

"That's right," said the president, so eager for a look at the stack of files that he carried them to a better-lit part of the balcony.

Hating to be in the spotlight, Harriet slipped back to her office as soon as the first barrage of fireworks went off.

———

**Hotel Washington, Fifteenth Street and
Pennsylvania Avenue**

The CNN producer nodded to Larry King, indicating that he and
Ann Richards—King's guest for a special live-from-Washington
Fourth of July broadcast—would be off-mic for the duration of the
pyrotechnics and patriotic music coming from the Mall.

Looking up from the Hotel Washington's rooftop terrace, King
said to the former governor, "You know, these fireworks look like big
splooges to me. I can't see the edges or the individual shoots." The
diverging red, white, and blue streams of a giant crossette, which had
just raced into the Washington sky and beautifully exploded, were
more or less lost on him.

"Honey," asked Richards, "have you had any cataracts done?"

"I know I've got *one*. But it's not ripe yet. Not ready for slicing."

"Larry, you're *over*-ripe. In more ways than one. Get the damned
thing taken care of."

King took a cup of coffee from a crew member and mused for a
moment, before brightening. "I could broadcast with the eye patch!
Do a show about the procedure—do people some good!" He sipped
the coffee and pointed across Fifteenth Street, toward the Truman
Balcony. "So, what do you think they're saying down there?"

"Some deep conversation about Schopenhauer?" suggested Richards. "Who else is down there besides Shrub? Not that you can see."

"One of the guys with the big lenses saw Rove and the elder Bushes.
You know," he almost shouted, another show idea occurring to him,
"I'd love to have you and Barbara on together! Team you up for lit-
eracy or animal rescue or something else. Would you do it? The numbers would be great."

Richards rolled her eyes. "I think that's a little too much white hair
and poison for one TV screen."

"Think about it!"

The show in the sky soon moved through a deafening crescendo.
"Oh, good," said Richards, pointing to the balcony. "The smoke is
obscuring them all from view."

King nodded to the director, who'd just told him they'd be back in three. The host explained the rest of tonight's drill to Richards: "We'll do two more blocks, six minutes apiece. And we'll mix in clips of what some prominent people around the country were doing to celebrate today."

"Prominent like who all?" she asked.

"The *American Idol* girl—am I right?" he yelled to the producer. "And we've got John Edwards visiting a homeless shelter."

"Really," said Richards. "Is this shelter in New Hampshire or Iowa?"

"Fast thinking, Ann! They do say poverty's going to be his signature issue."

"I met him at a party down here a couple of months ago—needless to say, they didn't bother campaigning in Texas last fall—and he gave me the creeps. I think he's his wife's Manchurian candidate."

"Great film," said King. "Sinatra shouldn't have kept it out of circulation for so long. But I guess he had his reasons, after Oswald and everything."

"All this reminds me of something. Have you got a matchbook?" A crew member looked at her with a bit of alarm, as if she might be getting ready to smoke on the air. "Oh, don't be so damned horrified," she responded. "That's just the antediluvian way we had of trying to find something to *write* on in a bar. I'd settle for a piece of *paper?*" She raised her voice in the direction of four young techies looking at consoles and laptops. A waiter brought her the hotel concierge's business card.

"I'm remembering this young man," she explained to King, "who e-mailed me and whom I never got back to. I met him at that same party with Edwards."

LUBBOCK GUY, she wrote on the concierge's card.

"You don't still have his e-mail on your computer?" asked King.

"Sure I do, Larry, along with two or three hundred other ones that I've neglected because I'm doing things like talking to you. But my girl in New York will find it." She added the words BUSH BASH to the little card.

14

AUGUST 11, 2005

Prairie Chapel Ranch; outside Crawford, Texas

Condi looked out the window of the guesthouse into the still-early light, contemplating a small row of oak trees. Today would be hot and clear. She'd arrived late last night, having slept through most of the flight from Andrews; she'd found Laura still up reading, but the president had already gone to bed.

She hoped that once today's war council concluded, her boss would invite her to bike one of the trails he'd laid out at his ranch. She liked it here and got to come often, as recently as a week ago for the Colombian president's visit. But her favorite memory of the place would always remain the night before Thanksgiving, nearly two years ago, when she and the president slipped away, baseball caps pulled down low, to begin their surprise trip to Baghdad from the airport in Waco. *We looked like a normal couple*, he'd later told the press, a statement she cherished in a number of ways.

Karen Hughes, who two weeks ago had finally gotten through the Senate, was in the adjoining room. The president wanted to talk to them both about public diplomacy before Dick and Don and everyone else got here after breakfast.

And there he was! Combing her hair and adjusting her pink blazer, Condi could see him crossing over from the main house.

"Welcome to Prohibited Area 49, ladies!" Bush cried toward their screened windows, referencing the restricted airspace over the ranch and making it sound a little like Roswell. "May I come in?"

"Yes, sir!" boomed Karen.

"Condi, you up?" called the president.

He kissed both of them once they'd gathered in the living room. "Nice to have my judgment *confirmed*," he said, hugging Karen, whom he hadn't seen since the Senate vote. "Bolton must be furious. I didn't have to ram *you* through." The new UN ambassador's troubles with the Foreign Relations Committee had exceeded Karen's, and a "recess appointment," with predictable howls from the bypassed Senate, had proved the only way to get him up to Turtle Bay. "At least Dick's happy with that," the president added. "And there isn't much that makes him happy these days."

Condi could see that Bush, who would have just had his "blue sheet" intel briefing, was genially caffeinated. But he was so invested in today's meeting, so determined that it lead to progress and clarity, that she feared he'd turn testy and bite some heads off before they were through.

"Was up in Illinois yesterday," he told her and Karen. "Signing the transportation bill at a Caterpillar plant." He laughed. "Half of the pork in it is aimed at Hastert's district."

"You'll never guess what I discovered at the Greenbrier last week," said Condi, herself too keyed up about the day ahead to realize she was changing the subject.

"You've been to the Greenbrier since you were here for Uribe's visit?" asked Bush.

Condi smiled. She prided herself on the shortness of her vacations and hoped that Karen would follow her example.

"Okay," said the president. "I'm guessing you discovered the bunker." He referred to the once-secret Cold War facility beneath the West Virginia resort; it had been designed to house the top figures of the government, including the whole Congress, in the event of nuclear war. "Dad only told me all the details when my security clearance finally matched his," Bush joked.

"Nope," said Condi, who knew all about the bunker. "I discovered *golf*."

The president winced a bit, and Karen looked at Condi as if to say: You just made a mistake. The boss's reason for having given up golf in '03—not wanting to look like a callous man of leisure in the middle of a war—was well known, and Condi could now feel herself backpedaling. "Oh, there were no cameras around! And I kept up with all the preparations for the withdrawal from Gaza. I was on the phone with the Israelis half the time I was there."

"How'd you do?" the president asked. "On the course."

"I took three lessons from the pro. I think I could get serious about it."

"Oh, Condi," said Karen. "You always have to get the merit badge in everything!"

"Let's sit down," said Bush.

Condi imagined that he wanted to talk about Karen's maiden diplomatic voyage, a speechmaking trip to Egypt, Saudi Arabia, and Turkey that was planned for next month; a bit early, thought the secretary of state, who hoped the new appointee was by now better informed than she'd seemed at the announcement of her nomination back in March. Condi had the awful feeling she hadn't cracked that little souvenir atlas.

"What can your two top diplomats help you with, sir?" asked Karen, buoyant and self-amused. Condi thought: *Bob Zoellick would be surprised to hear that.*

"It's diplomacy," said Bush. "But the domestic variety. The Sheehan woman."

"Oh, God!" said Karen. "I passed her little squatter's spot coming in last night. She's all over cable news—she's just *made* for MSNBC." Cindy Sheehan, whose son had been killed in Iraq last year, was demanding a meeting with the president.

"This isn't going away," said Bush. "A bunch of other women are now out there with her. They're calling it 'Camp Casey.'"

"For General Casey?" asked Karen, taking the name to refer to the current commander of U.S. forces in Iraq.

"Her son was named Casey," explained Condi.

"And they've got a hell of a lot of press with them," the president continued. "I sent Hadley out there one afternoon when most of the reporters were gone. He talked to her for half an hour. Not good enough."

"Do you want me to strategize this?" asked Karen.

"Well—" said the president.

"I'm not sure sending the national security advisor was the best approach," said his former communications director. "Maybe *I* should go out there with the cameras *on*, and talk to her mom-to-mom."

Condi frowned.

"The thing is," Bush explained, "I *did* meet with her, last year, alongside a bunch of other families. I apparently put my arm around her and *called* her 'mom'—I always do that; nobody ever takes offense, and neither did she. *Now* she says it was conde-. . . condo-. . .'" His tongue twisted over the last few syllables.

"Condescending," said the secretary of state, who felt for him. The president had already met with over *nine hundred* families of the killed and wounded, almost always without any reporters tagging along.

"But as a mom *myself*—" Karen offered.

God, thought Condi, this was as bad as Barbara Boxer, even if it was coming from their own side of the war debate. *Only* a mother, not a childless woman like herself, could *possibly* understand the carnage.

"In May, over in Iraq," said Condi, "I met with wounded Iraqi soldiers and wounded Iraqi *women*, civilians, and they definitely didn't want cameras on themselves."

"We could bring her in here," Karen suggested. "Just do a still photo."

"Write me a memo with some options," the president told Karen. "Okay for me to borrow her for this?" he asked Condi.

"Of course." The hesitation in her voice came not because Karen was so busy, but from the certainty that doing anything further with this situation would only make it worse.

"We can move those numbers," Karen declared.

"Which numbers exactly?" Bush responded.

Condi thought he should have nothing but troop levels on his mind today.

"More than fifty percent of the American public think the war was a mistake," said Karen, whose expression seemed to indicate that people just hadn't had the right messaging, and that with it their conversion could be instant.

Condi would die if her new undersecretary wormed her way into this morning's war council by wearing her old communications hat and arguing that she needed to advise the president on how to handle the lunchtime press conference. Walking over to a bureau to get her folders, the secretary of state tried to remind herself that it was Don she really had to worry about.

"This Sheehan person is *not* Terri Schiavo," said Karen.

"How so?" asked the president.

"There are things we can do with the optics of this one."

An hour later, in the living room of the main house, Rumsfeld found himself being handed a Xerox of the snowflake he himself had written two days before to his chief factotum, Steve Cambone: *What do you think about initiating a program of finding ways to reduce the number of things that are classified, and to speed up the process of declassification?*

Dick Cheney, who didn't say how he'd gotten hold of the memo, asked his old boss: "Somebody getting ready to write his memoirs?"

Rumsfeld, with the twinkle that narrowed his eyes to tiny slits, replied: "Just shaking things up a little—though long ago the Old Man did tell me what a crimp classification puts into the memoir-writing process." Cheney didn't need to be told that the Old Man was Nixon. "Out there in San Clemente," Rumsfeld continued, "the poor s.o.b. had trouble getting hold of even his *unclassified* papers. Particular circumstances, of course." He twinkled again while recalling the web of legislative and judicial constraints in which Nixon had to operate after his resignation.

Throughout this exchange, the downward line of Cheney's mouth didn't move. In fact, it never shifted during hilarity, rage, perplexity, or serenity. Even so, since the reelection Rumsfeld had noticed the vice president's overall demeanor betraying impatience and loss of influence, things he himself was feeling to a lesser degree. At least none of *his* aides had yet been caught up in this Valerie Plame fiasco.

Both men bristled when Condi Rice entered the room in her pink-and-white parfait of an outfit. Before sitting down she smiled and waved to everyone as if she'd arrived to entertain them at the piano.

"Okay," said the president. "We're going to start with Zal"—the still-new ambassador in Baghdad, Zalmay Khalilzad, who gave the room a quick briefing about the slow progress of the Iraqi constitution. Its drafting was unlikely to be complete by the August 15th deadline. Steve Hadley backed up the ambassador's recommendation of support for a two-week extension.

"I don't like it," said Bush, with a sigh. "But does anybody object?" No one did.

Rumsfeld, looking toward the flat-screen TV that could support videoconferencing, wondered whether Khalilzad's three-minute presentation had been worth the long flight from Baghdad, that twenty-three-hour round-trip he himself had gotten used to making for every nine hours he spent on the ground over there. He'd done it about ten times now, his last visit only two weeks ago, and that gave him an advantage over Condi, whose latest in-and-out had occurred in June. Recency always counted: whoever'd been there last seemed to know the most, since nobody really knew anything for sure.

The defense secretary nodded to Allison O'Connor, who sat with three other NSC staffers in chairs placed some distance from the main participants. Rumsfeld wondered if she'd been around long enough to know that when the Council met in Washington this was known as the fart-catchers' row. His own feet were planted on a carpet Laura Bush had brought home from Afghanistan; he fiddled with a piece of the jigsaw puzzle that lay on a coffee table and never seemed to show, from one visit to the next, any movement toward completion.

Talk in the room had already drifted to Iran. Hadley informed them that the ayatollahs were suddenly reopening a nuclear plant, and Rice presented an update on the decision being made to grant or deny a visa to Ahmadinejad, the civilian Iranian president who wanted to make some appearances in New York, beyond the gates of the UN, next month. The sticking point was his close resemblance to somebody involved in storming the American embassy and seizing the hostages back in '79. "People at State have studied the video frame by frame, as if it were the Zapruder film," Rice explained. "There's still no consensus."

"Better safe than sorry," said Cheney.

Rumsfeld felt glad that Andy Card, away on vacation, wasn't here to mediate and soothe. Both he and Dick were eager to have a go at Condi this morning.

"Let's get to the main event," said Bush. "Five months have passed since General Casey said he thought we might begin to draw down by about thirty thousand troops. And that was *before* the insurgency went into its 'last throes.'"

Most people smiled at the crack, knowing that their own turn to be frat-paddled would probably arrive. The line of Cheney's mouth didn't move.

"Mr. President," said Condi, "because of the insurgency we are now in charge of *fifteen thousand* Iraqi and foreign fighters who've been jailed. We're having to build a fourth prison up in the north. I wish it were otherwise, but we need to maintain a full complement of troops just in order to keep doing *that*."

"Actually," Rumsfeld replied, "aside from speeding up the Iraqis' ability to do that for themselves, what we need is a full complement of American *civilians* on the ground. If the Department of State insists on running virtually every aspect of the Occupation, then it ought to *run* it, and get more people over there to do what needs to be done."

"Well," responded Condi, "last month, along with the sixty, ninety-eight, and then thirty-nine people killed in three separate car bombings, the Egyptian ambassador and two Algerian diplomats were murdered. We'll get in as many civilians as it's safe to."

"If you wait for that, it'll never be safe," Rumsfeld retorted.

Cheney weighed in with an observation from a well-regarded NSC staffer back in Washington: "Feaver says the fundamental problem is that the public—the American public—doesn't understand the strategy."

Rumsfeld felt he ought to support Dick on this, but since he didn't understand the strategy himself, he didn't want to exhibit any enthusiasm for it. For one thing, he knew the public would soon be feeling even worse, when the total of U.S. soldiers killed went above two thousand.

"We control forty percent of the Triangle of Death," said Cheney, referring to the bloody area south of Baghdad. His tone gave no clue as to whether he found this distressing or hopeful.

"Didn't we control ninety percent of it two years ago?" asked the president. "Hadley, pass around that handout."

The sheet of paper was an op-ed by Henry Kissinger that would appear in tomorrow's *Washington Post;* it had been sent to NSC principals a day ahead with an octogenarian's courtesy and desire to stay in the game. Rumsfeld thought he saw Cheney brighten as Hadley handed him a copy: the vice president still saw Kissinger all the time. As for himself, he'd had a more than sufficient dosage of Henry under Nixon and Ford.

Hadley had taken the liberty of underlining Kissinger's key points, or what everyone now called "takeaways." Among them, after a long comparison-and-contrast of Vietnam and Iraq, was the former secretary of state's declaration that "Victory over the insurgency is the only meaningful exit strategy."

"He seems *not* to support Casey on a troop reduction," said Condi.

The president, his head bobbing forward with each couple of words, quoted with contempt—and in a German accent—something near the end, about how any *withdrawal schedule should be accompanied by some political initiative inviting an international framework for Iraq's future.* "Oh, swell," Bush commented, "let's turn it over to the UN, 'cause they did such a great job in the run-up to the invasion. Maybe appoint Jacques and Gerhard joint viceroys."

The president didn't see Kissinger as often as Cheney did, but he saw him often enough, and he respected him, even if the former secretary's grave doubts about the Freedom Agenda were well known. But his own frustration over this meandering discussion had started to boil over. He directed everybody's attention to something early in Kissinger's piece, a sentence that he himself, not Hadley, had just underlined: *Every soldier withdrawn represents a larger percentage of the remaining total.* "Anybody care to explain what that means, besides not a damned thing? It sounds like something out of one of Rumsfeld's snowflakes."

All eyes upon him, Rumsfeld twinkled. Dick had gotten his; now he had, too. "What troop level *do* we need, Don?" Rice asked. Ultimately, the chain of command for that decision would be Casey to Rumsfeld to Bush. "The Joint Chiefs might be able to weigh in with a recommendation," Condi continued, "but I hear that even they can't get information out of you." She said it with a smile, pretending the defense secretary's withholding nature was just an endearing quirk.

"You seem to do pretty well getting information from your own sources," Rumsfeld replied. Most people in the room knew he meant Phil Zelikow, who'd become one of Rice's top aides after running the 9/11 Commission. She'd already sent him twice to Iraq and was preparing him for a third visit next month. "I believe your most important set of eyes and ears," Rumsfeld continued, "has said Iraq is a 'failed state.'"

Rice appeared shocked that Phil's eyes-only assessment had found its way to him.

"That 'failed state' business is crap," said Cheney.

Hadley tried to move things in a more pacific direction. "We have to start better protecting people over there, ordinary Iraqis, if we're going to maintain their confidence."

"We have to get them *under* our protection first," said Bush.

"But of course 'stuff happens,'" said Rice, quoting one of Rumsfeld's more notorious remarks, about the looting that had followed the rout of Saddam's Baathists.

The president threw his pencil onto a hassock. "You know, there used to be hog barns where we're sitting. We knocked them down to build the house. I suspect the animals inside 'em had more productive conversations. And were better behaved."

Condi cast a pleading look in Bush's direction, as if to convince him she'd only been defending him and the whole mission, while Rumsfeld wondered: What was the mission *now*? Did Bush *have* a position on troop strength? Even an inclination toward one? Maybe to go with Casey's recommendation? Stay the course? Double down?

As the conversation went on, none of the fundamentals became any clearer. Iraq remained the biggest known unknown of all, with only twenty minutes to go until the outdoor press conference at which Rumsfeld and Dick and Rice would stand behind the president, a new row of fart catchers, squinting into the sun.

"I've got seven interagency groups working Iraq policy," said Bush, "and I can't even get a goddamned big-picture plan from a handful of my top people. I think it's time for our break." He nodded at the principals. "Gentlemen, ladies." Rumsfeld noticed the use of the plural; the president knew that Allison O'Connor was in the room.

———

"What's the T-shirt mean?" asked Allie. Rob, a guy from the motor pool charged with giving her a tour of the ranch, wore one that said: THE PRESIDENT'S 100-DEGREE CLUB.

"You've got to bike ten miles or run three once the temperature gets there."

"Does the president do it with you?"

"Sometimes," said Rob. "Sometimes he just watches."

They were riding in an old-fashioned, open-air jeep, but the way Rob turned to her and laughed reminded Allie of her heavily armored Baghdad drives with Fadhil, once he'd finally gotten over his reluctance even to have a woman next to him in the passenger seat.

Some tall grass peacefully brushed Rob's side of the vehicle. Allie imagined there must be barbed wire around the whole ranch, but she couldn't see any. The Brazos River lay in the distance, and some cedar elms could be spotted far in front of them. "God, those are beautiful," said Allie, pointing to a clutch of wildflowers that looked like giant daisies with red sunbursts painted over all but the tips of their petals.

"Firewheels," said Rob.

The name came back to her from the long-ago year in Texas.

The president would by now be giving the press his no-change-in-troop-levels message, from a lectern set up near the house. Allie knew it would sound more like a default than a decision. Rumsfeld hadn't been willing to be the only man in the room who'd speak in favor of outright reduction; so he'd continue to proceed like the insurgency itself, by sniping and indirection.

All at once Allie saw a gaggle of sound trucks and satellite dishes. Her sense of direction had never been strong; she assumed that Rob had circled back and run into the press conference. But as they got closer to all the media machinery, she realized that they'd come upon the Sheehan encampment at the ranch's main gate. BUSH LIED THEY DIED read one sign above a cluster of small wooden crosses someone had managed to plant in the bone-dry ground. She recognized Cindy Sheehan, who wore a white T-shirt with a giant question mark slashing through a giant "W." Other women surrounded her like an object of devotion; further away a couple of dozen supporters sat in lawn chairs lined up beside a long banner: SUPPORT OUR TROOPS—BRING THEM HOME.

"Can I get out for a bit?" Allie asked Rob.

Finding the spectacle ridiculous, he said, "Suit yourself." He parked twenty feet past the gate. Once out of the jeep, Allie got close enough to Mrs. Sheehan to hear the woman defending herself, in a girlish voice, to a radio reporter. Yes, some of her in-laws had made statements against her, but she wasn't dissuaded; the whole vigil here would be moving to Washington after Labor Day. "We're bearing witness to my son's premeditated murder."

The phrasing was absurd, but as Allie looked at the fervent, tearful faces, she wondered if their collective exaltation was any more detached from reality than the factionalized derangement she'd participated in this morning.

She walked around for a bit and found herself behind a very tall woman on the edge of a group wearing CODEPINK shirts. It took her a moment to realize who this woman was, and the recognition was not mutual. Turning around, Karen Hughes asked her, almost accusingly, "Are you *old* enough to have a child in the military?"

The more pressing question: Was she still young enough to have a child at all? This morning the numbers going through her head had actually been very different from ones involving troop levels: eighty (days since things had started with Ross) and seventy-one (days since her cycle had started to seem off). She'd refrained from doing a test, for fear that the result would be negative.

Realizing her thoughts had drifted, she at last extended her hand to Hughes. "We've met. Back in March. I'm on the NSC staff. Allison O'Connor."

"Oh, one of us!" Karen said, with theatrical relief.

Under the baking sun, Allie could feel the frozen condition of her own smile. What could she say? *No, not exactly?*

"I've decided to wade into this," Karen informed her, nodding toward the scrum of microphones and cameras around Mrs. Sheehan.

"How?"

"I'm going to speak to her as a mother."

"But your own son isn't old enough for the military, is he?"

"Oh, yes he is!" said Karen, brightly. "He's on his way to Stanford!"

"But not to Iraq," Allie said, as politely, and logically, as she could manage.

Karen, who didn't acknowledge the point being made, plunged a hand into her canvas bag to answer her buzzing cell phone. "I remember when there was no service this far from the house. I suppose we can thank her for *that* at least." She nodded toward Cindy Sheehan as she flipped open the phone and said, "Oh, hi, Laura!"

A breeze brought five words, twangy but insistent, to Allie's ears: *Karen, do not go there.*

———

Bush milled around the living room with his plate of Mexican food. Even so, he was not in a social mood; nor was he eager to get to the business of the afternoon session, which promised only more of the same.

Rumsfeld approached. "Mr. President, this is Allison O'Connor. You met on *Air Force One* coming home from Fort Bragg."

Bush managed a smile. "Oh, yeah. 'Embrace the suck.' A little too much suck *here* to embrace, don't you think? What brings you down?"

Rumsfeld answered for her. "Ms. O'Connor is doing some work on the legal ins and outs of stop-loss deployments. I'm sorry we didn't get up to that this morning."

Bush cut him off by shifting his glance. He wasn't about to hear his defense secretary tell him that having to extend tours of duty, however unfortunate that might be, was another argument for a drawdown. "Did you get a look at the ranch?" the president asked Allie.

"I liked it," she replied. "Especially the firewheels."

"Laura calls 'em Indian blankets. Hey, how does somebody with no Texas accent even know 'firewheels'?"

"I needed a little reminding of it out there, but I lived for a year in Lubbock, a very long time ago. You and I actually met *before Air Force One*."

"You're kidding."

"In the mayor's backyard. At the Bush Bash. Nineteen seventy-eight."

He laughed—"An early display of my political genius"—but Ms. O'Connor's reciprocal chuckle got lost in a burst of applause that suddenly filled the room. The elder Bushes, joining everyone for lunch, had come through some sliding glass doors. They would be staying for the weekend, after everyone cleared out tonight.

"Dad! Lubbock girl here!"

The forty-first president waved, and smiled with his charmingly small teeth.

"Mother! This here is Allison O'Connor. She was at the Bush Bash in '78."

Barbara Bush gave her son a scolding frown, as if to say: *Why would anyone want to be reminded of that?*

"I'm not sure why that always gets under her skin," he explained to Allie. "I guess she still thinks I threw away that election. Well, Allison, welcome to the ranch. I'm going to go get organized while my dad and Rumsfeld pretend they like each other." He winked, and hoped his anger wouldn't keep rising like a sneeze all afternoon. If things went on like they had earlier, he was going to end up acting like Carrie at the goddamned prom.

He turned back to Allison O'Connor, apologetically, and said, "I don't think we'll get into stop-loss today."

"That's all right, sir. I'm involved with a lot of other things, even a bit of the Iraqi constitution."

"What's your feeling about where we left things this morning? I know you wouldn't have an opinion on exact troop levels, but—"

"Oh, I have an opinion, sir."

"You do?"

"Zero."

He laughed, and then saw that she was serious.

"I guess I should be asking if there's a bus station in Crawford," she added. "I suddenly have a feeling that's how I'll be getting home."

"Rumsfeld!" Bush called out. The defense secretary came over, looking relieved to get away from 41.

"Ms. O'Connor says zero is the right troop level. That your opinion too?"

"Our consensus this morning was to stay steady for the moment," answered the defense secretary.

"Yeah, some consensus," Bush replied, turning back to Allie and giving his cabinet officer the brush. He was enjoying the chance to be aggressive, to feel stimulated as well as peeved. "Sure it wasn't Brent Scowcroft who put you with the NSC?" he asked her. The name of Dad's old national security advisor, against Iraq from the start, rarely got mentioned in the White House.

The woman held his gaze.

"You like the constitution they're writing?" the president asked.

"It's got many good elements."

"Well, do you think any of those will ever establish themselves with zero American troops?"

"No, sir," she replied. "That would be a miracle of nation-building."

He was surprised that she'd escalate things into sarcasm, taking his stance against all that nation-building stuff in 2000 and flinging it back at him, as if she were Maureen Dowd mixing it up with Dad. A part of him liked it, and another part was infuriated.

"How can you be doing stop-loss work if you think those forces shouldn't be there at all?"

"You've got to keep things legal as long as they *are* there."

He felt himself holding *her* gaze, as she continued: "After that you leave a war with the army you have."

Another play on one of Rummy's contemptuous throwaways. *You go to war with the army you have.*

He turned to the rest of those in the room and announced, loudly, that it was time to sit down and get started. And then he turned back to Allison O'Connor. "When this breaks up, I want you to come up to me and give the case for getting out now. And I want you to give it to me in twenty-five words or less."

15

AUGUST 26–27, 2005

624 Pirates Alley, New Orleans

A few minutes after ten p.m., the sky contained only two or three cirrus clouds, lines of frosting squeezed from a pastry gun. And yet all talk in the city was of a coming storm, a hurricane getting stronger as it moved westward over the Gulf. Two more days would pass before it got here, but even so, Allie had had to cancel her trip from Washington. The Louis Armstrong Airport was still open tonight, a Friday, but bound to shut soon. Once it did—she'd asked Ross in an e-mail this afternoon—how would she get *out* of New Orleans in time to make an early-Tuesday meeting set up by Rumsfeld?

With the arrival of this e-mail, Ross's spirits had dropped nearly as low as the barometer soon would. But he was determined to hoist them back up. An hour ago he'd come to the guidebook's tiny office in Pirates Alley, just beyond the cathedral, stopping to read a plaque that explained what his academic colleagues would call the church's previous "iterations": it had been flattened by a hurricane in 1723; another time laid waste by fire. But tonight everything round the cathedral seemed as serenely inert as Napoleon's death mask in the nearby Cabildo.

The guidebook project, approaching full swing, did most of its work out of Tulane. But Ross loved the hideaway office here, a poetic aerie inside a house where Faulkner once lived. It had been more or less donated, a well-below-market rental, by the excellent bookshop, three stories below, that now bore Faulkner's name. Ross's Washington assistant had this week dispatched to the address a few boxes containing WPA files from the original project.

Ross was continuing to develop an affection for his long-dead predecessor, Lyle Saxon, a lonesome, kindly writer who'd run the 1930s program out of the Canal Bank Building and must have spent half his time advancing money to the desperate writers in his temporary employ. The urgency of their dunning letters, which almost filled one of the file boxes, reminded Ross that the first guidebook had been a relief project, not the present feel-good show of national unity. His own patronage headaches from Mayor Nagin hardly counted by comparison, and this seemed all the more reason to do Lyle Saxon proud, to create something worthy to stand beside the 1938 volume in Lindy Boggs's house. Toward that end, Ross decided that he would tough out Allie's absence with a weekend of hard work.

At ten o'clock he went down to the Pirates Alley Café for a takeout sandwich and beer, and as the guy at the register packed the little sack and rang him up, the radio reported that Nagin might call for a wholesale evacuation of the city, albeit voluntary, tomorrow morning.

"*Pfff!*" the cashier scoffed. "Were you around for Ivan last year? Was supposed to be Armageddon. My boyfriend and I sat gridlocked, bumper to bumper, on I-10 for five hours, before everybody got told to turn around and go home. A lot of hysteria over nothing."

Ross could only imagine what Allie would be like for that long in an unmoving vehicle. "We should be okay here, no?" he asked. "The Quarter's a couple of feet higher than any other place in town."

The cashier nodded, with an additional prediction: "The guy who heads the Transit Authority will probably be making money off any buses they hire to haul people away."

"You've got that right!" Ross replied, disliking the merry, unearned knowingness he could hear in his voice, the same quality audible in his remark about the Quarter's position above sea level. Unlike Lyle Saxon's, his knowledge of the city was likely to remain spotty and shallow. If Allie had been able to get here, he'd have had a map in his hand the whole time he was showing her around. Even now, six months in, he had regular contact with only two or three people on the project, plus Emile Bourreau, the assistant concierge at the Monteleone, whom an hour ago he'd told he was heading down here to Pirates Alley.

Mrs. Caine, the preservationist realtor, had asked him to dinner on Saturday night, encouraging him to bring a friend, but she'd called back this morning to say she was clearing out for Baton Rouge, where she had a sister. She reminded him that he could call Father Montrose's parish number if the storm got really bad.

By the time Ross got back up to the office, Governor Kathleen Blanco had followed Nagin onto the radio, telling everyone "within the sound of my voice"—an old-time dramatic touch—how serious things were. Ross wasn't sure why he couldn't feel it. Maybe he was just unable to imagine wind and rain *together*. In Lubbock there had been plenty of the former but little of the latter, and almost never at the same time.

Listening to Blanco reminded him that he had now personally met two female governors. An e-mail from the other one had arrived two days ago, and he now reopened it with a click of his laptop:

Dear Mr. Weatherall:

I'm sorry as can be. Your e-mail kept falling to the bottom of my electronic pile.

That Bush Bash was a strange business. The fellow you ought to talk to is named Bill Bright—not that he's very—in Slaton. Some sort of builder, inherited a business from his father. Did one term, maybe two, in the leg. He introduced himself to me on a plane in the late eighties, I guess it was—my state Treasurer days. Started telling me the story of your Bash—very proud he'd set it up, but all the time displaying this sozzled Cheshire-cat look: "Of course I can't tell you everything"—wink, wink.

Now that another twenty years have gone by, maybe he'll tell YOU everything instead. That whole damned '78 race was through the looking glass. Hance himself is of course a Republican now—couldn't content himself with just remaining a Boll Weevil.

Anyway, keep sticking up for the arts among that crowd you're running with. And if you come upon our host Hitchens again, try talking some sense into him re Iraq.
  Sincerely,
  Ann Richards

Ross had planned on showing the e-mail to Allie over their first drink tonight—polishing their tiny pebble of ancient shared history into a bauble to be cherished, a token whose portent couldn't be ignored. Now, he supposed, he ought to just go ahead and forward her the e-mail.

For the next half hour he let himself be absorbed by the Saxon files. The warning voices on the radio made way for some Cajun rock-n-roll, which Ross kept low enough that a little after eleven o'clock he was able to hear, out in the street, a female voice, singing upwards, like a troubadour, toward his window.

Just you and I . . .

He raced to open the shutters and saw her, three stories below, her long reddish hair glinting in the outermost reach of a floodlight from the cathedral.

"Your man at the Monteleone told me you'd be here," she called up. "He says that you work too hard."

"You came!"

"Evidently. My big Tuesday meeting got pushed back to next Friday. I can't imagine the airport down here won't be back to normal before that."

Ross opened the window and threw her the building key, a gesture more romantic than necessary. He could have just buzzed her in.

She caught the key with one hand. Her other held a tiny fold-up umbrella, no bigger than a can of soda pop.

———

Prairie Chapel Ranch, outside Crawford, Texas; Saturday, August 27, 10:10 a.m.

Laura Bush stepped onto the limestone porch, where the president was listening to his own weekly radio address from an old leather-cased transistor at his feet. He had recorded the talk, now being broadcast from Waco, yesterday morning. The First Lady settled into a lawn chair beside her husband.

"So *you're* the person who listens to those," she said. Like State of the Union Skutniks, the Saturday-morning broadcast was a Reagan tradition that no subsequent president wanted to abandon, lest doing so make him ineligible for a piece of the Gipper's general good luck.

> *Like our own Nation's Founders over two centuries ago, the Iraqis are grappling with difficult issues, such as the role of the Federal Government. What is important is that they are now addressing these issues through debate and discussion, not at the barrel of a gun. The establishment of a democratic constitution in Iraq will be a landmark event in the history of the broader Middle East.*

"Why exactly *are* you listening, Bushie?"

"To see if what I recorded yesterday still holds a day later."

As the extended deadline for the draft constitution arrived, Khalilzad had reported that the Kurds and Shiites, who held most of the cards, were telling Saddam's once-mighty Sunnis: *Tough, no more delays. This is what the people will vote on in October.* A clash had taken place last night, when the negotiating parties more or less walked out on each other.

> *We saw unity earlier this month when followers of the terrorist Zarqawi tried to force Shiite Muslims to leave the Iraqi city of Ramadi. Sunni Muslims in that city came to the defense of their Shiite neighbors.*

The First Lady poured her husband a glass of ice water.

"Thanks, I guess I need it to wash down my wishful thinking," said

Bush. He didn't often allow himself such pessimism, even in front of his wife.

They were having a quiet weekend—the Sheehan show appeared to be running out of gas—but things here always remained busier than they'd been at Reagan's old Rancho del Cielo. (Had Dad had to go there during the whole eight years as VP? Maybe twice?) In the two weeks since the war council had taken place in Crawford, people continued to come and go, and so did he: lots of day trips promoting one thing or another. On Monday he'd be off to Arizona for some Medicare events. He was supposed to bring along a birthday cake for McCain; in return he'd get a lecture on torture. There'd also be, on Tuesday, some V-J Day commemoration out at the naval station in San Diego, which meant that more than three months had passed since V-E without any return signal from Vlad.

After hearing himself sign off on the radio, Bush put on his half-glasses and picked up some papers. Laura suggested he take them inside. In spite of all the canny tricks the house's architect had played against the sun it was already too hot out here on the porch. Back in the living room, she put on CNN at low volume. The administration's FEMA man, whose name Laura couldn't remember, was suggesting that everybody in southeastern Louisiana evacuate their homes. The storm could reach Category Five, a sort of meteorological DEFCON 1.

The president, though he might be known for mangling his own words, could nonetheless be irritated by others' linguistic imprecision. He remarked on how the terms "evacuation" and "watch"—the latter being the alertness level the National Hurricane Center had just recommended for New Orleans—seemed to fight each other: an immediate emergency versus a wait-and-see, like "red" versus "yellow" in that box of Crayola colors he wished Chertoff would finally ditch at Homeland Security.

"Your brother got lucky," said the First Lady.

The hurricane had poured a lot of rain on South Florida, but done little real damage before starting to grind its way west.

When Laura clicked off the TV, Bush picked up the latest draft of the Iraqi constitution. He gave his wife a second copy to look over.

We are the people of the land between two rivers, the homeland of the apostles and prophets, abode of the virtuous imams, pioneers of civilization, crafters of writing and cradle of numeration. Upon our land the first law made by man was passed. . . .

This preamble had a nice we-the-people touch, which some were sure to criticize as imperialistic influence. But he liked it. In fact, he should have quoted it in that radio speech. The rest of the translation, as the Articles got down into the weeds, lacked the silver tongue of a Gerson, but it would have to do, and enough Sunnis would have to get off their asses and vote for it on October 15.

Bush picked up the phone to call Joe Hagin, his deputy chief of staff, who would be in the air-conditioned double-wide parked by the ranch's main gate. "Hadley there with you?" he asked. During the August vacation, staff rotated through Crawford a couple of days at a time, and this morning Bush had gotten his intel briefing from the national security advisor himself. "Send him up to the house."

Steve Hadley's smooth and soothing face was the only one everybody in the West Wing felt pleased to see each morning. His presence here at the war council a couple of weeks ago had reminded Bush of how far removed Steve was from the hissing system of poisonous sprinklers they both worked amidst, those alternating spits of venom from Dick to Condi to Don.

The president handed Hadley the new constitution. "Where's the real sticking point? Show me."

"Article 7," explained the NSA. "It prohibits any publicizing of Saddam's Baath party, 'regardless of the name that it adopts.' The Sunni Baathists feel they won't even be allowed to make a sincere reinvention of themselves."

"So what are they going to do?" asked Bush.

"They'll try to get the constitution voted down by a two-thirds majority in three provinces. That would be enough to sink it."

"Can they manage that?" the president asked.

"Yes," Hadley replied.

Bush threw his glasses onto the sofa.

"But we can still pull it out," said Hadley. "The way we did in January. Excite people about the referendum. Get them to be in favor of starting over, of moving forward. That will overwhelm the sectarian difference."

"Think we'll get sixty votes on *Roberts?*" Bush asked, referencing his Supreme Court pick.

"Not my department, sir," said Hadley, with a laugh. "My expertise only *starts* at the water's edge."

The president, his glasses retrieved, resumed scanning the draft. He quoted from Article 2, sections A and B: *No law that contradicts the established provisions of Islam may be established. No law that contradicts the principles of democracy may be established.* "Good luck getting those two to dance."

Laura softly sang: "*Sharia, I've just met a law named Sharia . . .*"

Hadley made no comment.

"What's this phrase I keep seeing?" asked Bush. "*This will be organized by law.*"

Hadley explained it meant only that legislation would need to be passed in order to implement the constitution's broader directives— the same way, for example, that the American Founders' vision of a legislative branch had required a whole body of subsequently passed election law.

From her nearby chair, Laura read out Article 30: "*The State guarantees the social and health security of Iraqis.* They must be doing it with those private accounts of yours, Bushie. Good for you!"

Her husband cast her a genuinely wounded look.

"I'm sorry," said the First Lady. "Your mother's been gone two weeks but she's not out of my bloodstream yet."

The president asked Hadley to get his deputy back in Washington to request a clear plan from Khalilzad for getting this thing passed. Hadley immediately picked up the phone, and Bush could see him wince as soon as he got connected.

"What's the problem?"

"Hammering," said the national security advisor. "I'm going to switch to a cell phone. Less ambient noise."

"They're replacing the floor in the Oval Office," Laura reminded the two men. She and the president remained silent until Hadley was through with his call.

"I keep thinking about that redhead," Bush remarked.

"Reba McEntire?" asked Laura. "You're competing with Gampy?"

"No, the one on the NSC staff."

"Allison O'Connor," Hadley reminded him.

"Yeah," said Bush. "What do you think of her?"

"Very smart. An odd choice for NSC. But Don always has his reasons. And he always keeps a sharp eye on anyone whose salary he's paying." Ms. O'Connor has been detailed to the Council from the Department of the Army.

"I keep thinking about what she told me when we were alone."

"What's that, sir?"

" 'The longer we stay, the weaker we look. The weaker we look, the weaker we are.' "

Hadley cautiously assembled the elements of a response. But before he could volunteer one, Brett Kavanaugh, also on ranch duty this weekend, came in with paperwork for the president to sign: the declaration of Louisiana as a disaster area. Bush perused the document, which allowed federal officials to cooperate with local ones on whatever might be coming. "This will be organized by law," he muttered.

"Exactly," said Hadley.

"Sir," said a Secret Service man coming in from the porch, "the chainsaws and Mr. Hagin are ready."

The president and his deputy chief of staff were going to clear some dry-as-a-bone brush.

16

AUGUST 27–28, 2005

New Orleans

They'd finished touring the Gallier House in the Quarter and now sat in a dive bar on Decatur. At five o'clock this Saturday afternoon, skies were still no worse than cloudy, but Governor Blanco and Mayor Nagin and a state meteorologist continued to insist, from the bar's TV, on how bad things were likely to get.

"That guy," said Ross, directing Allie's attention to the mayor. "Did I tell you how he forced some distant relative onto the guidebook payroll?"

"No," she replied.

So he told her the story, and she suggested, "Maybe the woman's a plant, like me. She's going to dazzle you the way Rumsfeld wants me to dazzle Bush. Maybe you'll end up putting Mayor Ray on the guidebook's cover."

"Where do you and 'W' go from here?" asked Ross. "Seriously." It seemed somehow too grandiose, too ridiculous, to say "the president."

"Nowhere probably. Remember, I've so far gotten him to cock one eyebrow at something I've said. At this rate the boys will be home by 2505."

Nagin was now telling everyone to get out of town—even if the evacuation remained an urgent suggestion, something just short of mandatory. A pointless cheer went up from half the bar's patrons, mostly tourists without cars who were staying in hotels even bigger than the Monteleone. They wouldn't be going anywhere, voluntarily or otherwise. Two tables from Ross and Allie, a pair of white male locals, each wearing a wife-beater and sporting ZZ Top beards, laughed at the tourists and noticed Ross looking in their direction. "Hey, Gerald!" one of them yelled at the bartender; a piece of exhibitionism for Ross's benefit. "You staying open tomorrow?"

"Hell, no," Gerald replied. "I live out past the lake. They're going to have all the lanes running in the other direction. How could I get in here if I even wanted to?"

The other local offered a derisive memory of last year's false-alarm Ivan, and implored: "Shit, Gerald, where are we supposed to go?"

The bartender just laughed, knowing these guys would find someplace.

Governor Blanco backed up Nagin's call for a voluntary evacuation, but sounded hesitant about even that. Allie observed: "She's more concerned about pissing people off than making sure they're okay."

Gerald switched the TV to a preseason college football game.

Worried that the two locals would come over and get chummy, Ross took hold of Allie's hand on the tabletop, a privilege he didn't usually allow himself over supper at Whitlow's, back in Arlington. "Think we should talk to Emile—my guy at the hotel?" he asked. "See if we can keep the room and ride it out there for another couple of days?"

"I'd say it's high time," Allie answered, with no real alarm. She reached into her tote bag for a copy of today's *Times-Picayune*. "Did you see this?" Several pages in, after the storm news, an article discussed the FDA's just-reaffirmed disapproval of over-the-counter sales for the "morning after" birth-control pill. She put the paper in front of Ross. "In the name of *safety*," she said. "Actually, in the name of pleasing evangelical voters."

Ross sighed. This weekend, at least up until now, Allie hadn't been quite so relentless in her attacks on all things Bush, as if their first trip together were maybe not a honeymoon but at least a bit of a moratorium. This late in the afternoon Ross had let his guard down.

He read some details about how the pill worked, and asked, "This isn't something you've been taking, is it?"

Allie laughed. "Really? As a means of regular birth control it would be about on a par with the Occupation. A little more forethought might be preferable?"

"Well," said Ross, "you did tell me you had it covered." He didn't want to appear ungallant on the subject—making contraception "the woman's job"—but he now *was* looking for reassurance. Why had she brought this up? The last thing he needed . . .

"Yes, I did say I had the matter covered."

"As I'm sure you had it covered with Rolf." He couldn't resist hurting himself a little. Maybe poking at his own vulnerability would toughen him up.

"Right," Allie purred, making things worse. "Rolf, my *only beau.* Actually, you and I haven't been 'covering' the matter in the same way."

He didn't know where this was going. Had Rolf sheathed his playful, no-doubt-uncircumcised German manhood in condoms from the Green Zone's PX? Ross finally responded: "Do I have to ask what the difference has been?"

"You don't, but you can."

"Okay."

"With Rolf I took preventive measures; with you I haven't."

Starting backwards, he heard the scrape of his chair against the bar's wooden floor.

"But I haven't been—" he said.

"I didn't want you to."

"Well, we'd better start! *Why* didn't—"

It was her turn to take his hand, and with the one left free she reached back into the tote bag to extract what Ross immediately recognized as a sonogram picture. Shock competed with a nauseous sense of betrayal, his own, as he remembered twice living this moment with Deborah, once in the kitchen and once in the car.

Allie slid it in front of him. "Meet Holley. With an 'e.' My one tribute to the city of Lubbock, Texas." She caressed the black hairs on Ross's forearm. He didn't know if she was doing it from tenderness or to soothe the anger she must see rising in him. As he remained silent, she explained: "You can't see the sex in the picture—it's too soon— but I know it's a girl from the Down's test I had this week—"

"You *named* her?" he finally asked. "I mean, you didn't even think to *ask* me? Let alone ask me about—"

She put a finger across his lips. "Ross, she's *mine. I'm* keeping her."

The two locals watched them with increased attention.

Ross stared at her and felt himself coming out of a long, stupid sleep, as if Napoleon's death mask were dropping from his face. "Did you *plan* this? Is this what you wanted all along?"

She didn't speak, just maintained a look that seemed to say: *Now, now—you'll soon see this is no big terrible thing.*

But he persisted: "You decided it was *time* to do this? After a dozen years traipsing around the world? I seemed *suitable*?" He had a sudden, awful recollection of the couple of times she'd picked up framed pictures of his children in the Arlington apartment, and given them what now struck him as an *appraising* look.

She tightened her grip on his hand, but only slightly, as if what she'd done weren't odd, let alone monstrous. He was aware, in the midst of his revulsion, that he had left his own hand in place.

"Did you make a list of physical and mental attributes?" he asked, keeping his voice low enough not to intrigue the ZZ Top guys any further. "Did my blue eyes beat out whatever color Rolf's are? My nice symmetrical chest hair, just enough, not too much; did that tip things in my direction? The fact that I usually don't know how to get angry? What put me over the top?"

Allie took his hand to her lips and kissed it. The gesture broke something inside him, but he didn't know what.

"Where do I fit in from this point on? Will I be Holley's Uncle Ross? An uncle-with-benefits? Redeemable by Mommy whenever I come over after she's put 'her' daughter to bed?"

"I haven't figured things out that far."

"I'm sure you will."

She was the one to get up from the table, to tell him she was going back to the hotel. Anyone capable of this, Ross told himself, would also be capable of sharing the room, with equanimity, for however long it took the storm to come and go. He watched her head to the door, crossing the grubby barroom floor, and he realized that his youngest child was crossing it with her.

Back in Room 928 of the Monteleone, throwing her things into the rollaboard, she understood that she'd been mad to think it would all somehow go well. If something could be calculating and thoughtless all at once, this was it. *All* of it: she had never had a firm plan—only, after rediscovering Ross, a sudden last-chance feeling, panicky but also larkish. Her mother remembered him from Lubbock: *a lovely boy*, said the letter that arrived two weeks after the Karzai reception. She kept it near the old card: OMG!! I FORGOT TO HAVE CHILDREN.

He was still a lovely boy, though what business anyone had being boyish at forty-three in this barbarous world seemed open to question.

She would have the baby and figure it out later. She was, in this, as bad as Condi Rice and her Vulcans had been about Iraq. The arrogance of her to think that this disclosure was a sort of unilateral gesture requiring nothing much in the way of a response from him!— even though she had created the situation precisely because he was the kind of responsible man who made a good father. *Did you make a list of mental and physical attributes?* The best measure of his basic success with his children back in Texas, she had decided, were the agonies he seemed to suffer over his recent derelictions.

She zipped up the rollaboard and exited the room, not having heard, to both her relief and distress, any buzzing from the Black-Berry that would be in her jacket pocket. Down in the lobby she could sense a general nervousness. The hotel's storied rotating bar was loud enough, but the festiveness felt forced. The desk clerk seemed per-plexed when she told him she was checking out of 928; the room was in Ross's name, and she'd never really checked into it.

"I've been called back to Washington," she said, pointlessly invent-ing a story for herself as she handed over her plastic key.

"Ma'am, the airport is closed."

"I know," she said, unable to improvise another lie.

The clerk appeared relieved when he remembered something he could say: "Oh, I have a fax for you!"

She thanked him for the envelope and took it with her to a chair beside the lobby's grandfather clock. What she first saw confused her: the letterhead of the Titan Corporation of San Diego, California. But the text below it made things instantly, if blandly, clear:

> *The Titan Corporation, the largest contractor of translation services and personnel for the American effort in Iraq, regrets to inform those on this distribution roster of the death of Mr. Fadhil Hasani during the week of 15 August. Mr. Hasani was 32 years old and had provided the United States government outstanding service, through Titan, since May 2003. He leaves a wife and daughter.*

It's a person.

The distribution roster for this memo contained the names of several old Baghdad colleagues, plus a number of people who had arrived since Allie's January departure. The fax's cover sheet, mistakenly stapled beneath the letter, made clear how the news had found her here. Someone had faxed the original from the EOB, its first destination, to the in-case-of-emergency weekend address she'd left. The Baghdad origin of the electronic odyssey, as well as the non-anodyne version of the contents, could be found in Rolf's familiar handwriting on the cover sheet:

> *Fadhil and his wife kept living two or three miles outside the Green Zone, though most of the translators are now living within. Several notes got slipped under their door over the past couple of months. He was killed with three bullets to the head. Since he was a Kurd, no one seems to care much whether it was Sunni or Shiite militia who did it. So let's just apportion things the way our glorious new constitution might and decide that the Sunnis fired one and the Shiites fired two.*
>
> *I am heading home to Cologne, for good, tomorrow.*

She left the hotel not knowing where she was headed herself.

———

A day later, at eight p.m., Ross awoke to the sound of rain lashing Room 928's windows. He could see a strange color in the sky, not nightfall but some other, unfamiliar darkening. A curfew had taken effect at six o'clock, but people were still on the streets—no matter that Nagin had this morning made the evacuation mandatory: in fact nobody was supposed to be in the city even if they were *off* the streets. The news had been calmly delivered from room to room throughout the hotel, with the gentle knock that usually precedes an offer of turndown service. Until somebody made them, the carless guests were not about to share the Louisiana Superdome with the carless poor. And it seemed that there were no buses to take them away: all the ones available, Emile had told Ross early this morning, were already commandeered for relief work.

Ross threw on yesterday's Izod shirt and jeans. He'd shed them shortly after dawn, when he got back here from long hours in other Decatur Street bars, and then another couple on the couch in the guidebook office. Having found Allie packed and gone, he'd crawled into the hotel bed and been awakened by a series of vibrations: she had left behind her BlackBerry in the tangle of bedclothes. Would she be back for it? It buzzed all the time, but he never looked at the screen, not wanting to see who was calling her. All that counted was that she hadn't called him.

Now, at 8:10 p.m. on this Sunday night, he went down to the lobby and was surprised to see an elderly lady, carrying her parakeet inside a cage, checking *in*. Emile, finishing a double shift, told him there were at least a dozen locals who had newly registered, following an old custom of riding out storms in the hotel—keeping themselves watered at the bar and their cars dry in the Monteleone's parking lot.

Ross made his way to the hotel's front entrance.

"Sir," the flustered doorman told him, "the curfew . . . You're not supposed to—"

"I'll be back very soon, before it gets super-heavy."

He zigzagged from Royal to Bienville to Bourbon Street, without an umbrella, which the rising wind would only turn inside out. He did have a destination, albeit one with no easily explainable purpose. He was sure the house where he was heading would be sensibly deserted, but it might provide a spot on which he could stand, by himself, if only for a moment, without jumping out of his skin. *Just keep doing your work, and come see us again when you're further along with it.*

He passed two bars that were still open. One of the proprietors whispered, "Come on in," as if the curfew had turned it into a speakeasy. A few doors further down, he came to the sliver of an alley he was seeking. Near its end he reached a wrought-iron fence, easy enough to hop even when soaked to the skin. Once over it, he walked toward the swaying magnolia tree whose upper branches were already flailing in the wind.

And there it was, if only a silhouette under the blue-black sky: the statue of the angel that he'd seen from the hideaway on Mrs. Boggs's third floor. He dropped to his knees and put his arms around the stone creature, unsure whether he meant to be giving or taking shelter. As he shifted his legs, Allie's BlackBerry slid from his pocket. Lit up and buzzing, it slithered like a rodent across one of the garden's soaked flagstones. He wondered whether to abandon it here, in this watery world from which, unpaired, he now knew no ark would ever carry him away.

Part Two

SEPTEMBER 4, 2005– MARCH 21, 2006

17

SEPTEMBER 4, 2005

Above the Seventeenth Street Canal; New Orleans

Looking down on the houses, most of them still submerged but for their roofs, Rumsfeld remembered those candy dots on strips of paper that Joyce used to buy for the children. How—once the helicopter touched down, a few minutes from now—was he going to tout the waters' recession as a sign of the situation's improvement?

He did not want to be here, but everyone in the administration's topmost echelon had been instructed to show the flag, an exercise that, to Rumsfeld's mind, only implicated them in a supposedly general failure that was in fact quite specific: the fuckup of the past seven days belonged to the Department of Homeland Security, a vast modular monstrosity whose creation, he had warned Andy Card four years ago, would never succeed. Before half the people below this helicopter got a blanket or a can of Spam, FEMA—now trapped inside DHS—would be spending a month getting internal approvals to hire private contractors.

"We're passing over the levee," said Steve Cambone.

Waitin' for the Robert E. Lee, Rumsfeld thought, hoping the old song didn't turn into an earworm that would bedevil him for the next week. He could already see the titles of the first Katrina books that would start appearing a year from now: *Breach of Faith*? That would work.

Despite Cambone's pointing, he could barely make out Seventeenth Street, let alone the hole in the canal wall, but at least they were lower than 1,700 feet, the closest Bush's *Air Force One* flyover—Rove's genius idea—had gotten last Wednesday. The White House's excuse had been that the president's plane would "interfere with rescue and relief operations" on the ground. And what might *they* have been? From the look of it, nothing.

The chopper was now low enough that Rumsfeld could see some of the houses sporting spray-painted numbers—not the cheering Iraqi signifier that minesweepers had come through, but an indication of how many bodies had been found inside.

"How the hell did they not get word of these breaches up the chain of command until *Tuesday morning*?" he asked Cambone. His deputy of course had no answer, even after Rumsfeld added: "It's not a rhetorical question, Steve."

Late last week he had been forced to send in 4,500 troops from the Eighty-second Airborne. He hadn't wanted them here at all, but at least they wouldn't be policing, so you wouldn't have some kid trained to shoot anybody making a furtive move in Kandahar blowing off the head of some guy looting a sixpack from a 7-Eleven. The Louisiana National Guard, still more or less controlled by the state's incompetent governor, would remain responsible for restoring order. The guys from the Eighty-second would be doing "humanitarian work" instead, a term that always made its recipients somehow sound *less* than human, like statistical aggregates.

The helicopter flew over Jackson Barracks, here for 170 years, and now, after the breaks in the levee, more or less gone—drowned and splintered and deserted.

"Jesus," whispered Cambone. "Where did everybody from there go?"

"To the Superdome," Rumsfeld answered. "Once boats could get them to helicopters." The waters had risen twenty feet, a picture his mind could more easily host than the images of life inside that stadium-turned-shelter. But those pictures had gained mental admittance over the last several days: the gropings in the dark; the scrounging for water and bags of chips to stay alive on; the shit-smeared concrete floors. And why was it that most of these images derived from reporters inside the place instead of from DHS people, who kept claiming they couldn't get near?

"How the hell did *that* happen in the middle of everything else?" Rumsfeld asked, pointing below to a car that had been crushed by a train.

"The train was empty," said the helicopter pilot, who'd flown over this curiosity several times. "It wasn't moving until the wind pushed it."

Cambone handed the defense secretary the printout of a newspaper article about Condi Rice's rough week: she'd been seen shoe-shopping in New York, and gotten booed at *Spamalot* with Gene Washington, before she'd come to her senses and hightailed it back to Washington. Her defense? The State Department had been highly proactive *before* the hurricane—transferring the responsibilities of its New Orleans passport office to Miami.

"Really Janie-on-the-spot, isn't she?" said Cambone.

Rumsfeld couldn't manage a twinkle. Despite her stumbles, Condi had by the end of the week prevailed against him on the question of sending troops. People wouldn't like seeing them "in the streets," he'd argued; and she'd fought back, saying that they'd be "cheered." Even if she sounded like Dick talking Iraq in 2003—*They'll be greeted as liberators*—it was clear by Saturday that she'd been right. As for Dick, he knew enough to stay as far as he could from this new mess; Bush so far couldn't even get him to go down to the politically friendly Mississippi coast. Condi had just been dispatched to Mobile, in her native Alabama; and here *he* was in New Orleans, uselessly charged with pepping up the troops.

All of these trips had had to wait until Bush could make his own visit here on Friday, when he'd hosted a clusterfuck of a meeting inside AF1 on the airport tarmac. Nagin and Blanco spent most of it shouting at each other, and Senator Mary Landrieu, hapless at the best of times, kept blubbering like some hysterical Kewpie doll. "Brownie," the head of FEMA, was still off somewhere doing his "heckuva job," while Chertoff, his boss atop the jerry-built Homeland Security pyramid, waited for a decent interval to pass before firing him.

The helicopter made one last loop over the levee breaks, while

Cambone went through the rest of the news printouts. "Jesus," he told Rumsfeld after seeing one about other countries' offers of aid to New Orleans. "The government of Afghanistan wants to send a hundred thousand dollars." The secretary of defense, who usually delighted in ironies, shook his head. He looked down toward the Coast Guard station where they would land. "Let's get this thing on the ground," he said. "So we can have our fatuous press conference."

After touching down, while waiting for the blades of the propeller to slow, Rumsfeld asked Cambone, "Any word on Allison O'Connor?"

He'd called her six days ago, after finding out from another NSC staffer that she'd gone to New Orleans for the weekend. Her Black-Berry just rang. The hotel she was supposed to be at had no record of her.

"Nothing further," said Cambone.

"Tell Phil Lago I want to talk to him," said Rumsfeld, referring to the National Security Council's executive secretary. "And keep this quiet. I don't want 'NSC Staffer Missing in New Orleans' to become one more human-interest horror story."

A minute later, near the press ropeline beyond the helipad, he took the first shouted question from a reporter: "Mr. Secretary, how would you describe the current state of the relief effort?"

"Suboptimal," Rumsfeld answered.

———

Baton Rouge, Louisiana

"Thank you, Mrs. Caine," said Ross. "You've really been kind." The realtor had just brought him up a hurricane cocktail, complete with a little umbrella stuck in the orange slice.

"It'll put you in the mood for dinner. I still can't get over what you've been through. You remember Father Montrose? He'll be joining us tonight. He's been over in Thibodaux since Tuesday, doing what he can. He's eager to get back to New Orleans, but they're sayin' any returning is weeks away. He might even go to Houston in the meantime to help out the . . . displaced." Her delay in uttering the last word seemed to indicate a desire for something more genteel than "refugees."

Ross, still trying to find a flight to Washington, told her: "I think I can get home by Tuesday, if I fly from here to Nashville first."

"You're welcome to stay as long as it takes."

Mrs. Caine was more relaxed than she might have been, because she now had Ross's eyewitness testimony to add to news accounts of how well the Quarter had fared in the storm. And she enjoyed bossing around her timid sister, another widow, here in Baton Rouge.

"Sorry about this itty-bitty electric fan," she told Ross, retreating from the guest bedroom. "I know the air conditioning doesn't really get up to the third floor."

"I'm just fine," he replied. "I can't thank you enough."

Once she was gone, he positioned his chair in front of the weak electric breeze. He set the cocktail on the armrest and after two sips was near to dozing again. He hadn't realized how tired he was until he got here Friday night. Whenever he closed his eyes, the same sound came back into his ears: the scream of the wind early Monday morning, as he lay in his room in the Monteleone, still soaked from his foray into Mrs. Boggs's courtyard, while Katrina neared landfall. The sound wasn't the loud, flapping whooshes he remembered from Lubbock dust storms, but a keening, angry whistle that insulted everything in its path with a *get-the-fuck-out-of-my-way* madness. Within hours the noise had receded, but it still wasn't out of his head.

When he looked out the window on Monday afternoon, he'd seen a few loose bricks and fallen signs on Royal Street and concluded that things would soon be all right. And then came the news of the levees: half the city had drowned. The elevated Vieux Carré may have survived, like a louche version of Reagan's shining city on a hill, but soon enough, except for buildings like the Monteleone that had their own backup generators, all the Quarter's lights were out too.

The hotel began to empty on Tuesday morning; its guests were asked to buddy up in any available cars. Emile told him there would be no problem with his staying, and Ross gratefully pitched in however he could. Food was plentiful: the freezers held provisions for the twelve hundred or so people the Monteleone was used to having inside. But the elevators were out and the generators had only enough juice to keep the hall lights on at night. Ross carried up meals to the frailer guests, along with buckets of water for flushing the toilets. Once some looting began outside, Emile and other edgy staff patrolled the hotel's perimeter and parking lot. On Wednesday afternoon Ross saw a man on Royal Street break an antiques-shop window with one of the fallen signs.

The troops started arriving as fuel for the hotel's generator ran out. An extra shipment that the management had ordered before the storm got commandeered for the Convention Center and Superdome. Hellish stories had been drifting back from both of them all week. With the Monteleone's lights about to go out for good, Ross helped Emile and the others to lock up, after knocking on the door of every room to make sure no one was left behind.

Emile had relatives in Baton Rouge, so he took Ross with him in the last available hotel car, depositing him like a foundling on the front porch of Mrs. Caine's sister, whose name Ross remembered from the message canceling the dinner party a week before. Settled in the house, he charged his phone and called Deborah to tell her he was okay. Her relief upset him; he didn't feel worthy of it. And when she put the children on the line he experienced an absurd desire to tell them they would soon have a new baby sister.

He also called the Chairman, who urged him to get back to Washington as soon as he could: "There are lots of relief efforts to plan, and you're the only one that knows New Orleans." *No, I don't*, Ross had thought, before pledging a fast return.

Only now, two days later, did he feel ready to power up Allie's BlackBerry, however pointlessly: he'd still found no message from her on *his* recharged phone. Over the past week he'd gone out of the hotel only once, to look for her at the nearby Marriott Courtyard, which had been turned into a shelter. Even so, he felt certain she would have departed the city before the storm. Her refusal to contact him seemed not ominous but cruel.

Now, as soon as the progress bar indicated a strong enough charge on her phone, he was appalled by what he found: forty-two messages, most of them increasingly frantic repeats from Allie's mother and office, some of them left as late as Friday. There was even one, in the middle of the rest, from Rumsfeld.

Ross felt his thoughts tumbling like clothes in a dryer. To try and stop them he put Allie's phone underneath a pillow and turned on the television. He'd been looking at it for most of the two days he'd been here, continually disoriented by its filmed record of so many calamities he'd been nearby but unaware of. He was still realizing how much worse it had been than anything he imagined from inside the Monteleone. When he spoke to Mrs. Caine and her sister, and even to Deborah, he realized how they all knew more than he did.

The greatest surprise was that the natural catastrophe of the hurricane had been followed by what everyone now perceived as a colossal human fiasco, a debacle already starting to dwarf Iraq in the public mind. Right now he was seeing footage of George and Laura Bush at Red Cross headquarters in Washington. They were followed onscreen by John Edwards: "If this is 'a heckuva job,' I'd hate to see a bad one." The ex-senator was squeezing shut his eyelids, in an effort to hold back tears—or maybe to produce them.

Ross turned off the TV and dialed Allie's landline in Arlington.

Her phone rang and rang, summoning only, yet again, the sound of the keening wind.

———

2001 N. Clarendon Boulevard, Arlington, Virginia

Allie heard the phone and finger-stopped her ears against its ringing. With her hands so close to her face, she swore she still smelled filth and homelessness on them, no matter that she'd stood under the shower in Houston for half an hour on Friday, and then under her own, here last night, for at least that long.

Eight days ago, once she'd exited the Monteleone and gathered her wits, she'd found a room in a little hotel on St. Ann Street. The owner made it clear that it would be for one night only; he was determined to close up and get out of town on Sunday. That morning, beginning to understand the fix she was in, she decided to head toward the Jackson Barracks. With her multiple impressive IDs and Army connections, they would have to take her in until the airport reopened. She even had a telephone friend there with the memorable name of Merrily Smith, a woman who'd consulted with her about the deployment to Iraq of the Louisiana National Guard's 256th Infantry Brigade.

And so she walked the first mile down St. Claude, pulling her roll-aboard, until she found a renegade cab driver still cruising the streets who agreed to take her the rest of the way before the storm commenced. Sure enough, at the barracks there was a lovely clean cot for her, in a room with a lock, all of it quickly arranged by Merrily herself, who'd come in on a Sunday to help orchestrate the Guard's expected movement into the streets of the city.

By seven o'clock the next morning phone service was gone, and Allie's missing BlackBerry, which she assumed she'd dropped on the street on Saturday, seemed entirely irrelevant. She kept her wallet strapped to herself inside a fanny pack and guessed that the worst might be over by afternoon. And then, at 8:15 a.m., she heard a crash, and water began coming in under the door to her room. She opened it, and a lightning-fast slab of Lake Pontchartrain rushed in and pinned her to a bookshelf by the cot. She swam, indoors, for her life, making it to a staircase and then, on foot, to the highest point inside the barracks. She stood there with a captain and a nurse, who told her that the levees had been breached. Hours passed, all of their panic rising with the waters, until their ears popped at the same moment in response to the sudden, enormous rise in barometric pressure that told them the hurricane was moving away. Before long they ventured out onto the roof, realizing they were waiting not for a helicopter but a boat.

A pink house floated past like a merry pleasure craft. Was there a person, at the window, trapped inside it? Or had she only imagined that?

At five o'clock a motorboat came near. Its pilot signaled them to get back inside and climb out one of the windows closer to him. In minutes he had them at the banks of the Mississippi, where a Chinook chopper pulled them up above the city and delivered them, in less time than the average ride on a ski lift, to the Superdome. As soon as they were inside it, she and the captain and the nurse got separated and never saw one another again.

Now, closing her eyes, once more in her own apartment, she can remember the four half-lit nights in the death star of the stadium: the lines for water; the shaming improvisations performed whenever she needed the toilet. Twice she'd received the gift of a half sandwich from people who had brought their own food, as the mayor had suggested in his final evacuation order.

She remembers the sound of the creaking, leaking roof, more frightening than the screams of anger and the speeding rumors of people dying in their seats.

She never tried to use her pregnancy to any advantage, but wrote out a card with Holley's name and her own and put it in the fanny pack, so that if they both died in there someone might find a record of the baby's preexistence.

While under the dome, she had wanted a gun more than she ever wished for one in Baghdad.

Where, she had wondered day after day, was the Army? She'd felt as if Bush had taken her advice about a zero troop level and applied it to New Orleans instead of Iraq.

Then, early on Friday, the soldiers started to arrive. Too dazed to figure out whether she was offering assistance or asking for a favor, she identified herself to a sergeant. That afternoon they put her on a bus to Houston, where she narrowly avoided being herded into the Astrodome: she had to remind the relief people that she still *had* a home, and could get to it if they would only take her to the airport named for the president's father. Once they did, at a hotel on its edge, she telephoned her mother, who greeted her voice with cries appropriate to a New Testament miracle. And then, at last, yesterday, they found her a flight to Reagan. Back here, inside the apartment, she ordered in food, threw up most of it, and called no one.

The baby could certainly have died, but every instinct and physical sensation convinced her that it was still fine. She had decided to keep the card she'd written inside the stadium as a souvenir of what they'd survived together. Tomorrow she would go to the doctor and let people at work know she was alive.

Had Ross been sensible enough to remain inside the Monteleone? Did she have a right to worry about him? Lying here in the dark without contacting him seemed more respectful than selfish.

On her bureau sat the picture of Fadhil's daughter—IT'S A PERSON!—a baby made fatherless by men with guns rather than the blunders and ego of a woman who now felt sure she had no right to be a mother.

18

SEPTEMBER 15, 2005

Jackson Square; New Orleans

Bush sat silent in the armored SUV. Its high beams seemed to wish they were searchlights able to rake the dark, deserted streets for signs of life.

The president occasionally still wondered if he should have gone to the Superdome two weeks ago, once everyone realized what a disaster Rove's flyover had been. Would the crowd inside the stadium have killed him? There were times in the last two weeks when he would have welcomed the fate.

There was no one to blame for the heckuva-job-Brownie remark but himself—his penchants for nicknames and pep talks. What he should have done is shout "I am *pissed*!" the way Nagin had on the radio. He liked the guy even if he'd seemed half out of his mind that day on *Air Force One*, and even if he was crooked, as Jindal said. He certainly thought better of him than of Landrieu, who'd been *completely* crazy, with all the shrieking and tears. He'd kept wishing Blanco would give her a sisterly snap-out-of-it slap, but that would have required somebody bringing the governor to *her* senses first. Her basic reason for not letting them put her precious Louisiana National Guard under federal control? She hated Rove too much for that.

And then he'd had to contend with Rumsfeld not wanting to use the Army—as if it were his own private force. How had Rummy gone, in the space of two years, from being U. S. Grant to being George B. McClellan? Adding to the pileup: he had Condi telling him he now had "a race problem," and Dick needing an engraved invitation to get himself down to the Gulf Coast.

Bush felt like the blank eye of the hurricane as it appeared on those weather maps, surrounded and taunted by swirling fury. *Nothing worked.* He'd gotten rid of Brownie and made Dad and Clinton revive their tsunami act, only to have even that undone by Mother's little Marie Antoinette moment among the refugees shipped from Superdome to Astrodome: *Everyone is so overwhelmed by the hospitality. And so many of the people in the arena here, you know, were underprivileged anyway, so this is working very well for them.* He'd thought of asking her if she'd hired Nancy Reagan as a speechwriter, or considered going shoe-shopping up in New York with Condi, but in the end he just sucked it up along with everything else.

Out in the dark, as the SUV drew closer to the French Quarter, he could make out the Day-Glo letters embossed on a T-shirt: SCREW FALLUJAH, SAVE NEW ORLEANS.

———

Three cars behind, in this motorcade trying not to look like one, Ross tried to locate himself. Power had returned to parts of the Quarter, and he sensed they weren't too far from either the Monteleone or Pirates Alley, but the darkness remained overwhelming: there was no one to turn on the lights in buildings that *had* electricity. The SUV's illuminated dashboard looked bright enough to start a fire.

Ross had returned to Washington nine days ago, and soon succeeded in learning, without any details, that Allie was alive and back at her desk. When he got to his own office, the Chairman barged in, informing him that every agency in the government now had to make daily reports to the White House on its Katrina efforts. They were all doing a catch-up scramble that would never erase the public's first impressions of indifference. Ross was told that he would be overseeing a program of small emergency grants to the Gulf. In the short run he'd be doing it from here in D.C., and later from down in New Orleans. It was imperative that money get there fast: mold was already growing on books in the libraries and pictures in the museums. Katrina really *was* Iraq: all these threatened cultural treasures would need to be frozen like the Jewish archive out in College Park.

"What kind of oversight will we be doing on these emergency applications?" he'd asked the Chairman, mindful of Nagin's sticky fingers. "I mean, it's Louisiana we're talking about."

"Next to none," the Chairman admitted. "If some of the money gets skimmed, it'll just be water under the bridge—or over it."

Within days Ross began authorizing checks and working with the First Lady's office on a couple of bigger grant programs, the kind that might put a whole new roof onto a gallery or theater. And before he knew it, he was receiving word that he'd be one of a dozen or so officials on the plane to New Orleans for the president's big rebuilding speech.

There had been no sign of George W. Bush on the flight down: the last one on and the first one off, the president spent the trip inside his cabin—brooding, the reporters speculated. Ross had pocketed two cardboard *Air Force One* coasters, wondering if his children, at this point, would even accept them.

He finally recognized that they were in Jackson Square. The portable, self-powered lights on giant stanchions reminded him of the vertical beams that sometimes now illuminated the towerless Ground Zero. Tonight the tungsten lamps threw St. Louis Cathedral into sharp relief and made him recall how, little more than two weeks ago, the church's regular floodlights had caught Allie's auburn hair.

The president, in rolled-up shirtsleeves, soundlessly crossed the cathedral's lawn. The deep surrounding darkness felt more remarkable, and weirdly miraculous, than the silver patches of emergency lighting. Bush might as well be stepping through an Anne Rice novel; Ross half-expected him to be as pale as Tom Cruise, or wearing Napoleon's death mask.

There was no introduction, and the president's delivery was subdued:

Throughout the area hit by the hurricane, we will do what it takes, we will stay as long as it takes. . . .

Ross could imagine Allie saying, "Sound familiar?" The space between Lake Pontchartrain and the Mississippi had become the ground between the Tigris and Euphrates. But even now, if only from old reflex, he found himself rooting for Bush, hoping this moment might equal the one with the bullhorn a few days after 9/11.

The breaks in the levees have been closed. The pumps are running, and the water here in New Orleans is receding by the hour.

Ross looked toward Pirates Alley. He wanted to check on the guidebook office—for looting, not flooding—but had been told it was out of the question. After the speech the plane would be leaving as soon as they could get back to it.

Our goal is to get people out of the shelters by the middle of October.

Where would they be putting *him* until the toilets at the Monteleone were once again flushing? The Chairman had mentioned the possibility of a Navy ship docked at the Toulouse Street Wharf.

Four years after the frightening experience of September the 11th, Americans have every right to expect a more effective response in a time of emergency. When the federal government fails to meet such an obligation, I as president am responsible for the problem and for the solution.

This apology might be called manly, but things here were so bad it seemed to Ross that nobody in the government ought to be focused on anything *but* this domestic wreckage. He'd seen the same T-shirt everyone else had. Couldn't they maybe SCREW FALLUJAH for *now*?

Silence, no applause, greeted the end of the speech—an expression of gravity, not contempt. Bush went over to accept quiet greetings from those in attendance, even Kathleen Blanco. He affectionately patted Nagin's bald head, which the mayor had reportedly found time to shave during his shower on *Air Force One*.

Ross hadn't let himself expect what happened next, but here it was happening. The president was coming toward the second-row group he'd been placed in, and Andy Card was all at once presenting him to Bush, like some small holding in the president's portfolio. "This, of course, is Ross Weatherall, one of your appointees to the NEH's National Council, who's now on the staff over at NEAH. As you know, the First Lady is taking a special interest in their relief activities."

"Good man," said Bush. "Where you from?"

"Dallas, sir, before coming to Washington. But I grew up in Lubbock."

"I saw a Lubbock gal last month! On the NSC staff."

Bush was enjoying the connection but restraining his expression, taking care that no cameraman noticed him having even a moment's good time in this expunged city.

"I know her. Or used to," said Ross.

Bush's look turned quizzical, and Ross realized his response must have sounded odd. "We were at the Bush Bash together in '78," he added.

Cameras or not, the president couldn't help laughing at Ross's trace of pride in having attended that long-ago event. "That party's starting to sound like the Alamo—one jam-packed little fiasco! Years from now, as my legend grows, people who *weren't* there will be claiming they *were*."

From now on, Ross expected, all the president's humor would be of this gallows variety. He sensed Bush's desire to linger a bit, rather than fly straight out of this place he'd only have to keep coming back to for the next three years.

"Okay, Weatherman. Keep me informed—directly—of what you're seeing down here. You heard that, Card?" Bush asked his chief of staff. "I mean it."

"Yes, sir," said Card and Ross, simultaneously, as Bush moved on to the next person.

He had a nickname. But its conferral in this Purgatory, and his exile from Allie's inevitable mockery of it, kept him from feeling the slightest peace or pleasure.

19

SEPTEMBER 24, 2005

The White House

India, the Bushes' black cat, jumped out from behind a chair in the Red Room and dashed into the White House's crowded main hall. Post-9/11 security had accustomed the shy animal to long stretches of tourist-free tranquility, even on Saturday mornings, when the public floors could be quieter than the Residence. But now, upon waking from her nap, the cat had been startled by a general hubbub. Dozens of authors filled the corridor, all of them here for a breakfast kicking off this year's National Book Festival, an event the First Lady had made popular with the local citizenry and *de rigueur* for members of the administration.

India darted between Tom Wolfe and Supreme Court Justice Stephen Breyer, a fan of the novelist. She left a black hair on a pants-leg of the writer's all-white suit.

"Whose path did she just cross?" Breyer wondered.

"Couldn't be mine," said Wolfe. "*Charlotte Simmons* came out a year ago." The less-than-rapturous reception for his latest book had to indicate that any spell of bad luck lay behind him, not ahead. Breyer, however, had his own recent grimness to cite: fellow justices, his ideological opposites but genial colleagues, had this summer fallen off the bench like sparrows from a tree. Sandy O'Connor's retirement announcement had been followed by Bill Rehnquist's death, which had prompted the president to reposition his nominee for O'Connor's replacement, John Roberts, into the slot to succeed the chief justice. So once again it was the naming of Sandy's successor that everyone now awaited.

"Willie!" called the First Lady, urging the errant cat to move upstairs.

"I thought her name was India," said Barbara Bush, who with her daughter-in-law was advancing toward Breyer and Wolfe.

"It is," said Laura. "But in public it's now Willie." She explained that there had recently been a strong protest against the fifteen-year-old feline outside a U.S. consulate somewhere on the subcontinent. The demonstrators had been unaware that India was named for one of the president's old Texas Rangers, Rubén "El Indio" Sierra. "It's just easier this way," said Laura.

"What a ridiculous fuss over an animal," her mother-in-law responded.

Larry King, walking behind the two first ladies, asked Barbara Bush: "You're not sentimental about the four-footers, are you? Remember when I asked you if you missed Millie?"

"I do," said the elder Mrs. Bush. King had wondered, on national television, if she pined, post-presidentially, for her late spaniel, a much-publicized resident of the first Bush White House and the focus of a best-selling book. She had answered no. "I heard from both my sons and from Karl Rove," Barbara Bush now reminded King. "They said that I'd just cost the family the animal lovers' vote. For God's sake, Larry, we're talking about a *dog*." She looked the cable host up and down. "At least you've got a tie on today."

Then she pointed to John Irving. "Isn't that the *Garp* man?" she asked her daughter-in-law. "Are you still reading his books? He looks awfully fit for a writer."

"He wrestles," Laura Bush explained, before they all, including Irving, reached Wolfe and Breyer.

"Oh!" said the associate justice. "Maybe I can arbitrate this from the bench?" He pointed first to Irving and then to Wolfe, who in a ferocious essay had lumped the other novelist with rivals he considered insufficiently realist. Irving had responded that Wolfe's own fiction read like a bad newspaper. Both writers shrugged politely at Breyer's offer, declining to make a fuss in such a dignified venue. Laura Bush returned their smiles. She wouldn't mind a literary quarrel; it would be more fun than having to hear, as she now did each year, from writers refusing invitations to the festival because of George's Iraq policy.

A waiter passed with a tray of mimosas. "Take one—everybody," Barbara Bush commanded. "Alcohol is healthier than the water here." She explained that she and her husband, and even Millie, had years ago all come down with forms of Graves' disease, a thyroid condition, and that the White House pipes were suspect.

"Lincoln used to hear rats inside the upstairs walls!" Larry King observed.

"They've moved to the West Wing," Barbara Bush replied.

The current First Lady's chief of staff signaled that it was time for her boss to make welcoming remarks in the State Dining Room. Mrs. Bush nodded. Once those in the hall assembled by the food, they heard her tell them that, in addition to all the festival's usual literary setups out on the National Mall, they would find inside the Library of Congress pavilion a Veterans History Project that was gathering personal recollections from the nation's past and present soldiers. She also pointed out Condi Rice, who had been at last night's dinner in the Jefferson Building and was with them all again this morning. "The president will be down a little later," said Laura. "In the meantime you can see that I've brought along my mother-in-law, an author herself, as well as an avid reader—and critic."

The president was in fact already here, in the hall outside the Dining Room. At this event he always stayed to the side, trying not to take the spotlight off his wife. He looked from a distance at the authors lining up with their buffet plates, and saw Condi talking to Jim Billington, the librarian of Congress. Or was it David McCullough? Both of them looked like white-haired professors out of old movies.

Bush had liked the Texas version of this festival that Laura put together when they were in the governor's mansion. Now, though, he always had to be on guard against some asshole historian or New York editor looking to have a heroic moment by making an anti-Iraq comment that would allow the guy to say, on the Acela ride home: "Boy, I really gave it to him."

"Hello, darlin'," said the president, waving to Harriet Miers, who was also in the hall, putting in a loyal appearance and allowing herself a break from her usual Saturday labors. Bush hoped that Laura had some Grisham-type legal novelist on this year's roster, somebody who might put a little sparkle into Harriet's day. As he regarded his White House counsel, the president had the same thought he'd been having all week: Why not her? So what if she's never been a judge? Roberts had only short experience on the bench and lots of SCOTUS justices had had none. And so what if she wasn't some fancy-ass intellect like Breyer over there? She'd been the head of the Texas Bar Association before she'd gone to work for him a dozen years ago. A smooth technician; no ideologue—and a woman. Confirmable? Certainly more so than Priscilla Owen, the conservative judge he'd really like to pick. Of course, if he did choose Harriet, everybody would laugh at the supposed parallel to Dick in 2000, saying she'd been charged with finding someone to fill the job and decided to select herself.

Carrying their now-full plates, people started spilling out of the State Dining Room. Here was Condi coming toward him—with another blue-suited, white-haired professor? No, as the guy got closer he realized from his face-lift that this was actually Buzz Aldrin, the astronaut. They'd met, maybe fifteen years ago, back when Dad was talking about going to Mars. For all he knew, the government was still committed to that on paper. (Oh yeah, bound to happen!)

He and Aldrin shook hands and quickly ran out of pleasantries. But then Bush had an idea: he took out a little photograph he liked to keep in his wallet. Condi—trying to avoid Tom Friedman, nearby with a question about the next vote to be held in Iraq—recognized the picture.

She knew that the president had gotten it from Don.

"You've been up even higher than where it was taken from," the president informed the astronaut. "Can you tell what it is?"

Aldrin, who had worked out the rendezvous mechanics of lunar landing, couldn't quite figure out the image: big clusters of bright lights with a large swath of darkness above them. Some galaxy picture from the Hubble?

"South Korea," the president explained, pointing to the big blooms of illumination in the satellite photo. "North Korea," he then added, tapping the black stretch above them.

"It shows you what freedom can accomplish," Condi observed.

Aldrin, still regarding the dark square inches of the Democratic People's Republic of Korea, said, "Looks like it's been bombed."

Not yet, thought Bush.

"We *are* making progress with them," Condi informed the onetime astronaut. "Despite that little glitch with the agreement." She smiled with a charming chagrin and explained how the off-and-on "six-party talks" designed to prevent a nuclear North Korea had last week yielded what looked like a breakthrough: the North would drop its nuclear program and allow inspectors in, so long as the U.S. pledged not to invade.

"What was the glitch?" asked Aldrin.

The president answered for his secretary of state. "Next day Son of Kim says not so fast. You've got to give us a light-water reactor first. Strictly for peaceful energy purposes, of course." He winked at Condi.

"Even so," Condi gently insisted, "we're on the right track." She'd briefly believed that the agreement had given her a victory over Cheney, who liked multilateral diplomacy even less than the one-on-one kind.

"Buzz," asked the president. "You got a book out that you're pushing here?"

Aldrin nodded. "It's called *Reaching for the Moon.* An autobiography for kids; it leaves out the complicated stuff."

"Like how to rendezvous in lunar orbit?" asked Condi.

"More like all the drinking and depression that came after."

The president could see, a few feet away, what looked like a third wife. Buzz, he now remembered, was a bit of a mess, but he felt an odd, particular sympathy for him. Being the second man on the moon was a little like being 43 only because 41 had been your booster rocket.

It was time to make an I've-got-to-go-mingle move. He didn't want to stand here and run the risk of meeting Aldrin's latest wife, or hear how hard Condi had worked with the other foreign ministers involved in those six-party talks, along with all the other stuff she'd done up in New York at the opening of the General Assembly, that annual waste of time made even worse this year by Clinton's coming down from his Harlem office to announce his "Global Initiative"—and getting more press than the people who were still in power all over the world.

Before peeling off from Buzz, who could hardly be given a nickname on top of what he already had, the president decided he had one last thing to add: "Not many books come out of North Korea."

"I don't imagine they do," said Aldrin.

Condi wondered where this was going.

"But I did get hold of one of them not long ago. A present from Kissinger," the president explained, more to Condi than to Aldrin. "Called *The Aquariums of Pyongyang.*" He took care pronouncing the city's name. "Not many actual aquariums there, I would guess. But this book was by somebody who wound up in a concentration camp, as a kid, with his whole family. He got out and lived to tell the tale." Bush had even underlined pieces of the text: *Keeping us calm was apparently the guards' main responsibility. It was common knowledge that people in our situation often preferred to take their own lives. The guards wanted none of that. Suicide was a manner of disobeying, of showing that one had lost faith in the future traced out by the Party.*

"I gave a copy to Putin when he was here last week."

Condi looked positively alarmed.

"I thought it was a fair exchange," the president continued. "He came here with some rare edition of *The Brothers Karamazov* for Laura." The scene with the Grand Inquisitor was known, from an interview she'd given, to be a favorite of the First Lady's.

"Stay in orbit, Buzz." The president patted the astronaut's shoulder and made his departure. He had to get out of here altogether and fly to some emergency-operations center in Austin about fifteen minutes from now. Another hurricane, this one named Rita, was on its way. Yesterday he'd been out at NORTHCOM in Colorado, looking over the Defense Department's storm-relief assets, ready to deploy them at a moment's notice.

He walked past Jerry Ford's portrait, waved to the national archivist, and sidestepped an editor still trying to get Dad to write his autobiography. Grandmother would have applauded the modesty of his refusing to do one back around '93—and Mother had approved of it too. "More sales for me," she'd reasoned—and sure enough she cleaned up with her own memoir. All the personal appearances she made for it, when she wasn't already down in Florida campaigning for Jeb, had only added to its success.

"Mr. President."

"Weatherman! Who let you in here?"

"NEAH is helping to run one of the pavilions," explained Ross Weatherall. "There's a Book Relief Project designed to get reading materials into the hands of kids made homeless by Katrina. I go back to New Orleans tomorrow."

"Good man," said Bush. "Let me ask you something. I've got Putin on the brain. He and I had a little meeting here and then talked to the press a day or two after you and I met down by the cathedral. Exactly what supplies has Russia sent down to the Gulf? Putin said they'd dispatched some right away." Vlad had also done him a rhetorical solid with the reporters, referring to "Mother Nature" as the cause of the storm, instead of making it sound, the way the press now did, as if Bush himself had dumped a giant cauldron of water onto New Orleans.

Wasn't this, Ross thought, really a question for Brownie's replacement, or for the secretary of state over there? "I'll get you an answer this afternoon, sir."

"Good. I want one. By the way, Rumsfeld tells me that Ms. O'Connor, your old Lubbock pal, has returned to Iraq for a while. I hope he brings her back here soon. She's kind of *my* Grand Inquisitor, and it wouldn't hurt for me to go another round with her." The president could see an expression of puzzlement come over the younger man, and assumed it must derive from the Grand Inquisitor reference: he had a bad habit of talking to people as if they'd participated in whatever previous conversation he'd had with someone else. But now he noticed the Weatherman's sort of green-around-the-gills look, and realized that this Lubbock girl was more than just an old friend. *They've been fucking*, the president intuited.

He clapped Ross on the arm. "Go get some books to those kids. And remember that you're going to give me your impressions—directly—of things down in New Orleans."

"Yes, sir."

Okay, thought the president: this was enough grinning and hand-shaking for Laura's show. To the nearest agent, he pointed upwards, meaning he was ready to make a quick stop in the Residence, not the Oval, before they left for Austin. Heading upstairs, he reflected again on Putin's recent almost-across-the-board helpfulness: not just blaming Mother Nature, but saying he hoped Iraqi voters would approve their new constitution. On North Korea, however, in stressing diplomacy, Vlad had said one shouldn't aggravate problems and bring them toward, as the translator put it, "extremalities." Well, nobody had been talking out loud about any dire response, so Bush now concluded that if tough actions were on Putin's mind, it was because *he'd* put them there on V-E Day. Vlad might not be open to them *yet*, but it did sound as if he wasn't misunderestimating the old extremalities.

20

OCTOBER 19–21, 2005

The Green Zone, Baghdad

Since January, the eager beaver named Kevin, whose surname Allie now knew to be Barden, had acquired a proud blond mustache and a good deal more responsibility. In fact, he was now, by the standards of the Green Zone, an old Iraq hand whose service had lasted more than a year and would soon be coming to an end. A job with Bechtel awaited him in California. But this morning Kevin continued to buzz in and out of the office where they'd found a desk for Allie these past several weeks. Each time he passed her he would display a new bundle of tally sheets from last Saturday's referendum on the constitution.

The results from the provinces had started coming in only yesterday and were being touted as evidence of a splendid democratic success. Turnout had neared ten million, and the yes vote might end up as high as seventy-five percent. Most crucially, only Salah ad-Din and Al Anbar—*two* provinces rather than a fatal three—had voted "no" by more than two-thirds. (Allie had been hearing that the count in Ninawa, where the no vote had been kept to fifty-five percent, would have made old-time ward heelers in Chicago blush.) Saturday's violence had indeed been less than what was feared, but since the violence reached spectacular levels nearly every day now, the insurgents may not have seen much point in making a special effort for the election.

Allie had personally asked Rumsfeld if she could return to Baghdad for the referendum and the start of Saddam Hussein's trial. "You're the only person to request Iraq for R-and-R to get over New Orleans," he replied, having heard the story (minus the closely guarded fact of her pregnancy) of how she had escaped the storm. "Sure," he finally agreed, "but I don't want you there past Thanksgiving." She assumed he was thinking that any persuasiveness she might have with Bush would dwindle if she stayed away from Washington longer than that. On the other hand—as they talked, she could see the ledger filling itself out in Rumsfeld's quadratic mind—a substantial visit would allow her to return with fresh evidence of the Occupation's fatigue and futility. When she'd spoken to the defense secretary via videoconference on Monday, he had seemed almost disappointed in the referendum's apparent success.

Here in the Republican Palace, wearing loose, unrevealing clothes (something she could get away with for another month at most), she had been shuttling between the U.S.'s election-advisory operation and an annex of its Regime Crimes Liaison Office. The American hand on the bicycle seat seemed especially firm when it came to the trial of Saddam, and she was now assisting in consultations between the U.S. Army and the infant Iraqi judiciary.

With some of the morning already gone, it was time for her and three others, including ubiquitous Kevin, to make the fast drive across a portion of the Green Zone to what had once been the headquarters of Saddam's Baath Party. The place had won out as the symbolic choice for a location in which to try the former dictator and seven codefendants. In looking at the structure, Allie's eyes always had trouble distinguishing 2003's bomb damage from the then-still-incomplete construction of the building's extension.

She took a reserved seat in the gallery next to Kevin, who was aglow, as if he were looking down on the proceedings of the First Continental Congress. Nearby sat two U.S. Army generals, a human-rights lawyer from London, and a pair of election observers, one from Uruguay and the other from Denmark, their work in Iraq now done until December, when they would return to monitor the voting for parliament.

Allie studied a fidgeting Iraqi attorney, so unprepossessing it appeared that he should be trawling a bail bondsman's district, hustling up work. The human-rights lawyer noticed him, too, and shook his head as if to say: *See? Inadequate representation. This is a show trial.* But the attorney's hapless aspect, Allie now understood, was really a manifestation of the nervousness he felt while awaiting the arrival of his once-omnipotent client. The man snapped to attention and brought his hand to his heart when Saddam Hussein, roughly but recently groomed, shuffled in wearing shackles.

Only at this moment, because of some obscure security regulation, was Rukia Hasani, the widow of her slain translator, allowed to join them in the gallery. She took the empty seat near Allie, who along with everyone else, including the human-rights lawyer, smiled protectively. It was Allie who had arranged for the young woman to come.

On Monday, in the midst of a sandstorm, she had at last ventured to Rukia's home, which was now inside the Green Zone, a small apartment found for her and her infant daughter by the Titan Corporation, Fadhil's old employer. The California-based service had also furnished Rukia with a large plant, which Allie could see needed watering. The baby, Pirnaz, was down for her nap as the two women visited and Rukia told her story with a surprising proficiency in English, something she'd acquired from her now-murdered husband.

Rolf had had things wrong. Only Fadhil's mother was a Kurd; his father was Shia, one of 148 local men rounded up by Saddam Hussein in the summer of 1982, after a party of assassins tried and failed to kill the Sunni dictator as his motorcade made its way through the Shiite-majority village of Dujail. Like the other 147 men, Mr. Hasani had been tortured and then killed—in Abu Ghraib. Fadhil had been nine years old.

On Monday, Rukia had explained: *Fadhil did not work for you.* She had gestured, while speaking the pronoun, to the Green Zone beyond the apartment's window. *He did not work for the money. He worked, how do you say it, to keep the tables turning.*

The Dujail massacre made for easy pickings in the orchard of Baathist atrocities. A compact, provable abomination, it could be made to stick to the lead defendant and his cohorts as a sort of surrogate charge, avenging other enormities that would have to go unpresented for a lack of time or evidence. The strategy was an exponentially expanded, war-crimes version of the one Allie remembered her prosecutor friends employing when she lived in New York during the crime-ridden early nineties: if you could get somebody on one murder, the dozen others he'd committed were, however imperfectly, taken care of.

You go to war with the army you have.

Last summer, word had gotten out that Dujail would be a judicial focus, and shortly after that Fadhil had been murdered by Sunni insurgents: a gesture of disapproval. The shooters had never been caught, but Rukia knew there could be no other explanation. Her husband's connection to Saddam's crime, however peripheral his victimization, was enough for his killers to make a point. Like the massacre itself, he could serve as an example.

Now, two days after her visit from Allie, Rukia leaned forward to look at the prisoner who had been transported here this morning from the Americans' Camp Cropper. Asked by the judge to state his name, he refused. And when the judge then answered his own question—"You are Saddam Hussein al-Majid, former president of Iraq, born in 1937"—the prisoner erupted with rage over the "former" and what he declared to be the court's lack of jurisdiction.

The ranting reminded Allie of Ceauşescu in his last minutes, and for all the meticulous legal work she'd been helping with, she wished for a moment that Saddam, like the Romanian, could simply be taken out into a courtyard and shot. Rukia directed her attention to the copy of the Koran being brandished by the dictator as both shield and justification. She squeezed Allie's arm and laughed, more loudly than the human-rights lawyer thought was strictly appropriate.

The session ended up feeling like a preliminary hearing instead of the start of a trial. After three hours of judicial contretemps, the proceedings were recessed, in part because of a witness shortage. A number of those who had been expected to testify from behind a curtain had decided at the last minute that too much risk remained and thus failed to show. The judge pledged to alleviate this difficulty, along with a host of others, by the time the trial resumed on November 28.

After the adjournment, Allie and Rukia were driven by a new Aussie security man—Tim Gleeson was long gone—to Rukia's home. While they were en route, the Green Zone's p.a. system, or "Giant Voice," blared updates about which roads to avoid. At one point it drowned out 107.7 FM, Freedom Radio, which was playing inside the armored vehicle. The station's newsman had been reporting a pro-Saddam demonstration in the dictator's hometown of Tikrit.

A translator accompanied Allie and Rukia, a young man who had worked with Fadhil and was now invited to have supper and to smooth over any linguistic confusion that might arise between the two women. Laughter from Rukia's baby greeted the three of them even before the apartment door was opened by the silent aunt preparing supper. Pirnaz was wearing her IT'S A PERSON bib.

Allie recognized a framed copy of the picture she had on her desk in Washington: the baby and Fadhil.

"You have, yes?" asked Rukia.

"I do," Allie replied. She'd been staring at the photo. "I never asked Fadhil what the numbers on the pin signify."

Rukia, unsure that she had the right English for the explanation, exchanged some words with Fadhil's old colleague, who then told Allie: "Two, eight, nine, one, seven, eight. It's a backwards scramble of the digits for July 8, 1982."

"Do you have the pin?" Allie asked Rukia.

"No, they tore from his body. The killers."

"Because they knew what it meant?"

Rukia laughed. "Because they thought the gold was worth five American dollars."

After handing the baby to Allie, Rukia helped her aunt serve the meal, commenting most of the while on the various ways in which life inside the Green Zone was an improvement over what she and Fadhil had experienced outside its walls. For one thing, fewer blackouts.

Conversation flagged as the adults concentrated on their food, but then a loud whisper from Rukia, in English, ended the lull: "*You too!*"

The exclamation brought puzzled looks from Allie and the translator. Smiling, Rukia got up from the table and made Allie join her in the small kitchen.

"You are having baby," she said softly.

Allie's look of disbelief derived from the uncanniness, not any lack of truth, in the other woman's realization. With delighted certainty, Rukia explained: "Each time you look at Pirnaz, you touch and rub stomach. Yours, not hers. You have baby coming—but no man?"

Allie nodded—yes on both counts—but she indicated that they should get back to the table and not give the translator any gossip to take back to the Republican Palace. Returning to her chair, she thought: *I don't know what I am doing; only that I'm doing it myself.* She remained in free fall, and most nights dreamt not of the dangers that lay outside the Green Zone but of things she remembered from inside the Superdome.

The silent aunt, the first to finish eating, turned on the television. Al Jazeera was reporting on the now-almost-complete election returns, replaying recent clips from two Sunni clerics, one who'd urged participation in the referendum (if only to vote no) and another who'd demanded that people remain at home. Then, putting the results into "the broader context of U.S. policy," the anchor introduced some video clips of Bush, Rice, and Karen Hughes—selections from the latter's September forays into Egypt, Turkey, and Saudi Arabia, where she went about hugging children and boldly telling the Saudi women that they should be allowed to drive; she'd been shocked to learn of the prohibition. Rukia's hitherto mute aunt murmured something as the television showed the undersecretary of state kicking a soccer ball. The translator relayed her comment: "Big feet."

"Would Fadhil have testified at the trial?" Allie asked Rukia.

"No. He was little boy on the day," she answered, referring to the reprisal kidnappings twenty-three years earlier in Dujail. "His mother hid him in basement. I tell you the other day: they kill him just because he was Shiite, connected to those who now seek justice. As a—what do you say?"

"Symbol?"

"Yes. No reason other than that. That is enough. He grew up Shia in village surrounded by Sunni."

"Did he ever see his father again? After the kidnapping?" The word puzzled Rukia; the translator was about to step in when Allie tried "abduction" instead.

"Once. Inside Abu Ghraib. Before Mr. Hasani was hanged—we think. That was 1985. Fadhil was never told where his father was buried. Or if."

Allie had grimaced at the utterance of the prison's name. "Why do you make face?" Rukia now asked her, scoldingly.

"The awful things that the army, my army, did there."

"Is as nothing!" Rukia replied, with a force that startled everyone. "Is as nothing, compared!"

Not wanting to scale the iniquities, Allie put a comforting hand on Rukia's forearm. "How long will you stay here? Will you go home soon?" The young woman's family lived in the north.

"I will be here in November. I will listen to rest of testimony about Dujail, and then about Anfal, too." A cousin of hers had died in the poison-gassing of Kurds, in Halabja, in 1988; she explained this rapidly, in Arabic, through the translator. Then, after lifting her daughter away from her aunt, she held Pirnaz in front of Allie. "She is Shia *and* Kurd. They"—the Sunnis—"would be happy to kill her just for existing. You are here, fighting different war from the one you came to fight. But you are *here*. Do your job! Only you can fight this to finish. Finish your job, you Americans!"

After a few seconds of silence, Rukia pointed to Saddam Hussein's face, which had returned to the TV screen. "I will stay here, in Baghdad," she said, "until they snap his neck."

———

New Orleans

Cable had come back to the Monteleone, which had technically reopened, though most people staying there were staff who'd been displaced from their homes. Ross himself, again in town on his NEAH per diem, had been welcomed back as a Katrina veteran by Emile, who even put him into Room 928, to which water, along with television, once more flowed.

On this early Friday afternoon, C-SPAN was covering the dedication of the *Air Force One* pavilion at the Reagan Library. The president, on an elevated platform with both Laura and Nancy Reagan, was paying tribute to his predecessor's willingness to fight the Cold War, over the long haul, to a successful conclusion: *Like the ideology of communism, our new enemy is dismissive of free peoples, claiming that men and women who live in liberty are weak and decadent. And like the ideology of communism, Islamic radicalism is doomed to fail.*

Ross found himself resisting the comparison, not because he judged it untruthful, but because he had only enough mental room to think of the battle for New Orleans: in the streets outside, General Russel Honoré was turning out to be a more successful version of General Casey in Baghdad, beating back the consequences of a literal flood rather than a human insurgency. Ross could no doubt add some more reflections like this one to the ever-expanding, undispatched e-mail to Allie that sat in his computer. He wondered how long it would be before a night arrived when he brought one drink too many up from the Carousel Bar—room service had not yet come back—and loss of inhibition sent his finger to the send key.

Come back to me.
When will you talk to me?
Please tell me you won't stay over there for the birth.
I'll agree to it. Holley is yours.

The diary-like e-mail contained all these draft pleadings and pledges, along with details of his work on behalf of "Recovery" down here. *NEAH is partnering with a person at State so that we can send abroad 15 New Orleans jazz bands to thank countries that have donated aid.*

He had gotten the president the detailed information on the Russian contribution: a breakdown of the sixty tons of items, everything from tents to medicine to stuffed animals, all of it flown here on three IL-76s. He'd in fact obtained the data from someone on the NSC staff, taking advantage of the opportunity to fish for further wisps of information about Allie.

Her colleague added the Superdome story to what little else Ross knew. When he'd first gotten back to Washington from Baton Rouge, and it became clear she wouldn't answer phone calls or e-mails, he'd driven the three blocks of Arlington from his place to hers and sat inside his parked car, the visor of his baseball cap pulled low, like some sad John Cusack character, until he'd seen her go in and out of her apartment, twice. After that he'd learned from Bush about her impending return to Baghdad. "What a brave woman!" the NSC guy had responded to his pseudo-casual mention of her name. "Do you know the story of her escape from the floodwaters, Mr. Weatherall? No?" The man was more than eager to furnish details. At the office a day later, by coincidence, Ross signed off on an emergency grant to the Jackson Barracks Military Museum and Library, for help with storage and mold abatement.

Now, as Bush talked from the television about Reagan and *Air Force One*, he looked over the latest section of manuscript to come in for the guidebook, the work of an aging minor novelist who had known John Kennedy Toole. It included a quick write-up on Memorial Hall. What the man submitted was vivid and at first glance appeared accurate, but Ross knew he would have to suggest that, where the building's Confederate museum was concerned, the text become a little more . . . penitential. He would have to do it gently, since the guy was supposed to provide copy about the whole Lee Circle neighborhood.

If they got that chapter right, it might be showcased in January, when the agency hoped to present a preview of the guidebook, several printed signatures of it, at a little ceremony. They would emphasize that the material was ahead of schedule, a fact that would please

NEAH's congressional overlords, Republicans especially, and seem encouraging, in a general way, about the region's convalescence. Blanco's office and Nagin's had agreed to participate, promising the appearance of both governor and mayor at a party Mrs. Boggs and Mrs. Caine would host.

The phone rang.

"Ready?" asked a cheerful Father Montrose, down in the Monteleone's lobby. He had offered to show Ross the Holy Cross neighborhood, a small piece of the Ninth Ward, and they would be seeing it in great protective style: a Humvee driven by a National Guardsman, something Mrs. Caine had arranged, was parked outside on Royal Street.

"Church-state alignments are sort of fluid down here, aren't they?" asked Ross, with a smile to both the priest and soldier.

"Don't say 'fluid'!" pleaded Father Montrose. "We've had enough *fluidity.*"

Within minutes the vehicle, which carried a Saint Christopher medal, had them in the stricken district between the Industrial Canal and Jackson Barracks. Ross craned his neck through the Humvee's window, trying to guess which rooftop Allie had stood on.

The first of Holy Cross's old residents had arrived home only a few days ago; many, of course, would never be back. A pair of buses, one of them outfitted as a soup kitchen, stood gleaming in the sun, and Father Montrose marveled over the sight of them, as if they were the Twin Towers restored to life. Several FEMA trailers were in place a block away, most of them still untenanted.

"Aside from showing me around, what will you be doing today?" Ross asked the priest.

"Saying Mass, of course!"

"Where?"

"Next to one of the buses."

Father Montrose had once taught at Holy Cross High, whose pummeled building he now pointed out. After more than a century here, the school had been forced to move to less-ravaged Gentilly. Near its old front lawn, the priest and Ross stepped out to meet, as planned, a community gadfly named Gary Fowler, a large, bald black man with two earrings. "Glad to get you outta the Sliver by the River!" he shouted in welcome, using the new name for the city's higher, unflooded ground. He greeted Ross with special warmth and told him he'd heard from Father Montrose about all the good things his little piece of the government was doing.

"Yeah," said Ross, abashed at hearing praise from someone who had been up against it in ways he couldn't imagine. "We're doing a heckuva job."

The three men set off on foot over the cracked gray mud that still covered everything. The Humvee driver stayed in his vehicle. Gary, with exuberance, drew Ross's attention to a dozen different things, explaining to him the distinctions between a camelback and a shotgun house, though so many of the lots now contained only foundations he had trouble finding more than one example of the former. The water, he told Ross, had risen seven feet high; had mostly receded by mid-September; and then risen again when Rita came through.

"That just about did in the last of my optimism," Father Montrose confessed. "But nothing keeps Gary down for long."

Ross could see and smell sewage and mold everywhere. "How are you going to feed the people who're coming back?" he asked the two men. "That soup kitchen can't handle too many of them, I'd guess. Where was the grocery store before it washed away?"

"Wasn't one here *to* wash away," said Gary, explaining how far the residents had to go to shop even before the storm. For the foreseeable future, food would have to be trucked in from afar, since the old grocery one whole neighborhood over *did* wash away. Gary seemed amused by this one of the Lord's mysterious whims; Father Montrose's expression showed less forbearance toward the Almighty.

A clarinet, far in the distance, could be heard playing "Don't Fence Me In."

"Where's that coming from?" asked Ross.

"Probably on top of the levee wall," answered Gary.

"Somebody's playing while *sitting* on it?" This seemed somehow an impossibility; if the waters had been a nuclear explosion, the broken levee was the plane that had delivered the bomb.

"More likely walking on it," said Gary. "Happens all the time.

Between the breaches! Hear how the sound's moving away a little?"
He knew the girl who was playing, he said. He had taken a clarinet out
of one of these houses—it had been dry as a bone in its case on a high
shelf above the water-rise—after he'd seen two bodies, a man's and a
woman's, being removed from the property.

"How did the girl get the clarinet?"

"We gave it to her," explained Father Montrose. "The day before
yesterday, when she and her mother came back from Arkansas." Both
the priest and Gary looked at Ross, as if to say: You have a better idea
of what we should have done with it?

Inside the soup-kitchen bus Gary introduced Ross to Mrs. Carlotta
Watson and then bustled off to the next task at hand, leaving him to
make conversation on his own, to extract from the woman, as politely
as he could, her particular story of the days after August 29th.

"Did you know Gary before the storm?" he asked.

"Everybody knows Gary."

"I'm glad to have met him. Just an hour or so ago."

"Where are you from?"

"Washington, D.C.," Ross replied, quietly, without the bright
Potomac-feverish manner he'd exhibited to new acquaintances during
the first months of the year. Even so, Mrs. Watson's glare told him
he would have been better off saying "Lubbock, Texas." She quickly
made it plain that her recent experiences had erased any need to make
a distinction between bureaucratic failure and active malevolence.

Her twenty-five-year-old daughter, half dead from an infection,
had been evacuated from the ICU at Chalmette Medical Center when
the generators failed. She ended up being sent to an airport hangar
with a makeshift clinic, where the young doctor who began to treat
her—"a volunteer, a nice girl who'd come all the way from Indiana in
her car"—was pulled away from her patient and told either to unload
palettes of toilet paper or leave: there was no record of young Dr.
Chang's name in whatever vast electronic file of the nation's physi-
cians the man from FEMA had insisted on checking. Someone else
succeeded in locating the name two days later, which was two days
after Marguerite Watson died.

Ross asked Mrs. Watson where she was now living and she told him: with a woman she knew only well enough to dislike, a Good Samaritan who made her feel bad about herself. Her application for a FEMA trailer had recently been rejected because she had been informed that she owed the federal government four hundred dollars. A U.S. Treasury aid check had reached her on September 10th, and when Gary managed to cash it for her, she did not know—FEMA's instructions for spending it not having arrived until the fourteenth—that it was only for housing, of which, of course, there was none to be had. Last week she had gotten, along with the trailer rejection, a bill for the four hundred dollars, which she was told she had improperly spent on "other life expenses."

"Actually," said Mrs. Watson, "it was death expenses. A part of my daughter's funeral."

———

After dinner, in the Pirates Alley office, Ross brushed off the last of the mud his pants had picked up while he knelt during Father Montrose's fast outdoor Mass. He had attended politely, but experienced little of what he'd felt afterwards inside the bus-turned-soup-kitchen, where Mrs. Watson had dozed off. His application of an old manual can opener to tins of tomatoes and beans had seemed more Eucharistic than Father Montrose's makeshift consecration. The sensation that he was being directly and immediately useful brought him a fragile serenity, something he wasn't getting from putting his signature to mold-abatement grants. He had fed three people this afternoon; tonight he was just taking up space in the world.

The office radio was broadcasting a report on Condoleezza Rice's trip to Alabama with the British foreign secretary. She'd shown him the sights of her segregated Birmingham girlhood. Jack Straw had also gone to her speech at the university in Tuscaloosa, and the station had some sound bites from it: *And of course Birmingham was the city where my friend Denise McNair and three other little girls were blown up one Sunday morning while they were going to Sunday school at the Sixteenth Street Baptist Church.*

Ross looked up from his desk and waited for what he felt certain would come next. And it did: *Today we face the same choice in the world that we once confronted in our country. Either the desire for liberty and democratic rights is true for all human beings or we are to believe that certain peoples actually prefer subjugation.*

So now, thought Ross, the Islamists were the KKK as well as the Cold War Communists. Everything had to be some goddamned *other* thing, bigger than itself; not just informed by precedent but a reincarnation of it. The new guidebook would be a typological fulfillment of the old; one testament piled atop another. Even Holley would be a new joint manifestation of himself and Allison.

All these thoughts—repetitive, stale, academic—felt like another kind of mold, what would grow on *him* if he didn't let his anger, over what he'd seen this afternoon, start burning it away.

He clicked open the Word file of his ongoing memo to George W. Bush, the newest portions of which—unlike his draft e-mail to Allie—he sent every few days. He scrolled through the Russian figures he'd forwarded; moved down past Bush's pasted-in reply (*Generous of them. Keep these coming, Weatherman*), and then began typing what was actually in his head:

> *Mr. President, this afternoon I dished out some canned fruit to a boy who'd never tasted a peach. How, I thought, can this be? And how is it that people down here are dying because of decisions being made by idiots in a Washington office ten blocks from yours—people hired by people you appointed. . . .*

The waters, the ones inside him, were beginning to rise.

21

NOVEMBER 2, 2005

The State Floor of the White House

"*Oooh*," said Merv Griffin. "Am I with Nancy Reagan or Nancy *Drew*?"

"Who's going to stop me?" asked the former First Lady, opening the door to the State Dining Room for a peek at tonight's table settings. "I mean, for God's sake, my *portrait* is hanging downstairs."

Merv and Nancy had in fact just taken a sentimental turn past the First Lady paintings in the Vermeil Room, where her Shikler competed with Jackie's in ethereal, El Greco–like elongation. On one side of them, Pat Nixon's eyes brimmed with tears, and on the other, Lady Bird Johnson remained recognizable, even while raised to a peak of attractiveness she'd not scaled in life.

"It's just force of habit," Nancy explained to Merv, her escort for the evening, as they entered the still-empty dining room. The other hundred and thirty guests honoring Prince Charles and his new wife were gathering for cocktails down the hall in the Blue Room. "We did so many of these dinners," said Nancy. "And something always went wrong."

Sure enough, she saw what it was tonight—and so did Merv, whose *oooh* now ended in a disapproving collapse. He and Nancy stared at the faux pas: every place was set with Hillary Clinton's pineapple-colored White House china.

For a long moment Nancy was silent.

"I don't blame *her*," she said at last, meaning Laura Bush. "She's been very nice to me. She's smart, and she's preoccupied with other things."

"But," said Merv.

"I *do* blame that chief of staff she has. Not up to it."

"Absolutely," Merv agreed. "*Knowing* you were coming."

"Yes," said Nancy. Knowing she was coming and not using the beautiful red-rimmed plates the press had practically broken over her head during Ronnie's first term—no matter that the taxpayers hadn't shelled out a dime for them.

"Medallions of buffalo tenderloin!" enthused Merv, picking up a menu card. "Wild-rice pancakes and roasted corn! Sounds like Wild West fare to go with those fancy saddles the Bushes are giving the prince and—what are they calling Camilla now?"

"The Duchess of Cornwall," Nancy reminded him. "I'm not sure I would have gone that far with the menu."

"Let's get out of here," said Merv, urging her away from the table.

A minute later they were braving the crush inside the Blue Room, brushing up against the vice president and his eldest daughter, Liz, who had been slotted into a deputy assistant secretary's job at the State Department.

"Liz and Dick!" proclaimed Merv.

Cheney laughed; his daughter looked puzzled.

"You're too young," Nancy told her, as maternally as she could manage.

The vice president, recalling their May encounter at the fundraiser for the *Air Force One* pavilion, gave the former First Lady a courtly kiss and a mischievous greeting: "We've got to stop meeting like this."

"Oh, we will!" said Nancy. Since Ronnie's passing, thoughts of death were never far away or even unwelcome. She waved to Cheney's wife, Lynne, who stood a few feet away next to their other daughter, the lesbian. Mrs. Cheney had a nervous chaperone's aspect, because the daughter had brought her girlfriend. Nancy wondered: If Patti had gone that route, taken up with some butch but nice antinuclear activist, would it have been any worse than the male yoga teacher, briefly a husband, the one whose name usually now escaped her?

The president and Laura entered the room; just barely, it was so crowded. The Marine Band's "Strolling Strings" played a light, low-key version of "Hail to the Chief," appropriate for what wasn't technically a state dinner—not unless word came halfway through that the prince's mother had just dropped dead. Nancy thought of all the protocol screw-ups bound to occur on such an ambiguous occasion, and then remembered with relief that this problem now belonged to that East Wing chief of staff who'd loused up the china—not to her.

She nodded to the president and he nodded back.

Bush was still half-in and half-out of the packed Blue Room, able to see down the hallway to the spot where back in September he'd pondered the idea of picking poor Harriet for the Supreme Court. He thought about the ensuing monthlong fiasco, which had ended only yesterday with the announcement of Sam Alito's nomination—four days after the withdrawal of Harriet's. For all he knew, she was in her office even now, tidying up from the search she'd made, this time for her own replacement. "Loyalty" didn't begin to cover the extent of her devotion. He could have invited her to this thing tonight, but that would have amounted to one more mortification. Tonight, after turning out her office light, she'd head back to that apartment she'd rented, without even asking the realtor to see it, the minute they'd prevailed in 2000.

The whole ordeal involving Harriet had begun with that look on her face—all fear and no joy—when he told her she was his choice. And she'd been right: the thing was doomed from the minute she started going to all the Senate offices she'd walked John Roberts through a couple of months before. Being remembered as "staff" made it hard for all those upper-house blowhards and would-be presidents to adjust their vision and see her in Roberts's role. And when she started answering their questions, it became apparent—at least that's what people said—that she just wasn't on a par with John. (But this story that she'd tripped up on the meaning of "probable cause"? It had to be a new urban legend.) All of their *own* bastards—like Kristol, Quayle's old egghead, and Frum, who'd written two speeches here before going off to write a book—had kept it up against Harriet, in print and on cable, for weeks.

Time to plunge into the room. Ten minutes of chatter, then the pictures, and he could get this dinner back on schedule. The prince was just ahead of him, talking to Tom Brokaw, telling the newsman "how interesting it was to hear, from the president, just now upstairs, about all the Earth-friendly features of his ranch house. Remarkable, really, what it does with rainwater and so forth."

"Sounds interesting for sure," said Brokaw, with that leaky lisp.

"Yeah," said Bush, looking at the now-retired anchor. "I know that comes as a surprise to you all. I'm usually not happy unless I'm out there scorching and plundering the planet." He made himself wink at Brokaw; the anger was gone by the time his eyelid reopened.

The prince, unruffled by the sarcasm, kissed Nancy Reagan.

"I see I don't need to introduce you two," said Bush. *She was at your wedding to your first wife, after all.* He recalled Mother making fun of Nancy's big garden-party hat.

What the president didn't know, thought Nancy, is that Charles, charmed by her in '81, still wrote to her from time to time, occasionally even sharing his troubles.

Bush told the prince: "I'm remembering the first time I met your mom—I suppose I should say Her Majesty. It was here at a dinner Dad and Mother gave."

Charles smiled with unexpected broadness. "She recently reminded me. Gave us both a briefing before we came over." The Duchess of Cornwall, until earlier this year Mrs. Camilla Parker-Bowles, had joined the little cluster by the president, who continued with his anecdote: "Her Majesty asked me if I was the black sheep in my family. Pretty intuitive! I conceded the point and asked who was the one in *hers.* She never answered." Everyone laughed. "I was often 'inappropriate' in those days."

He could see they were all thinking *when you were still boozing,* but he'd realized in telling this story that his bit of banter with the queen had occurred five years after he'd exiled whiskey from his life. He wondered for a moment what parts of himself had never changed with the end of the drinking. The fast gear-grinding of his moods, from third to reverse and back again—what would it take to put an end to that?

"So who would it have been?" Camilla asked Charles. "The black sheep." It was a nervy question to pose, given that her own dark wool had so recently been bleached to something lighter.

Charles's syllables turned to a mush of mumbling, scarcely audible inside the Blue Room's din. "Black sheep? Our family? Rather hard to say. Fergie, I suppose. Was she still on the scene in—when was this? Ninety-one? Ninety-two?"

Nancy was carefully appraising the former Mrs. Parker-Bowles, this horsey homewrecker. You had to grant some esteem to any woman who could make a man leave a wife fourteen years younger than herself. Even so, Nancy had never thought Diana to be that beautiful—the nose was too big. And *dumb?* She could hear herself posing the question in Joan Rivers's voice. *Please!* That night Diana had been here, at the start of Ronnie's second term, dancing with Travolta and lighting up with a sudden, evident sexuality. Nancy could remember thinking: *Honey, you're barking up the wrong tree—again.*

She could tell that Camilla liked her, maybe because they both belonged to the sorority of second wives, though Jane Wyman was so far in the past that fewer and fewer people remembered any of that. With demure mischief, Nancy now drew the duchess's attention first to Laura Bush's burnt-orange dress and then to Condi Rice's red one—clearly both de la Rentas—and finally to Oscar himself, a guest tonight, standing beneath a portrait of William Howard Taft that made the designer look all the more elegant and slender.

"Do you think the two ladies chose their dresses together, as a little surprise for him?" she asked Camilla, before realizing that the duchess didn't have the faintest idea what she was talking about, and probably didn't even know who'd designed what she was wearing herself. Just as well, thought Nancy: that boxy jacket over the wide taffeta skirt made her look like a Dutch door. Oh, well. She supposed there was less likelihood than she'd imagined of something simpatico developing between them.

Looking for a different subject altogether, Camilla said, "A genealogist has informed me that I and the president's mother, Mrs. Barbara Bush, are eighteenth cousins, once removed."

Strike two, thought Nancy.

The duchess took the prince by his elbow. "Time to move you about," she said, propelling him, not gently, in the direction of the secretary of state.

"A pleasure to see you again," the prince told Condoleezza Rice. "Will you be playing the piano for us later? On the way in Mr. Ma told me that you'd performed with him once." Like de la Renta, Yo-Yo Ma was here in something of a dual capacity: he was a guest, but he'd also be playing the cello for them after dinner.

"I accompanied him, *very* badly, at a ceremony for medal-winners in the arts, back in 2002," Condi said, surprising the prince with her precision. She realized he could hardly be expected to match this exactitude about his own forty-year blur of ribbon-cutting apprenticeship. He could also, she worried, detect a trace of longing in her phrasing, *back in 2002*. That time before Iraq, those months of emergency unity after 9/11, a period for which she was already nostalgic in the way that ordinary Brits, folk a generation older than the prince, liked to sit around on Christmas watching movies about the Blitz.

"Mr. Straw, the foreign secretary," Charles reported, "had a bang-up time at that restaurant in Tusca—"

"Tuscaloosa," Condi explained. "Jim 'N Nick's Bar-B-Q."

"He met your aunts," the prince added.

"He did indeed." Condi politely turned her attention to the duchess. "Did you enjoy Anacostia?" Earlier today Camilla and Charles had visited a charter boarding school in one of the city's poorer neighborhoods.

"Oh, very much so," said the duchess. "The children were quite game. They'd ask one anything."

As the three of them chatted, Condi thought about the barnstorming through Alabama, a trip Jim Wilkinson had been determined to have her make, to build her up in the media in support of an eventual run for office. She hated herself for having gone along with it, for letting herself be, even more than usual, the sunny voice of moderation and competence and racial transcendence—another Colin with the female angle added for good measure. She'd allowed herself to stand in the Sixteenth Street Baptist Church, in front of the stained-glass window still pocked with a hole from the bombing; an hour later she'd extolled George Wallace for having built up the tech sector of state public education.

No, she would never cross over to the electoral side of politics. People told her that was the only way to achieve real independence, earned autonomy, in the political world she'd chosen to conquer step by step, rung by rung, as if moving through Iraq: *clear, hold, and build*—how she'd described America's stick-to-itive strategy to the Foreign Relations Committee a couple of weeks ago. No, if Charles Windsor here could inherit his one lifelong job, she could be appointed to all of hers. The ballot box, the great prize of the civil rights movement, would turn her into Pandora if she approached it: the world's evils might not escape from under its lid, but every compromise and stifling and self-suppression to be performed would fly out and devour her with shame.

She had learned, long before becoming the nation's chief diplomat, simultaneously to conduct one discussion with the live people in front of her and another with the forces in her head. The First Lady now approached, with a polite "May I?", unaware that it was this other, internal discussion she was really interrupting, not the one Condi was having with Charles and Camilla.

"The duchess was telling me about the school visit she and the prince made today," Condi explained to Laura.

"We brought a great many books from home with us. Made a little donation," added Camilla.

"Oh!" cried Condi, turning directly to the First Lady. "That reminds me! I haven't thanked you for my e-reader!"

"When we had the Book Festival back in September," Mrs. Bush explained to the royal couple, "Secretary Rice told me that she'd never really done much reading for pleasure." It was true, said Condi. She'd been reading all her life, but almost always as a matter of study, the book in one hand and a pencil in the other.

"Why an e-reader, then?" asked the prince. For weeks Condi had been wondering the same thing.

"You can't underline and annotate it," Laura explained. "Can't turn it into work." She was certain that Condi had never yet even booted up the device. If she had, she would have noticed that it had been stocked for her with six novels.

As Mrs. Bush excused herself to greet the mayor of Washington, Condi noticed Rumsfeld coming toward her. He'd been leading General Honoré around the room like a prize horse, as if to claim credit for recent success with *that* Occupation, the one of New Orleans, but the general had now set off on his own, and the chairman of Sotheby's had captured Charles and Camilla. There was no chance of her escaping Don.

And he was angry; the tiny eyes were shooting lasers instead of the usual twinkles. He was still, she knew, irked about her recent Senate testimony, her *clear, hold, and build* trinity, which he would have heard as stressing the military over the political, and which would have sounded like *forever* to him.

"Sending Zelikow back to Iraq for a fourth trip?" he asked her. "I've heard as much."

"I'm still waiting for the Pentagon to do something about what he found on the third one," she answered, referencing Phil's discovery that the IEDs going off in Iraq were deadlier than ever because Iran was supplying the insurgents with new parts—a donation the Shia mullahs were not really making to the Sunnis, but in behalf of chaos.

"You should have emphasized the handover, not the 'building' we're doing," said Rumsfeld.

The bicycle seat, *again*, thought Condi. "I guess I was just trying to speak 'the common language of the heart,'" she said, scornfully employing one of Karen's dippier expressions.

"You appointed her," said the defense secretary.

Mocking the phrase just now had been a terrible slip, Condi realized, a revelation of her own doubts about Karen—something Don would undoubtedly try using to his advantage. "The president appointed her," she lamely replied. Her anger, at Don and herself, swelled. "Have you had a handshake with the prince yet? You can add a picture of it to your collection."

He knew of course that she was making a reference to Saddam;

Rumsfeld was the only one in the administration who'd ever met the dictator and been photographed doing it, back in '83, during Reagan's tilt toward Iraq. And yet, thought Condi, Don had been the first to urge a move against Baghdad, the morning after September 11. Just as he was now the one who wanted out the fastest.

She detested him, and because she did she found herself, at moments, actually *liking* him: he was the rare person whose respect she didn't crave and whom she didn't want to please. In that sense he was like her new e-reader—an object on which she didn't have to perform any work. As he walked away, she looked over at Dick and felt the same curious affection. The president was approaching his veep, and in Bush's eyes Condi detected anything *but* affection. Things between those two grew worse by the week, with the president lately angry over Dick's lukewarm public defense of Harriet. Neither Cheney nor Rove had wanted the nomination to be made, but as the weeks of the White House counsel's agony wore on, only Andy recommended that the boss stop the bleeding and shut things down before she was mortified by a televised confirmation hearing.

Condi turned away, but wondered what was being said across the room.

"So how do you see this playing out?" the president asked through especially pursed lips.

"Karl could give you a better reading of that," Cheney responded.

"I want to know what *you* think." Half the press still believed he was Dick's Jerry Mahoney doll. But if they looked a little closer they'd see some wooden-teeth marks on Dick's neck. He almost wondered if Cheney, once Harriet's nomination was made, had *wanted* a crash-and-burn spectacle, one that would make a point about the need for conservative purity, the sort of thing that Dick and his brainiac friends in the Federalist Society thought essential. (God, was he getting as paranoid as Nixon? A moment ago, at the sight of Roberts taking a drink from a tray, he'd wondered if the only reason the new chief justice had extolled Harriet—which he *had*—was that he wanted to shine all the brighter.)

Dick knew his question about things "playing out" referred to a story in this morning's *Post* by one of the two Danas (Priest? Milbank? he could never keep them straight). The article had drawn attention to all the "black-site" prisons the CIA had set up in other countries over the past four years, and then revealed the "rendition" of second-string terrorists to jails in Morocco and Jordan and some dubious old East Bloc countries turned allies, what Rumsfeld liked to call New Europe.

Yes, Bush thought, a few days after 9/11 he had signed the order allowing all of that. Those little partnerships had begun to sprout and shift—Thailand was in, Thailand was out—and before you knew it, things had been going on for years, the arrangements becoming a very regular, very irregular government program. The number of terrorists swept up had grown with the funds available; it might as well be fucking Medicare Part D.

Now it was all in the *Post*'s glaring light of day, and there was no getting around the fact that it was Dick who'd let this get out of hand. Condi had been trying to put the damned thing on a sounder legal footing and been thwarted by Cheney and Don all along the way. And then last month Dick had backed him into a corner by trying to exempt CIA guys from torture prosecutions. Ninety votes against that in the Senate! Now, just to stand firm, he might have to veto the whole Pentagon budget, which wouldn't even reach his desk if it didn't keep the CIA guys accountable. No, he didn't think "enhanced interrogation" was torture any more than Dick did; he had no illusions about the people they were fighting. But if you listened to Dick—or to the two Danas, for that matter—you'd conclude that those techniques were the things we were fighting *for*, an end in themselves instead of a nasty, regrettable means toward something good.

He motioned for Rumsfeld to come join them. "Work this out," he told both men. "Even if you have to bring in Pelosi and Reid and kiss McCain's ass. *Work it out.*" Otherwise it was going to be the levee that broke and let the whole Freedom Agenda drown.

He started walking down the hall with Cheney and Rumsfeld, the three of them on their way with everybody else to the State Dining Room, and he was getting an over-the-shoulder look of disapproval from Mother, who wanted him to know he should be paying more attention to his non-administration guests. From her point of view his little gab with Dick and Don was like reading the paper at the breakfast table. He shot her his own comically wounded look, and hoped the expression would also convey a little assertion: *You know, by now I've been doing this longer than you and Dad did it.*

Rumsfeld seemed to want to make the most of this unexpected moment, good party manners or not.

"Would you like to hear from Ms. O'Connor over in Iraq? Directly?" the secretary asked the president.

"Sure," said Bush. "You can tell her I'm already hearing from her boyfriend, the Weatherman. Getting plenty of visionary advice from him." Some of it had come the other day: *The waters have washed away a lot of illusions here, Mr. President. I've begun to think we should delay the guidebook; wait until we can produce a book about a whole new city that's been remade more justly than the one before.* He'd almost replied to this with a joke—something like, "Hey, you're at the Arts endowment, not Faith-Based Initiatives"—but decided he didn't want to alienate the guy more than he already had. And he was eager to know where Ms. Allison O'Connor fit into his story.

Rumsfeld looked curious, as if with this reference to a "boyfriend" he'd just been tossed an "unknown unknown" that needed to be turned into something else.

"The Weatherman?" Don asked as they entered the dining room.

"A nickname," the president answered. *You figure it out.*

He sat down to a bowl of celery broth and shrimp, across from the Prince of Wales, whom he'd started to think of as POW. He wondered if Charlie would start plucking the little crustaceans from the soup, fearing they'd suffered some inorganic mistreatment. On his right he was delighted to have David Herbert Donald, the author of maybe the best of all the Lincoln biographies he'd read in this house. He introduced the prince to "Professor Donald, from Harvard," who was here with his daughter-in-law.

"Professor *Emeritus*," Donald corrected; a gentle joke about advancing age.

"Like *President* Emeritus over there," said Bush, pointing to his father and resisting the envy that overcame him whenever he was feeling sorry for himself. He wasn't envious of the neat and successful little war against Saddam that Dad had conducted; it was the chance that 41 got to watch all those Communist dominoes fall into place as New Europe, after someone else had given them the push.

It was a mean thought, but he was in a mean mood. He shifted his gaze from Dad to Mother, who was giving Jenna's new boyfriend the third degree. Already impatient for them to clear away these green, drowned shrimp, he turned to Professor Donald and asked: "Is it too late for me to grow a beard?"

The historian hazarded a guess as to what was bothering his host. "This morning's paper?"

Bush answered with a barrage of rhetorical questions, the sort Lincoln himself always used: "Didn't Lincoln suspend habeas corpus just when he was issuing the Emancipation Proclamation? Were those two things a contradiction? Or was the first maybe *necessary* to the second?"

"Well," said Donald, "he suspended habeas corpus just before he took big losses in the midterms."

Bush scowled, as if his guest had overstepped. But he quickly banished the facial expression and said, "Touché." Then he darkened again, with the thought that Lincoln had issued both those sweeping legal commands only when he was realizing he knew as much as his officers about what worked, and what didn't, on the battlefield. God knows he wasn't feeling that himself.

"'A streak of ruthless determination,'" he finally said.

"Pardon?" asked Professor Donald.

"I'm quoting you—about Lincoln."

"Oh," said Donald, cautiously, wondering if the president was really going to enter into a discussion of those black sites.

"I've got it, too," said Bush. "But it comes and goes."

"Then it can't be ruthless," Donald reasoned.

"Or useful," Bush added.

22

NOVEMBER 16–17, 2005

One Observatory Circle, Washington, D.C.

Dr. Kissinger's limousine proceeded along Massachusetts Avenue, passing the Vatican embassy. POPE HIDES PEDOPHILES read the banner held by a solitary man on the sidewalk, the same man Kissinger had seen the last time he passed here on his way to someone's memorial service in the National Cathedral. In fact, he'd seen this protester dozens of times before that; for years. Whether the fellow was noble or crazy, it was hard to tell; but his persistence was unsettling. A kind of Buddhist monk who never burnt out.

As his car went through the gates of his destination, Kissinger looked at the observatory dome beside the vice president's official domicile. He wondered for a moment whether the daily sight of it, and a sense of the astronomers' celestial business, impelled Cheney to take a long, semi-cosmic view of things. The pinpoint pictures of a spy satellite were one thing; but a useful proportionality might be supplied if they were laid next to pictures made by a telescope photographing the whole of the heavens.

Kissinger supposed that the years had by now rendered him a bit Chinese when it came to these things.

With the assistance of his driver, the former secretary of state made it up the steps into the white brick house first used in its vice-presidential capacity by Nelson Rockefeller, his real patron, beyond anything Nixon had been. Kissinger's ancient form, more or less spherical these days, huffed and puffed as it padded into the dining room. Cheney—eighteen years younger but not, with that heart, the actuarial favorite here—rose to greet him. They took possession of a pair of club chairs, off to the side of the room, for some pre-lunch conversation. This almost-monthly meal usually took place downtown in the EOB, and in recognition of the change of scene, as a kind of substitute for a house tour, Cheney pointed to a couple of paintings on the wall, abstract pastels selected from the National Gallery by his wife. Kissinger recognized them as the work of Helen Frankenthaler, thanks to his years in and out of Rockefeller's many mansions: the governor had been a prodigious collector of both women and modern art.

Cheney had proposed today's different location. With the president in Asia, the red-hot-center appeal of the White House, still potent for Kissinger, would be diminished.

"It's a good thing they hadn't acquired this place in Agnew's time," the former secretary mused, in his guttural growl, about Nixon's corrupt veep. "He would have stripped away the copper piping before any of his successors got to use it."

Cheney displayed his slanted smile. Three decades ago he and Henry had shared the Nixon and Ford years, sometimes locking horns toward the end. His memory preferred the moments when he'd had to separate Kissinger's giant ego from Moynihan's—two Harvard hot-air balloons in a continual belly-bumping contest.

When his guest arrived, the vice president had been looking over the typed pages of a speech he would be delivering tonight. He liked to have a good advance command of his text but tended to forgo any preening preparation before the office teleprompter.

Kissinger, pointing to the sheaf of papers, asked: "Is that going to be what Kristof recommended?" The *New York Times* columnist had declared the need for Cheney to give a "Checkers speech" telling the public whether or not he had asked the now-indicted Scooter Libby to leak the name of Joe Wilson's CIA-agent wife.

"Kristof can't be much of a student of the boss," Cheney reflected. The "boss" of course meant Nixon. "He's hoping for a confession, and the boss didn't go in for that."

"Well," said Kissinger—the "w" sounding even now more like a "v"—"at least not until he was out of office."

"My subject tonight is what you Ph.D.s, like Lynne, call 'revisionism.'" The vice president located a key line in the draft and read it aloud: *"What we're hearing now is some politicians contradicting their own statements and making a play for political advantage in the middle of a war."*

Kissinger nodded, worrying his lower lip with an index finger.

"I have another one coming up next week at AEI," said Cheney, referencing the conservative think tank. "I talk about *shameless* revisionism in that one." The slash of his mouth, self-amused, seesawed in the opposite direction from the one it had traveled a moment before.

"Where is the speech tonight?" asked Kissinger.

"Down at the Mayflower. Frontiers of Freedom Institute, or something like that." The White House had decided on a new rapid-and-sustained response to congressional criticism. It remained unclear whether Scott McClellan, the still-callow press secretary, would be up to such a task at each noontime briefing, but Cheney had decided, with tonight's speech, to send a strong signal of the new approach.

Kissinger could hear Nixon's morose voice in his head. *It depends on who writes the history.* "Maybe it's still a little early in the war to be talking about revisionism?" he asked.

"Henry," replied Cheney, "the participants—the legislators who voted for war—are already practicing it. Saying they didn't have access to the same intelligence we did before they cast their vote. It's a crock." Bush himself had begun the counterattack at a Veterans Day speech last week in Pennsylvania—*it is deeply irresponsible to rewrite the history of how that war began*—while his vice president laid the wreath at Arlington.

Kissinger nodded, apparently conceding the point, though Cheney knew from long experience that this didn't mean he *actually* conceded it. "You're talking about things like that piece by little Johnny Appleseed," the secretary grumbled. John Edwards, Cheney's opponent in last year's vice-presidential race, had finally published his op-ed about his war vote, "I Was Wrong," in Sunday's *Washington Post.*

"Yeah," said Cheney. "Of course, the translation of 'I Was Wrong' is '*They* Were Wrong.'"

"That goes without saying," Kissinger replied. "And there's an argument for letting it remain unsaid. Think of the uncountable hours the boss spent letting the antiwar movement get under his skin. You've already lost the battle for public opinion. You now need only to worry about losing the war."

Cheney, determined never to apologize for the uncomplicated relief he'd felt last year after telling the self-cherishing Senator Leahy to go fuck himself, gave Kissinger a look to indicate that he would take this recommendation of restraint under advisement.

For his part, the former secretary decided to change the subject. "All the Europeans have been calling Condi about that other *Post* piece—not Edwards's, but the thing about the black sites."

"Did she tell you that?"

"No," said Kissinger, almost offended at the suggestion that he would need to depend on Condoleezza Rice to know this. "The Europeans tell me this."

The vice president picked up a phone. He asked an aide to go into his briefcase and bring two copies of "the Zelikow memo" to the dining room.

"What is this?" asked Kissinger. "The latest from Condi's eyes and ears in Iraq?"

"No," explained Cheney. "A little project Zelikow is working on back here, along with Bellinger, Condi's legal guy, and Gordon England—whom Rumsfeld lent out, reluctantly, from DoD. An attempt to regulate the interrogations and renditions." The vice president turned to the sixth page of the document, which contained a passage he read aloud and found especially distasteful: "*'There is a risk that some intelligence may be lost when enemy captives are ultimately placed in a less coercive regular detention system. As in our prior wars, this risk should be recognized, but accepted as necessary to maintain the integrity of the system and our common, fundamental values.'*" He looked up at Kissinger and said, "If you accept *that* risk, you put *everything* at risk."

It was difficult to tell if Henry was nodding assent or nodding off. A Navy steward's tinkling of a small bell revived him. The lunch plates were on the table. Once there himself, Kissinger asked Cheney about his recently resigned chief of staff: "Do you miss Libby?"

His host answered, unhesitatingly, "Yes. The indictment is crap. The president ought to pardon him, sooner rather than later." He looked closely at Kissinger, attempting to discern whether his guest believed, like the prosecutors, that Scooter had lied in order to protect him. Kissinger, opening his napkin, appeared all at once expressive and inscrutable, like a stone gargoyle atop an Oxford college. "The boss was never the same after Haldeman left," he finally said.

"I don't change much," replied Cheney.

———

Videoconference between 2206 Kalorama Road, Washington, D.C., and the Republican Palace, Baghdad

"Did I get you out of bed?" Rumsfeld asked from a secure connection on the second floor of his seven-bedroom home. A slice of moonlight glinted on the computer screen. The house's shutters were open far enough to reveal the pool and gardens below.

"I don't sleep a lot these days," replied Allie. It was 8:30 p.m. in Washington; 3:30 a.m. in Baghdad. She had, an hour ago, gotten a message on her new BlackBerry requesting that she arrange a video call with the secretary of defense for sometime tomorrow afternoon. She'd decided that now was as good a time as any, and after a quick relay of messages Rumsfeld had agreed. A soldier from the Republic of Georgia, the easternmost piece of Rumsfeld's New Europe, had just run her from the Rashid to the Republican Palace.

"I'm seeing trail mix on your desk," said the smiling defense secretary. "Is that a midnight snack or an early-morning breakfast?"

"Just a craving," Allie replied.

Rumsfeld seemed intrigued by the wording. "How's the work going?" he asked.

"They've got me involved mostly with the tribunal. I'm with some very good people. When it starts back up, I think you'll be seeing something much tighter, much better arranged, than the opening session."

In the weeks since that chaotic afternoon, she'd regularly been seeing Fadhil's widow and daughter. The loose blouse she had on now was a present from Rukia, who continually urged her to get back to America with her own as-yet-unborn girl. *Allie, you forgive me, but is crazy for you to be here.* In between such importunings, she listened to Rukia's tales of the reprisals visited upon the other Shia families of Dujail, not just Fadhil's, after the assassination attempt in '82. Inside one of her Velcro-fastened pants pockets Allie now carried a relic she had been unable to refuse: a bloodstained two inches of rope acquired years ago by a friend of Fadhil's father on a visit to his own son in Abu Ghraib.

"And yourself, sir?" asked Allie, archly casual. "How are things in your world?" She knew, of course, that he wanted something.

Rumsfeld ignored the question, choosing instead to enter his mental landscape of categories and classification: "The trial: where would you say it belongs on the spectrum of 'clear, hold, and build'? We've been hearing a lot of that phrase."

"Yes, I know," said Allie. She'd noticed it not just in Rice's testimony but in Bush's Veterans Day speech. "I'd say it's 'build.' Saddam was 'cleared'—or cleared away—in '03. By showing the justice behind that action, this tribunal won't just consolidate it. The trial will offer the Iraqis a better judicial world than what they're used to." She noticed Rumsfeld's right eyebrow go up: the twinkle below it crumpled, like a piece of spun sugar, into skepticism.

"I'm still trying to get the president to stop at 'hold,' and to stay even *there* only temporarily."

"Yes," said Allie, "I know." She wasn't inclined to elaborate on the assessment she'd just given him.

"I'm hoping that your latest observations over there will strengthen the case you were making to him in Crawford. He'd be glad to hear from you—a personal debriefing, perhaps. Don't you think it's maybe time for your strange R&R over there to come to an end?" The twinkle was back.

"He *told* you he'd enjoy hearing from me?"

"Yes, he says he's also getting reports from your friend Mr. Weatherall in Louisiana."

She stared at him for a second. Her hand involuntarily seized a piece of carob from the trail mix.

"No, Allison, you haven't been surveilled. The president briefly mentioned to me a friend of yours in New Orleans that he nicknamed 'Weatherman.' It didn't take much more than a little flipping through the Federal Directory to figure out whom he was talking about."

Rumsfeld's *twinkle* seemed to be twinkling. Allie couldn't tell whether the delight was simple self-congratulation or something truly sinister. All he added, neutrally, was: "I'm now guessing why you were in New Orleans when the hurricane struck."

"Would you like me to brief the president before or after my leave begins?"

"Leave?"

"Yes. Pre- and post-natal. I'll need a few months."

He said nothing. Allie wondered whether the admission of her pregnancy, which there would soon be no concealing, had even been necessary. The fact of it might already have come to Rumsfeld through his cherished deductive capacities, or from the surveillance he denied having undertaken.

"Anytime before New Year's would be all right," the defense secretary finally replied.

"I'll be home by December eleventh."

"No need to say more," Rumsfeld added. "'Don't ask, don't tell,' and all that sort of thing."

"I might remind you that those kinds of standards don't apply to civilians—leaving aside whether they should apply to the military. Which, by the way, they shouldn't."

Realizing that this was genuine frost, not banter, Rumsfeld offered what seemed to border on an apology. "I really don't mean to pry, Allison."

"You already have, sir. And you've probably leapt to several incorrect conclusions."

"Perhaps *incidentally* incorrect. But correct in the main. And 'conclusions' are what I'd actually like to speak of. If we don't bring this war to our own conclusion, the other side may bring it to theirs."

"I take it you mean the Democrats, not the Sunnis."

"That's right," said Rumsfeld.

"I've seen the Murtha story," Allie informed him. An old-school Pennsylvania House Democrat, a bemedalled Vietnam combat veteran, had just turned against the war in a speech rebutting Cheney's of the night before. He'd come close to calling the vice president a draft dodger, and had capped things off by introducing a resolution to withdraw troops from Iraq.

"As of tonight he's the latest media hero," Rumsfeld said. "You won't be hearing much about his old willingness to take bribes—are you old enough to remember the Abscam investigation?—or the suspicions surrounding all those Purple Hearts he collected."

"Why not let him pass his resolution?" Allie suggested. "Have the Democrats force you out of Iraq and then blame the collapse on them."

"For one thing," Rumsfeld replied, "he can only pass it with Republican votes, which he won't get. And for another, passing it would permanently weaken the presidency. Fighting against that is the biggest bond Cheney and I have—ever since the days of Nixon and the War Powers Act."

"The imperial presidency."

"Long may its scepter wave! You know why Cheney and I have credibility on this? Because we both served in Congress and know you can't run a war out of there. The president needs to perform a withdrawal on his own terms, not with Nancy Pelosi prodding him in the back with some rolled-up congressional resolution."

"Clear, hold, clear out," said Allie. "Before the Sunnis or the Democrats force Bush's hand."

Rumsfeld appeared puzzled by the sarcasm in her tone. "What happened to 'zero' being your preferred troop level? You don't sound very fervent about finding a quicker way to get to that."

"You mean, am I going 'wobbly' on you?" She could count on his remembering Mrs. Thatcher's spine-stiffening words to the current president's father in advance of the Gulf War. "Or to put it more precisely: Are you worried that I'm wobbling on my wobbliness?"

"Are you?" asked Rumsfeld.

Allie decided to say nothing more than "I'd be happy to give the president my most recent impressions."

The secretary sent another quizzical look across the six thousand miles between them. He appeared to be wondering how the formerly "known known" on his monitor might be turning into a less-certain isotope of her former self. "Happy Thanksgiving, Allison. We'll be glad to have you home before Christmas."

Once his image left her screen, Allie pushed a button and let the Georgian soldier know she'd be ready to leave in five minutes. She decided to do a quick log-in to her e-mail, where she again found YOU AND ME AND MUCH MORE, the subject line of something from Ross at neah.gov, the boldface indicating that after five days in her in-box it remained unopened. For the first time, however, she noticed that the document contained 146KB of text, which suggested even more than "much more." But still she didn't open it.

From the other Velcroed pocket of her pants, the one not occupied by the bloody relic, she extracted a letter that Dr. Asefi had sent to her from Kabul via Washington. It had arrived this morning and she now reread it:

Dear Madame O'Connor:

Greetings to you—and a puzzle for your entertainment!

Here are eighteen pieces of a torn watercolor. If you can fit them back together you will see the picture of a pretty girl in a pink dress. Separately they look like rose petals, do they not?—but they are even more lovely whole.

Quite apart from those oil paintings that you heard about, these pieces come from a large case inside our humble National Gallery. There are many more thousands of such little pieces, created by the Taliban (such artists without knowing it!) when they tore up all the drawings and unframed watercolors with human faces that they could find. Most of these were never, I admit to you, very good, but if I might, I would invoke what the English especially like to call "the principle of the thing." I ask with all humility—having received permission of Mrs. Morris to put the question to you—if you might be able to direct us to someone

*inclined to help in the restoration of these pictures. Mrs. Morris men-
tioned that you are providing similar assistance to treasures (I hesitate
to call these rose petals such) that were found in Iraq.*

    With the greatest respect and good wishes,
    Mohammed Yusef Asefi, M.D.

    P.S. We are learning many *things from Iraq!*

She knew what the postscript meant. Since Afghanistan's September parliamentary elections, too successful for their taste, the Taliban
had imported a tactic from the Iraqi insurgents: the suicide bomb. It
was one of the few forms of cruelty they hadn't used previously. Last
week one such explosion, in Kabul, had killed eight Afghans and a
coalition soldier.

She put the letter and its paper petals back into the envelope.

Kevin, the eager beaver, had left Iraq for his new stateside job at
Bechtel, and now, at four a.m., stepping out of the Republican Palace,
Allie thought she almost missed him. If he'd still been here, she would
have given him the thrill of waving at Rumsfeld's video visage.

The Georgian soldier's English, if not so good as Dr. Asefi's, was
passable, and as they drove back to the Rashid she listened to him tell
her that he'd recently climbed up into one of the hollow metal hands
of Saddam's giant crossed-swords monument and taken pictures to
send home to Tblisi. General Schwarzkopf had wanted to blow up this
monstrosity during the Gulf War, but now, fifteen years later, some
preservationists, Iraqi and American, insisted that the 130-foot-high
swords should forever continue to meet in midair above the parade
ground, and that the little necropolis of dead Iranians' helmets at
their base should become just a curious archaeological detail to be
explained by tomorrow's guides to tomorrow's tour groups.

Allie realized that she wanted this monument destroyed. Its sustained existence somehow thwarted any actual future that might be
created here, born from what she was beginning to tell herself might
have been the right war for the wrong reason. What had unsettled her
most as she sat opposite Rumsfeld's image was not the fear of being

spied on or further enmeshed in his schemes, but a growing, slightly sickening sense that an American departure from Iraq might be worse than staying. For weeks, while working on the tribunal and hearing more and more of Fadhil's life and death, she had been able to feel the shift occurring in the pit of her stomach, another gestation happening someplace close to where Holley swam in amniotic peace.

Back inside her room in the Rashid, knowing she would not sleep any more tonight, she whispered to her unborn daughter: "Let's do a puzzle. Let's make something pretty." At a small table, she went about reassembling eighteen pink shards into the picture of a living creature.

CNN Headquarters; 820 First Street NE, Washington, D.C.

Larry King, broadcasting from the capital this week, promised viewers now tuning in "a powerhouse panel to discuss the fast-moving political developments of the last couple of days": former Texas governor Ann Richards; ex-Senate majority leader and presidential candidate Bob Dole; and, via satellite from New Orleans, former senator and recent vice-presidential nominee John Edwards.

King asked Richards and Dole, both with him in the studio, for thoughts about tomorrow's scheduled House debate on Congressman Murtha's resolution to withdraw American combat troops from Iraq.

"Well," said Richards, "who's got more military credibility, Larry? A decorated combat veteran or a president who made a few beer runs in a National Guard jet—on days he even decided to show up at his post?"

"Harsh!" said King, turning to his other guest. "Speaking of distinguished combat veterans, what does Bob Dole think?"

The former senator looked into a middle distance between his microphone and the studio's glassy backdrop. He spoke in a low rumble. "I think Hunter'll do a passable job managing the Republican side of the debate in the House."

"That's Duncan Hunter of California?" asked King, repeating information that had just come through his earpiece.

Dole realized he was already down in the weeds of procedure, one of the tendencies that had made his run against Clinton so hopeless. He tried to talk past the parliamentarian in his head: "I'm with McCain on this. I'd echo what he said the other day: it's a lie to say that the president lied to the American people about how and why we got into this war."

"Ann," said King, "the White House press secretary, Scott McClellan, says that Murtha, for all practical purposes, is now siding with Michael Moore and the president's most radical opponents."

"Oh, God, Scotty McClellan. Another *shrub*. His *mother* used to be a thorn in my side down in Texas."

"How so?" asked King.

"She got herself elected to the state Railroad Commission when I was governor. You know, Scotty's dad wrote a book that more or less has LBJ pulling the trigger against JFK in Dallas. The truth-telling gene in that family is a little recessive, Larry."

"Interesting stuff! Okay, they tell me they're ready with our remote feed from New Orleans—is that right? Yep, there he is, live from the Crescent City. Greetings, Senator Edwards! You've got some enthusiastic backup there!"

A gaggle of UNO students cheered. Edwards, wearing the same sweatshirt they all had on, said, "Thanks, Larry."

"What's the gathering down there?"

"I'm here in New Orleans fostering relief efforts and continuing to talk about poverty as the moral issue of our time, what's been turning the United States into two nations rather than one. I've been speaking on so many college campuses that I hope I have the right sweatshirt on tonight!" He flashed his recently whitened teeth as the UNO students cheered. "The only places I've been more often than campuses are homeless shelters," he added, performing a fast, seemly retraction of the smile. "But what I'm most excited about at the moment," he declared, brightening again and pushing back his forelock as if he were about to roll up his sleeves, "is a program for our great young people, like the ones behind me, called Opportunity Rocks. One of its goals is to get college students to spend their spring break, only a few months away, down here in New Orleans—not to party, but to rebuild, to do something for their fellow citizens." The students applauded. "We need effort and sweat, just as our country desperately needs leadership."

"Your op-ed piece about the war has been getting a lot of attention," said King. A graphic of the essay went up onscreen.

"I *was* wrong," said Edwards, with the solemnity he'd displayed in his mention of homeless shelters, "and I'm glad I found the courage to say so, because that's just a small fraction of the courage our troops continue displaying in this military misadventure that's been forced upon them."

King asked permission to digress for a moment: "I know that our viewers are as curious as I am to know how Elizabeth is doing."

"She's doing great!" said Edwards, tempering his delight with a trace of thanks-for-asking abashment. "She's gotten good reports from her doctors, and she's just signed a contract to write a book that I know is going to provide a lot of inspiration to a great many people."

"Terrific!" said King. "Do you miss the Senate?"

Edwards appeared surprised by the question. "I, we don't, I mean, something like the effort here, with these great young people, is the kind of thing that I was always fighting for in the Senate and in the campaign last year. And I'll continue to fight for it. You know, I've been reading a lot about Robert Kennedy lately. He was a figure who energized and roused a lot of people like my good friend there, Ann Richards."

The former governor was startled. "Oh, sure," she said at last, trying to keep her eyebrow from arching. "Bobby Kennedy was on his way to becoming the biggest force in this country."

"Thanks, Senator!" King called out to the screen.

"Thank *you*, Larry."

"We'll be back in just a minute with our guests—plus your phone calls!"

As the first commercial began, Richards turned to Dole and said,

"I met him exactly once in my life. I think you were at the same party, given by that British guy—"

"Hitchens?" asked King.

"That's the one," answered Dole.

"Well, I hope the wife makes a lot of money from that book," said Richards. "She's going to need it. They finished building that house in North Carolina. Somebody showed me one of those aerial pictures of it—you know, that Google spy-in-the-sky stuff? It looked like a combination of Tara and Jonestown. Massive. Insanely so."

"Why didn't he take the DNC chairmanship?" Dole asked her. "He could have had it, couldn't he?"

"You know how he'd have seen that job? As having to spend two years gettin' other people elected instead of four years gettin' *himself* elected—no matter that he would have collected a bushelful of IOUs to cash in during '08."

An assistant producer handed King an anonymous fax just received from someone at the Center on Poverty, Work and Opportunity. The host read the organization's name aloud to his guests.

"That's Edwards's outfit down in North Carolina," explained Dole. "It's a PAC masquerading as a think tank."

" 'The senator,' " King read, " 'currently receives fifty-five thousand dollars a speech to talk about poverty as the moral issue of our time. Most of our fundraising goes to cover his travel and expenses.' " King paused, and handed the fax back to his staffer. "Sounds disgruntled!"

"Sounds perceptive," said Richards. "Now, Larry, you let *him* plug Opportunity Knocks or whatever the hell it is, plus his wife's book. When we're back on are you going to let me plug one of *my* good works?"

"Sure. What is it?"

"A big benefit in New York next Monday night to support Women's Voices for Change."

"Is that a *real* PAC?"

"Hell, no. It's an educational foundation with a cute name. They spread knowledge about the problems of menopause."

"No kidding!" said King. "You know, I'm getting an idea for a whole different show!" He pointed back and forth between Richards and his other guest, by now the longtime spokesman for Viagra.

"Don't go there," harrumphed Dole.

"Which is what Viagra has forced so many menopausal women to say," Richards added. "It's a real testament to Bob's pitchman skills."

"You said you met Edwards only once?" Dole asked her, eager to change the subject.

"That's right."

"I met her, the wife, twice. Down at North Carolina events. Things I was at with *my* Elizabeth."

"The Tar Heel State's senior senator!" exclaimed King. "A great lady!"

"The first time I thought Mrs. Edwards was crazy about *him*, her husband. The second time I realized she was just crazy, period."

"Honey," replied Richards, "they're bound to go farther than we did."

"And we're back!" King said into the microphone.

23

DECEMBER 5, 2005

The White House; 10:18 a.m.

Bush surprised Karen Keller, his personal secretary, by reentering the Oval Office after a hallway chat with Andy Card. The president was due on the State Floor in twelve minutes for a children's holiday event, after which he'd go directly to North Carolina for a speech trumpeting the success of his tax cuts and pleading for pension reform. There would be a lip-service mention of Social Security but nothing more; the springtime initiative was politically dead.

"Big wheel keep on turnin'," sang the president, hurrying past Mrs. Keller's desk. They'd had the Kennedy Center Honors last night, and Tina Turner had been a lot more fun than Robert Redford. With "Proud Mary" he was saluting his own work ethic, his determination to make the most of the next twelve minutes and still achieve an on-time arrival at the kiddie party. Three documents lay on his desk, one of them a nine-page printout of the Weatherman's latest e-mailed jeremiad from New Orleans. These still came in every couple of weeks, and, angry as they might be, he did read them for what Laura would call their "vignettes" of people's struggles and successes. But, whoa, what was this shit about John Edwards? Bush sighed, supposing he'd have to deal with that, too, in his response.

He missed the days of g94b@aol.com, the address he'd retired, along with the habit of e-mailing, when the campaign started up in

2000. And he didn't have Dad's talent for the two-sentence handwritten note, which artfully evaded anything substantive in the way of a reply but still left the recipient feeling like a million bucks. So with the Weatherman he did the best he could: a few inked annotations in the margins of the printed e-mail. The secretary then scanned the hard copy and sent it back to rweatherall@neah.gov.

He put his first marking on page two, next to a new story about the girl who plays the clarinet atop the levee: *glad you followed up—I can get M Spellings, SecEd, to rec charter school for her?*

———

Ross was four hours and 250 miles out of Dallas, nearing Snyder and heading northwest on 84. This morning's business with Deborah in the Dallas courthouse had taken twenty minutes. They had now "filed," jointly, and their divorce would be final at some point late next year, though things between them could hardly feel more final than they did already. The pages they'd signed read like an overdetailed submission from a contributor to the guidebook: too much information in every sense of the term. *On or about May 31, Ms. O'Connor became pregnant by* . . . Deborah would have full custody of the children, whom he had not seen at Thanksgiving. Christmas, along with everything else in his life, remained up in the air.

He had put in for a week off, to do what he had to in Dallas and then go on to Lubbock, unannounced, for visits with his brother Darryl, who disapproved of the divorce, and his widowed mother, who was indifferent toward it. He didn't want to see either one of them in his current state, though he was trying to exercise some discipline, working long hours and drinking little and running each morning whether he was in Washington or New Orleans; he made a peculiar sight racing along the still-depopulated pavements of the Quarter. While in Lubbock, he also intended to check on a displaced Louisiana family that, according to a recently made FEMA friend, had been resettled in an apartment off Fourth Street, not far from the Tech campus.

Asthmatic as a boy, Ross remained sensitive to small variations in altitude, and as he drove with the window down, heading toward the West Texas Caprock, his lungs could feel that he was two thousand feet higher than the Dallas he'd left behind and below. Along with the air, the sound of the radio was thinning too, the signal from the NPR station in Abilene weaker than it had been fifteen minutes ago. But the news still came through: the announcer explained that the day after tomorrow, Pearl Harbor Day, would also mark the one-hundredth day since Katrina had made landfall. She went on to present some statistics that made the recovery seem like a new presidency, something to be judged on the extent of its transformative first-hundred-days effects. The numbers spoke mostly of failure: in New Orleans, ninety percent of buses were still not running; seventy percent of restaurants remained closed; so did 115 of 116 public schools.

Ross decided to get rid of this rental car in Lubbock and get back to the Quarter by Wednesday night, before the hundredth day had fully passed. It was a meaningless commitment, but one he would make to the place he now considered home, even if he still resided there less than half the time, in a hotel, at the government's expense.

NPR's delivery of statistics gave way to a loud cry in Arabic. The announcer translated the recorded snippet: *I am Saddam Hussein!* The fallen dictator had shouted the words, a querulous protest against lèse-majesté, at today's session of his trial in Baghdad. He and his brother then complained about what they were having to put up with in jail—to a witness who had lost seven of his own ten siblings in the Dujail massacre.

Ross switched off the radio—the story only made him think of Allie—and put on a CD by his favorite Texas band, Explosions in the Sky. "Your Hand in Mine" only made him think of her more. He had at last sent her his e-mail—by the time he did a scroll as long as a staircase runner—and had yet to receive a "read receipt," let alone a reply to his litany of observations and pleadings and animadversions. The band's country jangle of strings and chimes, along with the beauty beyond the car—not a cloud in the sky or a curve in the road—made him angry at her for always mocking this flat and windy stretch of the world, as different from Dallas as Baghdad was from New Orleans. For a moment he wanted to forget his just-made pledge and stay here the whole week, to stand on the sidelines at his nephew's Friday-night football game for Lubbock High.

He drove into Snyder, finding coffee and wi-fi inside the Student Union of Western Texas College. His open laptop revealed that he *did* have mail from the president of the United States, or at least from Karen E. Keller at whitehouse.gov—complete with an attachment and a subject-line proviso that told him all this was for his EYES ONLY.

It was strange to see Bush's penmanship along the right margins of his own e-mail. The president's script was clear and unpretentious, with a friendly, bouncing quality, but a closer look always revealed something oddly disjointed, a tendency to put spaces between syllables as if they were whole words: *wor king, impor tant*. The pen didn't want to stay down on the paper.

Ross rushed through the comments, almost always evasive, without bothering to reread the adjacent portions of his own prose:

appreciate what you're seeing

great progress

God bless her!

This last jotting commented on his story of a chambermaid in the Monteleone who now volunteered four nights a week at a church pantry.

Ross found one argumentative patch with a higher-than-usual incidence of spaces within words; a response to his own mention of John Edwards's criticism that the administration had never done enough to promote the home ownership it claimed to recognize as the best basis for a prosperous and stable society.

Edwards wrong. Dem policies had mortgage rates at 14% when Reagan and my dad took over in '80. I like Habitat for Hum., but Carter will never hammer together enough houses to = the # people couldn't buy when he was prez.

Ross was preparing a surrebuttal in his head when his eyes traveled farther down the e-mail and spotted this:

Our Lubbock friend, Ms. O'C, is on my calendar for 12/15. SecDef DR tells me she's been at Saddam's trial, home next week.

So here he was, being updated on his treacherous beloved's activities by the president of the United States, and entertaining the absurd feeling that he didn't like his unborn daughter being exposed to the atrocious tales and invective of a war-crimes tribunal.

December 15; a week from Thursday. He couldn't remember if he was even supposed to be in Washington then.

Back on 84, driving northwest again, he tried to understand the president—a man he now regarded as a maestro of catastrophe, someone whose sympathy for those suffering might be genuine enough but was too little visceral or sustained to be of use. Could it ever be tethered to fruitful action, or would it always float free, like his handwritten syllables, amiable and testy by turns? New Orleans needed something drastic and concerted, from whatever political direction it might come—even the suspect Edwards.

Ross recalled a visit, made with Father Montrose, to a man breathing on a ventilator because he'd nearly suffocated from mold inhalation. The sight of him in his hospital room had once more inflamed Ross's desire to *fix* things—along with a wrath he'd never before felt toward the world. And if it had taken self-pity to unleash it? Then good for self-pity. If Bush felt sorry for himself over disappointments in Iraq, why couldn't *he* turn that to domestic advantage and become righteous, not just bare-minimum right, about what needed to be done along the Gulf?

He ejected Explosions in the Sky and replaced it on the CD deck with a copy of Edwards's speech to the Center for American Progress in Washington. Mrs. Boggs had passed the disc on to him; Father Montrose's superior had also received one in the mail from Edwards's new organization. Through the rental car's excellent speakers, Edwards's liquid Southern voice spoke the sentences that had provoked the president's annotation when quoted in Ross's e-mail:

> *We ought to have a new WPA where we make sure that the people who have lost their homes and lost their jobs and are now displaced are able to rebuild their own city. . . .*

Ross had refrained from quoting the part that compared FEMA-trailered "Bushvilles" to the Hoovervilles of yesteryear. Next time he wouldn't be so polite.

Still suspicious of liberal pieties, as he'd been his whole adult life, Ross nonetheless hungered for passion, just as he had hungered for a different sort of it before blundering into his romance with Allie. He craved directness; he *needed* to be hammering houses together, whether or not Bush was right about the history of mortgage rates.

Should he be asking for reassignment to another agency?

Back here in Texas for the past few days he had been remembering and reconsidering the young man's crush he'd long ago developed on George W. Bush, a kind of political and personal calf love for somebody who'd thunderstruck him as the anti-Darryl. He tried thinking about it now—tried letting go of it—but he suddenly saw a road sign telling him that Slaton lay only three miles up ahead. His eyes, for less than a second, looked toward the closed laptop on the passenger seat, which contained last August's e-mail from Ann Richards: *That Bush Bash was a strange business. The fellow you ought to talk to is named Bill Bright—not that he's very—in Slaton. Some sort of builder. . . .*

He turned off 84 and soon found himself on Ninth Street, the main drag of Slaton, a town smaller than Snyder. He parked in front of a bakery whose arched pillars at the end of the sidewalk looked like hitching posts in an old TV western. "On the Atchison, Topeka and the Santa Fe" played inside; brochures were available for the town's old train station and Harvey House. Ross ordered a bear claw to go with the student-union coffee still out in the car, and asked the girl behind the counter if she knew of a builder in town named Bright.

Actually, she said, his office could be found just four or five doors down.

Ross ate the pastry without going back to the car. He was brushing crumbs from his hands by the time he stood in front of BRIGHT BUILDERS, through whose large window his eye caught a poster for Tony Sanchez, the Democrats' candidate for governor in 2002.

"He's right back there," said a woman at the front desk, the only other person here except for the proprietor, a man whose scraggly white hair descended way past his collar and whose large belly extended far beyond his belt. A moment's inspection of the sun-reddened face behind a pair of wire-rimmed glasses showed someone who might not be far into his fifties. Ross could only suppose that he *had* once met this man in Mayor Granberry's backyard. "Could I talk to you?" he asked.

"You already are."

"Could I ask you about an event that took place up in Lubbock, way back in 1978? The 'Bush Bash'?"

The man's laugh sounded hearty enough, but gave little clue as to whether it was friendly or hostile. "You a reporter? A biographer?"

"No. I was there."

The man shot him a skeptical look.

"I was sixteen," Ross explained.

"Drink any beer that night?"

"At least two. And I signed up for Bush."

"Taught you about losing, I guess. Good early life lesson."

"Did you set it up? The event."

"Sort of," said Bright. "But I wasn't the prime mover."

"Was it sabotage? I mean, you do seem like a Democrat." Ross pointed to the Sanchez poster.

"Who you been talkin' to?" asked Bright.

"Ann Richards." The answer sounded so offhandedly pompous that Ross had to remind himself it was true.

"Never met her," Bright replied.

"She says otherwise," Ross insisted. He could hear himself trying to sound hard-boiled and film-noirish. The result was ridiculous, but he stood his ground.

"I guess she meets too many people to keep them straight," Bright responded.

"She said you bragged about it."

"Who exactly are you?" asked the builder. "Maybe I can interest you in a house as well?" The remark was only half-sarcastic; part of its tone belonged to an ever-hopeful salesman. "I can build you three bedrooms on the edge of town for a hundred and nineteen thousand dollars."

Ross experienced an involuntary vision of himself and Allie and Holley in a small development flung up as quickly as the American presence in the Green Zone. Then New Orleans again took over his thoughts: if one could build that cheaply, why not right away erect a whole new city next to what was left of the old one, instead of persisting with all the current complicated, well-reasoned schemes for recovery that would die before any review process or "impact assessment" could run its course?

Bright handed him a business card.

"Is there anyone else I can find out from?" asked Ross. "About how the event started and then wound up the way it did?"

"Why do you care?"

"I'm just interested in twists of fate these days," Ross answered.

"Twists are always twisting," Bright replied. "Look at how old Kent Hance ended up. Ten years after beating W, he was a Republican delegate to the convention nominating W's daddy for president."

"Yeah," said Ross. "In New Orleans. In the Superdome."

"Proves my point. Twists are always twisting."

After a pause, Ross asked: "Was Hance behind it?"

"Why would he be?"

"Because it did him a lot more good than harm," Ross answered, exasperated even now by the thought that Kent Hance, making money off a bar, had gotten all that hypocritical mileage out of the horror of beer-drinking.

"Didn't do Bush much harm," Bright retorted.

"In the long run, no. But in the short?"

Bright didn't answer.

Trying reverse psychology, if that was even the right term, Ross finally attempted to appear indifferent: "Well, I suppose there's no way of knowing."

"The hell there isn't!" cried Bright, who tugged on a locked metal desk drawer and said no more.

24

DECEMBER 15–31, 2005

The Oval Office; December 15; 2:15 p.m.

Mistakes had been made. The speechwriters had avoided using the word, as well as the passive voice so mocked when Dad was handling Watergate contrition for the RNC all those years ago, but there was no getting around the fact that for the last couple of weeks he'd been *apologizing.* Sort of.

Anti-revisionism had been replaced by another strategic zigzag, a limited, modified mea culpa: small guilty admissions sprinkled atop a robust assertion of the Iraq policy's bedrock rightness. The media, of course, rushed to these contrite crumbs like goldfish racing to the surface of the bowl they never looked beyond. Each morsel of regret was reported as if he'd performed a Shiite's holiday self-flagellation. He had so far conceded, in a Naval Academy speech, that the "security forces" in Iraq could have been better managed; acknowledged, before the Council on Foreign Relations, that "hold and rebuild" had required a little recalibration; admitted, to the Philadelphia World Affairs Council, that the transition to democracy still needed speeding up. Yesterday, in a fourth speech, he'd summarized these three so-sorries and added another—just to make it a grand slam—about the intelligence failures.

The rationale for this new give-a-little tactic? If they swaggered a bit less, they'd gain support for the fundamentals: no retreat from the freedom = security agenda (safety at home depends on success in Iraq) and no deadlines or timetables for troop withdrawals.

Yesterday's remarks had been delivered at the Woodrow Wilson Center, another egghead venue like the CFR and that place in Philly. Just down the street, inside the Reagan Building, it seemed to provide the right atmosphere for a slight, nonparanoid repackaging of things. But of course, what the eggheads really wanted was an exorcism: hot Jimmy Swaggart tears streaming down his face; a strangled cry about having been a false god; an offer to turn around in the pulpit and submit to a stoning.

But he wasn't finished yet. Here on his desk was the draft of Iraq remarks he would deliver this Sunday night, live from the Oval to the whole country.

He pushed the typescript aside and buzzed for Condi and Hadley to come in and get him ready for McCain. He kissed his secretary of state and gently clapped his NSA on the back. "Hey, Sadly," he said to the latter, reviving a nickname Steve had briefly acquired from an uncharacteristic display of discouragement. "I can't remember. Were you in the audience yesterday?"

"No, sir. I held the fort here and left in-person attendance to the two secretaries."

Condi *had* been there, right next to Rumsfeld and close by a bunch of diplomats and members of Congress. The whole thing had looked like some mini-, made-for-TV State of the Union.

"It was smart of you to host those Democrats in the Roosevelt Room beforehand," said the secretary of state.

"You think?" Bush asked. He knew she was aware of his doubts about this whole new concession tactic. "Well, McCain will be here in nine minutes."

These days he needed to look at the clock less than ever; instinct and compulsion kept him as punctual as the sun. John would be arriving to discuss his goddamned "anti-torture" amendment to the defense appropriation bill. It had gotten through the House yesterday, 308–122, helped by a regiment of nervous Republicans that McCain had hectored into seeing things his way. Which meant that there was now nothing to do but accept it, pretend that it had always been what the newly felonious Martha Stewart would call "a good thing"—no matter that Cheney had had three meetings with McCain, letting him know the troubles his good intentions would soon cause the CIA.

On top of all else, they were about to lose reauthorization of the Patriot Act in the Senate. Could the week get any more fucked?

Condi saw his long face. "I know this is hard, Mr. President. But it's the right thing to do. And you've done the right thing on matters like this before. Remember Uzbekistan in May."

Bush looked at her and Hadley with annoyance. He had 191 countries and fifty states to keep track of; she might give him a little extra *hint* of what she had in mind from that far back. Was he supposed to just stand here while the Final Jeopardy theme played?

"Oh, yeah," he said. It had come back to him. Last spring, over in Uzbekistan, Karimov had violently suppressed some anti-corruption protests. Condi had issued a strong condemnation, and Rumsfeld then just as strongly suggested that she shut up, since we needed the Uzbeks' airfield for operations in Afghanistan. "I remember what you said," Bush assured her. "'Human rights trump security.' Don reminded me of it the other day."

"I never said that," said Condi.

"She didn't," Hadley agreed.

"It's what Don wanted to *imagine* I was saying. In the NSC meeting. But you sided with us back then, Mr. President," Condi reminded him. "Now you should actively side with McCain."

"And back in May we lost the airfield," Bush responded.

Hadley hastened to reply. "I don't think we'll lose anything with this amendment. It's a good compromise." He'd done most of the negotiating himself, in McCain's office, and it hadn't been easy, with the senator puffing up like an adder every ten minutes.

"If you sign off on this," said Condi, "it will be easier to push back on the measures you *really* don't want." Kennedy and Kerry were demanding a census of the black-site prisons.

"Well, Rove had better make damned sure to reward those 121 Republicans who stayed with me. And he ought to send a Christmas turkey to this guy Jim Marshall"—the one House Democrat, from Georgia, who had voted against the amendment.

"We need to keep McCain with us—and he *is*, on the basics," said Condi. "You'll be great with him today." She checked her watch.

"What have *you* got next?" asked the president.

"Ellen Johnson Sirleaf at two-thirty. The president-elect of Liberia."

"You're going to be late." Bush spoke the words like a fatal diagnosis. Condi's face fell, but she refrained from pointing out that she could be back at State in under five minutes. The president walked her to a different door from the one through which McCain would be entering.

"Karen around?" he asked Condi.

"Oh, yes." The sigh accompanying the words betrayed her feeling that the undersecretary of state for public diplomacy was in town a bit too *much*. After flopping in the Middle East, Mrs. Hughes had spent a few days in Asia and a few more in Central America, but that was the extent of her international travel during the last three months. "I saw something this morning," Condi remarked, as encouragingly as she could, since the president was not prepared to admit to himself what she already had—that Karen was not working out. "She's got an event next month in connection with Eid al-Adha, the Muslim holiday."

"Good," said Bush.

"At the Islamic Society of Frederick, Maryland."

The president's bad mood came back in full force, and he returned to the earlier subject. "Well, I guess none of us will have to spin 'torture' anymore, now that John has his way. We'll just have to spin the damage done by some suitcase nuke when it explodes in Times Square."

Both Hadley and Condi knew there was no point in replying. There was also no time. Just as Condi exited, McCain entered the office with Virginia's John Warner. The national security advisor remained, and the four men now present sat down on two couches.

"Okay, boil it down for me," said the president, looking at Hadley instead of the senators.

The national security advisor went over the wording—prohibitions against torture and descriptions of correct interrogation procedure—that would now go into the Army Field Manual.

"What do *we* get?" asked Bush, pointedly making McCain the adversary.

Hadley described the bone that had been tossed the administration's way: while intelligence officers accused of misconduct would have no immunity from prosecution, they would be granted a certain latitude in their defense—if they could provide evidence of having been led astray by 'good faith reliance on advice of counsel' prior to the questionable interrogation.

The president turned to McCain. "You good with that?"

"I can live with it," said the senator. "Especially since it's been on the table for about a month." The big smile he flashed said: *You're only taking the deal now because the House vote was so lopsided, and because you've cratered in the polls.* The grin swelled McCain's golfball-shaped cheek; he looked as if he'd made a hole in one inside his own mouth.

Bush nodded, and exhibited some okay-our-business-is-done body language. Should he allow a moment for small talk, even a joke, before they let the press in? Okay, he would try: "Did you ride over—"

But he stopped himself before he could add "on the Straight Talk Express?"—that fatuously named hot tub of a campaign bus for all the adoring media who'd six years ago covered McCain (mostly with kisses) during the primaries. Instead, he finished the question by saying "together?"

"Well, yeah," said Warner, with some bafflement.

The president searched for a bit of Christian charity within himself, remembering that McCain's facial golfball came from the way melanoma surgery had affected his jaw muscles. He also tried to remind himself of how much water John had carried for him ever since Iraq began, and especially in the past month: *It's a lie to say that the president lied. . . .* Even so, whenever they were in the same room all the anger from that old do-or-die South Carolina contest, all the dirty tricks and sanctimony, came right back and overwhelmed the two of them.

"Is Dick busy?" McCain asked cheerfully. He would love to be grinding the vice president's face into this loss over the amendment.

"Yeah," Bush answered, without smiling. "So's Porter." Goss, the CIA chief, liked the amendment no better than Cheney did.

The president thought back to his visit to Seoul last month, to the momentary signal he'd finally received from Putin about North Korea—an encouraging one. Looking at John, he now vowed to himself that if a joint operation actually came off, McCain wouldn't find out about it even ten minutes before his darling press corps did.

"Shall we?" asked Bush.

The four of them straightened up for the entering media. The cameras did their cicada overkill, a hundred hums and clicks, while he paid tribute to McCain as, what else, "a good man," one "who honors the values of America." He reminded the newspeople of today's parliamentary elections in Iraq, hoping they'd find a little airtime for that story too. The voters over there were bravely overcoming the "rejectionists"—a new term they'd been slipping into his speeches, like some piece of slang that Barbara and Jenna had picked up at the mall in Austin.

He listened to McCain praise him and Hadley for helping "to resolve this very difficult issue." For a moment he considered joking that the talks had been a form of "enhanced interrogation," with John as the inquisitor, but he stopped himself, knowing that the same reporters smiling at him now would within minutes be contrasting his "insensitivity" with McCain's moral heroism.

Click. Whirr. Click. Whirr.

McCain broke the silence. "We've sent a message to the world that the United States is not like the terrorists."

Click. Whirr. Click. Whirr.

"I think we send that message every day," Bush responded.

———

Five minutes later, Mrs. Keller showed Allison O'Connor in.

"You catch any of that?" Bush asked his latest visitor.

"A little bit." Fox News had been on in the waiting area.

"What'd you think?"

"Sir, the best way to protect everyone is to keep them from participating in anything over the line. Any Army officer will tell you this."

Bush scowled. "We're not talking about just the Army. We're talking about civilian intelligence officers too."

"They'll tell you the same. How many men from Dujail were tortured because, ostensibly, they might 'know something'?"

Bush, who knew from the tribunal reports what had long ago gone down in that Iraqi village, snapped: "You're going to equate a dictator's reprisals with an interrogator's attempt to prevent a terrorist act?"

"Are you *sure* there's no element of reprisal in the latter? Ever?"

With a steely look: "Yes."

"Then you have more certainty than I do."

"Actually, you seem pretty damned certain about most things." He wondered why he'd let Rumsfeld put him through this. He wanted to change the subject and get her out of here fast. "Heard anything yet about the Sunni turnout?"

"It's up substantially, even in Salah ad-Din province. I just heard from an NSC colleague." She waggled her BlackBerry.

A large smile signaled Bush's mood swing: Salah ad-Din contained Saddam's hometown of Tikrit. "Today, Salah-whatever; tomorrow maybe Anbar!" he exclaimed. In the latter province, a year after the bodies of American soldiers had been dangled from a bridge, the Sunni insurgency remained full-on. The week before last, ten Marines had been killed in the abattoir that was Fallujah. "But I suspect you differ," he added, knowing she would wet-blanket any optimism he displayed.

As it turned out, she didn't. She raised her plastic water bottle and said, "Tomorrow maybe even Hong Kong," without any sarcasm that he could detect. The Chinese had been coming down hard on pro-democracy demonstrators there. Bush thought he could hear a slight longing—even an uncertainty—in her voice. This was not the same woman who'd been at Crawford in August.

"The Chinese are ignoring the obvious," he responded. "People want to be free."

Ms. O'Connor smiled with a softness he couldn't recall. Did she just lack the energy for more argument, even though both of them knew that argument was Rumsfeld's purpose in arranging for her to be here today? *Christ, wait a minute.* He'd just noticed: *Was she pregnant?* "I may be doing a little ignoring of the obvious myself," he blurted, sounding half-paternal and half like a frat boy.

Allie felt a measure of relief at having this out of the way. Her choice of outfit had a deliberate oh-fuck-it aspect: a dressy, unbuttoned blouse over a shell top that hid nothing of what her late father would have called her "condition." She even managed to smile again.

"I know from Rumsfeld that you've had a hard time since August," said the president. "I also know we've got a mutual friend."

"The Weatherman."

"Yeah," said Bush. "But it's really none of my business."

She realized that he knew or had figured out more than he was admitting. She could sense disapproval (of the adultery, and the drama) mixed with approbation (she was clearly keeping the baby) as well as a certain plain human sympathy. Altogether: compassionate conservatism.

"Even so," said Bush, politely prying, "are you set up all right?"

"Yes, thank you, sir. I'm taking a bit of a leave soon. My mother will run my life for a while."

"I know a little about that! But once she's through with you, he, or she"—he pointed to her midsection—"will start running it."

Flooded with a surreal sense of her immediate circumstances, Allie tried bringing the conversation back to their business, which was ill-defined enough. Instead of telling him that the baby would be a girl, she handed him a memo.

"What's this?"

"My thoughts on the setup of the tribunal. We've done a good job, given the situation. We can hold our heads high, legally."

"Thank you. I should have had you in here with McCain and Warner." He was darkening a little, and so was she. Allie felt a *can-I-go-now?* look coming over her features. For the sake of courtesy she tried finding more to say as he glanced at the memo. "I've been listening to your speeches," she told him.

"What did you hear? 'Mistakes were made' or 'Stay the course'? We're not going to zero, Ms. O'Connor. And there'll be no deadlines."

"I'm not suggesting that."

"You suggested it at the ranch."

"You said yesterday that the intelligence was wrong but that we still made the right decision to go into Iraq."

"Yes," he said. He waited a few seconds for her to say more. "I'm bracing myself now for some *logic*, which half the time I find is just games."

Actually, she had begun leaving logic to Rumsfeld, had started replacing it with a new instinct that told her even "known knowns" could only arise and remain in place through a certain amount of faith, and fierceness. "Doing the right thing for the wrong reason has begun to speak to me," she finally said. She handed him an envelope containing the small length of bloody rope she'd received from Rukia. A card, also enclosed, explained the object. "Keep this with Officer Howard's badge." She referred to the shield of a dead New York policeman, which Bush had carried in his pocket throughout the fifty-one months since 9/11.

———

The Blue Room; 7:05 p.m. the Same Day

As soon as he entered, Karen Hughes gave the president a hug and pushed him a gentle few inches toward some mistletoe. Looking up at it, Bush said, "The way things are going I'm surprised this isn't the sword of Damocles."

"Those bastards," whispered Karen, who knew her boss must be thinking of the same sudden development that had everyone here talking: a *New York Times* story, just up online, revealing how the National Security Agency, with the president's authorization, had been listening in on lots of domestic telephone conversations.

"I pleaded with Sulzberger," Bush told Karen.

"I'm sure you did! And you don't do pleading often or easily."

The president had had the *Times*'s publisher, Arthur "Pinch" Sulzberger, son of "Punch," down here ten days ago, and asked him not to run the story. The guy was all geeky humor at the start, implying that they could work this matter out, scion to scion, Punch's Pinch to 41's Shrub. He'd seemed surprised to find the president of the United States so goddamned *serious* about the whole thing. And then he'd quietly dug in. By the time it was over, all he would offer was a short, unspecified delay in going to press.

"Timing's a little suspicious, don't you think?" Bush asked his one-time press secretary.

"A *little*?" replied Karen. "The same day as McCain and just before the Patriot Act debate? These horrible people. Do you know what's all over the European news? Not the Iraqi elections. Oh, no, perish the thought! All they're talking about is the execution of that gangbanger in California. Believe me, I've *tried* to get them to change the subject."

Her BlackBerry buzzed. "Al Jazeera," she said with an eye-roll, after checking the screen. "Sorry." She shut off the device.

"Actually," said the president, "you ought to take it."

He walked off to get into position for another hundred photos; he'd already done at least that many with the guests at this afternoon's party for the military. Eight holiday mob scenes down; eight more to go. The thought of passing the halfway point put a spring in his step. But en route to his designated spot in front of the Christmas tree, he decided he'd better have a quick word with the vice president.

"I think you should go up to the Hill tomorrow and calm people down about this NSA business." Of course, Dick was more likely to inflame at least half of them, but things might be reaching the point where the true-believers needed to be firmed up. Six months from now the Alamo could be falling, and he didn't want to die there alone. "I know you've got a lot on your plate," he added. Cheney was getting ready to leave for Kabul and the swearing-in of the Afghan parliament. For God's sake—and for all the credit they got—by this point they'd helped set up more elections than the League of Women Voters!

Cheney nodded. "I wonder how many of Sulzberger's employees are heading home over the Brooklyn Bridge tonight." A plot to bring it down had been exposed by exactly the sort of NSA intercept the *Times* had now revealed and deplored.

"Thanks, Dick." He patted Cheney's arm and went over to kiss his mother, who would be here with Dad for most of the next ten days, until Christmas at Camp David. She stood near a gingerbread house while a nervous female Marine explained how one of these had been a feature of the decorations ever since the Nixons lived here. Mrs. Bush leaned over and looked into one of the little baked windows. "I think I see a tiny microphone."

A nearby NSC staffer, whose name the president tried to recall, complimented him on yesterday's speech at the Wilson Center.

"I could have done without the Harry Truman reference," said Barbara Bush.

"Overkill?" asked her son. He had pointed out how the democracy-building American occupation of Japan had eventually proved skeptics wrong. "Should have kept that more *subliminable*?"

The NSC man laughed more heartily than was necessary.

"No," said Mrs. Bush. "I just didn't see why you had to mention that awful *man*. Truman."

At this particular party, mostly for White House staff and agency appointees, there was less to worry about from overheard remarks than at the festivities already held for the press and Congress and diplomats. A good thing, too, thought the president, because Mother, who like all Bushes read the poll numbers, looked in a mood to bite off one of the gingerbread chimneys.

Laura signaled for him to hurry up and take his place between the Christmas tree and the Marine photographer's big Sunbounce panel, which would keep everybody free from harsh shadows and lit with holiday sparkle.

Those who'd already had their pictures taken began to head for the State Dining Room, passing as they went, on an easel set up in the hall, the painting Jamie Wyeth had done for this year's White House holiday card. It depicted the first family's three pets on a snow-covered South Lawn. On a table not far from the easel stood three little topiary sculptures of Barney, Miss Beazley, and the variously named cat. "Oh, God almighty!" said Barbara Bush as she passed them.

Near the Dining Room's huge and slightly monotonous buffet stood Mary Matalin, who'd given up political consulting and senior-staffing with Cheney to take an editor's job at Simon & Schuster. She asked Karl Rove: "Are you going to do a book for me?"

"It's a little early for that, isn't it?"

Matalin's husband and political opposite, James Carville, answered for her: "Not if they throw the book *at* you."

Mary gave out with a long-suffering groan over her rabid spouse, whom she'd once described as looking like an eel that had swum too close to a nuclear reactor. She turned to Scott McClellan, who was trying not to notice Rove, and put her arm over his shoulders: "How about you, honey?"

"A book from me? Who would be interested?"

"Come see me in '09."

Michael Gerson stood in a corner with just a cup of coffee, ostentatiously lost in thought, as if minting another *Bartlett's*-bound quotation for the Freedom Agenda. Coming over one of the thresholds into the big room, Paul Wolfowitz nervously ran a comb through his abundant hair. He held hands with his Saudi-Libyan girlfriend, a British citizen who'd been to LSE and Oxford and who'd had to depart the World Bank for a perch in Liz Cheney's shop at State when her paramour had taken over at the Bank's H Street headquarters.

"That the one who kept him from getting the CIA job too?" Carville asked Matalin, in nothing close to a whisper. His wife nodded, recalling how Wolfowitz's estranged wife had written Bush a letter of warning about the relationship. Scooter Libby had kept the envelope from reaching the president, but even so . . .

"Shaha! Paul!" cried Karen Hughes, who'd helped to implement Ms. Riza's new arrangement at State.

"Christ," said Carville. "Looking back, we could have done a little better by Monica."

Matalin noticed a man standing a few feet away, beside a marzipan Jefferson Memorial, chewing on a tiny lamb chop. His boyish features reminded her of Tom Hanks nibbling the ear of baby corn in *Big*. When she made her way over to say hello, he introduced himself as Ross Weatherall and also presented his NEAH boss, who was standing beside him. Mary remembered that the Chairman was a composer and said she thought the music tonight was wonderful. A portion of the Marine Band, seated in the State Hall, was playing "Have Yourself a Merry Little Christmas."

"That song always makes me want to kill myself," said Ross.

"Doesn't it?" said Matalin, as if discovering a shared fandom.

Karen Hughes joined them and became quickly bored by the Chairman and Ross's descriptions of their work, though she did remind both men of the fifteen New Orleans jazz bands State had sent on those thank-you tours of Katrina-donating nations. She then swooped down from her great height onto Harriet Miers a few feet away, giving her a big bless-your-heart hug before tapping the shoulder of Allen Weinstein, the national archivist, whose voice had been reduced to a whisper by Parkinson's: "Here's the woman," declared Karen, pointing to Harriet, "who should be running the George W. Bush library that you'll be building!"

Weinstein tried, above the conversational surf and the Marine Band, to explain that Ms. Miers would perhaps be better suited to the boosterish foundation that always operated in uneasy partnership with the government's supposedly neutral direction of each presidential library.

"Well," said Karen, before running off again, "I'll let you two work out the details of all that!" Weinstein and Harriet relinquished each other in grateful, mutual embarrassment. The archivist nodded hello to Ross, who once they were in conversation did his best to explain a bit about NEAH's help in preserving the rescued Iraqi Judaica. His information, alas, was anything but current: ever since Allie's self-sequestration began, he had lost track of the project.

The president and First Lady entered the Dining Room to applause, the loudest of it coming from staffers who knew just what a strain all the handshakes and photography inflicted. Bush would stay for only a few minutes. He greeted Wolfowitz near the buffet and asked if it would look rude to plunge his aching hand into the bed of chopped ice supporting the shrimp. He nodded to the woman who'd caused Wolfie so many problems; gave Mary Matalin a kiss; and ignored Carville. After shaking hands with the NEAH Chairman and the archivist, he surprised them all by placing a gentle hand between the shoulders of Ross Weatherall, whom he led off for a private word.

"I saw your friend this afternoon." He expected the Weatherman to say, "She told me," but received a look of curiosity, an eagerness for information, instead. So he added a question: "Everything okay in your life?"

Though he'd had nothing stronger to drink than the teetotaling president, Ross blurted: "I've been looking for her tonight. I see a lot of NSC people here, but—"

"You're not in touch?"

"No, sir."

"You need to correct that."

"I've been trying. It's very complicated and—she's stubborn."

"Actually," said Bush, with something of a smile, "I noticed some flexibility this afternoon."

Toward Iraq? Ross wondered. Toward *him?*

Bush winked and walked away, then turned back around after a few steps to say, "Work it out," as if issuing an executive order.

———

Prairie Chapel Ranch; December 31, 2005; 8:05 p.m.

Mrs. Welch, Laura's mother, dozed on a couch. She'd been here for a couple of days. They would be having the quietest possible New Year's Eve, a holiday that now inspired in Bush the full contempt of the ex-drinker. He looked out into the moonlight, toward a distant cedar, before returning to some paperwork on the clipboard atop his lap. He made a pencil mark by one passage of legalese:

The executive branch shall construe Title X in Division A of the Act, relating to detainees, in a manner consistent with the constitutional authority of the President to supervise the unitary executive branch and as Commander in Chief and consistent with the constitutional limitations on the judicial power, which will assist in achieving the shared objective of the Congress and the President, evidenced in Title X, of protecting the American people from further terrorist attacks.

He picked up the phone and asked an operator to get hold of the White House counsel. Harriet—home, sure enough, on New Year's Eve—was soon on the line. He said he was sorry to bother her but had just been reading through the signing statement for the McCain legislation. He read her the sentences he'd marked. "Do the words mean what I think they mean?"

"Not to put too fine a point on it," Harriet answered, "they mean that you can do what you want. You remain the final arbiter of things, whatever the act might say."

Which is what he'd surmised: the hardliners in Cheney's shop had prepared this. "Has Hadley seen what I've got in front of me?"

Harriet said she didn't know.

"Okay," the president replied. "I hope you've got some champagne in the fridge." She assured him that she'd be with some downstairs neighbors at midnight.

He picked up a Sharpie and autographed both the bill and the addendum, feeling fresh anger toward McCain—though nothing like the anger John would feel once he read this signing statement. He also experienced a new flash of ire toward Tom DeLay, who could have kept the GOP House members in line on this if he hadn't gotten himself indicted for corruption, an offense that sickened the president more than any dovishness on either side of the aisle.

Dick would see this signing statement as a victory, but he shouldn't.

The president was tired of his number two's in-the-bunker zealotry, even when he shared it. The only thing that irked him more than Cheney's Svengali reputation was McCain's should-have-been-president stature. The press had constructed both images. Well, Dick wouldn't be learning about North Korea much in advance of John.

He needed to brace himself for tomorrow's San Antonio hospital visit: more missing limbs and PTSD.

From there it would be directly back to the White House, where he would see everything, all of it, through.

25

JANUARY 15, 2006

623 Bourbon Street, New Orleans

"Lindy, darlin'," said Mrs. Caine, "there'll be *no* taking no for an answer. We are having a *huge* bash for your ninetieth in March, even if, sadly, you won't be here."

Mrs. Boggs joined her guests in taking a wistful look around the courtyard, where it was just warm enough on this January evening for a round of pre-dinner cocktails. The hurricane's damage to everything—the house, the garden—wasn't catastrophic, but severe enough in combination with her advanced age to have convinced the evening's hostess it was time to move, and soon, closer to her children in Washington.

Ross could see what the storm had done to this spot he remembered from August. The angel statue was gone; it had broken, Mrs. Caine explained, when the magnolia tree, also now carted away, had fallen. Looking down, Ross thought of Allie's BlackBerry slithering across one of the flagstones after he'd fallen to his knees here, hours before Katrina made landfall. He now asked Mrs. Caine about damage to the house's interior, and the realtor gave a little shudder. "That lovely little writing room on the third floor," she said, shaking her head and tsking forlornly. But she began to effervesce once she remembered that she would soon be hired to *sell* this house, perhaps even to a friend of someone overhearing what she said to Mr. Weatherall. "But once it's fixed up, what a nursery that little room could make!"

The slow pace of the city's recovery was the chief topic of conversation here tonight and throughout New Orleans. The president had visited on Thursday, speaking at the Convention and Visitors Bureau along with the mayor, but not the governor.

Ray Nagin was again among Mrs. Boggs's guests tonight. "I can't say I blame Governor Blank for ducking W," he said, loud enough for his backhanded compliment of Kathleen Blanco, whom he detested, to be heard by Mr. Capehart of the Chamber of Commerce and just about everyone else as well. "She won't ever have to deal with any video of her clapping when Bush said, 'Yeah, let's rebuild the levees, but I can't promise we can make them withstand another category-five storm.'"

Mrs. Boggs remarked, appreciatively: "Not being there *was* a bit of mischief on Kathleen's part." The governor had made a point of going off to the Netherlands—to talk with flood-control experts—while the president was in town, and she was even skipping this little dinner connected to the guidebook being produced by Bush's NEAH. Ross had stayed on the sidelines at the convention center, presenting a sample chapter, "The Garden District," to local businesspeople, emphasizing the economical speed with which the guidebook project was running. He and the president had only waved to each other after the speech, whose stay-the-course message Ross had found wan and exasperating.

"Four months is a long time," Father Montrose said to the mayor.

"Yeah," said Nagin, "but we got through them." He raised his glass, saluting the city's grit; everybody else in Mrs. Boggs's courtyard raised theirs as well.

"I'm talking about the four months *ahead*," said the priest. "That's a long time for people to wait before they're told whether or not they're welcome to come back to their own city."

Nagin gave him a hard look. The mayor had been on the defensive for days, ever since his own Bring New Orleans Back Commission recommended a four-month freeze on reconstruction work in the hardest-hit neighborhoods. During this period a decision would be made about whether to rebuild at all. Was the mayor, people won-

dered, doing the bidding of the municipal establishment that had
taken a chance on him in '02? Would this black man who'd come from
nothing deliver to them a less poor, less black, storm-scrubbed city?

"Father, I think you need a little patience," said Nagin. "If you've
got enough of that to wait for the Second Coming, you could spend a
bit of it on our construction issues. If anybody tries to rebuild some of
these houses before the new infrastructure is figured out, well"—he
tossed an ice cube from his drink into Mrs. Boggs's fountain—"those
houses are likely to dissolve on you just like that."

"Shall we?" asked Mrs. Boggs, inserting her frail form between the
mayor and the priest and urging her guests inside. Mrs. Nagin sooth-
ingly took Father Montrose's free hand and sat herself beside him at
the big dining-room table under the bronze chandelier. Mrs. Caine
was on Ross's right. Curiously, between Mrs. Boggs at the head of the
table and Bobby Jindal, the Republican congressman, there was an
empty chair.

While a maid set out the appetizer of Creole shrimp and deviled
eggs, Nagin asked Ross how his second cousin's niece was getting
on in the guidebook office. Ross told the mayor that she'd decided to
move on, but assured him the young woman was being supplied with
good references and some job leads. Nagin responded with a skeptical
glance; his wife looked embarrassed.

Mrs. Caine announced to the table that Mr. Weatherall had a treat
for them. When he'd been here last March, he'd confessed to the old
WPA guide's neglect of number 623 Bourbon Street, this beautiful if
bruised house they were all in tonight. "He told us he would try to
make amends in this update that's aborning, and I think he now has
something more to tell us about that."

Ross stood up, as if to give a toast. He took a sheet of paper from
his breast pocket and explained that soon, following the old entry for
number 601, there would be another for number 623. The new passage would begin with the house's construction in 1795, tell the story
of Mangin the blacksmith, who'd made it his dwelling and his forge,
and end with a reference to how the structure "eventually became
the home of Lindy Claiborne Boggs, member of Congress from 1973

through 1990 and U.S. representative to the Holy See from 1997 to 2001."

"I feel like a statue!" exclaimed Mrs. Boggs.

Though everyone laughed, they all appeared to be having the same unfortunate thought: the stone angel destroyed in the courtyard seemed to make even statues an emblem of transience, not immortality.

Once Ross sat down, the mayor pointed to the old guidebook that had been set out on a nearby table. "How much of that one was about Uptown rather than every other part of this city? Was it anything like proportionate? You going to fix that?"

Ross recited some page-count statistics about the greater justice that would be done this time around to Tremé and the Lower Ninth and other neighborhoods.

The mayor, turning folksy, flashed everyone his biggest smile and announced, "*I've* got the draft of something in *my* pocket. I wonder if I can get all of your thoughts on this." It was a brief Martin Luther King Day speech, to be delivered at City Hall tomorrow morning. "Maybe you can help me to get it sounding eloquent and off-the-cuff all at once," Nagin joked, before reading from a single sheet of paper: " 'When I woke up early this morning, and I was reflecting upon what I would say that could be meaningful for this grand occasion, I decided to talk directly to Dr. King.' . . ."

"Sounds like Hillary gabbing with Eleanor Roosevelt's portrait," said Congressman Jindal.

Nagin ignored him and continued with his text: " 'Now, you might think I'm experiencing post-Katrina stress disorder. But I was talking to Dr. King and I just wanted to know what he would think if he looked down today at this celebration. What would he think about Katrina? What would he think about all the people stuck in the Superdome and the Convention Center with us unable to make the state and the federal government come do something about it? And he said, 'I wouldn't like that.' "

Mrs. Caine ventured an objection. "Well, I don't like it either, but I don't think that we can speak for the dead with any certainty."

Nagin took no notice of her; he was seeking approval, not correction. " 'As we think about rebuilding New Orleans'—this part, by the way, is me, not Dr. King—'surely we need to recognize that God is mad at America. He's sending hurricane after hurricane, laying stress and destruction on this country. Surely he's not approving of our being in Iraq under false pretenses.' "

Eyes turned toward Ross and Jindal, the supposed Bush partisans. Mrs. Boggs sought to take the pressure off them by saying, softly, "Mayor, I think God works in *mysterious* ways. We can't really be sure, can we, of what He means by sending us these trials?"

"Well, Lindy," said Father Montrose from the other end of the table, "we do need to divine His meanings. Or at least to try."

"Thank you. That's just what I'm doing," said Nagin. He went back to reading—a few lines about the need for black unity and self-discipline—before saying, "Now let me give you my peroration here. 'It's time for us to rebuild a city that's a chocolate New Orleans! And I don't care what people are saying Uptown or wherever they are. This city will be chocolate at the end of the day! This city will be a majority African-American city. It's the way God wants it to be.' "

He wasn't finished, but Jindal put a stop to the oration. "Let me tell you what this is really about," he said, looking at Ross, the out-of-towner, who remembered the tension that had simmered between the mayor and the congressman at this same table last March. "Ray's a little concerned about his reelection a few months from now. He's worried about all those absentee ballots that'll be coming in from still-displaced black voters—aren't you, Ray?" This April, Nagin would be facing Mitch Landrieu, Blanco's lieutenant governor, a white liberal and part of the latest family gumbo to feed the state's politics: Landrieu's father had been mayor, and his sister Mary was the senator who'd come unglued on *Air Force One* a few days after the hurricane. "You see, Mr. Weatherall," explained Jindal, "Ray is like most of us politicians. He needs to have things both ways."

Nagin swelled formidably, after a great inhalation of breath. Though still seated, he now loomed over the slightly built congressman. "I'm telling these black folks that I'm going to bring them *back*."

"That four-month moratorium won't even be over by April," Father Montrose reminded the mayor. "Are you going to let the evacuees help to reelect you and then give them the bad news that your commission has decided against their returning after all?"

Nagin stayed focused on Jindal. "God, Bobby, three years ago I even endorsed you over Blanco in the governor's race! Before you went and lost. Why are you being so nasty to me now?"

"With all due thanks, Ray, that old endorsement of yours just proves my point. You're all over the place, always have been. You're happy to make opposite promises to the Uptowners and the poor." He paused. "But I'll give you another chance to support me for governor next year."

The congressman may have hoped this joke would lighten the mood, but it failed. Silence prevailed at the table for nearly half a minute, ending only with simultaneous commotions from the kitchen and the front of the house. As the chicken Oscar entrée came through the swing doors, Mrs. Boggs's maid went to answer the doorbell. Sarcastic tones and scolding could soon be heard in the vestibule. The politicians at the table recognized the sound of an underling being chewed out.

With a gentle assist from Mr. Capehart, the Chamber of Commerce man, Mrs. Boggs rose from her seat to greet the new arrival, the owner of the reprimanding voice.

"Our surprise guest," she announced. "I wasn't sure he'd make it!"

A short-sleeved Senator John Edwards, pushing down a boyish cowlick that had been gelled into place an hour before, cried, "Lindy!" He took both her hands. "I'm so sorry I'm late. A logistical screwup. I'm in 'the valley of staff.'" He let out a knowing, put-upon sigh and proceeded, with a smile that rivaled Nagin's, to shake hands with everyone around the table. "Please, everyone, go ahead and eat. And please forgive me for how I look. I've been working 'in the bowl' all day."

The phrase signified the lowest-lying and most-devastated portion of the city, but Edwards's use of it—one could almost hear the quotation marks—seemed so odd and self-congratulatory that Nagin and Jindal shared a furtive, unifying glance, one that seemed to say: *Does anyone else here realize what an asshole this guy is?*

Edwards took his place in the empty chair beside Mrs. Boggs, while one of the catering people brought him some chicken Oscar. The server's momentary presence prompted the senator to inform the table: "You know, I've recently been in San Francisco. The hotel workers out there are beginning to unionize with some real effectiveness. I'm hoping to help their counterparts in New Orleans to do the same."

Jindal was ready to point out that a period in which hotels were struggling to reopen and workers had no homes from which to commute might not be the optimum time for a union-membership drive, but what was the point? Edwards, he could tell, had acquired this focus-grouped position—something to help him stake out a spot on the left edge of the Democratic establishment before '08 arrived—as if it were a chip that had been inserted in his brain. "Hillary with you on that?" the congressman settled for asking.

Edwards smiled. "She's a remarkable woman. I first met her about ten years ago, when she was still First Lady. Elizabeth and I went to the White House with our boy Wade, after he was a finalist in the Voice of America essay-writing contest." The senator bit his lip. Everyone here knew the terrible story of his teenaged son's accidental death.

"I'm sure she was lovely," Mrs. Boggs said of Mrs. Clinton.

Edwards expressed agreement with this estimation of his likely primary opponent two years from now. After a pause, he continued in a kind of confiding whisper to the whole table: "I don't know when, or if, I'll announce in '08 . . . so much, really all of it, depends on Elizabeth's health."

Everyone murmured "Of course."

"Is that *blood* on your shirt?" Mrs. Caine asked Edwards, with sudden alarm. "Just to the side of the pocket."

"Oh," said the senator, looking down at the stain as if he hadn't noticed it before. "I got caught on a nail while repairing a house in the Lower Ninth this afternoon. I'm fine, ma'am." His eyelids fluttered, but his tiny cowlick stood firm. While waiting for several admiring glances to run their course, he failed to notice, in his right peripheral vision, the disapproving expressions of Nagin and Jindal. "I'm always trying to be the man my wife thinks I can be," he added quietly. And then, as if to say "enough of that," he began speaking of the spring-break volunteer proposal he'd been pitching at his campus appearances and on *Larry King Live.* "Easter is such a special time," he observed, looking down the table to Father Montrose's clerical collar. "You know, my son died on Maundy Thursday."

Jindal whispered to Nagin: "Do Baptists observe that?"

Nagin whispered back: "Somebody ghostwrites this guy's *conversation.*"

"A few of those spring-break students can stay here!" Mrs. Boggs suggested.

"They could do a little work on *this* house!" joked Mrs. Caine.

Amidst the laughter, Ross remembered the thoughts he'd had during his long Texas car ride last month, the ones about wanting to get his hands dirty, to feel his own muscles hammering houses together. So what if it meant getting stabbed by a nail? And so what if there was something maybe a little smarmy about Edwards?

People in New Orleans sometimes had to remind themselves that they were allowed to discuss things besides the storm—the way several years ago New Yorkers had learned to give themselves permission for talk that didn't include 9/11. Over the next half hour, Mrs. Boggs's diners turned their attention to the house's furnishings, the food on their plates, and then, as always in this city, to food more generally. Tonight's chatter finally came around to the Super Bowl playoffs, with Edwards confessing that he'd taken a break from his reconstructive labors to watch a few televised minutes of the Carolina Panthers beating the Chicago Bears. Shortly after this admission, the senator became the first to rise from the table, with a sheepish apology for "eating and running."

"Oh, he's *running* all right!" joked Jindal, with the same sort of edge he'd displayed toward Nagin.

Edwards mentioned a small group of hotel workers he'd promised to meet with before the night was over. Ross, suddenly eager for a private word, followed him to the door.

"You won't remember me," he said, apologetically, "but we met last spring at Christopher Hitchens's party." He described his job at the agency.

"The NEAH does some fine work with education," Edwards quickly averred. "I've been supporting an effort in North Carolina to provide a copy of *To Kill a Mockingbird* to every junior high school student in the state."

"We're trying to get all sorts of books into the hands of people displaced by Kat—"

"You know, my youngest son is named John *Atticus* Edwards. We call him Jack."

Ross responded by saying that he had been impressed by Edwards's speech to the Center for American Progress and had personally drawn President Bush's attention to it. He now seemed to be gaining Edwards's attention too. "My praise of some particulars didn't please him." Ross promised the senator that he would pass along the spring-break idea to the White House, and that he would pitch in himself when the students got here. As it was, on his own trips to the city he'd begun helping out in the same soup kitchen where the chambermaid from the Monteleone volunteered.

"Stay in touch with our efforts," said Edwards. Ross shook his hand and went back to the dining room to say his own goodbyes.

The maid opened the front door for the senator, revealing a group of demonstrators on the sidewalk near his SUV. Their signs proclaimed: MAKE THE FEDS PAY and WE NEED A LEVY FOR THE LEVEES and CAT-FIVE-FORTIFIED OR NOTHING. Edwards regarded them with a wounded look until his aide, bringing him toward the car, explained that the protesters were there not to criticize *him* but to put pressure on the mayor, whose evening whereabouts they'd managed to get hold of. Reassured, the senator went over to shake hands with them.

Mrs. Caine and Father Montrose were also leaving the house. The realtor introduced herself to Edwards's young aide, who was now waiting for his boss, a few feet away, to finish up. The senator, without having been asked, had begun autographing the demonstrators' signs.

"Where do you go next?" Mrs. Caine asked the staffer.

He smirked. "Wherever his wife tells him. Or wherever she doesn't know about in between."

Even in a city as indiscreet as this, the boy's response startled Mrs. Caine, who could see in his face the very real resentment that had motivated it. She was also surprised that he was wearing, with nothing atop it, a T-shirt that hadn't seen the laundry for some time. "Things do get rather warm here," she remarked, "but shouldn't you have on an actual shirt?"

"I had to give him mine. He liked the blood on it. I got between a pliers and a nail this afternoon."

"Interesting," said the realtor, as she scrutinized the senator, still in curbside conversation. Turning around in search of Father Montrose, she saw him standing next to Nagin. The mayor, still none too pleased by the priest's moratorium remarks, was writing out some sort of note for him. Father Montrose waved, indicating that Mrs. Caine should probably grab a ride home with someone else.

Ross returned to the hall just after the priest finished with Nagin. "Can I interest you in a nighttime adventure?" Father Montrose asked, waving a card with the signature of the now-departed mayor. Ross assumed that this might be the launch of another gentle flirtation, like the one the priest had attempted outside that bar on St. Ann last March. He asked, with a smile, "Is that a free drinks card?"

"More like a wartime safe-conduct pass. From the mayor—but really from Frank Minyard, a friend of mine for forty years."

Ross thought he recalled the name from the news.

"He's the city coroner," Father Montrose explained. "This adventure involves a favor I'm doing for a parishioner whose stepdaughter disappeared in August."

Ross felt he could hardly say no, and a moment later found himself in the priest's Chevy Caprice—no Humvee this time—heading toward a warehouse on Poydras Street. The business district seemed only normally deserted, like any other on a Sunday night, until one remembered that things here would still be close to lifeless tomorrow morning.

A city security guard, impressed by the mayor's signature, let them enter a chilled, cavernous space containing what Ross for a moment took to be an art installation: a hundred or more large white boxes. Were they meant to represent FEMA trailers?

"They're caskets," said Father Montrose. "Very plain ones. The unclaimed and the unknown. My parishioner believes her stepdaughter may be inside one of them."

For a second Ross thought that they were about to look inside each box. But the priest explained: "She just wants me to walk among them and pray. You're welcome to join me."

Ross imagined the bodies in various states of active decomposition, just as somewhere tonight Holley was accruing more and more life and form, awaiting her emergence from Allie into the world.

"Father," said Ross. "I have a daughter."

"Yes, that lively fourteen-year-old you've told me about."

"No, another daughter. One a couple of months away from being born." As if he were Catholic and this dark warehouse a confessional, Ross imparted the story of his lover and newest child. The priest, accustomed to impulsive bids for absolution, listened calmly, and when Ross was finished he put a purely pastoral hand on his shoulder.

Glad that his face wasn't fully visible, the younger man asked: "Father, was God in the Superdome?"

The answer he expected—a faithful yes, with a few mutterings about His inexplicable ways—didn't come. "No," said Father Montrose. "I don't believe He was. The devil may have been." He then repeated his invitation: "Would you like to walk and pray with me?"

"Shouldn't we be concerned with the *living*?" Ross replied with some fierceness. The priest gently responded: "Dear boy, these *are* the living."

26

FEBRUARY 24, 2006

Residence of the Vice President; Observatory Circle, Washington, D.C.

It wasn't yet noon, but with only a week or two of her pregnancy to go, Allie had started feeling tired more or less constantly. She stared at the soothing pastel Frankenthalers on the wall of the Cheneys' living room, thinking she might fall asleep even as she eavesdropped on two NSC colleagues making nervous jokes while they all awaited the vice president's arrival.

"Did you know," one asked the other, "that Bush put Harry Whittington on the Texas Funeral Commission? He might have gotten bumped for conflict of interest if he'd disclosed plans to go hunting with the boss!"

The other staffer hid a smile behind his hand. It had been thirteen days since Cheney had accidentally shot and wounded one of his fellow quail hunters down at the giant southeast Texas ranch of Anne Armstrong, a Republican stalwart who'd been Ford's ambassador to Britain. Whittington had not, as Cheney believed, been a good deal off to the rear collecting his kill from a previous covey. He was close by, and got a face full of birdshot the next time the vice president fired.

"They could have gotten him to take care of Terry Schiavo," the second NSC man whispered. "Made it look like an accident. Would have solved the whole thing."

Both of them were getting the giggles, like two boys in the back of a classroom. "By the way," whispered the first. "The boss's gun was made in Italy. Just like Oswald's. *Think about it.*"

This last joke was not on Cheney but on the press corps, which had spun itself into a frenzy of indignant speculation over the vice president's tardy disclosure of the hunting accident to a little Corpus Christi paper rather than one of the national dailies or the AP. The damage to the administration's press relations, which were bad at the best of times, had been surprisingly serious.

Mary Matalin now entered the room with the VP. More than a week ago she'd been summoned from her editorial job in New York to do damage control for her old boss. Still around and looking tired, she had wound up dueling over the incident with Don Imus on his radio show, and trying to appease the first family. Laura Bush was even more annoyed than her husband about how things had been handled.

Allie felt certain that she again owed her own presence here to Rumsfeld, that he had inserted her into this meeting whose agenda would consist of the accelerating calamities in Iraq. Two days ago, Sunni insurgents had bombed the Golden Mosque in Samarra, destroying the dome of this Shia holy of holies, and since then the Shiites had been conducting reprisals against Sunni mosques, twenty-seven so far.

Before sitting down, Cheney shook Allie's hand, saying he remembered her from Crawford last August. The tilt of his mouth indicated wry recognition of her impending motherhood. She'd gained a minimum amount of weight over the last several months, and was carrying her little girl small and wide, but her body language by now conveyed the single word *soon.* Monday would be her last day on the job; Holley would come a week or so after that.

As he settled into his chair, Cheney appeared to be looking, still, for Scooter Libby. But the meeting's participants consisted of only the vice president, Allie, Matalin, Steve Hadley, and the two other NSC staffers, both Iraq experts, who had recovered their sense of decorum. One of them poured himself a second cup of coffee, and Cheney, taking notice, observed: "Careful. That stuff can be addictive—like oil."

Matalin and Hadley laughed politely but exchanged surprised glances at this sarcastic reference to Bush's just having urged the country, in his latest State of the Union address, toward less reliance on fossil fuels, a prescription the former CEO of Halliburton regarded as soft-hearted nonsense. Had things gotten to the point where the president and his number two openly made fun of each other? One had the feeling that Bush was probably repeating all of the hunting-accident jokes that Leno and Letterman kept making each night.

Cheney got down to business: "How do we help Khalilzad?"

Hadley responded first. "By making plain that he's not to blame for what's going on right now, even if some groups are making him out to be." The ambassador to Iraq had several days ago made a statement that seemed to suggest the U.S. might begin to withdraw if the Iraqis didn't speed up their formation of a new government. Had he thereby encouraged the fanatics?

"Zal's now saying that we'll help them rebuild the dome," one of the NSC staffers noted.

If that's so, thought Allie, Rumsfeld will be moving to recall him: he won't want an ambassador who's nation-building, literally, from here to high heaven. She had heard only this morning from Rukia, who had been visiting angry Shiite relatives in Sadr City, about the sudden, chaotic swelling of vengeance. American troops were constantly patrolling the Green Zone's perimeter, and a daytime curfew, which sounded like a contradiction in terms, had been put into effect.

"There was a spike in attacks on Shiites in the days before the mosque was hit," Allie pointed out. Cheney just nodded, but she had an odd feeling that a couple of the others were raising their eyebrows, as if her observation indicated some bias toward the Shia, whereas current U.S. policy was to bend over backwards to the Sunnis, so as to increase their participation in Iraq's political process. She did sometimes now find herself feeling that such bending had reached a limbo-dancing extreme, leaving everyone to forget that the Sunnis' oppressive minority rule over the Shiites was what the U.S. had overturned in Iraq.

The conversation shifted to the continuing uncertainty about who would be the next prime minister and what it would take to get the current one, Ibrahim al-Jaafari, to step aside. "You've got to have faith," said Mary Matalin, in her curiously appealing monotone. "Look at how long it took to get Sam Alito in there." The newest Supreme Court justice, at last sworn into the seat Harriet Miers might have assumed, had provided the president's numbers with one of their few recent upticks.

"Khalilzad's problem is that he's a Sunni," declared Allie. "It hardly matters that he's also an American. How is he credibly supposed to go after the Shiite militias that are rampaging now?"

"By letting the Iraqi police do that job," said one of the NSC men, expressing, Rumsfeld-like, something between a hope and a position.

"The Shiite militias are *inside* the Iraqi police," Allie reminded him.

"Any chance," the vice president asked, "that the parliament will meet on Saturday, as it's supposed to?"

"No," said Allie.

"The biggest worry is provoking Iran," argued Hadley. "Giving them any excuse to intervene on behalf of the Shiites."

As the meeting proceeded, Allie imparted some news from the continuing Saddam tribunal, but otherwise kept quiet. Discussion zigzagged to a pessimistic close with a brief debate over whether Iraq could now be judged, officially, to be in a state of civil war. Opinions varied, but there was unanimity that the term must not be publicly employed, no matter if the reticence recalled such long-ago absurdities as insisting that Korea was a "police action" and the invasion of Cambodia an "incursion."

Once they adjourned, Allie decided to walk back toward the office along Massachusetts Avenue. She was vain about her ankles, didn't like their temporary swelling, and would get a little exercise before she had to hail a cab. It was a nice, globally warmed February day, and she had on the lightest of her two winter coats.

She had passed Thirtieth Street, reaching the point where Whitehaven ran into Massachusetts, when a man standing on the corner reached into a large box of Danish pastries and handed her one. "Come join us!" he urged. He was trying to lure the scant pedestrian traffic to the Embassy of Denmark a block or so down Whitehaven: Would she care to add to a show of support for the Danish cartoonists who'd been threatened with violence for some satirical drawings of the Prophet?

Allie could see news cameras and free-speech signs even from here: MUSTN'T HURT THEIR FEELINGS read the lettering on one, beside the sketch of a suicide bomber. She agreed to take a look at what was going on. "We're waiting for the Hitch," another young man informed her as she neared the embassy's grounds. Christopher Hitchens, whom she often read, and whose heresy about the war she was coming to share, had organized the protest. She stood and watched it, feeling sure she shouldn't be here, suspecting that even nonverbal participation violated the terms of her employment.

Hitchens, bearded in what appeared to be a temporary way, arrived to cries of "Speech! Speech!" He responded with some oh-twist-my-arm reluctance while climbing atop a large white rock, as if it were a soapbox in Hyde Park, at the edge of the embassy's lawn.

"Brothers and sisters!" he began, in a gentle, good-humored way, before gravely speaking of the West's growing appeasement of Islamofascism, a word Allie knew was no more likely to be spoken by the White House, for all its Freedom Agenda, than the term "civil war." The Hitch continued: "We know who our friends and allies are, and they should know it, too. I would remind you that Denmark is a coalition partner in Iraq, and that our invertebrate State Department, manned by officials like the absurdly supine Mrs., or should I say 'Ma,' Hughes, should be—instead of attacking the cartoons—attacking those who would physically assault the cartoonists. You may and you should applaud."

Lusty cheers followed, and Hitchens signed off in the comradely mode of his more thoroughly leftist youth: "Solidarity with Denmark. Death to fascism." His tone was so even and seductive that an auditor had to supply any exclamation points for the marching orders. Climbing down from the rock, Hitchens let himself be chatted up by a man who'd taken a train in from Baltimore to be part of the event.

"How good of you to come," said the writer, before expostulating further on the enemy: "Yes, they're permitted to deny the Holocaust, but Allah forbid that we should be skeptical about a ninth-century imam being in a state of sleeping-beauty occultation before he once more quickens."

He noticed Allie in her open coat. "Good afternoon to you *and* the young lady," he said in greeting. As the father of two boys and a girl, he was willing to hazard a guess about Allie's lateral expansion, different from the frontal protuberance of a baby boy. "It's cheering to see a mother-to-be who's not marching reflexively for 'peace,'" he added. When he saw her warm to the flirtatiousness, he asked: "And where have you both come from?"

Saying "the vice president's house" would sound both indiscreet and provocative; but saying only "Arlington" might dully waste the opportunity to strike a conversational spark with this unlikely ally Ross had been so excited to meet last spring.

"Baghdad," she half-honestly answered.

"Really," he replied; a sexy, simple declarative. "In what capacity were you over there? Not with the just-mentioned invertebrates, I hope?"

"No. I'm a lawyer with the government. Involved with the tribunal and the elections." She decided to leave the Army and the NSC out of it.

"Well, they too, the Iraqis, will soon have a government. An elected one."

"Not soon enough, but yes."

Before he could ask who she thought might take over from al-Jaafari, she said: "I suppose someday my daughter will wonder: 'What did you do in the war, Mommy?'"

He brightened at this antique reference to his native land's popular culture. But Allie earnestly added: "What do I tell her was a good reason for it?"

He ticked off several, with a precision that made them feel like integers in a code or password. "There was the enemy's genocide against the Kurds, and a cornucopia of human-rights abuses year in and year out. That ought to have been enough for anyone. Colin Powell—a semi-invertebrate, let's say—never needed to hold up that vial of poison at the UN to make the real case. Tell your daughter it was to stop the export of a lethal Baathist form of fascism, one enforced by a crime family to rival the Korean Kims. Tell her that when Qaddafi, terrified by the American victory in Baghdad—the mission *was* accomplished—surrendered his own WMDs, he surrendered them to Tony Blair and George W. Bush, not Kofi Annan: the biggest nonproliferation accomplishment in history. A *smashing* success. The setbacks, however huge—and I'm sure you've seen more of them than I—don't even enter into it as a matter of proportion." He took a pause that seemed theatrical and heartfelt all at once. "Tell her that you were there for the beginning of the war, and that she must see it through to its end."

Startled by the last suggestion, Allie said, "I should leave you to your fans."

"The implication being that you're not one of them? I'm hurt."

"I'll let you know what she decides," Allie replied, tapping her abdomen and a bit recklessly handing him her card. She walked off through Dumbarton Oaks Park and then down R Street, realizing that the path she was now on would make it impossible to get back to Mass. Ave. anytime soon. But she wasn't in the mood for the office and decided to venture into Oak Hill Cemetery, green Georgetown acreage suffused with the remains of the city's nineteenth-century gentry. Excepting herself, she could detect no living creature here besides a solitary groundskeeper.

Threading the landscape of headstones, mausoleums, and weirdly inventive sculpture, the whole thing a chess board of death and status, she soon enough found herself next to an obelisk commemorating the life of Edwin M. Stanton, Lincoln's secretary of war. The top of it disappeared into the lower branches of an oak tree, making the marker seem cut off or unfinished, like the Washington Monument of Stanton's time.

Lowering herself onto a marble bench, she began to contemplate this resting place of Donald Rumsfeld's distant predecessor. Some of what little she knew about Stanton came from Ross: the Lincoln era lay somewhat after his own period of academic specialization, but one evening when they were talking about the current SecDef, he had contrasted Stanton's penchant for bombastic certainties about anything in front of his face with what she'd told him of Rumsfeld's appetite for vast and gnomic speculations.

Rumsfeld had called her yesterday, saying he hated to bother her at such a crucial time, as if the weeks before birth were a kind of military deployment, Operation Desert Shield on the brink of becoming Operation Desert Storm. He spoke about the bombing of the Golden Mosque, and seemed to find opportunity in the ensuing chaos: if this were cast as a test of the Iraqi authorities, one it was *failing*, there could be a new reason for pulling out instead of stepping up. Make it seem as if *they* were letting *us* down. He talked as if he believed all this, and she had merely listened; he was obviously coaching her for the meeting with Cheney, though he never acknowledged being the source of her invitation. "Damn it, Allison," he'd eventually added, "what's happened to you? Where's a display of the satisfaction that comes from looking like you were right?" He meant, presumably, right about the depths of futility to which the American effort had sunk, a point even lower than it had been when the two of them first met.

She'd joked about how such a display would be presumptuous, as if presumptuousness weren't what had first brought her to his favorable attention. And then, more exasperated than she'd ever heard him, he added another question: "What's this piece of rope you gave the president?"

"A souvenir" was all she would say.

Her usefulness to him was ending, and they both knew it. She could display no satisfaction, because last year she had been telling him something like the opposite of what she now took to be the truth; namely, that for the sake of justice the Sunni boot had *had* to come off the Shia. It would have happened eventually, but with even more appalling violence, if the Americans hadn't been there as both catalyst and buffer.

She took a last look at Stanton's pillar, considering how the Civil War had been set in motion by the abstract principle of federalism and then only later electrified by a commitment to people's freedom.

Why should it be impossible to think that the war in Iraq, undertaken over a mirage of chemical weapons, would reveal its true meaning in retributive justice and then a tormented sort of liberty? It seemed clearer and clearer to her that this was about carrying on, maybe even all the way to peace and reconciliation.

Her BlackBerry, beside her on the bench, had downloaded seven e-mails while she'd been inside Cheney's house. The second of them, she now saw, was from Ross, its subject line "#7." He'd taken to numbering his communications, which remained unread, but undeleted, in her in-box. Sitting here, doubly alive amidst nothing but death, she finally, after so many months, gave in to an impulse to see his words and imagine his voice:

Good morning. Here on the fifth floor of the Old Post Office, right in Washington, D.C., we have something strongly in common with much of New Orleans, and that's a dearth of potable water. It's been this way for years—signs above the drinking fountains say DON'T DRINK. There's no prospect of improvement, either, because fixing the building would cost a sum roughly equal to the agency's budget. So we all drink from plastic cooler jugs.

It may be a good thing that I'm not allowed to act as Holley's father. At this point I'd be an irresponsible parent. I'm on the verge of quitting my job here and heading to New Orleans for good. I can't see myself continuing to edit a guidebook and signing emergency-grant checks to little historical societies so that they can dry off their collections. I need to be down in Louisiana humping jugs of clean water to houses that are being rebuilt, and then falling into the sleep of the just at some rooming house—not a per diem bed in the Monteleone. But then how do I help support my two children, the ones to whom I am supposed to be a father, to the extent that the courts will allow me to be?

You'll be glad to know that I'm good and estranged from GWB—and don't even care that I'm writing this on my .gov account. I'm aware of moving to the point where you are, and I'm preoccupied by the impend-

ing birth of a child for whom no court will ever give me standing or sympathy.

I hope you are drinking the cleanest, freshest and sweetest water to be had, and that Holley will wait long enough inside you to be born on the first day of spring.

Allie rose from the marble bench and thought: Moving toward the point where *she* was? Once he got there he would find that, in some purely political geography, they had reversed places. As she walked one of the cemetery's well-tended paths, passing the graves of people who had lived only to her current age but still died as grandparents, Stanton's obelisk gradually disappeared from view. When it was fully out of sight, a sudden, sharp and then spreading pain doubled her over, making clear that her daughter would not wait even for tomorrow, let alone the first day of spring.

27

MARCH 21, 2006; 10:00 A.M.

Austin, Texas

"What are you up to this morning?" asked Larry King.

"Why are you calling me at home instead of the office?" asked Ann Richards, accusingly.

"I hear you're under the weather, Annie."

"I *hate* being called by that name. It makes me sound like Ma Ferguson."

"Who?"

"Google her. And I am *not* 'under the weather.' I have cancer, as you well know, thanks to that woman in the *Times*." The paper had run a profile of Cecile Richards, Ann's daughter, who had just taken over Planned Parenthood in New York; the reporter had mentioned the recent diagnosis of the subject's mother.

"I know what your next question will be, Larry. So I'll answer it now. I am not going to do one of your I-urge-you-to-get-tested shows."

"Not calling to ask! Honest. Just calling to say get well. But *shouldn't* people get tested?"

"People should avoid half a lifetime of my foolish behaviors, like Olympic-level drinking and smoking. After you're through Googling 'Ma,' read the Wikipedia article on esophageal cancer. I did. I had so many of the risk factors on their list I thought the next one down would be 'served as governor of Texas.'"

"What are you doing right now?"

"I'm lying in bed, and I'm not too weak to get up, if that's what you're thinking. I'm just too ornery and self-pitying for it this morning. So I'm staring at your network, which keeps showing the presidential seal affixed to an empty podium, which will be no less empty once Shrub comes out and gets his press conference started."

"How about calling in to the show tonight?" King suggested. "Whatever Bush says is bound to come up!"

"I'll be busy *throwing* up. I have a treatment this afternoon, so I guess that'll mean a second puke today, after the one this press conference brings on. Larry, I've got to go."

———

James S. Brady Press Briefing Room; The White House; Washington, D.C.

Taking the podium, he thinks: This'll be the last one of these under Andy. For days now he *keeps* thinking that this or that will be the last occurrence of whatever it is before Andy Card departs. A White House shake-up is coming—the press knows it, though he won't admit it when they question him now. It'll be another week before Josh Bolten is announced as Andy's replacement; after that, hapless little McClellan—let down by Rove, let down by Dick—will be on his way out, too. Bolten will do the canning.

Until next week the press will be saying that the absence of a shake-up means he's paralyzed, that his administration is out of gas. Then once he does it, they'll say he's panicking, about the midterms and everything else.

"Good morning," he says, before reading an opening statement in which somebody thought it would be a good idea to remind people we're now "marking the third anniversary of the launch of Operation Iraqi Freedom." As if the time had really flown.

He goes on to talk about progress, to praise Zal Khalilzad and say, "We've got a strategy for victory."

What they need in addition to that is a strategy for keeping Congress at bay, now that Democrats are beginning to talk about Feingold's proposal to "censure" him in the Senate, as if he were Clinton and Iraq were Monica, something reprehensible but maybe not criminal. A week ago both houses had formed the Iraq Study Group, a blue-ribbon wind machine, and he'd had to say yes to that: *Sure, we appreciate having help and input from anyone. . . .*

"First question, please."

*

Office of the Secretary, Department of State;
Washington, D.C.

Do you agree with Mr. Allawi that Iraq has fallen into civil war?

Condi Rice—writing an e-mail to her assistant with instructions to pack workout clothes even though today's trip will only be an overnighter—heard the question and looked up at the TV. She heard herself whisper *No, no, no.*

Bush said that the former prime minister was a good man, but that he himself would have chosen different words.

Well done, thought Condi, even if the truth was that nothing had stabilized in the month since the Golden Mosque explosion. She wondered all the time now if they weren't circling the drain. Maybe Don was right and they ought to be wrapping things up over there, one way or the other.

In his answer to the next question, the president warned Iran to stay out of Iraq, and to step away from any further development of nukes.

Good, Condi thought. But please don't leave the impression that we're going to open a third front in the war on terror.

She was tired, and had to remind herself that she didn't *do* tired. In recent weeks she'd been with the president in Kabul and India, by herself in Indonesia, and then somewhere else she couldn't even recall at the moment. This afternoon she was off to Nassau so that fourteen Caribbean foreign ministers could yell at her about whatever part the

U.S. was supposed to have played, *two years ago*, in getting rid of Aristide from Haiti.

The president was now back on the Iraq Study Group. When around him, she continued to pretend that she'd been only grudgingly in favor of its formation, though in fact she thought it a good idea, something that might not only buy them time but also diversify responsibility for whatever happened next over there. The group would be headed by Jim Baker and Lee Hamilton and have Bob Gates among its members. Its existence reminded her—and made her long for—41's calm, Pax-American world, where she had been a happy ingénue instead of a failing star.

*

2001 N. Clarendon Boulevard; Arlington

Mr. President, your decision to invade Iraq has caused the deaths of thousands of Americans and Iraqis, and wounded thousands of others for a lifetime. Every reason given, publicly at least, has turned out not to be true. My question is, why did you really want to go to war?

Bush's reference to the third anniversary had left him open to this sort of expansive retrospection, and Helen Thomas, who everyone knew had at least two screws loose, was going to town with it, talking about oil as a motive, getting the president to sputter "excuse me" and "hold on," making him look like a rageaholic ready to beat up on a woman older than his mother. Allie listened to him make the WMD argument as she nursed Holley, who was wearing her Arabic IT'S A PERSON! bib, already a hand-me-down, sent from the Green Zone by Rukia, with a card on which she'd learned to make lots of x's and o's. Another card, from Dr. Asefi, stood beside it: a beautiful, hand-painted whimsical landscape in six different shades of pink, dominated by herself wheeling a baby carriage; in one corner of it a little black arrow pointed to what lay unseen on the other side of a hill: *Papa?* read an even tinier caption.

Bush began giving what now struck her as a better justification for the war:

Liberty isn't America's possession. Liberty is universal. People desire to be free. And history has proven that democracies don't start wars. And so part of the issue is to lay down peace, to give people a chance to live in a world where mothers can raise their children without fear of violence. . . . A democracy in Iraq is going to affect the neighborhood, *is going to inspire reformers in a part of the world that is desperate for reformation.*

She began singing, without irony, the Mister Rogers song: *It's a beautiful day in the neighborhood.* Holley's eyes, as she rocked her, remained contentedly shut. "Mother!" Allie called out, laughing, before she remembered that Patricia O'Connor, her constant companion and attendant for the last three weeks, had just gone back to Philadelphia. Were she still here, Allie would have said: *Come listen. I'm already getting stupid. I knew this would happen.* What would she be like six weeks from now, when she returned to work?

*

Office of the Secretary of Defense; the Pentagon

Secretary Rumsfeld has said that if civil war should break out in Iraq, he's hopeful that Iraqi forces can handle it. If they can't, Mr. President, are you willing to sacrifice American lives to keep Iraqis from killing each other?

Rumsfeld, composing a snowflake, heard his name and looked up at the television:

I think the first step is to make sure a civil war doesn't break out, Bush replied to the reporter.

Rumsfeld recalled being behind a similar podium, briefing the press day after day at the start of the Afghan war, a rejuvenated bantam rooster whose sparring sex appeal almost left Maureen Dowd susceptible. Now he was just one more person who, like the wars, had been around forever.

He went back to his snowflake, this one addressed to General Pace and Undersecretary Eric Edelman. He wanted them to consider a suggestion from old Van Galbraith, his eyes and ears at NATO, that the U.S. conduct an "Aegis/Middle East missile defense exercise focused on the Black Sea, Persian Gulf, Gulf of Oman or the Eastern Mediterranean." He closed with a request: "Please let me know what you think."

He wouldn't admit what *he* was thinking, or at least *wondering*: Would a clean, fast, useful war in the skies over Iran provide a way out of Iraq, something to divert not the enemy but ourselves?

Out-of-the-box as all that might be, it was another snowflake that still had most of his attention, the one on his desk that wouldn't melt, addressed only to himself three weeks ago:

From: Donald Rumsfeld
Subject: Turning Responsibility of Detainees Over to Iraqis

On February 28 I told Generals Casey and Abizaid and their team to get us positioned so we are putting pressure on the Iraqis to take over responsibility for the detainees.

He'd gotten no satisfactory answer in the twenty-one days since. And now there were too many corpses in the streets for the Iraqis to start worrying overmuch about men still alive within prison walls. Their detention appeared to be indefinite.

As did the American Army's.

He switched off the television.

*

9 S. West Oak Drive, Houston

Barbara Bush heard her eldest son getting testy with NBC's David Gregory. George hated being interrupted as much as he hated being late, and he hated Gregory as much as he hated *others* being late. She smiled approvingly and felt a revival of her flagging interest in this press conference. Her attentiveness was sustained when her son swatted another question (*Do you now have in mind a target date for forming the unity government?*) as hard as he swatted Gregory: *As soon as possible. Next question.*

"Good," said Mrs. Bush. "I don't know why he put up with Helen for as long as he did this morning."

The former First Lady's husband, at the other end of the couch, chose to focus on the subject matter of the latest question. "He's gonna need to send Condi over there; maybe with Blair's man, that Straw fellow. She told me they work well together. Maybe they can get this al-Jaafari guy to step aside a little faster. Gotta get this show on the road."

"It's a show that never should have opened. And I'll never stop wishing that you'd told *him* that, three years ago. Maybe Jim Baker and Bob Gates can tell him *now*."

Forty-one pretended not to hear. He watched his son admit that the political capital he'd hoped to use for Social Security reform had wound up being spent on the war.

"Why would he say that?" Barbara Bush asked. It was as bad, in its way, as reneging on "Read my lips" had been twenty years before.

She was horribly irritated. All of this should have fallen to Jeb, the son she admired more and loved less. Averting her eyes and ears from any more, she got up and walked to the next room. Her mind went back, as it often did, to '78, and how she'd secretly wished for George's loss that year. Now she wondered if she'd been right to. Had he beaten Kent Hance he might have had a conventional dead-end career on the Hill, immune to the oddball rise that now had him playing—fatally, she feared—in the world's traffic.

———

624 Pirates Alley, New Orleans

Bush was back to talking about the "shake-up" that everyone seemed certain would occur. And the question led him, for the first time this morning, to the storm:

We've been a remarkably stable administration. And I think that's good for the country. Obviously, there are some times when government bureaucracies haven't responded the way we wanted them to. And, like citizens, I don't like that at all. I mean, I think, for example, of the trailers sitting down in Arkansas. Like many citizens, I'm wondering why they're down there. So I've asked Chertoff to find out, what are you going to do with them?

How, thought Ross, could he bring this up without even knowing the answer? More than a month had passed since he last sent an e-mail to the president, but that didn't mean he couldn't write one now:

That trailer story, you're right, is extremely depressing. People will say, how can they ever help us rebuild if they can't get this *straight? (Do you remember my writing you about the ridiculous denial of a trailer to Mrs. Watson right after the storm?) Please go back on the air when you have an answer, a piece of good news. There are plenty of places the trailers could be put in Louisiana. If you could just get people back into their home state, with a feeling that they were moving closer toward their actual homes, that would have a good effect.*

Most of the people who are still gone are ones who evacuated them-selves, before the storm. They did what the government told them to do. Doesn't the government therefore have a special responsibility to them?

Bush had been here again, briefly, on March 8th, and Ross hadn't gone to see him. The president's message, delivered in the Ninth Ward that day, six months after the hurricane, had been about getting the debris out of people's yards. A worthy, necessary, goal, but the way it was stated made people who weren't even *here* seem sloppy and negligent. The *city* had hauled the stuff into their yards, to get it out of the street.

Trash removal was a lot of what Ross had been doing for the past week. He'd taken five half-days of vacation to volunteer for cleanup work, most of it in connection with Opportunity Rocks and the seven hundred spring-breakers who'd heard John Edwards's call and come to town. They'd run out of tents to put them in, but the former senator had flown in—for one day—to cheer them on.

At the moment, Ross was finishing up some agency business; but he was already dressed in work boots, cutoffs, and an SMU T-shirt, ready to join the students for another afternoon of hauling. He didn't want to finish a memo about the Marigny section of the guidebook; he preferred to keep going with this new e-mail to Bush—urging a Category Five standard for the levee replacement; telling the president he wasn't pushing back hard enough against those legislators who wanted some of the latest $4.2 billion Katrina appropriation used as reimbursement for states (their own) that had taken in refugees and spent money on services for them. Why couldn't the White House suggest that these states just regard their own efforts as a matter of Christian charity? A temporary faith-based initiative?

"Ross!"

He heard a woman calling up from the street and thought back to Allie's arrival here on the Friday night before the storm. *Just you and I . . .*

It was probably the waitress at the café where he was forever leaving behind a notebook or his keys. He went to the window. Actually, he didn't know the woman, though she looked distantly familiar. He held up his index finger in a just-a-sec gesture and clomped down the steps in his work boots, through the downstairs bookshop and out into the street.

"Hello," she said. "I'm Patricia O'Connor, Allison's mother."

She was a small, athletic woman with short gray hair, wearing a windbreaker. His memory made an effort to peel away thirty years and see her as he thought he remembered her from Lubbock: a busy, kindly, make-the-best-of-things person.

"I don't know what to say," he stammered, as if he were a sixteen-year-old boy who'd been caught knocking up her daughter.

She handed him the picture of a very small baby, its fingers fussing with one another as if performing an isometric exercise.

"Why did you come?" he asked. "She'll kill you if she finds out."

"No, she won't," said Mrs. O'Connor. "She'll only want to. As it is, she thinks I'm home in Philadelphia."

"The baby," said Ross. "Holley—"

"She came a little early. She's fine. So is Allison." She took one of his hands between both of hers. She looked him long and straight in the eye. "I'm not going to tell you what to do. But do *something*." And then she was gone.

He went back upstairs and sat for a minute. He then moved to the computer and composed an e-mail to the Chairman: *I hereby resign as Director of the NEAH's Homeland Heritage Division.*

Hitting SEND, he remembered that it was only now the first day of spring, and he allowed himself, for a moment, to believe that everything, somehow, might yet be all right.

Part Three

APRIL 26, 2006–
JANUARY 25, 2007

28

APRIL 26–29, 2006

U.S. Embassy Compound, Baghdad

Donald Rumsfeld and Condi Rice emerged from separate armored Rhino GXs. As her door thunked shut, Condi thought not of the insurgent bomb it might have had to stop, but of the invective soon to be hurled her way in Massachusetts. Before leaving Washington a couple of days ago, she'd accepted an invitation to be the Boston College commencement speaker. Jim Wilkinson was delighted, but she was having second thoughts. Once the announcement got made, there would be the inevitable student and faculty complaints, and a few weeks after that all the turned backs and little protest messages masking-taped to mortarboards. The hippest of the left-leaning would accuse the college of helping Bush to "blackwash" the war, of putting a sweet coat of racial diversity upon the administration's criminal aggression.

Even at this moment, it was easier to think about Boston than to think about Don. They weren't arriving separately just here at the compound; they'd arrived separately in the *country*. He'd come directly from D.C., while she'd contrived bits of business that would allow her to reach Baghdad only after stops in Athens and Ankara. The president wanted the two of them to make a joint show of support for Maliki, the prime minister–designate, who more than four months after the elections had just told them he needed one more week to finish putting his government together. But here they now were, she and Don, walking twenty feet apart from each other into a press conference at this unfinished embassy by the Tigris—price tag: six hundred million dollars! A slender podium was ready for each of them, like candidates in a debate, and she noticed a Rumsfeld aide dropping a sheet of paper on *her* little lectern before scurrying away. Don noticed him too, and smiled.

The paper was one of his goddamned snowflakes, she realized, silently uttering a swear word she almost never permitted herself.

April 05, 2006
To: Stephen J. Hadley
From: Donald Rumsfeld
Subject: Iraq Visit

I am convinced Condi and I should not go to Iraq together at the end of this month. I think the Straw-Condi visit looked heavy, and I think it would be a mistake to replicate it, so I am going to plan to go separately.

DHR.ss
040506-01

He had of course been overruled, and besides that, if she and Jack Straw hadn't come here a few weeks ago, there's no telling when al-Jaafari would have finally stepped aside for Maliki. So why was Don putting this little memo, evidence of his own failure and need to reverse himself, in front of her eyes as things here got under way? To get into her head, as if they were about to face off in one of his high school wrestling matches; to make her feel that *he* was the one unafraid to speak his mind, while she still Photoshopped her views into alignment with the president's. He was telling her that he had come here to project division, not unity.

And it was showing. The photographers were engaged in a more frenzied level of clicking than usual, hoping for a shot that would convey the bad body language. All she needed to do was blink her eyes or brush her hair back, and that would be the image they used, freezing the instant as a display of her frustration.

A woman from Bloomberg News asked whether "security was a factor in your secret arrivals in Baghdad. And if so, does it say something about conditions on the ground?"

"I'm afraid those conditions are still not as good as we want them to be," Condi responded. "But we're doing everything we—"

Rumsfeld interrupted. "I guess I don't think it says anything about it. I just don't see anything in your question."

"Of course," said Condi, as if apologizing for his rudeness, "we want to see security improving all the time."

Rumsfeld mutely looked at a sheet of paper, not a snowflake but a list of topics they'd covered with Maliki. Condi knew that unless she began speaking to these items, there would be only silence. "We discussed infrastructure," she explained to the Bloomberg woman. The president had insisted that this be on the agenda, even though Don could barely be persuaded of a U.S. responsibility to keep the lights on, let alone to rebuild anything. "And we devoted a good deal of time to the militias situation," Condi went on. A whole Shia brigade, really a vast anti-Sunni death squad, had insinuated itself into the security forces. "As you know, the prime minister–designate has candidly admitted his own less-than-complete confidence in these forces. But I told him that I've seen, in my life's experience, how police forces can become stronger, fairer, more committed to a just enforcement of the law for all. I've seen the police department of Birmingham, Alabama, evolve from its days under Bull Connor into something truly professional."

The reporters waited for Rumsfeld to say something too, but he just kept doodling on the paper in front of him. So Condi went on speaking, about Maliki: "I found him very focused and very clear. He understands his role and the role of the new government—that it has to demonstrate it's one of national unity, one on which all Iraqis can rely." The prime minister had assured her and Don that he wouldn't be anyone's puppet, a word she couldn't now use with the reporters, lest even its utterance suggest the possibility of such a thing.

Rumsfeld remained silent; he didn't look up. So Condi gave a signal with her eyes to Sean McCormack, an assistant secretary standing nearby: *Shut this down.*

"People at State are feeling very excited and optimistic about Nuri Kamal al-Maliki," Condi declared with a smile, before someone posed a direct question to Rumsfeld, about reforming the militias, and finally provoked his engagement. He replied to it while looking at Rice, not the reporter: "The first thing I'd say is that *we* don't do it. The Iraqis do."

The signal she'd given McCormack was becoming more urgent; but the press were determined to persist. A next question, for both her and Rumsfeld, concerned the prospects for U.S. troop reductions. It was more properly his to answer, but she decided to field it before he retreated into his silence and this fly ball dropped between them. "General Casey wants to see how the new government does," she replied, more candidly than she might have.

"Are any of the Iraqi leaders in favor of troop cuts?" the reporter followed up.

"None that *I* talked to," said Rumsfeld, whose laughter gave the media permission to laugh too. "I indicated my own desire for reductions, needless to say." He was cementing his counterintuitive brand, reminding them that he wished to be in the vanguard of a retreat that could be spun into a victory, a fine known known.

Since he now seemed to be paying attention, one of the reporters asked him, once more, about a remark Condi had made a few weeks ago in England. She'd mentioned the "thousands" of tactical errors the U.S. had no doubt made in Iraq, and Rumsfeld had immediately struck back hard: *I don't know what she's talking about.* The press were now urging him to hit her again. "She's right here," he replied. "Why don't you ask *her*?" He resumed doodling, looking up only far enough to see her squirm.

"I didn't mean 'thousands' literally," Condi explained. "We'll all have plenty of time when writing our memoirs to figure out just how many there were. My point was that you adapt to situations, make necessary changes when particular things aren't working."

Rumsfeld had actually begun gathering his papers. He waved good-bye as a reporter asked one last question about the "context" of their visit: four different major explosions had occurred since their separate arrivals. Condi was now picking up her own papers, including the snowflake. She was not going to be left alone out here, like Princess Di in front of the Taj Mahal.

"Ma'am, are you and Secretary Rumsfeld—"

"The secretary of defense and I have a great relationship and we're having a great time here in Iraq!" She waved and exited.

Once away from the reporters, she raised her voice to McCormack and Wilkinson: "Get me into a room with him! *Now!* Do it!" Startled, Wilkinson pointed to a small space they might use. "Everyone out of here!" Condi shouted to the three Americans and lone Iraqi in the room. She waited, alone, until Sean and Jim brought Rumsfeld to her. He was smiling.

She balled up the snowflake and threw it on the floor. "Those thousands of tactical errors?" she shouted, once the door was closed. "Why don't you request a *list* from General Eaton? And General Zinni? And General Swannack? And General Newbold? I'm sure they can come up with five hundred apiece!"

A recent "generals' revolt" had seen several retired commanders publicly call for Rumsfeld's dismissal over mismanagement of the war.

"Along with that request," she continued, raging now, "you can send them a thank-you note! For the decent interval they've given you!"

Don just waited and twinkled. The generals' criticism had indeed forced the president into a full-throated defense of his defense secretary. Bush couldn't have it look as if he were being pressured into firing him.

"'Decent interval' is an interesting phrase," Rumsfeld finally replied.

"Yes, it is. It also stands for what you want *here*, before the American army leaves and everything we've tried to do collapses."

One of Rumsfeld's aides knocked hard on the door. The president was on the line. Back in Washington, where it was early morning, he'd watched a video feed of the press conference and now wanted to speak to both secretaries. The aide put the phone, set to speaker, on a table. Rice and Rumsfeld were soon left alone in the room with it, and with facial expressions—maskings of anxiety—that were nearly identical.

"Madame Rice?" the president called out. She braced herself. He often lightly teased her about the "language of diplomacy," but this sounded as bad as the time he'd mocked David Gregory, at a joint press conference with Chirac, for asking a question in French. "Was that a display of *unity* just now? How about you, Secretary Rumsfeld? Any thoughts on that?"

"We expressed no policy disagreement," Rumsfeld replied.

"To start with," Bush responded, *"anybody* would know that the kind of display I requested entailed a joint airport arrival."

"Sir," said Condi, "the scheduling—"

"You'd better be *departing* together—and I'd better see you in a group hug with Maliki."

But it was already arranged for Condi to spend the night in Baghdad, her first ever, once Don had gone. "Everything has been—"

The president cut her off. "I'd advise neither of you to sleep too comfortably between now and Monday morning." They were due to brief Bush jointly in the Oval Office. General Pace would be there, too.

The phone clicked off. She looked at Don, who'd already turned around to leave. The two of them were now scorpions in a bottle, and the president had just stoppered it.

———

White House Correspondents' Association Dinner;
Washington Hilton Hotel

If only Laura could do it *this* year too, he thought, as he got ready to go up to the microphone. A waiter removed what the menu card called *mustard-rubbed filet mignon*—his own portion of it so little touched that the food taster might as well have eaten the whole thing. He stared out into the ballroom, this hellish basement bunker with its clamshell ceiling, huge and claustrophobic all at once. And then he got up to get it over with.

"*Ladies and gentlemen, I feel chipper tonight. I survived the White House shake-up!*"

Bolten was in; Rove had been pushed to the side; and McClellan was leaving, to be replaced by Tony Snow, a nice guy who'd even done some speechwriting in Dad's White House. The black-tied, mustard-rubbed press here would forgive Tony the last several years he'd been with Fox, since he'd come out of the *Detroit News* long before that.

Okay, here came the shtick they'd worked out: this comedian named Bridges, stepping up to a podium right beside his own, would pretend to be his alter ego, saying all the things *he* supposedly wanted to but couldn't. "*Where's the great white hunter? Shot the only trial lawyer in the country who supports me!*"

And now he speaks a line of his own: "*Cheney's a good man. He's got a good heart.*" Take a pause; let them think about the cardio problems. "*Well, he's a good man.*" You could hear the gasps from the crowd. He looked to his right, toward Laura, who was smiling quietly. She'd told him not to cut it.

He phoned the rest of it in, so detached from the comedian's voice that it really *could* have belonged to him. The bit was over soon enough, and the press gave him plenty of applause—their way of feeling big about themselves. He sat down. Once the main comic finished—poor Bridges was only a warm-up act—he could get out of here.

It took only a couple of minutes to realize that the guy now up at the mic was coming at him hard. "*I stand by this man. I stand for this man because* he *stands for things, not only for things, he stands on things. Things like aircraft carriers, and rubble, and recently flooded city squares.*"

"Who is this asshole?" Bush asked Laura.

"Stephen Colbert. But it's not really 'him.' It's his persona."

"His *what?*"

She urged him to nod toward McCain, who'd just smiled at her. But he looked at Scalia instead, and glared at Helen Thomas when he felt pretty sure the reaction-shot camera had trained itself on another part of the dais.

"I believe the government that governs best is the government that governs least. And by these standards we have set up a fabulous government in Iraq!"

Don't look in my direction, fuckwad, or you'll *really* have crossed the line tonight.

Lèse-majesté? He had less *majesté* than ever. Out in Rancho Mirage last week, ancient Gerry Ford, whom he'd dropped in on as a *courtesy*, had lectured him on Iraq as if he were still Dad's son, the wayward prince who needed another tutorial from Dick.

General Pace looked ready to walk out. Good man. He could teach Condi and Rumsfeld a thing or two about displays of unity, and maybe he would when he joined them in the Oval on Monday. Karen Keller, his secretary, *was* walking out, bless her heart.

Then he realized, to his surprise, that the discomfort was pretty general. This guy was *not* going over; the media looked uneasy, a little *guilty*, as if Colbert were playing *their* alter ego and saying what they'd like to say without their usual pretense of "objectivity." Even some of the Democrats were shifting in their seats. Steny Hoyer, Pelosi's shadow, shot him an apologetic look.

He should talk to Tony, ask if they had to do this next year. Didn't Nixon once skip it? Probably not until his death spiral.

He could dimly remember this dinner when it wasn't such a freak show, before that kid from the *Baltimore Sun* brought Ollie North's secretary as his date and, before you knew it, the event became nothing but starlets and celebrities you'd half heard of. The kid's name? He tried to remember it. *Kelly*—later became a Democratic Clinton-hater, God love him. And then got himself killed three years ago, while he was embedded during the invasion.

"Mayor Nagin! Of the Chocolate City! Welcome to the Chocolate City by the marshmallow center!"

Sure enough, there was Ray-Ray, out in the audience beside his own brace of starlets, standing up and beaming as if he'd *achieved* something.

Bush stared up at one of the ceiling clamshells and started thinking might-have-beens, an infrequent indulgence and always a bad sign. How different things would be now if Kelly had been embedded in a tank racing toward a Baghdad warehouse found to be stuffed with poison gas and chemical weaponry. How different things would be if Hinckley had finished off Reagan in the driveway outside this hotel, putting Dad in the White House eight years ahead of Nancy Reagan's astrological clock, and knocking *him*—what would he have been in '81? thirty-five?—into some peaceful outer orbit where he stayed for good, a celestial spot where all the passing stars and planets looked happy, like stitched baseballs under the lights.

Colbert had finished, and Laura was doing that thing she sometimes did when some lefty writer got up on a soapbox in the East Room. She was splitting the difference, appearing to clap but not actually touching her hands together, so as not to add to the approving noise. She was also leaning into him to whisper. "Be prepared. This is going to go over better on YouTube than it did in here."

The Wyoming, Apartment #702, 2022 Columbia Road NW, Washington, D.C.

"Here's to a hanging judge," said Christopher Hitchens, raising a glass of Johnnie Walker Black and Perrier. "Well, without the actual hanging." He remembered that he was an abolitionist when it came to the death penalty—even, he supposed, for terrorists. But one could still relish the fact that the "sentencing trial" of Zacarias Moussaoui—who would have been the "twentieth hijacker" had he not been arrested a month before 9/11—was now reaching its end. Moussaoui had pled guilty, with various emendations and retractions, and a jury, not a judge, was tonight deciding his fate, choosing between life in prison and lethal injection.

The circle of guests around Hitchens, a small ring within the great crush of his annual after-party for the Correspondents' dinner, lifted their glasses in an awkward toast.

"What's *he* doing pre-sentencing?" asked Michael Kinsley, cocking his head toward Scooter Libby, the vice president's diminutive former chief of staff, who'd come over on his motorcycle and wore a leather jacket.

"He's pre-*trial*," replied Hitchens, who had made Libby one of his quixotic causes. "He's over at the Hudson Institute for the moment."

"Thinking and tanking," said Kinsley. "Well, at least he diverts you from David Irving." The Hitch continued to champion the Holocaust-denying historian's right to publish along with his release from jail on the European Continent.

The Chairman of the NEAH gave his old friend Kinsley an amused you-never-change look, and then asked Ross Weatherall, standing with him on the edge of the group: "Sure you aren't going to miss all this? You can still change your mind." He explained to Kinsley and Hitchens that he'd persuaded Ross to stay on at the agency until June 30th, after which Ross intended to "go off and build houses for the poor." The Chairman affected an aesthete's incomprehension of such an ambition. "At least we get to keep him until the new guidebook is locked up."

"Along with Libby," said Kinsley.

Ross laughed—too heartily for the Chairman's taste, he realized. It was one thing to appreciate the editor's sarcastic bent, but enjoyment of the joke *itself* seemed to strike his politically appointed boss as excessive, a demonstration of disloyalty from a man on his way out.

"I wonder," Kinsley continued, "if Libby knows that Joe and Valerie were next door." Wilson and Plame, the husband-wife intelligence team whose female half Libby was charged with helping to "out," had attended the dinner.

"At ABC's table," Mary Matalin confirmed. She turned to Ross: "You look a lot happier than you did the last time I saw you. Was that at a Christmas party?"

Ross said yes and reintroduced himself, knowing his mid-level obscurity would necessitate his forever having to do this if he stayed in Washington. Nagin had come in a little while ago and given him a what-the-hell? look. *You're* important enough to be here?

"I'm much better, thanks," Ross assured Matalin.

In fact, he was soaring, having yesterday received an e-mail from Allie.

She'd proposed that he meet her downtown at the National Archives on May 11th, a week from Thursday, to see if they might resume conversation about the Iraqi Jewish archive *and something else*. Which had to be Holley. Ross was convinced that he was about to meet his new daughter under the dim, soothing lights that helped to preserve the Declaration of Independence and Constitution—as if they were undergoing a quiet Lamaze birth, like the one Deborah had given Caitlyn fifteen years ago.

He had, since yesterday, mentally surfed this miracle, undulating between reverence and rage. One minute he'd marvel at Allie's generosity; the next he'd bloom with fury. Who manipulates the father of her child like this? Even so, after eight months, long since he'd given up on the possibility, she had *responded* to him.

Tony Snow, the incoming press secretary, arrived at the boisterous apartment.

"Mission accomplished?" asked Hitchens.

"What mission would that be?"

"Getting Bush out of there alive."

"Could you *believe* that Colbert guy?" asked Snow. "Were you there?"

Hitchens shook his head no. He wouldn't be caught dead at the dinner itself, even if the Hilton was literally next door.

Someone called out: "Here it is!" Footage of Colbert's performance was being broadcast on the eleven o'clock *local* news; such was the sensation it had already made.

"This is a man who believes Wednesday what he believed Monday, despite what happened Tuesday!"

Standing near the television, Larry King asked Bob Dole: "You're one of the funniest men in public life. Does Bob Dole think that's over the line?"

"Or maybe just too close to the bone?" asked Kinsley, who'd joined those wanting to see the routine a second time.

When Dole didn't answer, King, with his professional horror of dead air, asked a different question: "What was your funniest line at the Al Smith dinner? That event's usually a riot! You must have done it in '96, when you were running."

"Was never invited."

"You're kidding me!"

"The cardinal wouldn't have Clinton because he'd just vetoed the partial-birth-abortion ban. So they couldn't have me either."

King marveled at the loss of such a booking opportunity. "A shame! Not that abortion's a subject either of you could have touched."

"Same with the altar boys," said Hitchens. "Touched as a delicate *subject*, I mean. I'm sure a few of the lads got fervent squeezes from God's intermediaries if they remembered where to kneel during the invocation."

Dole and King didn't know what to say, so the CNN host asked the former senator: "Have you called Ann down in Austin? You ought to. It's bad."

Ross, uncertain of whom they were speaking, suddenly noticed John Edwards. A blond woman was videotaping him watching Colbert. He had a faintly amused but mostly furtive look.

"Close," the videographer said. "Want to try it once more?"

Edwards apologized for the distraction to those by the TV. He explained that the woman, "Rielle," was shooting "webisodes" of his latest antipoverty speaking tour, which had him teamed with Danny Glover, the actor.

Was he here, too? people wondered, looking around.

Ross carried two snapshots in his wallet: the photo of Holley from Mrs. O'Connor, and a picture of himself, with Father Montrose and Gary, the guy from near the Industrial Canal, all three of them in Opportunity Rocks T-shirts. His high spirits over Allie's message made him take out the second photo and present it to Edwards—after introducing himself to the ex-senator for the third time. Edwards dropped a hand over his shoulder while Rielle Hunter shot a few seconds of video.

The Chairman, witnessing all this, smiled, but shook his head in a way that fell well short of jovial. "Maybe it's a good thing that you're leaving."

Ross didn't care. He was floating rather than flailing. Allie's e-mail, as yet unanswered, had been like the first gust of air he'd caught the time he went paragliding in the Rockies. He ran off the edge of the mountain, fearing he'd fall like a stone to the ground below, and then discovered he was rising instead, caught and saved by the updraft.

Donatella Versace made a late entrance with Jonathan Rhys Meyers, the young Irish actor, her escort for the evening. Meyers was in fact on the company clock. Along with having signed to play Henry VIII in *The Tudors*, he was about to become "the face of Versace," at least the male one, in all of the company's advertising. "Isn't he way too skinny for Henry the Eighth?" asked Mary Matalin.

"Isn't he way too hot?" replied Andrew Sullivan.

Donatella jumped up from the couch she'd just sat on. "I see it!" she cried, racing toward Edwards and touching his face. "The little mole! It's back!" She caressed its minuscule convexity.

Rielle Hunter turned off the camera.

"The tiniest implant," whispered Edwards.

29

MAY 11, 2006

Rotunda of the National Archives, 700 Pennsylvania Avenue, Washington, D.C.

Dr. Asefi looked at the vaulted ceilings, then swept his eyes across the murals and exclaimed: "I feel like the Nukak-Makú!"

"The new *what*?" asked Karen Hughes.

Allen Weinstein, the national archivist, attempted to correct her, but his whisper disappeared in the echo of everyone's footfalls.

The undersecretary of state repeated her question.

"He's referring to that Colombian tribe," explained Allie, in a voice that carried strongly, to Weinstein's relief. The primitive Nukak-Makú had been all over the news and Internet this week, after vacating the Amazon jungle for a nearby town on account of Colombia's civil war. With a shrug, Mrs. Hughes thanked Allie for the gloss.

Dr. Asefi had come to Washington at the urging of Mrs. Morris in Kabul. State Department staffers there hoped that his courageous story might inspire Americans to maintain their commitment to Afghanistan, an effort now nearly five years old. The physician-painter would address selected groups in D.C. and New York before heading to Texas and California for several days. Mrs. Morris had advanced the plan through Allison O'Connor (whom Karen Hughes remembered with vague unpleasantness from Crawford last summer) and finally through Condi Rice herself.

But Mrs. Hughes could still not see the sense of it. Her job was to sell America to the Muslim world, not vice versa. This morning's traipse around the Rotunda just took time from her own initiatives, which now included sending American sports figures abroad, maybe even into Islamic hotspots. She had her fingers crossed for Cal Ripken, Jr.

Weinstein pointed out the Magna Carta to Dr. Asefi.

"I'm never quite sure why that's *here*," observed Mrs. Hughes. "It's English."

Weinstein tried to clarify its generative relationship to the rest of the legal instruments displayed nearby, but as the group moved toward those, their echoing steps once more drowned him out. Allie tried filling the gap, but Dr. Asefi's playful eyes assured her there was no need: he knew what the Magna Carta was, the British having for so long turned his country into the Great Game. He made a joke about the dimness of the lighting, telling his guides that *this*, unlike the room's architectural grandeur, made him feel right at home: "Mr. Karzai hasn't figured out how to keep the electric on all the time." Allie remembered the brief blackout in Kabul: *I want a kiss.*

Mrs. Hughes, with too-evident haste, moved the doctor from one piece of democratic writ to the next. "I'm afraid I have to scoot," she soon explained. "I've got an early lunch back at the office."

Weinstein had another appointment as well, but he assured Allie and Dr. Asefi that a fine lunch had been set for them, as well as Ms. O'Connor's expected guest, in the Madison, one of the smaller conference rooms on this floor.

"I hope the food will agree with you," said Mrs. Hughes to the Afghan, before she rushed off.

"I am a gastroenterologist by day," Dr. Asefi reminded her. "I know many tricks for warding off upset. But I am sure it will be delicious."

Allie was glad to be shorn of the undersecretary and archivist, and ready to make Dr. Asefi the charming buffer in her peace overture to Ross, which she had decided on, with considerable hesitation, two weeks ago. She led the physician in the direction Weinstein had indicated. When he softly coughed, several times, Allie asked if he could use a lozenge.

"It's my Bamyan cough," he answered, smiling. "I'm afraid nothing will help. It comes from, what do you call it? Stress." He'd had it ever since the winter of 2001, when the Taliban blew up the giant Buddha rock sculptures, two provinces west of Kabul. It was then he'd realized he had to speed up his work on the paintings.

———

Office of the Director, Homeland Heritage Division, NEAH,
1100 Pennsylvania Avenue; 12:15 p.m.

Three blocks from the Archives, Ross exited his office, where he'd already boxed up his souvenirs from last year's inaugural. He carried a folder under his arm while walking to the elevator. He'd been boning up on the Iraqi Jewish archive, what he felt sure would be Allie's pretext for today's meeting. He wanted her to find him on top of the figures for NEAH's contribution to the project; the deadlines for further granting opportunities; and the list of personnel who had been interfacing with counterparts at the Archives and State. Of course, by the time this peculiar miscellany of Judaica got unfrozen, he would be long gone from the government—and no longer using words like "interfacing." Whether Iraq was safe enough for the repatriation of the restored collection would be up to others, and maybe Allie herself.

At 12:25 he bounded up the Archives steps, past the rectangular stone memorial to FDR—the exact size of the president's desk, as Roosevelt had directed. The block was actually smaller than the desk in the Old Post Office that would soon belong to someone else, a piece of furniture that could take up half the room he pictured himself renting in New Orleans once his per diem and the Monteleone were things of the past.

As he entered the Madison Room, he saw two figures at a small table; a waiter was clearing their lunch plates and bringing them coffee. It took Ross a moment to register that one of the people seated was actually *her*: thinner in the face; the cascade of red hair trimmed and disciplined; the freckles—he could see as he got closer—fewer than last summer or long ago. The past year had aged her, and this observation brought him a flash of encouragement. If his own sorrows were making him younger, less cautious, maybe hers had produced someone gentler, less vigilant.

He had imagined this as the moment he would kiss her, but she gave him only a friendly wave, as if he were a colleague she'd not seen since some last biannual colloquium. The slender, bearded man she was with, about Ross's own age, stood up to greet him.

Allie introduced "Dr. Weatherall" as "a representative of our arts agency," and promised that he was "a real Texan."

"Howdy? Pardner?" the bearded gentleman asked, with a smile.

"Ross, this is Dr. Mohammed Yusef Asefi. You'll remember I told you about the extraordinary things he did in Kabul."

"Oh, yes," said Ross, glad his nervousness would seem to derive from being in the presence of heroism. "It's an honor to meet you, sir."

Dr. Asefi reached into his briefcase for a photographic print of a painting, *Red Mountains in America*, by an Afghan artist named Muhammed Maimongi. "It comes all from his head," explained the doctor. "I suppose where you come from is not actually much like that?" The painted landscape, a sort of spiky canyon, did look more like the cover of a Ray Bradbury novel than any piece of Texas Ross had ever crossed, but he heartened Dr. Asefi by saying that "Kafka wrote a whole novel called *Amerika* without ever having visited here."

Allie explained the reason for Dr. Asefi's tour and gave Ross a copy of his itinerary. She then told the doctor about the Iraqi Jewish archive that she and Dr. Weatherall were working on. The strange process she described—the freezing and restoration of the materials—seemed to appeal to him, perhaps even remind him of his own applications and removals of water-soluble paint to the canvases in Afghanistan's National Gallery.

"Dr. Asefi and I have been wondering," said Allie, "if NEAH might help with another reclamation project—this one in Kabul."

The doctor again reached into his briefcase. He withdrew an envelope holding six fragments of paper covered with watercolor. He laid the pieces on the tablecloth and then reassembled them into the picture of a man in a long robe and turban guiding a flock of goats with a crook. One of the rips in the paper went straight through the muzzle of a dog sharing in the work. "The Taliban would not allow even the animals to be depicted," said Dr. Asefi. "Living creatures."

Ross tried to concentrate, but all he could think of was the photo of Holley in his wallet. He'd expected to be here holding and exclaiming over the baby's real self: *She's so much bigger already!* Was Allie even now just up to her cruel, pointless tricks? He began entertaining the possibility that she really was crazy, and had been made irretrievably so by the hurricane and the war. It beggared belief that she had not seen him since Katrina and that this was her idea of a reunion.

He looked at Dr. Asefi and recited a list of projects currently being funded by the Endowment's Afghanistan Initiative. Could he take these shards of paper back to his Chairman? he asked, before robotically continuing with questions: How many pictures were they talking about? If the work were funded, did Dr. Asefi imagine it being carried out here or in Kabul?

"Please take," said Dr. Asefi, gathering the paper fragments from the tablecloth and presenting them to Ross. "There must be several hundred pictures. If someone could be trained to do the work in Kabul, that would be most wonderful."

"Dr. Asefi makes no great claims for the quality of the art," said Allie. "But that seems less important to him—and to me—than the principle of the thing, the symbolism of the restoration." She looked at Ross. "It would be so much in line with the work he did on the paintings."

She was speaking without skepticism or the least hint of sarcasm. If the manipulativeness in her voice seemed as ever, the full sincerity felt new.

He made notes of what Dr. Asefi said, and smiled encouragingly. "It wouldn't surprise me if we could do something. But I'll have to turn this over to my successor. I'm leaving Washington on the thirtieth of June, at the latest." He phrased this, for Allie's benefit, as emphatically as he could, but she didn't seem surprised. Had she already found out? That wouldn't, he supposed, have been hard.

Dr. Asefi looked at his watch, rose from the table, and shook hands with each of them. "I am grateful to see Miss O'Connor again. And to meet Dr. Weatherall. I will be so lucky for anything you can do. Here is my 'contact info'—a phrase I have learned from my American friends." He handed Ross a business card.

"Are you going already?" asked Allie. The waiter had just brought Ross some coffee and dessert.

"I am afraid so." He explained that someone from Mrs. Hughes's office would soon be meeting him out on Pennsylvania Avenue, at the top of the Archives' steps. "May I ask, about the Capitol: Is it, from here, to the east or the west? Perhaps north and south?" He laughed.

"It's toward the southeast," Ross informed him.

"Surely they're going to *take* you there," said Allie.

"I have already been. I would just like to pray for a moment, before they pick me up. I wish to know what direction to face."

"Let me lead you out," said Allie.

"There is no need," said the physician, who began to leave but then startled the Americans by putting his hands on Ross's shoulders. "Daddy," he whispered, with a smile. "I am intuitive," he added, by way of explanation, before he coughed, waved, and was gone.

"I have a daughter," Ross said to Allie, as abruptly as he'd spoken those words to Father Montrose in the warehouse of coffins on Poydras Street.

"You do," said Allie.

"Why ask to see me *here*? Why this way?"

"Because I can pretend it's about something else. Because I'm still as tattered as those pictures."

"That's the only honest thing you've ever said to me." He paused, but just for a second, lest she again disappear under her old carapace of pseudo-certainty. "Show me a picture of *her*," he said. "Something more recent than what your mother gave me."

She looked surprised, just as he had been by his own ability to wait things out, without doing anything besides resigning his job, after Mrs. O'Connor showed up in New Orleans. He had stuck with the belief that his only real chance lay in a summons that came from Allie herself.

"Well, isn't she the sly one?"

"God bless your mama, as we might say in Lubbock. Nothing wrong with Lubbock, by the way. There never was." He heard a new assertion in his voice, as if he'd acquired power from his seven weeks of silence and from her own admission of disarray. Even so, he decided to proceed by indirection. "So this new project really engages you?" As soon as he asked the question, he felt a sudden, new anxiety: Was she in love with Dr. Asefi?

"Yes, I'm interested," she answered.

She was aware of how totemic she'd become: the pink watercolor reassembled from shards; Pirnaz's bib; the little piece of rope. "Will you build a house for *yourself* in New Orleans? Along with the ones you'll be fixing up for others?"

"How do you know about all that?"

She made quotation marks with her fingers and spoke in an affectionate approximation of his West Texas accent: "*'I feel I must do more for the city. I am glad that you gave me the chance to love it via the guidebook. But I believe the administration's efforts down here have been scandalously inadequate. . . .'*"

Her source was the president of the United States, who'd apparently shared his letter of resignation with her. Ross said: "*I* didn't hear from him; but *you* did?"

"He told me he's 'concerned about the two of you and this little girl.' He said you're 'a good man.'"

"How does he know Holley's a girl?"

"He's not without intelligence sources, you know."

Ross expected this remark to be followed by a cutting one about WMDs, but it wasn't. "And he's been in touch with me," was all she added.

"Why can't I build a house in New Orleans for the *three* of us?"

As soon as the question was out of his mouth, he hated himself for asking it. He'd rushed and overplayed a still impossibly weak hand.

"We've already lived there—Holley and I. We didn't like it." She reached into her wallet and handed him a card:

IF I AM FOUND DEAD OR UNCONSCIOUS: MY NAME IS ALLISON O'CONNOR. I AM PREGNANT WITH A GIRL TO BE CALLED HOLLEY.

She'd written it, he realized, in the Superdome. The note included her Social Security number and her mother's e-mail address. Ross knew he should say, now and unequivocally: *I want to see her. I want to see my daughter.* But he couldn't overreach again. He had to let the waters take things where they would.

"Here's something a little more handsomely printed," said Allie. She handed him a copy of the District of Columbia's birth certificate for Holley O'Connor, born on February 24. The child's middle name was Weatherall. On seeing this, Ross experienced a surge of contentment, but then, as always with Allie, felt himself tossed into a locked room: What new species of teasing was this? Some splitting of the difference that was supposed to make everything all right, since the playful choice of "Holley" hadn't quite done the trick?

"I want you to go to New Orleans," Allie told him. "You're right. Do your part to see things through there. Double down for a while."

Ross said nothing, just wished the sound of a crying baby might be there to cut the sudden awful silence in the room. "You mean I shouldn't cut and run? Isn't that always *your* solution to everything? From Iraq to us?"

She looked straight at him. "You'll find that I've changed my mind about one of those. And maybe both."

30

JUNE 12, 2006

Laurel Lodge; Camp David, Maryland

The windows looked out mostly on pine trees—not the oaks and cedars and scrub that provided the backdrop for last August's war council in Crawford. The meetings scheduled for today and tomorrow would be twice as long and several times better publicized than those of the past summer. This was to be a serious event, one that showed a capacity for fresh thinking and a refusal to accept the diagnosis that Iraq and its new government were in free fall. Tomorrow's program would include a little tech-civic spectacular: a joint meeting of the Bush and Maliki cabinets, each visible to the other via video linkup.

Today's participants, assembled by Steve Hadley, were more numerous than those at the ranch last year. The morning session now complete, a considerable line of people waited to get their sandwich wraps and iced tea from the buffet. In the center of the conference table, configured for a working lunch, sat a single brick, flown in from Baghdad over the weekend. It came from the house of Abu Musab al-Zarqawi, Al-Qaeda's man in Iraq: last Wednesday, after more than three years of trying, a bombing raid had destroyed him and his dwelling—a small, rare piece of good news from what nobody was supposed to call "the front."

"Wonderful," said Condi Rice, setting down her plate and noticing the brick. She welcomed any tidings that might help her to sustain or (more truthfully) recover her optimism. General Casey hadn't given them much that was hopeful on this morning's video feed; Ambassador Khalilzad had been somber as well. More and more, despite everyone's best messaging, the bombing of the Golden Mosque, now over three months ago, seemed to signal inevitable defeat.

Waiting her turn at the buffet, Allison O'Connor found herself next to Don Rumsfeld—positioning reminiscent of their first meeting in the chow line at Bagram two years before. But any easiness or teasing that once existed between them was gone. Rumsfeld hadn't been in touch since her return to work, though he had sent a baby present.

"My little girl loves the stuffed rooster," Allie told him. "I'm sorry I haven't gotten around to thank-you notes."

"Tell the little lady she's very welcome."

"I guess I should also thank you for getting me into the thick of things today." She was one of only a handful of NSC staffers who'd been put on the helicopters and into the vans early this morning.

"I didn't request you."

"Oh? Who did?"

"My guess would be the only man whose ear really counts." The defense secretary knew that his plan to insinuate Allie's once-dissident viewpoint into the president's awareness had by now failed, even backfired. But he had hardly abandoned his own position. He pointed to Michael Vickers, once a CIA officer and now a think-tank scholar. "He's the one to pay attention to," Rumsfeld told Allie. Vickers and three other men from outside the administration would be presenting policy alternatives over lunch.

Rumsfeld sat down across from Condi, the brick from Zarqawi's pulverized house on the table between them. "Well, at least you didn't shout at the screen this morning," the defense secretary told his colleague.

"I've never 'shouted' at the screen," Condi replied.

"I remember things differently," said Rumsfeld, smiling brightly. Two and a half weeks ago, during a White House video conference with Baghdad, General Casey had described the forty-eight new State

Department–sponsored civilians headed to Iraq as "paltry." Condi had startled everyone by replying, "You're out of line, General"—and Rumsfeld had shown no hesitation in telling her that she was the one who had overstepped.

The president now sat down next to Rice. His mood was not cheerful. "So what would you *call* that?" he asked his top cabinet secretaries. "A 'dialectic'?" He remembered the word from Yale. State and Defense had overseen two different portions of this morning's agenda, each looking anything but bold, headed with upbeat propositions that sounded complementary instead of creatively competitive:

> *With our current level of assistance, Iraqis can build capacity to meaningfully govern the country within the next few years. (State)*

> *With our current level of assistance, Iraqis can build sufficient military capacity to meaningfully secure the country within the next few years. (DoD)*

The president had been bored during the polite discussion of "challenges" presented by each theorem. He was losing patience with his whole team, especially Casey. Rumsfeld had sent the general a congratulatory snowflake about the Zarqawi strike before learning that Bush had reserved his own compliments for General McChrystal, lower down the chain of command, who'd actually ID'd the terrorist's corpse. All morning the president had looked as if his real business lay elsewhere, far from Laurel Lodge. He'd been much more buoyant greeting the guest experts than his own staff.

These outsiders knew enough about him to begin their lunchtime presentations exactly at 12:35, as the schedule specified, no matter that everyone was still mid-meal. The four of them had ten minutes apiece to argue a strategy.

Fred Kagan, an AEI fellow still in his mid-thirties, with the slack-bodied look of a chess-club president, said he would read from a memorandum of conversations he'd been having with retired general Jack Keane: "There are no grounds for optimism without a substantially larger commitment. America has repeatedly taken half-measures in Iraq—with terrible consequences. Minimum force levels have repeatedly proved to be *sub*-minimal."

Rumsfeld interrupted him. "Half-measures?" His tone implied that Kagan had disparaged the sacrifice made by the dead. Cheney nodded, his facial expression showing the way he and his long-ago patron managed to remain in strange, eternal agreement, even when they were actually at odds. Like Kagan, the vice president leaned toward deploying more troops, not fewer, but the speaker earned a frown from Cheney for a remark about things not having gone "according to plan." By a sort of metaphysical trick, while he favored moving in the direction the presenter was advocating, the vice president could still make himself believe that things *had* gone according to plan, that the Americans had been greeted as liberators and the mission accomplished.

Kagan went on: "An ill-conceived mission cannot have success. Iraqi control is premature; the Iraqis' own security is the urgent, current need."

"And how many more American troops do you think it will take to accomplish that?" asked Rumsfeld. "Thirty thousand?" He spoke the number so that it sounded astronomical.

"Thirty thousand might bring security to *Baghdad*," Kagan replied.

Rumsfeld flipped to a different tab in his briefing book, so audibly he might as well have shouted "Next!"

Michael Vickers took the floor a minute later. He stood up and looked at those seated through the oval lenses of his glasses, so small they almost exactly outlined his eyeballs. He declared: "We don't have too few troops in Iraq; we have too many." He favored a small rapid-response force and talked about how effective just fifty-five U.S. trainers had been in getting El Salvador's army to defeat the insurgency there in the early eighties.

"Fifty-five?" asked Condi. "Not forty-eight?"

The president, who remembered the latter figure from her recent argument with Casey, realized the extent to which Rumsfeld still provoked her. Everyone in this room hated losing an argument, but

Condi was the person who most hated losing *control*. Lately, Bush has seen her lose it, and his sympathy was increasingly mixed with irritation. He could hear Hadley, seated on the other side of the secretary, leaning in to mollify her. The NSA whispered: "Vickers has been saying all of this since '04. I wouldn't take it too seriously."

As lunch wore on, most of those around the table spent less energy listening to the presenters, whose arguments they already knew, than watching the body language of the president. The substance of the proceedings by now seemed a far cry from what Tony Snow had been selling to the media. The rest of the afternoon's agenda, pointlessly marked CONFIDENTIAL, looked to Condi like a program schedule for C-SPAN. Topics included: "Security and Reconciliation," "What Will Bring the Sunnis In?" and "International Compact," a joint presentation of State and Treasury with a "focus on concrete deliverables."

As for the troop-level argument, its outcome remained as unclear as it had been last summer. One still couldn't tell if either side, the double-downers or Rumsfeld's retreat-by-another-name faction, had the momentum. All Condi knew was that one side would eventually win. She didn't want it to be Don's, but if it was, she needed to be on it, neither too soon nor too late. As always, she had made it her business to update her knowledge of even the lowest-level participants here, and she hadn't failed to observe a new coolness between Allison O'Connor and her patron. Condi wondered whether the woman might feel flattered to be enlisted in a move against Don—as soon as the time came.

During a last break in the afternoon schedule, the president asked for a word with Allie. "Got somebody to take care of your little girl tonight?"

"No," she answered.

"Could you arrange it?"

"Yes, sir."

"Good. Cancel any plans you have through tomorrow, and talk to Bolten as soon as this thing breaks up."

She'd expected to be home in Arlington by six-thirty. The

nanny—an old friend of her mother's who must be eighty but had the energy of a college girl—had agreed to stay until eight if need be. But what then?

When the final topic had been inconclusively exhausted, the president went outside to do a press briefing with Cheney, Rice, and Rumsfeld. Through the window the quartet appeared less like game-changers than a tableau of wearying familiarity. Their own faces seemed aware of it; even Cheney looked apologetic. As Allie watched for just a moment, the chief of staff approached her and quickly whispered some instructions. She said, "All right," and stayed behind while almost all the others started for the helipad and vans.

She dialed Ross's BlackBerry. "Are you in Washington?" she asked.

"Yes. Twelve more days at the office." He was correcting proofs of the guidebook, which he would hand-deliver to the office in New Orleans when he went down there on his own, for the start of a new life, at the end of the month. "What can I do for you?" he asked. This was the only question one could *ever* really ask Allie. Since that lunchtime with Dr. Asefi, she'd returned two of his seven phone calls and e-mailed him one additional baby picture. That was it. He lately suspected—forget about a hand to overplay—that he held no cards at all.

Allie answered: "I'd like you to babysit your daughter."

"Where will *you* be?" He was angry yet again. *Can't the three of us just go have supper at the Olive Garden? Pretend we're one more happy, fucked-up American family?*

"I'll be out of the country. But they tell me I'll be home tomorrow night. I can't say more." She told Ross that she could call and set things up for him with Ms. Macmurray, her nanny. "She'll give you everything you need. There's breast milk in the frig for a two-a.m. feeding."

Ross said nothing, even as he calculated how fast he could get over to her apartment.

"Do you remember much from Caitlyn?" she asked him.

"Christ, I've been a parent for fifteen years, Allie. You've been one for fifteen weeks."

"Ross, I could probably get Anne Macmurray to stay—"

"So why don't you?"

She didn't answer. And Ross realized she didn't need to. *She wants me to meet my daughter.* This was just the sort of oblique way that would allow for that, something she would have realized the moment the occasion arose.

"When you get back home," he replied, "I'm going to be there."

———

Air Force One, en route from Andrews Air Force Base to Baghdad

The emptiness of the plane—it carried the smallest sprinkling of staff and military support—bordered on unreality. The Air Force officer who came searching for Allie had to glance into six vacant rows of seats, as if searching for a lost package, before he found her sleeping and gently tugged her blanket. "Ma'am, the president would like to speak with you."

She opened her eyes and looked at her watch. If they were four hours into this eleven-hour flight, it was well past Bush's bedtime. Even so, on her way to the president, what came to her mind was the schedule that Ross would be following tonight.

She carried her briefing book up the aisle, but found the president sitting behind a table with only a glass of water on it, not even the deck of cards she'd heard was ever-present during Clinton's time.

He did not appear happy; he looked, in fact, as if he were the one being interrupted by *her* summons.

"Want something?" he asked, pointing to the glass of water.

She hesitated before asking, "Could I have a beer? I guess I won't be breast-feeding anytime in the next four hours." A navy steward fetched a Lone Star and then left the two of them alone.

"I first drank one of these at Fat Dawg's," she told the president. "I had a fake ID that no one bothered to look at."

Bush laughed, half-happily, at this mention of Hance's old bar, and maybe, Allie thought, over the memory of his daughters' underage, overcovered escapades.

"Tell me about the Weatherman," he said.

"Back then?"

"Sure."

She explained what had brought her father down to West Texas and then led him away; how, yes, she and Ross had met at the Bush Bash, then gone to see *Hooper*, and later had their first kiss on Buddy Holly's grave, "right after he'd heard that you lost."

"Good thing you didn't have a date on Election Night 2000. He wouldn't have known whether to make a move for another six weeks."

She tried not to let out that sycophantic laugh people did in the presence of the boss, but she heard herself doing it anyway. Bush's mood was expanding, like a loosening belt, though the relaxation was taking the form of long conversational pauses, his relief from the seven hours of nonstop talk in Laurel Lodge.

Josh Bolten briefly broke the silence by handing the president a wire-service tear sheet. Back on Earth, Karl Rove had just given a speech to the New Hampshire GOP: *"If Murtha had his way, American troops would have been gone by the end of April, and we wouldn't have gotten Zarqawi."*

"Great way to make friends," said Bush, with pursed lips, handing the paper back to Bolten. "With all these funding votes coming up."

"I guess good news emboldens people," said Allie. The president knew she wasn't referring to Zarqawi's demise, but to a late-afternoon report out of the Justice Department: Rove, it had finally been decided, would not be indicted in the Valerie Plame affair.

"Two things you need to know about Karl," said Bush. "First, he's brilliant. Second—excitement tends to make him an asshole."

Instinct told her not to laugh. "What'll actually happen tomorrow?" She meant at Laurel Lodge, not the Republican Palace; she was thinking of all those discussions, supposed to be so decisive and newsworthy, that now wouldn't take place. The briefing materials the

NSC staff had taken weeks to prepare would be thrown away like an uneaten dinner when the guest of honor turned out to be in Iraq instead of Maryland.

The president, however, assumed she meant what would happen in Baghdad. "I'll try to give Maliki the kind of support my secretaries of state and defense didn't exactly convey several weeks ago. And I'll listen to Casey tell me about Operation Together Forward—have you heard this latest plan? We clear; they hold. Sound coherent to you?"

"It sounds a little like Vickers."

"It sounds like Rumsfeld." After a pause, Bush asked, "What made him foist you on me last year?" He laughed, but only to apologize for the wording; he wanted an answer.

"I think it was to shake you up with my oddball perspective."

"He thought that would be more effective than all these inside/ outside experts?"

She opened her looseleaf binder to a chart—

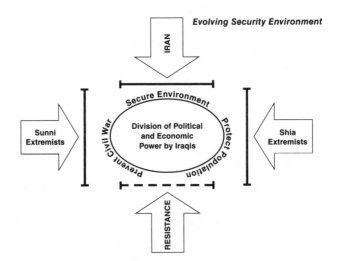

—and slid the absurd, meaningless graphic across the table to him. "When I look at this kind of thing," she said, "I don't feel quite so intimidated by all these people with their 'global security' degrees from Hopkins."

"That meeting today was a goddamned disaster. Everything came out status quo. Sticking with the muddle in the middle. And I knew it would be as bad as it was when they gave me a look at the agenda on Saturday. That's when I came up with this little change of plan for tomorrow. If we accomplish nothing on the ground, we'll still come out ahead of where that press conference left us this afternoon." He looked up at her and his scowl changed, with disconcerting quickness, to a smile. "You know, I think I get it now. I think Rumsfeld wanted you to be the 'office wife.' I see we've even put you in her clothes."

The pink-and-black top that Allie was wearing, along with the slacks, belonged to the First Lady. She'd been offered them before boarding the plane, and their fit was only approximate.

"Is there a particular reason you asked me along, sir?"

"Yeah. I want to meet that woman whose husband was killed by the militias. The one who gave you that piece of rope that you gave me."

She went on to tell him a fuller version of Rukia and Fadhil's story, beyond what had been on the accompanying card.

"This woman lives in the Green Zone? Get her to the RP tomorrow. See the Signal Corps guy way in the back of the plane and make it happen."

"Okay," Allie replied. "I'll try to focus on that instead of the corkscrew landing."

"You see that demonstration last week, the day before we got Zarqawi? The one that made me out to be the Antichrist, literally?" A local protest group had organized a 6/06/06 tableau outside the White House.

"I walked past it at lunch."

"Last summer you would have been *in* it. What's changed you? Besides this Hasani woman's story."

"You know what you said about Maliki at one point today? That you knew he would see this through—on account of how he stayed strong in opposition even after Saddam killed members of his family?"

"Yeah, though I haven't exactly seen into his soul, à la Pootie-Poot. In fact I've only seen him on a screen up to now. But I could sense pain and resolve. I'm looking forward to meeting him in the morning."

"I've begun to believe that this country"—she spoke as if they were already there—"wasn't maddened by religion. It was maddened by Saddam Hussein."

"Okay. It was Saddam and not all those generations of mullahs that made Iraq crazy. Why are you *now* thinking we ought to stay?"

"To force the bad to yield some good," she replied, with a speed that surprised them both. "I'm not a geopolitical thinker. I'm an Army lawyer." *And you and Rumsfeld have driven me crazy.* "I can't fully explain it."

"You sound like the Weatherman. The way he thinks something big and new ought to come out of the hurricane." He paused before saying: "You were in the Superdome."

She was taken aback that he knew this. But, as she'd told Ross, he wasn't without sources. Her expression indicated: *I don't want to talk about that.* And he got the message.

"I shouldn't be taking you away from your little girl."

"She's with her father."

Bush brightened. "I didn't think that was going to happen—from that time we talked right after you had her."

She saw him getting overly encouraged, as if she and Ross were some pet project, a faith-based initiative. "I don't know what's going to happen, Mr. President."

"I think I get him," said Bush. "He's past forty and he's cracking up a little. In a good way. A way I've seen. He feels goodness trying to break through him."

She worried he was going to ask if Ross had found the Lord. She hated this conversation, even more than she'd hated the one with a counselor that the OB-GYN doctor had made her see. She directed her next words more toward her lap than to the man across the table. "He's smart, but he's also boyish and guileless. If he were twenty-two instead of forty-four, and one of your daughters brought him home, you'd be thrilled."

"What I don't get is *you,*" said the president. "And I'll hazard a guess. *You* don't get you, either."

"If you had a chart of what's inside my head it would look like that monstrosity." She gave the open looseleaf a contemptuous push.

"Have another beer," said Bush. "My clock is way off, and I want to talk."

―――――

2001 N. Clarendon Boulevard, Arlington; 12:30 a.m.

The landline rang.

It was Anne Macmurray, to whom he'd said goodbye several hours ago, after hearing her life story; a pretty, elderly woman, long divorced, with grown grandchildren, who'd come to Washington twenty years ago to work for the nuclear-freeze movement. She'd written an unpublished novel and—Ross couldn't remember the rest. "You're *up*?" he asked her.

"Yes. I sleep less with every passing year. I just wanted to make sure everything is all right. *She's* not up, is she?"

Ross laughed. "No." Holley had remained oblivious to the ringing of the phone. "She's asleep next to her stuffed rooster, and I haven't stopped looking at her." The baby's hair, in the glow of the night light, was quite dark; it pleased him to have achieved that measure of genetic dominance, for there to be this persistent, visible reminder to the child's mother. "I have the alarm set to SOFT, in the other room, so I don't miss the feeding."

"I could call at two and remind you. I'm almost sure to still be awake."

"It's not necessary, Anne. But I'll look forward to seeing you in the morning."

"All right, Ross. Good night."

Over the next hour, when not marveling over his child, he let himself feel an alternation of resentment and gratitude toward Rumsfeld and even Bush for creating the night's strange circumstances. He also felt a weird, nostalgic desire to call Deborah: *Do you remember how* . . . ? Did the impulse make him despicable? Maybe just normal?

If Allie were in his position, she would have made the call, given in to the whim, not allowed it to subside, and only later let herself be surprised that indulging it had hurt someone else. He looked down at this little girl, who had shared those days in the Superdome, as if she might provide the answer—another piece of genetic information—as to why her mother was the way she was.

He sang a lullaby that the sleeping baby didn't need: *Just you and I . . .*

31

JULY 12–14, 2006

First United Methodist Church; Houston

At the sound of an old man's groan, a thousand silent people turned their heads toward the sanctuary. An emergency commotion now came from the spot. The assembled mourners, waiting for a memorial service to begin, wondered what it meant. An ambulance siren could soon be heard. Information then crossed the church in whispers, from one person to the next, like the brush of an angel's wing: Bob Lanier, once the city's mayor, was being taken away. His defibrillator had gone off, knocking him out.

"Jeepers creepers," said George H. W. Bush, when the news reached him in the front row. "I wonder if Cheney has to worry about that all the time."

"I shouldn't think so," replied his wife. "These days *he's* more lethal than his condition."

"Still," said 41. "Makes ya think."

The old mayor's collapse only added to the former first couple's recent intimations of mortality. Ken Lay, the disgraced head of Enron to whom they were bidding farewell today, had been only sixty-four when he died in Aspen last week—one day after the Bushes' eldest son, George W., turned sixty.

Today's service had drawn them down from the cool of Kennebunkport into the mephitic Houston heat, giving the Bushes a chance to add to the local display of loyalty toward Kenny, who'd still been awaiting his sentence from the court. True, he'd had coronary troubles—the top-notch treatment of which was one of the few reasons to live in this soggy medical mecca that sprawled ever more outward and upward—but Lay's relative youth and unfortunate circumstances made the death feel strangely like a suicide instead of something natural.

The delay caused by the ambulance was giving everyone in the church time to look around.

"Well, at least I don't see *her*," said Barbara Bush.

"Who?" asked her husband.

"Old Silverfoot."

The former president conceded that the absence of Ann Richards seemed odd; she had stuck up for Lay as much as a Democrat was allowed to. It took a minute before Bush remembered that Richards herself was sick.

"It's a lot worse than they've let on," said his wife.

Overhearing the exchange from the pew behind 41, Bob Mosbacher, once his handsome commerce secretary, leaned forward to whisper, "She's here in town."

"Not up in Austin?" asked Bush.

"Over at Anderson. In-patient."

The service began. A number of the tributes had an angry edge or undercurrent, as if Marc Antony were eulogizing Caesar. The general feeling in the church was that Kenny, whatever he'd been guilty of, had mostly been done in by inescapable economic forces and others' treachery. Over the course of an hour, George Bush looked increasingly preoccupied, as if the longer he listened the harder he was taking it. But when the service ended and people rose from their seats, he revealed a different source of agitation to his wife.

"I think we should go see her," he said.

"See who?"

"Ann Richards."

Barbara Bush reminded him that—aside from all else—they were supposed to be on someone's plane back to Maine in less than an hour. Lanier's unexpected defibrillation already had them cutting it close.

"They'll wait," said the former president. "Let's stop at Anderson on the way." He summoned the aide who these days spent a lot of time arranging his travels with Clinton. Within minutes, a visit had been set up. Yes, Governor Richards would be honored to see them, even though she tired easily.

*

The cancer center got her ready to receive the Bushes on the observation deck off the main building's twenty-fourth floor. Looking small in her wheelchair, Richards wore a bright-yellow sweater, even though up here the heat remained more fit for insects than humans. A piano player, who entertained patients and staff for much of each day, had been alerted to the Bushes' impending arrival. Knowing 41's love of country music, he launched into "Amarillo by Morning" when they came through the sliding doors.

In a whispered voice that retained its accent if not all its twang, Richards, unable to rise from her chair, smiled up at George Bush and said, "You've got your nerve. Up till a minute ago that guy had been in the middle of a *Guys and Dolls* medley." She accepted a kiss from the ex-president and a squeeze of the hand from his spouse.

The visitors sat down and didn't say much, knowing that one of Richards's main pleasures had always been to do the talking herself. "You know, for a while things were going just fine. I was getting the treatments locally, at the branch of this place up in Austin. I'd even drive to them in my old gas-guzzling Chrysler and get one of my kids to run me home. Then it got real ugly."

"The treatments or the disease?" asked Barbara Bush.

"Both." After a pause, Richards looked directly at the former First Lady and said, "I must say I never expected to see *you*." Minutes earlier, during one *Guys and Dolls* song, she'd even considered asking the fellow at the piano to play "Fascination" when 41 arrived. Those old rumors about him and Jane Morgan. . . .

"Something like this," said Bush, "makes politics—everything, really—seem pretty small."

Richards was enjoying his wife's discomfort, Bar's resistance toward dispensing any similar bromide. For a minute she let there be silence, as the old keynote-address quote practically hung above them like a banner. *Poor George! He can't help it! He was born . . .*

She at last relented, with an account of some bravely managed medical woe. "I always thought I'd just break in two at some point. Osteoporosis was really the only thing worrying me. I didn't figure on *rotting* from the center, which is what this feels like. Though I also feel like I'm on one of my exotic trips with Cecile—this time to outer space. Dear God, the *machinery* in there." She gestured toward the surgical acreage beyond the sliding doors. "Your son sent a nice letter. I had them fetch it from my room."

She took a folded piece of White House stationery from her sweater pocket and showed them the current president's handwritten message: *Laura and I have read about your battle with cancer. We wish you all the best and pray for your comfort. Knowing your strength and courage, all will be well.*

The president's father, these days the most sentimental of men, rubbed away a sniffle with his index finger. "Is there anything we can do?" he asked.

"Instead of just tiring you out," said Mrs. Bush, trying to speed things along.

"This visit's enough. I'm glad you came to see me. A week from now I'd say no—only because that's when the feeding tube goes in. At that point I'm going to become Greta Garbo."

Forty-one was tearing up. "I'm gonna go tip that fellow," he said, pointing to the piano player, who'd started in on "I Cross My Heart."

"George, it's not a cocktail lounge," his wife protested. But the former president, in an effort to keep from crying, had begun to cross the room. Bar, annoyed, was ready to say goodbye, and she couldn't very well say it by herself.

"How's your boy doing?" asked Richards. "Aside from being president."

"I'm not sure there *is* much aside from being president." Mrs. Bush could hear a curious humility in her own answer, the way it seemed to recognize occupants of the White House as underprivileged, or as being too dumb to have figured out the downside of things before-hand. "He'll have his life back, or some of it, in a couple of years."

Richards could feel several smart remarks rising to her lips—*Yeah, well, those two thousand dead GIs in Iraq won't have* their *lives back*—but she just wanted this woman to leave. She'd exhausted the fun to be had in observing her unease; and she was just plain exhausted herself.

Mrs. Bush then startled them both. "I never wanted it for him, you know."

Richards was struck by the remark. It felt real, not like small talk. "Not even the governorship?" she asked. The office young Georgie had seized from *her*? "Not even Congress?" She'd had so many fare-well letters these past weeks; even had a few from her ex-husband. This talk of Shrub—and his mother's contrary desires—was making her recall one note she'd had from that strange character in Slaton, the guy who liked to drop dark hints about the long-ago Bush Bash.

"You ever have anything to do with a fellow in Lubbock County called Bill Bright?" she asked the former First Lady.

Mrs. Bush flushed from the top strand of her pearls to her hairline, but said only: "Who?"

Richards looked away from her guest's suddenly pink skin and out toward the Houston skyline. She felt immediately thoroughly pleased with herself: "I should have guessed before now."

———

Strelna, Russia; July 14; 7:00 p.m.

"Yo, Blair!"

The president, coming out of Number Nine, had spotted the prime minister exiting one of the other seventeen cottages.

"Hello, George!"

The men and their wives approached one another; Cherie Blair gave Laura Bush a hug. Both couples had decided to forgo a golf cart for the short walk to Peter the Great's old summer house, and they now set off together, the Gulf of Finland behind them, the Konstan-tinovsky Palace just ahead.

"Pootie did himself proud here," Bush told Blair. Over the past five years, the Russian president had renovated the palatial compound, turning it into a conference center, for events like the current G8 meeting, as well as his own St. Petersburg residence.

"What are you two off to?" asked the prime minister. "I forget the schedule."

"Dinner with the Impaler."

"Ah, I'm afraid we have much more powerful company, George. We'll be with Frau Merkel—in the other wing of the palace, I sup-pose."

The Bushes had dined with the new chancellor last night in Ger-many, during a stopover on the way here.

"She really irks him, George. It's all about *deference*. He craves it every waking moment. When it comes to sheer touchiness, I haven't met his equal since Princess Margaret."

Bush wondered what it would be like having a royal family to deal with on top of everything else. He supposed the closest American equivalent was the "Club" of former POTUSes (plus the widow Rea-gan), even if that made him a prince as well as a president. Yester-day he'd had to issue a birthday proclamation for Ford's ninety-third, no matter that he was still stung by that little talking-to in Rancho Mirage.

"George, do we need to work up another joint statement?" Blair asked. Israel and Hezbollah had been clashing badly.

"I'll talk to Condi. They've put her and Burns with us at dinner tonight. She's even got a cottage."

"Burns is an effective fellow," Blair remarked of the U.S. ambas-sador to Russia.

"He's a good man. Clinton once had him in Jordan," said Bush. "Maybe he can be helpful with the Hezbollah stuff; he worked out a cease-fire down there in '01, just after I came in. He also did some good stuff in getting Libya to shed its nukes. You may have *heard* that that happened."

"You know, George, you *will* get credit for that. Be patient. You'll see."

The president pouted. Ambassador Burns had once told him the same thing. And William Burns *was* a good guy. But unlike Dad, or Condi, or Colin before her, Bush could still never make himself comfortable around the career people from State. For God's sake, Burns had once been *Madeleine Albright's* executive assistant. He and Condi would probably chat about Albright's *father*, Condi's grad-school mentor, over dinner tonight.

" 'Restraint,' " said the president. "That's the word we'll keep using. In a joint statement."

"Yes," replied Blair. "Keep the emphasis on not doing anything to knock Lebanon off its democratic path."

Years of working together allowed them to wrap up something like this with dispatch. Even so, Cherie Blair urged her husband along. "Hurry up, dearie. The frau has an even more Teutonic thing about punctuality than George." Always wary of the "poodle" factor, she occasionally turned Tony into that breed all on her own. She now pulled him toward the palace as if tugging on a leash.

Condi was already inside with Ambassador Burns. The two of them greeted the Bushes and said they weren't quite sure how private or friendly this dinner was likely to prove; the president's main meeting and press conference with Putin were both scheduled for tomorrow. As they waited for their host, Bush told his secretary of state what sort of Israel statement he wanted.

The Russian president's arrival increased everyone's uncertainty. For several minutes Putin stood with his wife, Lyudmila, at the entrance to the banquet room, conferring with an aide. He did not look pleased, and the American party wondered if his mood reflected irritation over the World Trade Organization—Russia still couldn't get itself admitted—or something else.

"Dangerfield," Bush whispered to Burns, who heard the remark as two words and tried to guess what set of perils the president was alerting him to.

"Rodney," Bush offered, by way of clarification. "No respect."

In a low-cut dress and with lots of blue eye shadow, Mrs. Putin seemed to both Bush and Condi heavier and more somber than she had in Moscow last year. Porter Goss, now departed from the CIA, had given them reports of her husband's philandering and abuse. Even beatings had been mentioned—before the president said he didn't want to hear any more.

Bush felt himself on edge tonight, unable to stop worrying that they'd all be interrupted by some terrorist incident, the way last summer's G8 in Scotland had been upended by the bombing of the London Underground.

Putin quickly disappeared and came back—this time actually entering the room and wheeling a silver bicycle in with him. "Happy birthday," he called out, with a heavy accent but no real cheer.

It was a fancy little piece of machinery with stylish, Sputniky ornaments. But it seemed pointedly less masculine than, say, a gun, or even the saddle that Bush himself had given Charlie Windsor a while back. "Blair got me a sweater," he informed the Russian president. "Burberry's." Everyone laughed.

"We all know about that," said Putin.

Yeah, thought Bush. *Along with everything else we're saying in those bugged cottages.* "I thought a few of these might be for *me*," he said, pointing to a golden bowl filled with Fabergé eggs. The objects were inviting to the hand; he felt an urge to pick one up and squeeze it like a baseball, but he resisted. A couple of weeks ago at Graceland, Koizumi, the Elvis fanatic, had impulsively tried on a pair of the King's curated sunglasses. Priscilla P. had damn near died, as if he'd used a piece of the true cross as a toothpick.

The two presidents sat beside each other. A first, fishy course was already on the single table. From the nasty looks of it, Bush thought he'd rather have one of the peanut-butter-and-banana sandwiches they'd offered Koizumi on the day of the Memphis trip.

"You know," said Putin, as if he'd picked up Bush's thought about the wired cottages, "we could have had you all stay on boats in the harbor, the way Gorbachev did at Reykjavik. Mrs. Merkel would have felt right at home." He explained how a little German fleet had occupied the inlet here for some of the war, until the Soviets succeeded in blowing up most of the ships.

"Does Angela know that story?"

Putin ignored the question. "The Swedes owned this whole place once. Now they're not even important enough to be part of the G8."

A few translators ringed the table like pieces of jewelry. Lyudmila was telling Laura about some recent misguided spelling reforms of the Russian alphabet. Condi pretended to take an interest in that while Burns strained to hear what passed between the presidents.

Bush waited for the conclusion of the main course—more fish—to ask if he and Putin could go off to the side and have a brief conversation about nukes, a word that seemed to require six syllables for translation.

"Ah, planning another crusade?" asked Putin, as they moved to a sort of love seat against the far wall. "This time in Iran? Will you be turning it into another fine democracy like Iraq? Something the Hunter would like *us* to take for a model?" Cheney had criticized the state of Russian civil liberties a couple of months back.

Throughout this little cascade of rhetorical questions, Bush saw the ex-KGB man maintain a smile as sharp and serene as his own mother's. The most recent annoyance now agitating Vlad was a meeting Bush himself had just had with a group of Russian dissidents, like the refuseniks of another era. He began complaining about it.

"I was actually talking about Kim" was all Bush replied, forcing discipline upon himself, resisting the maternally acquired instinct to strike back. The North Koreans had conducted a missile test the week before last, and tomorrow at the press briefing both he and Vlad would recommend a yes vote on whatever limp condemnation the UN was working up. This was the moment to press the idea he'd first floated during the V-E celebrations—a whole goddamned year had gone by since then.

"Democratization means imperialism," said Putin.

Yeah, yeah. It was like Dad used to say about the Chinese. You had to let them get through these little lectures before the conversation could get down to business. He looked over at Condi and knew how, once that happened, he would be getting far out in front of her and Don and even the Hunter. But he still wasn't ready to loop any of them in; he wasn't willing to see what he had in mind become one more sandbox battle between Condi and Rummy, or Condi and Dick. She wanted only State to be in charge of North Korea and along with Zelikow was now talking about negotiating a peace treaty, something apart from the never-going-anywhere "six-party talks." He'd done some bobbing and weaving on that more than a year ago, made her believe *he* was considering it. But none of it was going to happen, not after the other week's missile test. Rumsfeld wanted sanctions that would force Kim's generals to remove him in a coup—kind of like his Iraq policy: let the natives take it on! But Bush had decided he wasn't going to wait for that, either.

Vlad's imperialism tutorial still hadn't run out of steam. Bush again looked toward Condi, sensing how everywhere and nowhere she was these days. On Iraq he needed *direction*, something highly specific, but she still wanted to know what *he* thought before she'd think for herself. More and more she struck him as an isolated, artificial figure, with no place to go and nothing to contribute. He blamed himself for not making more demands of her, giving her occasions she could rise to. Even at this moment he could see her agreeing with both sides of the Russian spelling issue.

Pootie seemed to be yielding the floor at last, so he seized the moment. "They've tested missiles before. But the test of a *weapon* can't be many months off. You know what I've suggested in order to prevent it."

"And our Chinese friends?"

"*We* do it, but they know in advance. They condemn it in public and experience private delight. Like everyone did when the Israelis took out that Iraqi reactor twenty-five years ago." Time to flatter; *deference*, as Tony suggests. "*Sweden* can't do it. Only the two most powerful countries in the world can."

Putin paused, responding a half-minute later as if he'd just recalled some trivial matter he would attend to when there was time. "You'll have your answer this fall. When the leaves are falling on your bicycle path."

"Fair enough."

This wasn't destined to be a late night. Mrs. Putin seemed the only one who wanted to prolong it, so she didn't have to go home too soon with Vlad. It was barely past nine when Burns said goodbye and started back to his hotel. Lyudmila, needing some air, declared that she would walk Laura part of the way to the cottage. As they went off, Bush fell in with Condi. There was no sign of the Blairs on the path—maybe they were having a grand time with Merkel.

"I just talked to Jack Straw's successor on the phone, during coffee," Condi told him. "The 'restraint' statements are all set. They'll be separate, but they'll jibe."

Did she need praise even for *this*—which was beneath both their pay grades? He felt guilty for mocking her in his head, but he needed more from the person in her job. Would she flourish if he got rid of Rumsfeld? But what would *that* involve? Bringing in a defense secretary just like *her*?

"Well, I guess I can't complain that my wife is a clothes horse." He'd just recognized the pink-and-black blouse that Laura was wearing; realized she'd gotten it back from Allison O'Connor. He explained to Condi that it had looked very different without tonight's fancy skirt and jewelry.

"What did you have Allison do on the Iraq trip?" Rice asked.

"Wasn't time to do much. She met with their judiciary people." The Saddam verdict was probably still months away. "And she introduced me to the widow of her translator."

"Does she still hold Don's view of things?"

"At this point, anything but!" He laughed, but he didn't want to make this, too, about Condi and Don. He'd put O'Connor on the plane because she and the Weatherman, this peculiar couple collaterally damaged by the war and the storm, were on his mind in a personal way. He'd even told Laura about them.

"What did Allison think of the Camp David meeting?"

"She didn't talk about it much, other than to agree it was a godawful waste of time."

"I think Steve was badly served by the staff."

"Actually, *I* was badly served," said the president.

Condi felt depressed that she had nothing to offer him right now except her little back-and-forth on Israel and Hezbollah. So she asked, with a tinge of jealousy that would not bear much thinking about: "What *did* you talk about? You and Allison."

"Her home life. She doesn't have much of one."

His terseness, and Condi's own single status, didn't invite much in the way of a follow-up question.

As it was, he felt more alive to the echo of Allison's voice than to the actual one of his secretary of state. He could once again hear what O'Connor had told him amidst the low roar of the *Air Force One* engines: *I did a cruel thing to Ross. My stupid need to be contrarian didn't allow me to see it. But undoing it the way he'd like me to may be worse. There may not be a solution for me.*

"She said her whole life had been a series of evasive maneuvers— like the corkscrew landing she was dreading." Condi nodded, and he decided he'd probably said more than he should have. "I'm never going to get to sleep with these damned 'white nights'" was all he added.

32

AUGUST 29, 2006

**Warren Easton Charter High School, 3019 Canal Street,
New Orleans**

Now on the aisle in the fourteenth row, Ross had gained admittance to
this event with his old NEAH ID card, and he'd gotten Mrs. Carlotta
Watson in with him. He'd asked Gary Fowler where in Holy Cross he
might find her. That turned out to be a FEMA trailer that she'd at last
been lent. She had no recollection of meeting him last September, but
Gary had persuaded her to accompany Mr. Weatherall.

With so many emotional commemorations taking place around the
city today, one featuring George W. Bush didn't strike everyone as
particularly special, and the audience here was less handpicked than
usual for a presidential showcase. The last thing the White House
wanted on the first anniversary of Katrina was the appearance of
excessive PR management. Looking around, Ross could see a school
auditorium filled with ordinary parents, students, and minor community leaders, including Gary.

Coming into the building he'd even seen Gordon, last year's drinking companion in the Chart Room. This morning the conspiracist
had stood near the front doors beside a poster of Pete Fountain and
his clarinet—a tribute to one of Warren Easton's alumni. "No poster
of Lee here, you'll notice." The observation had left Ross and Mrs.
Watson baffled, until Gordon, with his vast and overlapping knowl-

edge of the Kennedy assassination, explained that for one month in the fall of 1955, before dropping out, at the age of sixteen, Lee Harvey Oswald had received the last of his formal schooling here at Warren Easton High. "Good to know," Ross had replied, noticing that Gordon didn't try to advance past the metal detector.

If the machine could detect thoughts instead of metal, he wasn't sure he'd have gotten past it himself. He had a long-shot plan for his attendance here today.

Before leaving the government he'd had a memo, from a deputy assistant secretary at the Department of Education, forcefully suggesting that the updated guidebook extol the fact that Warren Easton, a year after the storm, was reopening as a charter school. According to the memo writer, the guide's authors should take this opportunity to point out how charter schools were contributing to the revitalization of American cities. A paragraph of recommended text followed. Ross had pruned it back into something more objective, while acquiring, as he headed out the door, a final sense of being used.

On July 2nd he'd rented a small room on Dauphine Street. He'd awakened there this morning before bells began ringing to mark the moment last August 29th when the levees started to break. A nearby steeple was still clanging two hours later, one peal for each of the seventeen hundred people who'd died in the hurricane.

This afternoon he would go off to his part-time job at Catholic Charities, where he did paperwork and made phone calls for people seeking to return home for good. One day a week he worked with a group scraping mold: what the NEAH did through grants, he was now doing with his hands. He could feel his body regaining the tautness it had had when he was thirty.

Father Montrose, he knew, didn't entirely approve. He had made the connection for him at Catholic Charities, but expressed doubt that Ross was really experiencing a sort of Dorothy Day vocation. Was it instead maybe some temporary crisis of the spirit, a penitential impulse engendered by the calamity of a love affair—the one that produced the baby daughter whose conception had been revealed in the warehouse on Poydras Street?

As the live reporters and camera crews did their final setups, a woman on Mrs. Watson's right, a teacher told her and Ross that last year she'd caught her evacuation bus to the Superdome from here. As she imparted the recollection her voice rose with a sort of panicked giddiness; she too was still living in a FEMA trailer, and she nervously kneaded a tissue while the First Lady took the podium in advance of the president.

Mrs. Bush talked briefly about getting books back into schools, with an emphasis on thanking corporate donors that struck Ross as a bit heavy. She introduced her husband to respectful, nonclamorous applause. Ross could see the back of Mayor Nagin's shaved head bobbing in the front row between Bobby Jindal and Mary Landrieu. Bush himself was soon thanking all the officials, as if they, too, were selflessly helping out, like Target or Conoco/Philips. He launched, with a kind of slow reverence, into a *tour d'horizon* of last year's ordeal. *Those of you who were stranded on rooftops looked to the sky for deliverance, and then you saw the Coast Guard choppers come. Members of the Louisiana National Guard, who had just come back from Iraq, stepped forward . . .*

The "Cajun Navy" was praised for its volunteer rescues; even Catholic Charities got a shout-out.

The *mea culpa*, when it came, was forthright enough—*Government at all levels fell short of its responsibilities*—though Ross noted that it took up less than half a sentence before turning into a series of self-congratulations. *Every department of my administration has looked at its response to last year's hurricanes and recommended practical reforms, things to do to make sure that the response is better.* Yes, even NEAH, Ross recalled: the Chairman's daily reports on Katrina-related activity, mandated by the White House, had for months gone on arriving in his electronic in-box. They'd all sounded urgent, and been irrelevant.

After addressing the need for a new barrier system (still not Category Five) and faster debris removal, the president got around to . . . charter schools: *"It's good for New Orleans to have competing systems!"*

It was at this point that a Secret Service man took up position next

to Ross. "Please come with me to see the president as soon as he con-
cludes," the agent whispered.

"I'm impressed," said the teacher beside Mrs. Watson.

"Don't be," replied Ross. These last months his e-mails to Bush
had grown infrequent but more forceful; they expressed a citizen's
anger rather than the constructive criticism of someone who had been
until recently on the White House's personnel roster. The president's
replies had been brief and fairly gentle, and Ross had let him know
that he would be in the audience today.

Bush ended his speech with a call for return: *New Orleans needs
people—she needs those saints to come marching back, is what she needs!*

"My friend will come with me," Ross told the agent, who gave him
a doubtful look but relented when he saw him having to help Mrs.
Watson to her feet. This was a surprise to her; not a pleasant one,
either, to judge from her expression. But she agreed to accompany the
younger man.

They were led to a spot backstage near the edge of the curtain, as
Ross imagined how many times *The Member of the Wedding* and *Our
Town* had come to high school life here. A few feet away he could
see Nagin reluctantly conversing with Governor Blanco; the mayor
recognized but ignored him. Within less than a minute Bush himself
approached.

"What did you think?" the president asked. "I like the look of the
school."

"There are only twenty-two thousand students now starting school
in the city, Mr. President. Normally it's fifty-five."

Bush narrowed his eyes, and a nasty tone crept into his voice. "You
read that in the paper this morning."

"Yes, sir, I did." Ross did nothing to hide the hostile impulse that
had brought the statistic to his lips.

But Bush was smiling again. "We're in agreement. We both want to
speed up whatever it takes to get people back here."

"I believe we see things differently, sir. I see them the way Mrs.
Watson does. I've written you about her a number of times. She's the
lady who's suffered so much from FEMA's mistakes. Her daughter—"

"I remember the story," Bush said curtly. He clasped and held Mrs. Watson's hand and told her, softly, "I'm pleased to meet you, and I'm very sorry for your losses."

Mrs. Watson nodded with bare politeness. She glanced from the president to Ross, the look on her face conveying exactly what she understood of this moment: *This isn't about me; this is about the two of you. And that's the same kind of unholy blindness that killed my daughter and a thousand others down here.* "I'd like to sit someplace," she said.

A young aide led Mrs. Watson to a folding chair several feet away.

"Smell your hand, Mr. President," Ross suggested.

Bush looked at him angrily, letting him know he wasn't going to participate in some little stunt right after the ambush he'd just endured.

"It probably smells the same as mine right now. It's the odor of formaldehyde. People who live in the FEMA trailers, once they're able to get them, wind up reeking of it. Mrs. Watson says she keeps trying to scrub it off herself, but it never comes out."

Bush took a ten-second pause. "I appreciate your concern, Weatherman. Appreciate your commitment to this city, one way or another. I also appreciate your commitment to your little girl."

"Allison told me of your interest," said Ross. She had given him a predictably oblique and incomplete account of her airborne conversation with the president in June. What he wanted to know is why Bush cared.

"You don't write me much lately," said the president.

"Well, I'm on the outside now. Since the end of June."

"What precisely are you doing?"

Ross explained how this afternoon he'd be trying to help a displaced family return to New Orleans from Tyler, Texas.

"Good man. You need to get your own family moved here."

For a moment he thought Bush was talking about Deborah and Caitlyn and Archer, back in Dallas. Then he realized it was Allison and Holley being referred to. He wondered: Was Bush going to arrange Allie's relocation? Put her to work here in some structure General Honoré had left behind?

"I'm not sure she's ready for that, sir."

"Well," said the president, "she's a complicated person. Maybe she needs more incentive."

Ross was teeing up what had seemed the unaskable question. *Why are you taking an interest in the two of us?* But just then another young aide whispered something to Bush. With a wink, and a shrug of apology, the president was off to say a few words to Congressman Jindal.

———

The Carousel Bar, Hotel Monteleone; 7:45 p.m.

The Scott family, headed by a single mother, had achieved a 33.3 percent rate of satisfaction in Tyler, Texas. Mrs. Scott had found little work in fast-food restaurants, and her fifteen-year-old son, who believed Tyler to be "like *Friday Night Lights* with ugly people" had remained desperate to come home. Only the boy's younger sister, having discovered the Lord at a revival meeting for tweens, wanted to stay.

Ross was telling all this to Emile, who'd invited him to the Monteleone to reminisce about the adventure they'd shared twelve months ago. The men sat at the rotating bar, drinking pisco sours.

Emile had spent last fall living in the hotel as it struggled back to life. His own family returned to New Orleans in December, and they were all able to move back into their old house after New Year's. He counted himself lucky, but joked to Ross that he missed his commute from the eighth floor to the lobby.

The two of them were doing their best to inject some merriment into the anniversary, but Ross remained aware of the hair shirt he himself seemed unable to shed. His own part of the conversation kept returning to grimness and fuck-ups. He was now back on the Scotts: "It looks as if there could be steady work for the mother at a diner starting up on Claiborne. And there's a place for them to live in the Tremé. But the closest middle school to that hasn't reopened. The son's *old* school, in Hollygrove, the one he wants to go back to, *is* open, but he won't be allowed to attend if they move to the new neighborhood." The question of the family's return had still been open when he left the Catholic Charities office at six-thirty.

Emile nodded, though his attention was glazing over.

Ross noticed a couple sitting across the bar, a bit younger than himself and Allie. As they got up from their seats, he recognized them: they'd been guests at the hotel during the storm, ones who'd managed to get out relatively early.

"They're back," Emile explained. "Sort of a pilgrimage."

The couple seemed to recall Ross, too, and they came over to shake hands. "Why don't you come with us?" the man asked. They were driving to the Superdome for a candlelight vigil. "There but for the grace of God," said the woman. "You know?"

Ross could perceive her sincerity, but also an odd sort of envy, as if she wished she had a better I-was-there story than just a tale of having ridden out Katrina at the Monteleone. Even so, he agreed to go with the two of them, arriving at the Superdome after passing the bouquets and crosses that had been deposited today along Sugar Bowl Drive. A modest crowd stood behind a cyclone fence, half of them with their candles already lit. The others were waiting for a darker darkness, so that their lights would blaze a little brighter. The stadium's interior repairs had been completed—the Saints would again be playing football here in a few weeks—but the outside of the building seemed to Ross irredeemably ugly, like wet and slimy clay still spinning on a potter's wheel.

His daughter Caitlyn truly grasped how far down in the world he'd come when he turned in his BlackBerry to the NEAH and acquired a flip phone for himself. He was fingering it now, fighting the temptation to call Allie, knowing she would snap shut like the phone itself at any attempt to prod her into anniversary reflection. Even now she'd told him very little of what had happened inside the arena, and he still felt he didn't have a right to ask—no matter that the half-living Holley had been inside there with her.

Some cheers could be heard from about fifty feet away. A fit-looking man whose hair seemed immune to the late-summer humidity held a cordless mic while hopping onto a flatbed truck. When he turned around, Ross saw that it was John Edwards.

"I don't want to politicize a solemn occasion," said the former senator, "but we wouldn't be having this anniversary if the politics of neglect hadn't turned a natural disaster into a vast human tragedy!"

Ross felt a resurgence of the anger he'd displayed toward Bush this morning, and wanted to make his way to Edwards, hoping he wouldn't need to reintroduce himself yet again. Losing sight of the couple who'd driven him here, he approached the politician's aide, a different one from the guy he remembered seeing outside Mrs. Boggs's house in January. This new kid stood behind someone with a short blond ponytail who was videotaping Edwards's remarks. Ross stared at her, then recognized that this was the woman who'd been shooting a "webisode" at the last Hitchens party. He couldn't remember her name. "Ms. R.H.," the aide now called her, with some sarcasm. "I'm Rh-negative myself, but go ahead and talk to her. *Rielle!*"

As soon as Edwards finished speaking, the woman turned around to give Ross a big hello—"You look familiar!"—along with her business card:

BEING IS FREE: RIELLE HUNTER—TRUTH SEEKER

Ross introduced himself, and the aide, as if in competition with Ms. Hunter, gave him a business card of his own, with an address for the more conventional part of Edwards's operation, his One America PAC.

"Did you hear him?" asked an excited Rielle Hunter. "Whenever he tells me he wants to be like RFK, I tell him he's already *surpassed* Bobby!"

Edwards approached, and Rielle blotted his forehead with a pink tissue. Ross held out his hand and said his name, and this time Edwards said, "Yes!" He finally did seem to remember. "I'm looking forward to having you with us about four months from now," he added, with a wink reminiscent of Bush's this morning—in this case, a coy acknowledgment of his still-officially-undeclared candidacy. And then he went off to shake some hands.

"We're on our way to Missouri for Labor Day!" Rielle informed Ross. "We've just come from his *ginormous* new kick-ass house in Chapel Hill." While there, she'd videotaped Edwards's two youngest children. "So fucking *adorable*!" The ex-senator's wife and eldest daughter had been away. "And so much work to be done!" she added.

All the candles were now lit.

33

SEPTEMBER 12–14, 2006; 5:10 A.M.

Pictou Lodge Resort; Nova Scotia, Canada

"I'm going to open a window," said Condi, tugging on the blond hair of the naked Canadian foreign minister. She gave his well-developed chest a kiss before getting up from the bed.

"If you do, then I'm going to hog the blankets," said Peter MacKay. "Shouldn't a Southern girl like you dislike the cold?"

As he pulled the comforter in his direction, Condi admired the forearm flexors of Canada's Sexiest Male MP—the Conservative six-time winner of that title bestowed by one of the political papers up here.

Their just-completed lovemaking resembled the U.S.-Canadian relationship itself: affectionate; not especially dramatic; and unlikely to evolve. Peter, a player of rugby and hockey, might fit the athletic profile of the men she generally went for, but his being eleven years younger added an uncharacteristic loucheness and spontaneity to an encounter that was already nearing its end in the dawn's early light.

She had arrived in Nova Scotia yesterday around three o'clock, after a fifth-anniversary commemoration of 9/11 on the South Lawn of the White House and then a quick reception for foreign diplomats back at State. She was here to celebrate the help Canadians had given in 2001 to the thousands of passengers whose flights were diverted to Halifax after the second plane struck the Trade Center.

The Canadians always seemed to be assisting when Americans were at some low, victimized point: she thought back to the U.S. hostages they'd once managed to save from the Iranians. Since yesterday, on some small, personal level, Peter had been supplying more of a rescue than he knew. A Nova Scotian himself, he had, after this event, taken her—and a lot of press—on a long drive that ended with a tour of his hometown and dinner with his parents. The two of them had pulled off their private liaison here via a quick plan that necessitated making only a single member of Condi's security staff, the most reliable one, any the wiser. Peter had concocted the scheme well in advance. Now, just a couple of hours from sunrise, she remained more delighted by his ingenuity than bothered by his presumption. One couldn't say there'd been *no* buildup to this; the two of them had hit it off from the moment he assumed the foreign ministry last winter.

As she returned to the bed, he joked: "We're really speeding along here. You've already met the parents."

"Your father and *step*mother," Condi reminded him. "Which worked to my advantage. The stepmother always supports the step-son's choice of a girlfriend, because she always feels on shaky ground with the son she's inherited."

Peter smiled broadly and Condi felt the twinge of a particular post-coital sadness: it was a shame that this all had to be played for laughs.

"So," she added, commencing a list of his recent high-profile romances: "A cabinet minister's daughter; a female MP . . . Is there a pattern here?"

"If there is, I'm *really* trading up now!"

"I should say."

He was fully comfortable with this one-off sex in a way she never would be. If it hadn't been passionate for either, the pleasure for him had been more thorough, uncomplicated by any compulsion to think two steps ahead of his body. However politically well-connected his girlfriends might be, it was *she* who could never experience sex, or love, outside an intricate strategy of preparation, attainment, and advancement. A proper marriage had once been the end zone on this gridiron of calculation, but she recognized now that her aversion to risk had crushed any real chance of romantic success: she was always too afraid of losing ten yards on a penalty to make any bold play that might carry her down the field.

"You know," she said, enjoying the breeze from the open window, "I wish *I* could say 'cancer.'"

MacKay looked up with alarm, until he realized she was referencing some public remarks of his on the Israeli-Palestinian question, in which he had used the medical metaphor to describe Hezbollah. She was expressing a wish that in both her personal and professional lives she didn't always have to act as the cautious, calibrating steward of a superpower. What relief there would be in representing a mid-level country—or in being a mid-level person!

"Katyusha rockets," said MacKay, naming Hezbollah's weapon of choice. "Talk of them provides the oddest afterglow, don't you think?" It was clear that they wouldn't be going back to sleep. He put one arm around her as she rested her head on his chest.

"What did you think of the speech?" she asked.

MacKay assumed she meant the anniversary address that Bush had given from the Oval Office last night. They'd both seen the text before executing their evasive after-dinner maneuvers at the lodge.

"Not much," he replied. "As I think I already told you, no?"

"I'm sorry. I meant the speech from last Wednesday." The only one that had been on her mind. "The speech about the post-9/11 detainees."

"Ah," said MacKay. "Dubya doubles down."

"But he *wasn't* doubling down!" cried Condi. She sat up, outside Peter's embrace. "That's the trouble. Everyone heard it the way you did." In the East Room, with a group of 9/11 families for an audience, the president had promised to transfer some nonstate enemy combatants from the CIA prisons exposed in the press last year to the relatively more transparent walls of Guantánamo. But the speech, written by a hardliner who'd previously worked for Don, spent most of its time defending and justifying the very system whose need for dismantlement the president was conceding. The address had gone so far as to contain a nice-sounding endorsement of the "alternative" interrogation techniques whose existence Michael Hayden, the new CIA director, had finally admitted to the Senate Intelligence Committee. And there was no mention of actually *closing* the secret prisons.

Condi explained to Peter how she'd walked out of the Roosevelt Room last month believing that on this contentious issue she'd beaten Dick "bigtime" (one of Cheney's cherished words) and, to a lesser extent, had defeated Don as well—only to wind up, once the September 6th speech got made, feeling like the loser.

A rustle in the lodge's hallway signaled the arrival of the *Chronicle Herald*, left dangling from the doorknob by a hotel employee who believed only Secretary Rice to be occupying the room.

"I'm sure it's been swept for anthrax," said MacKay, getting up to fetch the newspaper in its little plastic bag. "We do look smashing together," he declared upon returning. Two pictures of them graced the front page, though the large, long headline came out of Bush's televised anniversary address: "The Safety of America Depends on the Outcome of the Battle in the Streets of Baghdad." Pointing to it, MacKay asked Condi, in an entirely businesslike tone: "Do you believe that? Honestly."

"Can we stick to the earlier speech?" she replied.

"Okay. What are you going to do about *that*?"

"Keep pretending it was a great victory. That we've judicialized the detainee problem and will now start punishing the 9/11 masterminds in the courts."

"Why not relitigate the issue? Within the administration, I mean. If the president inclined more in your direction than Cheney's—no matter what the speechwriter ended up conveying—why not pull him further?" They were both once more under the covers; Condi realized she'd overdone the open window. She answered Peter with a sort of absent defeat. "I need to pretend this is already a victory, because I have no other."

"How about nailing me? Doesn't that count? Kidding!"

She let herself be the silent little spoon for a few minutes, but before either of them could drift off she told him the story of how yesterday morning on the South Lawn she'd looked up at a low-flying plane making an ordinary approach toward Reagan and had a panic attack—thinking for a second that 9/11 was happening all over again; feeling, once the moment subsided, that she needed to chuck her job and go back to California.

"You just sagged for a minute," said the ever-ebullient MacKay. "That's all. Your subconscious knew that you were looking at the shuttle, and what made you buckle was actually an awareness of the more tedious parts to your life—all that back-and-forth New York–to-D.C. movement, especially when the UN has its opening show. Remember: that's next week, dear girl."

"But I felt *panic*."

"Anxiety is symptomatic of depression."

This seemed as unlikely to be true as the idea that she would ever allow herself to see a shrink.

"You know," she said, returning with a kind of wistful obsession to the detainee discussions before the September 6th speech, "it *felt* like a victory. I told the president, 'Don't let this be your legacy'—the torture, the secret prisons. And that *registered* with him."

"That's *not* his legacy."

Condi turned around, hopefully, but saw in Peter's face something like the prosecutor he'd been at the start of his career. "His legacy is Iraq," he told her. "And the goose is cooked."

*

At five-thirty that afternoon, after touching down at Andrews, she made a stop at her Foggy Bottom office. She was due at the EOB for a six-fifteen meeting with Nicolas Sarkozy, the French interior minister running to replace Chirac as president. If he succeeded, they would have a pal in the Élysée, and the Axis of Weasel—Gerhard Schröder now being gone—would be sundered. Sarkozy had been to a firehouse in New York yesterday, while the president was at Ground Zero reading the names of the deceased. A transcript of the Frenchman's subsequent Washington speech now sat on Condi's blotter: *Bin Laden targeted New York, but he might just as well have targeted Paris.* He'd made the remarks at the DAR's headquarters, a fact Jim Wilkinson took excited note of in the margin: *"We should have been there for this! JW."* The gall of him: he was thinking of the triumphant little Marian Anderson ironies they could have exploited. She wished she could respond: *Actually, Halifax was better. I got laid.*

Disagreement did appear between Sarkozy and Bush on global warming, of which the interior minister took the rational view. Why, she wondered, despairingly, couldn't their own conservatives shed their primitivism on issues like this? Everywhere else the center-right didn't seem encumbered that way. Peter had told her he planned to vote for gay marriage in the Canadian Parliament before the year was out. If only her own president could ease up on such things and still feel free and virile the way "Sarko" and Peter seemed to! Of course *they* didn't have Karl hamstringing them with that ticker-tape of polling stats that never stopped rolling from his mouth.

Under the speech transcript sat a pink telephone message only a half hour old. *Mrs. Reagan.*

She hadn't seen her since the Charles-and-Camilla dinner, and had never felt much warmth from her direction; mostly just a sense of being 41's protégée, and therefore the appendage of an appendage, a mere tertiary outgrowth of Ronald Reagan himself. No matter: Nancy was still NANCY, and Condi needed to return this call right away.

The operator found the former First Lady on her patio in Pacific Palisades. She told Condi she was having an enormous chocolate-chip cookie that Merv Griffin had brought when he visited yesterday.

"I can't believe you eat dessert!" said Condi.

"If you want to eat it, just don't eat anything else. Simple."

Condi again thought back to her early-morning conversation with Peter. She could suddenly, with a feeling of relief, imagine Nancy as *her* stepmother, taking care of everything. She settled for saying, cautiously: "Your call was such a nice surprise."

Nancy laughed her silvery laugh, recalling how often she'd heard words like that in Ronnie's time, when her telephone dialing struck terror within the administration. "*I* had a nice surprise yesterday," she told Condi. "Maggie Thatcher telephoned."

"Oh, it was such a thrill to see her yesterday morning. She stood with us on the South Lawn for the commemoration and then came to the reception here in the Franklin Room." The former prime minister had been stone-faced and mostly silent at both.

"It's hard for her to talk since the strokes," said Nancy. "She sometimes needs time to gather her words. You know, she did her eulogy for Ronnie on a video, even though she was sitting there in the cathedral."

"Yes," said Condi, "I remember."

"But she can still make herself heard when she puts in the effort."

Condi felt a sudden unease. Was Nancy teeing up a stem-cell pitch? Did that sort of science potentially help stroke victims, too? The president had vetoed another research bill in July.

Nancy went on: "She was also over at the Pentagon after talking to Cheney at the White House."

"Yes, it was a very busy day for her," said Condi. She was crestfallen over the picture today's *Post* had run of Thatcher being shown a souvenir ballot—by Don—from one of the Afghan elections.

"Rumsfeld said something to her about you."

"Oh?"

"Something on the order of 'The president does his best, but he's got Geoffrey Howe for a foreign minister.'" As Nancy well knew, this was a verbatim rendition of Rumsfeld's custom-tailored remark. Its substance, which both she and Condi understood, involved the plummy, too-moderate and eventually regretted foreign secretary who had served Mrs. Thatcher, a man so apparently devoid of ideological passion that an opponent once remarked upon how being criticized by Geoffrey Howe was like "being savaged by a dead sheep."

"What did *she* say?" Condi summoned the nerve to ask.

"To Don? To me?"

"Well—"

"I doubt she said anything to Don," Mrs. Reagan interrupted. "And she passed the remark on to me without comment."

"I myself don't see the analogy," Condi finally responded, with a stiff bit of bravery. "When Geoffrey Howe was—"

Nancy didn't have time for a tutorial. Actually, these days she felt she didn't have much time left for anything. And the girl was missing the point. "Condi," she said. The ensuing silence assured her that the secretary was listening. "You can bet that Don had Cheney say something similar to her before she stood out on the Lawn with you. Don and Dick are *married*. Just like Bush Sr. and Jim Baker were. Are."

Condi now felt a degree of panic not much lower than what she'd experienced yesterday outside the White House. She was in no position to criticize either 41 or Baker, which Nancy would be wanting her to do if the conversation started focusing on them.

"Those two, Dick and Don," Nancy continued, "kept Ford in and Ronnie out of the White House in '76. And they'd like you out of your job."

They couldn't oust her, of course—not with her even-now close connection to the president, not to mention the nasty bit of bad racial feeling such a dismissal would cause the administration's opponents to simulate. But Dick and Don could render her meaningless. She said nothing. Nancy waited.

"Condoleezza," the former First Lady then said. "What's that expression the lesbians—I mean the feminists—use? 'The personal is political'? Completely backwards. The political is personal, and nothing else. There are really no problems. There are only people who *cause* problems. Do what I always did to improve things. Get someone fired. You'll feel better."

"Yes," said Condi, with a politeness tinged by a sense of possibility.

"Get rid of Don. And get Laura to help you do it."

———

The Oval Office; September 14, 2006, 12:10 p.m.

The president had been up on the Hill for a meeting with House Republicans and then come back here for a one-on-one with Roh, the South Korean guy, whose nuke nerves were growing and who had no idea there was an elephant in the room: the proposal he'd made to Pootie in St. Petersburg two months ago. There was no point in springing that on the guy until an answer came from Russia. And the autumn leaves hadn't yet fallen.

During the next couple of weeks he'd have Musharraf and Karzai coming in here; in between them there'd be rush week at the UN, requiring his annual acceptance of the global cold shoulder. And before he could even have lunch today, there was a quick meeting on the schedule with this Hitchens character, something he'd long resisted despite the guy's unexpected support on Iraq. He'd finally given in to persistent nudges from Rove and Laura and the NEAH Chairman whose name he could never remember.

He remained wary of welcoming this loose cannon, who supposedly had a bug up his ass about even Mother Teresa. But here was Karen Keller bringing him in—no tie!—along with two folders of stuff for signatures. Bush looked out over his half-glasses and stood up to shake hands. This had been arranged as an off-the-record conversation, not an interview, so he was glad to see no pad or tape recorder on the man.

"I've appreciated your support," he told the writer. "I hear you're a complex, contradictory fellow."

"Actually, I'm a seamless garment of truth: happy to support you where I can; eager to oppose you where I must. I don't suppose I can convince you to sack Mrs. Hughes."

Bush pursed his presidential lips and shot him a that's-not-funny look.

Hitchens, having sat down without being asked to, pointed to the folders Mrs. Keller had brought and asked, "Anything interesting?"

Bush laughed. "First item's a little sad. A statement on Ann Richards's passing."

"She once called you 'some jerk.' "

"Thanks for the reminder."

"The other one?"

"An annual, like one of Mother's flowers." Bush turned the document so that it faced Hitchens. The president's yearly proclamation of Constitution Week was being issued "in accordance with the joint congressional resolution of August 2, 1956 (36 U.S.C. 108, as amended)."

"What's your favorite within the First?" asked Hitchens. "First Amendment, that is. Which particular freedom?"

Bush gave him a smile that said *nice try*.

"I'm relatively fresh from studying the whole document for my citizenship test."

"Good man," said the president. "Have you had your ceremony?"

"No, I took the test on the sixth of June, and I'm still waiting."

"Sorry things are slow. INS is a little preoccupied."

"One would think they'd be quicker signing up allies ready to pledge fealty—on D-Day, no less. But Chertoff promises to swear me in himself when the time arrives."

Bush wasn't surprised that this guy knew the head of Homeland Security. "Rove tells me that you get around." The Architect had also told him that the man was a prodigious drinker.

"My own personal preference—going back to the First Amendment," said Hitchens, "would be the lead item on the list: 'Congress shall make no law respecting an establishment of religion.'"

Bush just nodded. *Here comes the Mother Teresa shit.*

"I've been wondering about these three Republican congressmen who are threatening to hold up your defense-appropriation bill unless the military's chaplains are allowed to invoke Jesus' name a bit more particularly than they are at present."

"I take it you have an objection to their reform proposal."

"What I have," said Hitchens, "is a better idea. Eliminate the chaplains entirely. Madison was quite pointedly against having them, either in the foxhole or at the congressional rostrum."

"You know, there's a war on—"

"Something of which those three House members trying to give Jesus pride of place might well be reminded."

"—and I'm trying, have been for five years, to keep it from being one religion at war with another."

"You've been forced to make war on the one religion most bent on making government and religion indistinguishable. The further *we* stay away from doing that, the mightier and worthier a foe we shall be."

He couldn't get him out of here soon enough. "Christmas'll be coming along in a few months. We'll have a little manger and some Hanukkah candles upstairs. That too much for you? Got a problem with *that*?"

"A considerable one. The ecumenical is still theistic, and thus an unjust imposition on many citizens, including some future ones."

Rove was going to pay for this. The NEAH Chairman, too.

"I thought you'd want to be talking about Iraq," said the president.

"We *are* talking about Iraq, no?" asked Hitchens. "In some essential way?"

"I'd rather talk about North Korea. Rove says you were there a few years ago and saw people eating grass. Tell me more about that."

———

CNN Studios in Washington, D.C.; September 14, 2006, 9:10 p.m.

"With all due respect," said Molly Ivins, onscreen from Austin, "and given who the deceased is, or was, shouldn't we have more Democrats here?" Larry King's two other guests, all of them paying tribute to Ann Richards, were Barbara Bush, onscreen from Houston, and Bob Dole, across from the host in the studio. Mrs. Bush laughed at the Texas journalist's remark in the cheery American funereal way. Dole quietly harrumphed. Ann Richards's actual funeral would take place Monday in Austin.

Ivins was often compared to the late governor. They had been friends, competitors, and antagonists; she was lucky enough to be finishing last in their race with cancer. Still in treatment, she looked awful. Bits of a crew cut stuck out from under her turban.

"Bob Dole," said King, "you knew Ann at Verner, Liipfert, the big legal-lobbying firm here in Washington."

"Yeah. It was a good place for politicians who were past it." He muttered "Mitchell" and "Bentsen," then trailed off, and then resumed speaking. "I came in a little after Ann. She got trounced by Bush in '94, and Clinton did me in a couple of years later."

Ivins chimed in from a thousand miles away. "While they were at Verner, Ann and Bob made things as easy as they could for Big Tobacco."

"Would you say that's ironic?" King asked the Austin screen. "Given how Ann died?"

"God, Larry," Ivins replied. "I'd say it's *tragic*."

"Ann tangled with both Presidents Bush. We have a clip." The control room played the "silver foot" sound bite, and King asked the former First Lady: "Despite all that, do you have a favorite memory of Ann?"

"Oh, yes, she came to a party at the White House when George and I were there, and wonderful Charlie Wilson—such a handsome, colorful rascal!—brought her as his date. What charisma those two had!"

Ivins elaborated on the conservative Democrat who'd secretly helped the Afghan mujahideen get rid of the Soviets. "I like Charlie, too. They're making a movie of his life now. His *sex* life's a little more Clintonian than Mrs. Bush's party usually approves of."

"He always had the best-looking secretaries on the Hill," Dole observed, neutrally.

"Can you still even say something like that?" King asked with a laugh. "Different times!"

Ivins answered for Dole. "I don't know about the senator, but at this stage of my life—stage *four*, to be precise—I can say anything I like."

"Molly," asked King. "A favorite memory of Ann Richards?"

After a moment's consideration, the columnist answered: "A pool party in Austin, back in the seventies, when Nixon was throwing in the towel. We acted out the White House transcripts and Ann made a fine Haldeman. This all happened when Mrs. Bush's husband headed the RNC and kept telling us what a great guy Nixon was."

Barbara Bush smiled, jiggled her earpiece and pretended she hadn't caught the last sentence. "I'm looking forward to seeing Bob in person next month in Washington. The Navy is launching a carrier named for George Herbert Walker Bush. I couldn't be prouder, Larry."

"We'll cover that!" King promised. "You're a special lady. How do you manage to let bygones be bygones?"

"Oh, Larry, life is too short. One should enjoy all its fascinating people while one can."

"Ann Richards was certainly one of those," the host declared.

"And one of the quickest!" added Mrs. Bush.

Had she said too much to her on that observation deck at Anderson two months ago? She had seen her putting two and two together in a flash. Well, what did it matter? She was good and dead, and she'd taken whatever she figured out to the grave.

34

OCTOBER 7–9, 2006

Northrop Grumman shipyard; Newport News, Virginia

"*The* USS George H. W. Bush *is the latest in the Nimitz line of aircraft carriers. She is unrelenting; she is unshakable; she is unyielding; she is unstoppable. As a matter of fact, she probably should have been named the 'Barbara Bush.'*"

A distant peal of thunder injected some nervousness into the crowd's laughter over the president's remark. Even with its 4.5-acre surface—a quarter the size of the entire White House grounds—the ship being named for 41 seemed vulnerable to the approaching elements. But the incumbent president continued, paying tribute to his father's conduct on September 2, 1944: "*During that raid, his plane was hit by antiaircraft artillery, and it caught fire. Yet he stayed on course. He released his four bombs and scored four direct hits on that Japanese radio tower; he headed out to sea; he ejected.*"

Turning to look at the subject of his words, Bush saw Condi Rice a row behind the former president, leaning forward to give her old boss a grateful pat on the shoulder.

Doro, 41's youngest child, was soon cracking a bottle of sparkling wine against the carrier, and the sailors, to the sound of "Anchors Aweigh," were racing up the ladders to man the ship, like ants fleeing a spray gun, or specks in a videogame—a kind of virtual virtual reality. The current president had to banish from his mind the additional thought that they looked like a rewinding film of tiny bodies leaping from the Twin Towers.

As the band went into a Sousa march, spectators began to move and mingle a bit. The president considered Condi's gesture toward Dad and felt a tenderness toward her, an appreciation of her long loyalty to the family, something now being tested by a dubious (or was it?) quote in Woodward's latest, which had Dad incautiously observing that Condi wasn't really "up to the job"—her current one. The book was full of this stuff, and it was sticking, despite a week of all their guys trying to rebut it on the cable shows.

The truth is, she was *not* up to the job. (Would anyone be right now?) She'd arrived back from Iraq yesterday, full of gloom, reporting to him on all the pissy, mutual uncooperativeness of the Shia and Sunni guys she'd been in the room with. And when he asked her what she'd concluded, hoping for the sort of bold new certainty he'd been trying for eight months to hear from her and everybody else, she'd said she would "have to think about it." That was the best she could do? After being back there herself, and with all these policy reviews going on, including the one at State, not to mention all the reports coming to her from Zelikow?

Still. He looked over at her chatting with Jim Baker and Colin Powell, whose personal loyalty, unlike hers, had never passed from father to son. He waved her over.

"Can't tell you how much I appreciate your being here after the week you've had." She'd been to Jerusalem, Ramallah, Baghdad, and London.

"I'm taking Monday off!" Condi assured him.

"Good. We may need you over in China soon. I've already talked to Hoo-Hoo."

"About Korea?"

"Yes, ma'am."

On Tuesday the North had announced an imminent nuclear test. Hayden, over at CIA, believed this was for real and that they should expect it tomorrow.

"We could try to interdict some shipping," said the president. "But even that won't do much good." He slumped a little, still carrying the secret of how until this week he'd been prepared to go a hell of a lot further than that.

"I thought Chris Hill's statement was strong," said Condi, as encouragingly as she could. The U.S. representative to the six-party talks had declared: "We are not going to live with a nuclear North Korea."

Bush frowned: "What he said was diplo-speak for 'until we agree to do what I just said we wouldn't.'"

Condi let him go into a silence.

The president didn't want to have a debate with her. That would only add to the disappointment that had come with Putin's long-delayed, dismissive answer—rendered after a couple of crucial, cryptic post-Strelna conversations. *Any kind of raid on the facility would fatally destabilize Russia's 17-km. border with North Korea. Do the Americans even remember that our two countries share one? Besides, Mr. Rumsfeld, without even being aware of what you proposed, very recently gave me the impression that anything more than consultation privileges with NATO, let alone actual membership—your apparent blandishment—would be out of the question for decades to come. I have to believe, regardless of what you have suggested, that Mr. Rumsfeld's adamantine view belongs to his superior as well. If we were to cooperate in a raid, there would be no guarantee that America would not renege. Russia has been excluded from Mr. Rumsfeld's "New Europe" just as she was from Old Europe—and will no doubt be from Far-in-the-Future Europe too.*

"When did you last talk to Bob Gates?" the president suddenly asked Condi. Dad's old CIA director was now the president of Texas A&M, which also had Dad's library.

"Maybe a couple of months ago," Condi replied. "I'd have to check the exact date." She tried to figure out what had prompted the question.

The president again stopped talking and just listened to the band. This business with Vlad was a bitter pill. A strike against the North Korean reactors would have been quick and definitive—however risky. As they acted, the three of them—China joining in on everything but the raid itself—would have held their breath but managed to rein Kim in, made even *him* realize that there was no point in setting fire to Seoul, not with the three biggest powers in the world ready to crush him if he did. Now that Vlad had sent this idea south, his own presidency would come down to Iraq and Katrina. Not even to Afghanistan. Dear God, not even to 9/11.

Ten rows back he could spot Allison O'Connor with a group of NSC staffers who had, no doubt, been hoping for a morning with better weather. He looked to see if O'Connor's baby might be in her arms. He waved, and pointed her out to Condi, while trying to notice if the Weatherman had maybe come up from New Orleans to kick-start his reconciliation with Allison right here.

The two of them: little tumbleweeds of geopolitical destiny there in Granberry's Lubbock backyard all those years ago. He had no recollection of them on that night, of course, and he had no touch of the mystic. But his faith did give him a belief that the newer parts of the Bible are prefigured in the older ones. When he thought of those two, both about Doro's age, he somehow felt required to amalgamate not the past and the present but the miniature and the giant. If he could help to solve their problems, writ small in the ink of a double catastrophe, maybe that could lead him toward a solution for the catastrophes themselves. Ridiculous, yes. But even so.

Things were wrapping up here. The band struck up a couple of forties songs for Mother and Dad, one of which he recognized as "I Don't Want to Walk Without You." All the greatest-generation vets here today, half of them in wheelchairs, now sent his mind back to that World War II museum down in New Orleans, enormously expanded since he'd visited it before the storm. And then his thoughts returned to a conversation he'd had with the Weatherman down there, in August. *You need to get your own family moved here. . . . Maybe she needs more incentive.*

He had an idea.

———

Two Days Later, 5:30 p.m.; Watergate Apartment of Condoleezza Rice

"I'm so sorry I missed this year's Book Festival!"

The First Lady, on the other end of the phone, told Condi not to worry. "With all that you've been doing? Have you even had a chance to rest up from Iraq?"

The secretary laughed. "I've been home all day, and tomorrow will be almost as easy. I've got the Peruvian president, but it's a leisurely lunch at their ambassador's house. The briefing book is wonderfully thin!"

"Even so, they're wearing you out." Laura paused for a second. "At least they don't have you campaigning, like two years ago."

Any barnstorming, which had been iffy enough at NSA, was out of the question as secretary of state.

"Things don't look good, do they?" Condi half-asked and half-observed. Even stalwarts like Lindsey Graham and Kay Bailey Hutchison were openly questioning Iraq policy.

"I skipped going to Reno and Arizona last week," Laura confessed. "I just didn't have the heart for it with all these millstones around our necks."

Which ones did she mean? Condi wondered. "Neck imagery seems to be in style," she replied. "I saw awful political disarray in Baghdad last week, and I told some Shia and Sunni leaders that if they didn't start working together they'd all be swinging from lampposts six months from now. I couldn't believe the words came out of my mouth!"

Laura laughed. "Denny Hastert and Bill Frist ought to start thinking about that—at least as a metaphor. And so should our biggest millstone of all."

Get rid of Don. And get Laura to help you do it. It seemed she might not even have to ask.

"I tried," the First Lady continued, "to solve that problem, through Andy, after the '04 election. But Karl and Dick persuaded George otherwise. Even so, I'm certain that this is the moment to try again.

In fact, there's no time to lose." She paused for a few seconds. "I'm curious: Did you ever read *The Prime Minister*, Trollope, on that e-reader I sent you?"

"I'm so sorry. I'm afraid—"

"I shouldn't have asked. You have too much reading as it is, no matter how thin tomorrow's briefing book is. I was just thinking it might give you some ideas for this little effort I have in mind. But I'm sure you can come up with your own creative ways—"

The buzzer from the lobby sounded—proof, in fact, that Condi was already on it. But even now, caution prevailed; she wasn't sure she should tell Laura what she'd set in motion.

"It sounds as if you've got company," said the First Lady. "Let's talk in a day or two?"

"Oh, yes. Absolutely."

Only when they'd hung up did Condi realize that Don's name had never been uttered. After telling the doorman to send up the visitor, she looked over to one of her coffee tables and saw *State of Denial*, the Woodward book. A half-dozen Post-its bristled from its pages, which made her look more ineffectual than everybody else. The book even asserted that Don sometimes wouldn't take her calls.

Out in the curved hallway, Allison O'Connor went through a last security check from the guard who never stood more than five feet from the secretary of state's door. Given the dangers she remembered from the Rashid, Allie found this a bit much. She showed her ID and presented her special printed summons to Rice's apartment. Then she looked at her watch. Anne Macmurray had promised to stay as long as necessary with Holley, though Allie imagined this visit to the Watergate wouldn't run long. As it was, she had no clear idea why her presence had been requested. Was Bush trying to give her a new mentor? Had Rumsfeld constructed some sort of baroque trap, one that would require three trips through the looking glass for her (or Rice) to figure out its design and purpose?

The secretary greeted her in an elegant black pantsuit, a daytime-casual look that rendered her more done-up than her just-arrived guest usually managed to appear for a party. Allie worried that there might be some spit-up from Holley clinging to the sweater she'd thrown on before racing to the office this morning.

"Are you chilly?" asked Rice, showing her to a wing chair and wondering if she'd like a glass of white wine. "I always prefer things on the cool side, I'm afraid." She pointed out a Shetland blanket—a goodbye present from Peter MacKay last month in Nova Scotia—and told Allie she could use it as a shawl while they chatted. "But maybe you'd like a little tour before we settle down?"

Along with the apartment's views of the river, Rice indicated one of the Watergate complex's office buildings—"not the one where the break-in happened"—and pointed in the direction of a dry-cleaning shop whose owner displayed Condi's photo on the countertop. "Not an entire plus for business, I'm sure!" There was also the piano to see, and the elliptical. "I call it my bad-news bike," she told Allie. "I was on it last night when I got word of the North Koreans' test. Same thing back in January when Hamas won the Palestinian election!"

"I've been wondering," said Allie, "if we need better translators, or if the North Koreans are sillier than we think. That phrasing in their announcement about how the test was 'carried out under scientific consideration and careful calculation.' Well, *yeah*."

"Do you think Kim Jong-il calculates much? Perhaps he's just crazy?"

Allie picked up on the element of flattery involved in putting these questions to a subordinate so many levels below the asker. She decided to reply with a question of her own: "Did you see this report about the North Korean soldiers at Panmunjom, looking across at the Americans and making throat-slitting motions? I suspect that's as choreographed as all the gymnastics displays."

Condi nodded, thinking of the other neck imagery—the nooses, the millstones—she and Laura had shared. "The only good thing about this situation is that I'm not allowed to go to Pyongyang! Baghdad was awful enough this week. The *schools* there aren't functioning. Even the teachers are afraid to go."

"Sounds like New Orleans. More than half of the schools there are still closed."

The response seemed to strike Condi as a bit out-of-the-blue and faintly disloyal. Allie noted the reaction and added, "That's what my friend down there tells me."

The secretary returned the conversation to the Middle East. "We're still looking for that new way forward, just as we were in June." She knew this was the moment to plunge in, and she tried to channel Mrs. Reagan's force of will the way Nancy once called down messages from the planets and stars. "Do you know Ken Adelman?"

Allie had once met him, a Reaganite now on the Defense Policy Board.

"He had a shouting match with Don Rumsfeld a week or two ago; they're no longer speaking."

Allie laughed. "In my experience the secretary of defense never shouts. It's all the quiet, cryptic stuff he says that winds up deafening one."

"Steve Hadley is coming around to the Kagan view that we heard in June up at Camp David."

Allie nodded. "More troops, not fewer. And yourself?"

Condi envied this woman her directness, the slight overstepping that seemed natural to the overstepper and thus didn't offend. "It may turn out to be the only option, and if it does, we can't have the president being opposed by his defense secretary."

"How would you avoid that?" Allie was aware of the distancing quality of her own locution, as if she were speaking into a phone she knew to be bugged, trying to preserve deniability.

"By convincing the president to get a *new* secretary of defense." Saying this, Condi felt the way she had in Baghdad last week, when the remark about lampposts escaped her lips. But she made herself continue: "Don doesn't want to shoulder the burden *or* the guilt." She had gathered her courage and begun to press the seduction: "I hear from people that you're the kind of person we need more of on the ground over there."

Allie was not about to say *I have an eight-month-old baby.* "Well, I haven't accomplished too much during my short stints, especially the last one—not even twenty-four hours!"

Condi, in turn, was not about to point out that she'd been on Iraqi soil not much longer than that last week. After her meetings in the Green Zone, she'd rushed up to see the Kurds and then headed off to London. "You're being modest. When we were in Russia in July, the president told me how valuable you've been."

Allie felt skeptical. She'd done next to nothing in Iraq last June. Had Bush told Rice about the rambling personal conversation they'd had on the plane going over? That he valued her character and self-questioning? She could almost hear him saying it: *She's a good man.*

Condi continued: "If things go in the direction Steve Hadley is leaning, there'll be a longer-term U.S. presence, but one with fewer casualties."

"If that becomes the policy," Allie replied, "they're going to need a much better status-of-forces agreement than what's in place."

"It's not too early to think about that," Rice said, brightly. "And I mean think out loud, with the Iraqis. You may be what we require to start that process."

"Now?"

"Soon." Condi felt a thrilling sensation that she had stopped dithering and begun to *act*. It was as if on the piano a few feet away she'd broken off some too-long *ostinato* and gone into a soaring glissando. She told herself to keep rushing her hand across the keyboard. "I spoke to the First Lady. She agrees with the need for a change at the Pentagon. She's thought that way for a long time."

Allie could see the avidity in Rice's eyes. She recognized the irony of being asked to help take down the person who'd brought her in. But such recognition was weak compared to the excitement she herself had been experiencing when it came to the war itself, the daring, counterintuitive movement from opposition to support. Those things weren't, she was finding out, merely the two end points on a spectrum; being *for* something was a wholly different mental condition from being against it. Clear, hold, *build*.

Rice continued: "I would recommend having a personal conversation with the president about Don. It's not really the sort of thing for a memorandum."

5:45 p.m.; Holt Cemetery, Navarre Section of New Orleans

Having spent the last two hours digging a grave, Ross rested against his shovel. The hospital worker who had helped him went off for a smoke. They'd done the job inexpertly, but no one would criticize them for that. One of the now officially unidentifiable bodies from the warehouse on Poydras Street was getting buried.

Most of the graves in this potter's field had no headstones; the ones in evidence—sometimes just slabs of slate—tended to look like dominoes in mid-fall. The topmost point of a corpse would occasionally be indicated by a Magic-Markered cinderblock; other graves—including the one that belonged to Carlotta Watson's daughter—had only borders made from rotting wood. Here and there across the seven acres, one found fantastical arrangements, like a trellis resembling the peacock-tail costume of a second-line dancer: someone's act of intense, inventive devotion that would not long survive the weather. Shopping carts and busted wicker furniture suggested that those interred were somehow *still* homeless, as so many of them had been in life. Blue plastic tarps struggled to keep them dry, as if even now they were asleep on the sidewalk. A burlap bag, or human bone, would sometimes protrude through the dirt.

Father Montrose, with the last of the day's sun glinting off his bald spot, looked admiringly at Ross's once-more hard physique; the younger man appeared, in his sweat-soaked T-shirt, like a handsome new member of the working class. A tattoo, thought the priest, might soon be making an appearance. But Ross was also an object of perplexity; Father Montrose continued trying to estimate the degree of straightforward charity versus self-mortification in the work the younger man had been doing.

Ross's own thoughts remained focused on how the dead here, even amidst so many shabby tokens of their lives, were at least trying to *be* dead, realistically so, without the vampiric ambitions and expectations of all those lying in the city's countless elegant or gimcrack mausoleums. No artist had ever taken the impression for a death mask off anybody lying here.

"I still can't get over the bones sticking up out of the ground," he said, pointing to a cluster of them twenty feet away.

"People steal them," Father Montrose said.

"Why?"

"God only knows."

"Figure of speech?"

"Nope." Ross recalled his assurance in the warehouse: *These* are *the living.*

Father Montrose called out to Emmalina, the Holy Cross girl with the clarinet. After prayers were said, all four of them, including the fellow from the hospital, threw a solemn shovelful of dirt onto the white coffin, and Emmalina played "He Leadeth Me." The priest slipped the hospital worker, who would fill in the grave by himself, fifty dollars.

On their way off the grounds, Father Montrose and Ross and the girl stopped near a plaque commemorating the cemetery's name-sake, Dr. Joseph Holt, the Confederate surgeon and public-health pioneer who, the inscription pointed out, was buried in Greenwood. "Wouldn't be caught dead here," Ross surmised.

With the priest behind the wheel, the men drove Emmalina home. She chattered about her school: closed for all of last year, it was at last up and running. After dropping her off in Holy Cross, Father Montrose continued to Ross's place on Dauphine Street. En route, he asked, as delicately as he could, how long Ross thought his repentant labors would go on.

The younger man sidestepped the question. "Well, there's no shortage of work." The Scott family had come home, but thousands of others were still in line.

Father Montrose, via Mrs. Caine, had news to impart about Mrs. Boggs. The former congresswoman was nicely resettled near her daughter and son-in-law, just outside Washington. "She sends you her best and says to make sure she gets a copy of the guidebook!" It was due out in early December.

"I doubt I'll see those particular politicians again," said Ross. He was thinking of Jindal and Nagin at Mrs. Boggs's dinner table. "But I do hear pretty regularly from the Edwards campaign." He'd been getting e-mails from the One America guy and occasional video clips from Rielle Hunter. "I think I'm going to volunteer."

"Don't give your heart too cheaply," warned the priest. "Mrs. Caine told me—" He cut himself off, deciding not to pass on the bloody-shirt story he'd had from the realtor after last winter's party. "None of us wants to lose you," he said, "but maybe it would be better for *you* to be back near Washington? If the goal is to get to know your daughter?"

Ross smiled, evasively. He still hoped for some piece of fate that would bring the girl here, along with her mother, something that would resolve all three of them into happiness in this city he felt the need to call home.

"All right, dear boy," said Father Montrose, ready to offer contradictory-sounding advice to this betwixt-and-between fellow. "Don't work too hard, and don't drift."

Heading upstairs to his room at the back of the house, Ross decided he would check his messages and then sit out on the balcony with an Abita Amber. He was surprised to find an e-mail that the Chairman, his no-longer boss, had sent to his personal Yahoo account:

Ross, you apparently still have friends in high places. The director of the Smithsonian wants me to pass on the information below. I'm confused by it: does this mean that the government may not have lost you forever?

The museum director's message to the Chairman followed:

We are now, as you know, involved with the WWII museum in New Orleans. (Ambrose's old and much-expanded D-Day project.) They're an affiliate. We have just been told that the WH may want to create a program through them—something with a title like The Next Greatest Generation—that will get recent military veterans from the Gulf region to participate in the rebuilding of N.O. It will be run through the museum in an attempt to link the vets of different eras. The WH wants somebody with a military/legal background to go down and direct it. I've been told to get this to your Mr. Weatherall, wherever he may now be. Would appreciate your sending it on.

The Chairman appended a perplexed note: *You have the background for this, Ross?*

No, he didn't. This was the job the president wanted for Allison.

35

NOVEMBER 13, 2006

The Red Room; The White House

Rumsfeld walked toward three just-elected members of the 110th Congress—a female representative and two male senators, all of whom would be new to whichever chamber they entered in January. Each was here at the White House, along with a sprinkling of administration officials, for a welcoming reception. Tonight's effort at comity felt more urgent than what typically occurred at this event every two years: six days ago the Republicans had lost both houses in a midterm election the president himself conceded to be "a thumpin'."

The congresswoman-to-be, a Democrat, regarded the approaching Rumsfeld with surprise, as if to say, *You're* still here? His replacement as defense secretary had been announced from the Oval Office the day after the election; Rumsfeld would stay behind, more or less removing himself from policy decisions, until Bob Gates was confirmed.

He extended his hand. "Hi, I'm Don Rumsfeld."

"Gabrielle Giffords," the incoming legislator replied, with evident delight in the improbability of it all. "Everyone calls me Gabby."

"Oh, I know who you are!" Rumsfeld responded. "John McCain and I had to see a lot of each other—maybe too much—and he kept me abreast of Arizona politics. As topics go, it was a safer one for us than most others."

In the same spirit, as conversational refuge from the "thumpin'" on everyone's mind, Rumsfeld offered the first-termers some genial history, telling them he'd been at this very reception late in 1962, just before starting his six years in the House. "I'm delighted to see the number of women up," he added. "Hard as it is to believe, Gabby, I was *replacing* a woman back then: Mrs. Marguerite Church, who'd been born when Benjamin Harrison lived in this house!" He was dusting off the personable, relaxed Rumsfeld the public had seen during the early days of the Afghan war. "Mrs. Church was retiring, and my opponent was John Kennedy—John *A.* Kennedy. Of course John *F.* Kennedy hovered over the ballot. He'd handled the Cuban missile crisis pretty well a week or two before election day. We had a lot of national unity around such matters in those times. But I squeaked through." He'd actually won by sixty thousand votes.

Giffords and Sherrod Brown, who'd just captured the Ohio Senate seat, nodded, pretending that Rumsfeld's remark about national unity wasn't meant as scorn for Democratic opposition to the current war. For the few seconds of silence that ensued, the secretary surveyed the Thanksgiving decorations, taking note of a cardboard pilgrim whose cardboard musket was stoppered with an ear of Indian corn, like that Vietnam-era soldier having his rifle rendered impotent by the hippie's insertion of a flower. The sight somehow allowed the irony of his own current position to strike him with full force: here he was, unknown to the public as the person who'd actually argued within the administration for a faster *withdrawal* of troops; he'd been sacrificed to placate the opposition because he was almost universally perceived as the hard-line manager of an unpopular war.

"You ran up a big margin against DeWine," he told Sherrod Brown, with as generous a tone as he could manage.

"Well," said Brown, "it would have been smaller if—" He broke off.

Rumsfeld, touched by what he realized was an awkward courtesy on Brown's part, completed the senator-elect's thought: "You mean if they'd gotten rid of me the day before the election instead of after?" A number of Republican losers, incumbents and challengers alike, had all week been complaining that they might have finished first if the president had made the bold move of sacking his defense secretary two days sooner.

Michigan's Rep. John Dingell, a Democrat sworn in more than

fifty years ago by Sam Rayburn, joined the group and greeted his one-time House colleague from the days of the New Frontier and Great Society.

Rumsfeld grinned. "What the hell are *you* doing here? This is for members at the opposite end of life's timeline."

Dingell gave him a good-natured slap on the shoulder. "They bring me out for entertainment. Like one of those *Jurassic Park* things. What do you call 'em? *Animatronics*."

"They call them *dinosaurs*. You just reminded me," said Rumsfeld, before walking off several feet and returning with a squat ceramic vase, as wide as it was tall, that sported a big gift bow. "I've been try-ing to decide who should have this," he said, explaining that it was the spittoon—once a standard-issue item—that he'd found in his office in the Cannon Building in January 1963. He at last handed the recep-tacle to Giffords.

"Do you still have yours?" he asked Dingell.

"I think it's in the office somewhere. I make it a rule not to steal U.S. government property, Don." He put his arm around the shit-canned SecDef and abandoned the razzing in favor of a sentimental tribute. "You know," he told the three youthful legislators, "when it comes to smarts and innovation, I rank Don Rumsfeld right up there with Bob McNamara."

"He's talking about the whiz kid who ran the Ford Motor Com-pany," Rumsfeld explained, "not the guy who went on to run the Viet-nam War." He laughed, even as Dingell, in all sincerity, agreed. "Yes, that's exactly what I'm talking about. No small achievement, either."

"You know," said Rumsfeld, continuing to tutor the newcomers, "if John did any more favors for the auto industry, he'd get a free Ford 'escort' to take him to these events—and it would be Henry! This is really the guy for you to talk to, gentlemen and lady. He was on the Hill in FDR's time—as a page!"

"Well, not until his second term."

"Have him tell you about hearing Roosevelt's Pearl Harbor speech from inside the House." Rumsfeld could feel himself getting proud and wistful; he lowered his voice a decibel or two. "You know, my *dad* volunteered after Pearl Harbor. He was way older than any draftee they were taking. But he went in and we followed him to California. I was already a teenager when V-J Day came around. Hawked the newspaper with that big headline on the streets of San Diego!"

He could see that Giffords, Brown, and Tennessee's senator-elect Bob Corker—another guy, like himself, whose magnetism made you forget his short stature—were all marveling at his good cheer. He was wondering about it himself, in a curious, satisfying way. It was pleasing to be the phenomenon being analyzed rather than the analyst.

Joyce, who must have been monitoring him from a few feet away, concerned about the emotional drainage this event might later exact, came over and dragged him off, apologizing to her husband's four-person audience, telling them it was time for Don to go greet Pete Roskam, Henry Hyde's successor in the Illinois Sixth.

Rumsfeld twinkled, submitted to his wife's bidding, and waved goodbye.

Dingell, left with the trio of younger legislators, said, "Time was you could win a *world* war in three and a half years: Pearl Harbor to V-J Day. Now do the math from 'shock and awe'—March 2003—until tonight."

*

Across the room, and beside a portrait of Rutherford B. Hayes, Laura Bush gave Condi Rice a kiss on the cheek. "How many times have you had to be here today?"

"Only twice," Condi assured her. "Lunch with the Israeli prime minister and now this. Of course *none* of us will be back for a while!" Tomorrow night the secretary of state, along with the president and First Lady, would be off to Hanoi. Laura nodded while Condi observed with a grateful sigh how it still "seemed miraculous" for Americans to be making a friendly trip into what had for so long been an enemy target—no matter that it was old hat for people like Kerry and McCain to go there. Laura was struck by how often Condi, longing for the era of her professional youth, marveled over the Cold War's completion. The First Lady had more than once heard her tell the story of how, on 9/11, Vladimir Putin had magnanimously assured her that Russian troops would stand down while American forces went on high alert. The trust this seemed to show remained a matter of wonder to her.

A new member of Congress from California, a Republican, came over to shake the women's hands. As he chatted with Condi, Laura looked over at her husband, whose moods had been in even faster rotation since the election. Tonight George kept joking that come January, for anyone tuning in to the State of the Union address, Nancy Pelosi would be a lot easier on the eyes than Denny Hastert. He was alternating that line with the self-deprecating story of his long-ago loss to Kent Hance—"This is a party I never got to come to back in '78!"—once even recounting the Bush Bash debacle. Whenever he finished, she'd see him glowering, for a second or two, until he rewound the mental playlist of pleasantries.

Her own mood was oscillating. Being here tonight was like having to attend the opposing candidate's victory party—or like poor Gampy having to watch Clinton get inaugurated in '93. But part of her felt a certain celebration, too: with Don gone, there might be a minimal improvement in relations with this new Congress.

"Is Gene here?" she asked Condi, once the California newbie had moved on.

"I'm afraid not. He told me he'd be having enough of D.C. with the holidays that are coming up!"

"Well, we're looking forward to seeing him at Thanksgiving." They would all be at Camp David. Condi wished for a moment that she could instead invite—or even talk about—Peter MacKay, from whom she'd barely heard since September.

"I think that all of it helped," said Laura, fixing her eyes on Don Rumsfeld with some satisfaction. "Even getting whatshername, Ms. O'Connor, in on things."

Condi agreed. She had talked up Bob Gates at every opportunity once she realized why the president had mentioned him in Newport News: he himself had been thinking about getting rid of Don and only needed some pushing.

Laura leaned toward her and said, in a near-whisper, "I know you still have doubts about this 'surge.'" They both knew the president felt ever more inclined toward it.

It was becoming clear to Condi that the First Lady, having succeeded in the operation against Don, would be making this her new project of persuasion.

"Unlike you, I hate football," she told Condi. "But even *I* know that this is the last quarter—literally." There were two years left in her husband's eight. "So I hope you'll go for broke. And not be afraid to lose big."

Condi was startled by the way Laura formulated this; she also flinched at the apparent approach of Dick Cheney, though it turned out—to her relief—that the vice president was moving toward Vermont's Socialist congressman, the one now on his way to the Senate. She could hear Dick greeting him: "I'll finally be able to have a favorite senator from the Green Mountain State." He loathed Jim Jeffords, who'd deserted the party five years ago, and his detestation of Pat Leahy had passed into hot-mic legend.

Lacking any smile, Bernie Sanders declared, "Mr. Vice President, I'm not sure I will be giving you much more to like than Senator Leahy or Senator Jeffords did."

Oh God, thought Condi. It wasn't every day that Dick turned out to be the fun guy in the group.

*

"Sir," said Allison O'Connor, when Rumsfeld greeted her in the Cross Hall.

"Oh, it can be just 'Don' from this point on. Quite a 'surge' of people headed toward the State Dining Room, wouldn't you say?"

Allie brought a flat hand up to her brow, like a visor, and pretended to search the far end of the corridor. "Must be Steve Hadley leading the charge."

"Will you be bringing up the rear?" Rumsfeld asked. "Converted just in time to join the horde?"

"A sincere shift," Allie responded, aware of the defensive pomposity entering her voice. "Already made some months ago. As you know."

"But still, an unexpected one."

"To me most of all."

She could see Rumsfeld going into his gnomic mode. "The unexpected can remain un-understood. Or it can be comprehended. How is it in your case? Do you understand *why* you changed, Allison?"

A drinks tray passed and Allie took a glass of wine. "I've received a much better, closer-up education in Saddam Hussein since you brought me to the NSC. He did *not* keep the peace between Sunni and Shia, the way everyone now seems to say—once they stipulate, 'Well, yes, he shouldn't have sometimes massacred the Shia and gassed the Kurds.' And before they go into their yes-he-was-brutal-but-things-weren't-as-bad-as-they-are-now routine."

"You once told me that *we* made things worse."

"And we did, in the very short run. But all the United States did was hasten a reckoning that Saddam ensured would happen. Even so, if we're the ones who lit the match, we have the responsibility to put out the fire."

"By your logic," said Rumsfeld, "the old antiwar movement should have started supporting LBJ after Tet. The clearer it becomes that it's not about *us*, the further *we* should dig in."

"I'm not proceeding entirely by logic. You and your cat's cradle of knowns and unknowns can work that way. A fine lot of good it's doing!" She realized she was raising her voice, something she'd not done even in the Superdome.

"Then what are you going to substitute for logic?"

"Commitment, maybe. Something that was never my strong suit."

"Did you meet with the president lately?" Rumsfeld asked.

She made herself look straight at him and say nothing. He knew that she was answering yes, and they both knew what she and Bush had talked about: him.

"I've often wondered," she said, finally. "What kind of bicycle was it? Your own. The one whose seat your father must have taken *his* hand off."

"My older sister, actually, taught me to ride. It was a Schwinn." He shook her hand, and twinkled. "Goodbye, Allison. You're an experiment that failed."

"Goodbye, Mr. Secretary."

Rumsfeld returned to the Red Room. Allie just stood for a moment in the hall, deciding she would skip the buffet and head home to her daughter, who'd been left in Anne Macmurray's care. But the president himself suddenly appeared, as if he'd been waiting for her to be alone. He was, weirdly, holding a glass of milk.

"Sir," she succeeded in saying, "isn't that carrying the teetotaling a bit far?"

"I think I need some calcium. Laura tells me I've been grinding my teeth since last Tuesday."

"We have a new secretary of defense," said Allie, triumphantly. Her encounter with Rumsfeld had suffused her with anger.

"We do," Bush replied.

"And an evolving policy?"

The president's eyes narrowed into one of his accusatory looks; the good ol' boy suddenly imputing presumption to a buddy. "You know something I don't?"

"Not a thing," she replied.

The scolding expression vanished. "How come no 'plus one'?" he asked her. "I looked over the RSVP list. Was hoping the Weatherman might be on it. Making a trip north."

"We talk from time to time," she answered, cautiously.

"He mention any job opportunities?"

"He's been digging graves."

Bush seemed to think she was joking. "I'm talking about opportunities for *you*."

"He mentioned that there might be something for me in New Orleans. He didn't say what it was. But he thought it would keep for a while."

The president smiled. "It will. Let's say until Christmas."

She'd assumed that Ross had gotten some tip from his former Chairman, after confiding his family-geography woes. Now she realized that Bush was in on this.

"Go see him!" the president exclaimed. "Talk to him. Come New Year's we'll have a new policy and you'll have a new job."

"Is that an executive order?"

Did he know that his own secretary of state wanted to put her in Iraq? *You may be what we require to start that process.*

"It's executive clemency," Bush replied.

*

Back inside the Red Room, still holding the glass of milk, Bush tried to avoid Rumsfeld, but the departing secretary came up to him and said, "I imagine you've recently seen Allison O'Connor."

"You mean just now?"

"No, during the past few weeks."

"Sure," Bush said. Everyone had been in to see him about Rumsfeld. O'Connor had been early; others had been often; Dick had been chronic, pushing for his old boss's retention. He'd pretended to himself that he'd make no change before the election as a gesture toward preserving Rummy's dignity; in truth, he'd worried more about making himself look desperate.

"It could have been handled better" was all he said now. The whole thing had been a mess. On the first of November he'd told an interviewer he looked forward to Don's staying straight through January '09; four days later he'd met with Gates, in secret, at the ranch. The day after that he'd had Dick call Don with the bad news.

And now he was making things worse by starting to talk as if nothing had ever happened: "Pelosi's coming out for Murtha over Hoyer tomorrow," he told Rumsfeld. Since she was going to be speaker, the Democrats needed a new majority leader in the House, and there was a little race on for the job.

"Good," said Rumsfeld. "If she backs Murtha, she'll be starting out with a loss."

"That's what Rove says."

"Is he here?"

"No," said the president, "but he ought to be. Half the Democrats in this room owe their new jobs to him. They should be fighting one another to fetch his drinks."

"You know, I promised you a while back that I'd resign if we lost one house. I probably should have committed hari-kari when it was two."

Bush patted his arm, touched that Don was backing off from what-ever needling he'd seemed ready to engage in.

"How did the ISG interview go?" Rumsfeld asked. Earlier today, in the Roosevelt Room, the president had finally sat down with the Iraq Study Group, whose report, set to come out next month, he didn't give a damn about. He had enough competing recommendations already.

"Lee Hamilton asked me what 'victory' would be." He shrugged, still embarrassed that he'd had no clear answer.

Rumsfeld responded: "I hear that Casey weighed in by videolink." The general could be counted on to have supported a drawdown; men-tioning him now was an attempt to give that viewpoint a last hearing.

"I thought you were stepping back," said Bush. Humor and annoy-ance were both detectable in his tone.

Rumsfeld smiled. Flush with a momentary desire to feel useful and young, he seized an opportunity to run a little interference for the president, as if it were thirty years earlier and he was shielding Nixon from a demonstrator. Jim Webb, an antiwar Democrat in the Murtha military mode, a hothead who'd knocked off George Allen in Virginia, was coming toward them for what Rumsfeld knew to be a second and less-than-cordial run at Bush.

"Congratulations, Senator-elect," he said, blocking his path.

"Thanks for hanging on and helping me to get here."

"Did you use an ice-breaker that polite with the president just before?"

"He asked me how my son in Iraq was doing, and I told him that was between me and my son."

"He's your son's commander-in-chief."

"If you guys hadn't done things on the cheap and stopped the First Cavalry from going over in '03, my boy would be in a lot less danger now. He probably wouldn't be there at all."

"Well, maybe you'll soon get your wish for more troops, albeit a little late."

"It's already *too* late."

Webb turned on his heel and left. Rumsfeld gave Bush a chipper salute, consulted his watch, and walked away. He had told Joyce he would meet her at precisely eight forty-five, downstairs by the ladies' lounge. Nearing it, he looked into the Vermeil Room and saw Condi Rice standing beside Nancy Reagan's portrait, talking to a new Democratic congressman. He went over to shake the man's hand. "Well," he said, pointing to Mrs. Reagan's rapt visage, "we always obeyed *our* Nancy. Now you guys can obey yours!"

Condi knew that Don had never obeyed *their* Nancy. But she had. And now she would be rid of him. "Will I still be seeing you for carols this year at my apartment?" she asked.

"Why not?" asked Rumsfeld, affecting bafflement. He had no plans to leave Washington, even after Gates was confirmed. His facial expression made Condi see that; and he waited for her to ask another question.

She smiled and remained silent. So did the new congressman. Condi was recalling how, in the months before the invasion, back in '03, she had to get allies at DoD to sneak her some files she was perfectly entitled to see as NSA—ones Don had kept from her nonetheless. Well, now he could go pack up his snowflakes and write some convoluted, impenetrable memoir.

How had they ever lasted as long as they had? How had they even managed to function?

The answer to the last question, which she remained loath to admit, was that they *never* had.

36

DECEMBER 26–30, 2006

**Dining Room of the Hotel Monteleone; December 26;
1:20 p.m.**

"Emile," protested Allie. "You've spoiled us *already*."

The assistant concierge dismissed her concern. "For my comrades in arms? *Rien ne suffit.*" He put some custard on the table for the baby. Weeks ago he had arranged a steep three-night discount for his friend's lady and their child. He even booked mother and daughter into Room 928.

It had been Allie who suggested, in a Thanksgiving phone call to Ross, that the three of them spend Christmas in New Orleans. Ross was prepared to return, after each of their three evenings together, to his place on Dauphine Street, but on Christmas Eve, once the baby was asleep, Allie drew him back to the same bed in whose sheets he'd found her buzzing BlackBerry on August 28, 2005. While the baby slumbered in the crib across the room, the two of them made love almost in silence. Allie teased him, in a whisper, about his hot new gravedigger's muscles; neither said anything to indicate their shared awareness that they were crossing the highest of thresholds. As she held him Ross thought he would die of despair if she now absconded in another of her crazy, meaningless lurches.

I'm here, she'd said softly, seeming to realize, as did he, the tentativeness of that last word, so often joined to "now" with a mere conjunction. Permanence still lay somewhere else, and she acknowledged this in a sentence that both encouraged and warned him: *I'm not quite there yet, but I'm getting there.*

Yesterday, on Christmas morning, they'd taken Holley to mass in the cathedral, where she never once cried. Afterwards they pushed her around the Quarter in a fancy stroller Emile scared up from the hotel. Allie told Ross that he couldn't forever go on living in this city the way he was now, and he'd offered no argument, believing it best to let her define the details and timetable of getting to *there*. As it was, he worried that she regarded his apostasy from Bush—the trigger for his mendicant labors—as something he had designed to please *her* rather than a change derived from genuine internal need.

"Emile," Ross now said, reaching under the table for a box wrapped in fleur-de-lis paper. "I almost forgot. For you."

The package contained two volumes: the modernized *New Orleans City Guide*, bookmarked to the page that included the Monteleone, and the old WPA version. Each was inscribed to the concierge. Once Emile put on his glasses, Ross drew his and Allie's attention to a passage on page five of the 1938 edition:

> *The prevailing winds are from the Gulf, generally from the southeast. Tropical hurricanes, which harass most points of the Gulf Coast, very seldom strike New Orleans. Occasional fogs occur in the spring and winter months, particularly along the river-front, but are, as a rule, of short duration.*

He had expected Emile to laugh. But the concierge burst into tears, apologized, and went off by himself. The baby looked perplexed, but Ross and Allie understood. For the rest of their lives, the keening winds of Katrina would without warning make themselves audible, would begin to gust and whirl inside them. Somewhere the storm still raged, maintaining the undead condition to which all the city's aboveground, mausoleumed corpses aspired.

"We'll find him before dinner," Allie said, gently. "Don't feel bad." She arranged Holley in the stroller, zipping up her quilted jacket.

"How much do you think she's up for?" asked Ross.

"I'd say pretty much anything. How many items from that guide-book are you planning on showing us this afternoon?"

"Actually, I thought I'd let you set the agenda." He paused before continuing: "I've been wondering whether you want to go *back* anywhere—the barracks, or even the stadium."

Firmly, but without any drama, Allie replied, "No." She took his hand—never the easiest gesture for her to perform—and tried to convey what she was thinking: if they were truly, effortfully headed *there*, the commemorative destinations he had in mind needed to be understood as *elsewhere*. He had to free himself from the trap of the past, cease being the despondent victim who still couldn't believe her return. He needed to accept her resurrection as an accruing fact, not a miracle. Both of them were susceptible to revisionist personal history, one that saw the hurricane as the thing that had sundered them, whereas in fact they'd been sundered already.

"Okay," said Ross. "Let's roll." They pushed the stroller into the sunshine and cold. Holley's red-and-green Mardi Gras beads bounced against the outside of her jacket, catching the light. Allie asked him: "She won't swallow one if the string breaks, will she?"

"I'd never have figured you for a nervous mother."

He led the way, block after block, out of the Quarter and down Magazine Street, which ran parallel to Camp—some sort of fateful geography in Lee Harvey Oswald's life, if he correctly remembered yet another recent encounter with Gordon Novel. The three of them soon reached the destination Ross had yet to name, the World War II Museum. He urged Allie's gaze toward its inviting glass front.

Seeing the sign, she remarked: "Holley's a little young for this, wouldn't you say?"

"This could be Take Our Daughter to Work Day!" Ross answered, all at once incautiously bubbling over with enthusiasm for his scheme. He realized he was going for broke, pushing things past the edge, letting Christmas Eve's encouragement set free his neediness. "Come on!" he cried, holding a door for Allie and the stroller.

The three of them, ticketed, soon stood beneath a huge Dakota military transport plane suspended from the ceiling on wires. Only now, on this spot, did Ross at last explain what he'd heard from the Chairman and the head of the Smithsonian about a position here. "You'd be perfect for it," he declared. "I'll find a teaching job or something—" he started to add, stopping when he noticed that she was looking not at him but at the plane's stilled propellers, toward which Holley pointed.

The aircraft, Allie thought, was too cumbersome ever to have performed a corkscrew landing. She tried to think of the men and matériel it had ferried through darkness and sometimes toward doom, but with what any long view of the enterprise would concede had been purpose and fulfillment. There it was, still literally aloft, but carrying a semblance of accomplishment and finality.

"I'll take the job. But not until April," she added. "Will they hold it open for that long?"

All Ross could think of to say was: "Ask Bush when you see him on Thursday."

———

December 28; 8:30 a.m.; Prairie Chapel Ranch, outside Crawford

Condi took her coffee mug to the back porch, where the president sat with his. He was looking out at the lake and clearly wanted to keep doing only that for another minute or two. She sat down beside him, took notice of the white prickly poppies in the distance, and quietly picked a piece of lint off the black slacks she was wearing.

"I thought about getting up early enough to go fly-fishing," Bush finally said. "But I've had too many early mornings lately." Yesterday he'd been out in front of the reporters before seven a.m. to announce Jerry Ford's death. Recalling that now, he told Condi, "You know, this funeral is going to affect the timing of the speech."

She didn't need to ask which speech before pointing out: "It may also get in the way of consulting with Congress."

"Yeah," the president replied.

She'd arrived last night for dinner with him and Laura while the rest of today's participants were still flying in to Waco. She'd spent the night here; the others would now be driving from their hotels, in time to make the nine-thirty meeting.

"Things couldn't go on the way they were," said Bush, gravely. "Not with Casey and Rumsfeld." Just as Gates, at last confirmed, was replacing the old secretary of defense, David Petraeus would likely soon be succeeding the current American commander in Iraq.

"You certainly couldn't go on having *two* defense secretaries!"

Condi hoped, with this lighthearted remark, to dispel the mortification she heard in the president's voice. The situation *had* been crazy right up until Rumsfeld's departure ceremony two weeks ago. Both he and Gates were present for a crucial strategy session in the Solarium the Sunday after Thanksgiving. And Don had still been scattering snowflakes hours before exiting the Pentagon.

A few nights prior to that, over dinner with Gates at the Watergate Hotel, she herself had continued to express reservations about sending more troops; things in Iraq were simply too confused to allow their introduction. Yet the momentum in favor of a decision to mobilize them, a surge toward the "surge," now seemed unstoppable. Five new brigades would be going over, which would leave next to nothing at home. God forbid there was an eruption somewhere in, say, Asia. In the Solarium there'd actually been talk of the worst of worst-case scenarios: bringing back the draft. Still, even that political death-specter couldn't slow the drive to do what the president had at last decided to do. And with Don now gone, Dick could support what Hadley had been pushing without any awkwardness. The president would mostly be advising his advisors today. Every pursing of his lips or moment of exasperation, each pointed question and flared nostril, would indicate that he was now pulling the train.

"So are you really with me?" he asked her. "Out here last night you told me this was the last card. Are you ready to play it?"

"Yes," she heard herself insisting.

"What made you believe?"

"Talking to the Arab foreign ministers after we went to Amman the other week. They're more terrified of Iran than I ever realized. If Maliki collapses and the Shia take sole possession of things, Iraq will be a client state of Tehran. It's becoming clear that Iraq is really *about* Iran."

Bush scowled: "No. Iraq is about Iraq, in and of itself." *Don't make me enter the next damned place*, he was thinking. His still-fresh disappointment over North Korea had made him more determined to succeed at the war he was already fighting.

Condi, once more ill at ease, told him: "I was never really *against* more troops."

———

December 28; 9:00 a.m.; Ninth Ward, New Orleans

Gary Fowler was dubious and Father Montrose reluctant, but Ross had persuaded both to accompany him this morning. They stood on the edge of a cordoned-off yard behind a one-story brick house with a broken back window and crumpled metal awning. John Edwards had chosen the spot to declare his presidential candidacy.

Ross was in high spirits, not so much over the candidate—though Edwards did seem to be the only one who talked a lot about New Orleans these days—as over what had happened on Tuesday. He wanted to say things like "My fiancée is at the president's ranch," even if the small crowd here was decidedly anti-Bush (for that matter so was he) and despite the fact that he hadn't exactly asked Allie to marry him, a step that seemed small compared to the distance toward *there* that they'd already succeeded in traveling.

Standing with the press, Ross could hear beyond the thin rope line some chatter between two of the ex-senator's aides. He learned that Edwards had spent Christmas in his just-finished Chapel Hill megahome after finally unloading the six-bedroom in Georgetown for $5.2 million. For the past couple of days, he'd worked sporadically at a local food bank and on repairing this house, helped out by the middle-schoolers now standing within camera range wearing exhortatory sweatshirts.

The candidate at last came around the side of the house, emerging into view in an open work shirt and pair of jeans. The transmitter for a wireless mic had been attached to the belt encircling his trim waist. The script was so casual that he introduced himself; the students didn't realize they were supposed to applaud. "The two Americas I have talked about in the past" were, he insisted, "something I feel very personally." He praised the schoolkids and mentioned the springtime success of Opportunity Rocks. "Instead of staying home and complaining, we're asking people to help." It was unclear whether he meant with the campaign or with the rebuilding.

"Most of the good that's been done in New Orleans has been done by faith-based groups, charitable volunteers, people who cared enough to spend some time and actually do some work, get their hands dirty."

Gary, forgetting Ross's political turnabout, leaned into him and asked: "Sounds like your man's daddy, no? 'A thousand points of light'?" He laughed, long since resigned to the truth that these guys were all alike.

Ross conceded the comparison but still felt himself craving *some* sort of public faith, what Allie had weirdly found in the war—not that they'd talked much about that this week. If Edwards seemed more than blurry about his domestic plans, maybe that wasn't so bad? Maybe it left room for approaches that were truly sweeping?

The candidate at last got to Iraq: "It's time to actually start leaving. It is a mistake for America to escalate its role. It is a mistake to surge troops into Iraq." The debate in which Ross's perhaps-future-wife was participating this morning at Bush's ranch had lately, along with its foregone conclusion, come into the open.

As the minutes wore on, this hat-in-the-ring event retained its strangeness. CNN and C-SPAN were carrying it live, but the lack of any rah-rah or music—not so much as Emmalina on her clarinet— seemed gaudily prim, a pious refusal to insult the wounded location with any campaign frills. The result, under gray skies, was flat, as if the speaker were apologizing for, instead of announcing, his candidacy. For all that, Edwards's facial expression seemed unable to mask the feeling that he deserved a brass band.

Ross recognized Rielle Hunter with her camcorder.

"Where's Elizabeth?" a reporter shouted when Edwards was through.

The candidate replied that his wife was busy in North Carolina with her own good works. Ross, close to Hunter, heard her mutter: "Eating up a storm and raging at everything in sight. And, oh yes, shopping on the Internet." The man from Edwards's PAC, recognizable from August, did his own muttering to another aide: "Rielle should be careful. Mommy has spies everywhere." After recognizing Ross in turn, he said, "Hey," and handed him a new business card reflective of the PAC's metamorphosis into an actual campaign.

"You need someone here?" Ross asked, looking up from the card.

"We have New Orleans pretty well covered. You have any other hometowns?" the man replied, with a laugh.

"Lubbock, Texas."

"It's yours if you want to organize it!" All of them, he added, including Rielle, were on their way to Des Moines before lunchtime.

———

Prairie Chapel Ranch; 10:50 a.m.

They sat in the living room, an inner semicircle of blazers and sport coats—Cheney, General Pace, Hadley, and Gates—talking about where the additional troops would come from (the Eighty-second Airborne could contribute a brigade) and where they would be put. Four-fifths of them were destined for a tight series of rings around Baghdad. This would be a surge against counterinsurgency: making Iraqis in the capital *feel* more secure while they, almost incidentally, became so in fact. The soldiers' specific responsibilities would have to be hashed out with Maliki, who the president assured everyone had pledged to go after the Shiite militias more aggressively.

"A new status-of-forces agreement is going to be required," said

Condi Rice. She looked toward Allison O'Connor as she said this, and Gates nodded in agreement. "We'll need one," Rice continued, "to suit the new definitions of the mission, and then, assuming its success, we'll need a framework to solidify things for the longer term."

Allie could imagine Rumsfeld saying "Success would be bringing them *home*." But there was no longer anyone here with that point of view.

During a break for coffee, she chatted with Rice, and the president, talking to Josh Bolten, signaled "come here" with his fingers. When Condi stepped toward him, he had to correct her: it was Allison he wanted.

"Didn't have a chance to say Merry Christmas," he told her.

"Same to you, sir. Belatedly."

"Did you enjoy the day?"

"I spent it in New Orleans."

Bush brightened. "How is my ex-supporter?"

"How would you feel about my living in sin with him?"

She could see two reactions fighting on his face: pleasure in the news but also resentment toward the liberal bullshit he detected about his supposed religiosity, or maybe the marriage amendment. He was realizing that part of her would remain an unreconstructed pain in the ass.

"I'd say it's better than living apart," he told her. "Especially for your little girl. So: we've got a new policy here. Do you have a new job?"

"Well, that's an interesting program they've suggested for the museum. The Weatherman approves, and not just from self-interest."

Bush was smiling again. "He won *you* back. Maybe I can win *him* back in the New Year."

She grimaced at the idea of Ross's "winning her back"—the caveman feel of the phrase. Bush saw her expression and laughed.

"This job," she said. "Would late April be too late to start it?"

The president shrugged. "Talk to the Smithsonian guy. Tell him I said that's fine."

"It's the interim period I'd really like to talk to you about. I want to go back to Iraq."

Bush looked as if she'd just undone some cease-fire that he'd brokered.

"The status-of-forces agreement that Secretary Rice mentioned—"

"Right," he said, managing to sound neutral and annoyed all at once. "Makes sense. You being an Army lawyer. Was this Condi's idea?"

"Yes, but it's a good one. And I think I could be useful."

"You're not running away from—or maybe just trying to postpone—what you've decided about New Orleans?"

"No." The quickness of her reply convinced her that she meant it. Last night in the Waco hotel she'd posed the same question to herself, asked and answered it a dozen times. "I need to achieve something small and concrete there. It will give me strength to get on with things when I get back home."

She looked at Bush and seemed for a moment to understand herself *through* him. Half the time he was without self-confidence; the other half he spilled an excess of it. He was worn out from working the double mental shift, just as she'd been worn out by the gradual realization that she'd never truly had any belief in herself. The impulsivity, the flaunted skepticism, had been a membrane stretched thin over a black pond of self-doubt, a pool into which she'd never let herself look. She now wanted only to accept her circumstances—Holley, Ross, the skills she could deploy in Iraq—as if they added up to the religious faith most people simply inherit and assent to. Something not to question or scorn but to abide by; a vessel into which she could put her energies and life, instead of putting those things into perpetual flight.

Bush held her gaze but wondered about her commitment, remembering why Rumsfeld had brought her to Washington two years ago. On a human level, he didn't want her going back to Iraq, however briefly, and he couldn't be sure that his saying yes to the idea wouldn't derive just from feeling flattered about having one person around who'd been converted *to* the war.

"Accept the Louisiana job for April," he told her. "I'll tell Rice and Gates to have you in Baghdad by January fifteenth."

—

Café du Monde, Decatur Street, New Orleans; 11:58 a.m.

After the Edwards announcement, Ross mailed off the new guidebook to Mrs. Boggs—the last of his eighteen discount copies—and then went to have coffee in the Quarter. While CNN, mute and close-captioned, played above the counter, he asked himself, for the fiftieth time since Tuesday: Why had she said April? And he tried once more to settle for the Occam's-razor explanation: she just needed time. Who, after all, could wind up their affairs in only a couple of weeks?

His cell rang.

"I thought you'd wait until you were back in Waco."

"I've only got a minute. The four horsemen of the apocalypse, plus Rice, are on their way out to the reporters. They're going to give the press a statement before our 'working lunch.'" Looking at the TV in the ranch house's living room, Allie informed Ross that it was carrying the sound of some protesters down near the gate, though Mrs. Sheehan was long gone from their number.

On the café's silent television, Ross could see Bush approaching the press along with Cheney, Gates, Rice, and General Pace. A bank of standing microphones with wind-absorbing fuzzy covers waited for them like a flock of llamas.

"I need to make one more trip to Iraq," Allie told Ross.

"You mean another overnight?" He knew as soon as he asked that this couldn't be right; she wouldn't impart any such secret and spontaneous thing over the phone.

"No. Let me—I'm trying to be honest. I *want* to make one more trip. You'll understand why when the announcement coming out of all this talk today gets made."

"How long?"

"They'll make it a week or so from now."

"Not how long until the announcement. How long will you be *staying* over there?"

"About three months. Maybe two and a half."

He forced himself to say nothing, told himself he didn't *want* to argue, that this was just a last hurdle. What were three months when after that he would be granted what he'd never expected? *I'm not quite there yet, but I'm getting there.*

Or was this just one more display from a careless, rampant woman he would never grasp?

"There's no time now, but we *will* talk about this," she insisted. "I will explain. And I will keep my promise."

"Who'll take care of Holley?"

"My mother and Anne Macmurray. And while they do, I want you to think about getting away from Louisiana for a while. You can't spend another three months by yourself burying unidentified bodies and scraping mold. We need, both of us, to emerge from *all* of it. From both storms. *Then* we can go back to New Orleans and I'll take the job."

Neither spoke while Ross looked up at the muted TV. Through his phone, from Bush's living room, he heard the sound portion of the broadcast. The president declared that his advisors were "coming to closure on a way forward," and hearing the words, Ross thought back to a political-rhetoric course he'd once given at SMU. That line of Churchill's: *Now this is not the end. It is not even the beginning of the end. But it is perhaps the end of the beginning.* He scarcely cared if the words could be applied to the current war. He wondered only if they could be applied to himself and Allison O'Connor.

———

**Home of Rukia Hasani, the Green Zone, Baghdad;
December 30, 8:30 p.m.**

Rukia offered the Englishman, soon to be an American, a cup of tea.

"Very kind of you," said Hitchens.

Her aunt, perplexed by how this visitor had addressed tiny Pirnaz as if she were an adult, had several minutes before spirited the baby to the alcove kitchen, leaving the writer alone with her niece. The television, its sound off, played in a corner.

Today was Eid al-Adha, a Sunni holiday not being marked by Rukia. Her own holidays would begin tomorrow, though today had provided cause for Shia celebration in the execution of Saddam Hussein.

"It's good of you to welcome me here," said Hitchens.

"Miss Allison is my friend." Rukia was wary but had agreed to see him because of his slender connection to the American woman, which he'd explained: when getting ready for a Christmastime trip to Kurdistan with his son, the writer had made use of the business card Allison gave him at a demonstration back in February. He'd asked her for interesting people to see when he got down to Baghdad. Expecting to be directed only to American officials in the Green Zone, he was surprised to see that her list included the widow of her translator. "She told me some of your story," he said to Rukia.

"What is the news of Holley?" Rukia asked.

"I'm afraid I have no idea," said Hitchens. "I wanted to see you particularly to talk about today's . . . atrocity."

Rukia bristled. "Why that word?" She had an hour ago seen the video of the execution and—though she did not want to admit this to her visitor—been shaken by it. Before the lawful, judicial vengeance of the trial could be concluded, Maliki had allowed the hanging to be carried out at six a.m. by the Mahdi Army, the very Shia militia he had vowed to curb.

"Did you hear on the tape the cries of '*Muqtada! Muqtada!*'?" asked Hitchens, naming the Mahdi leader. He pointed to the television—the execution video was playing yet again—and requested that the volume be raised.

Saddam Hussein stood on the scaffold. The thick coils of rope above the noose, which had not yet been tightened, lay like a single giant epaulet on his left shoulder. Rukia wondered who would be taking a piece of *this* rope—to keep or bestow as a gift—like the bloody length of cord Fadhil had inherited from Abu Ghraib.

Mad cell-phone-camera gyrations, and then screams, as the drop neared. Rukia felt embarrassed by the bloodlust in the words she could make out.

"I don't understand your position," she told Hitchens. "Allison told me that you favor the American war."

Hitchens pointed to the screen. "What I don't favor is American helicopters ferrying a man, even him, to be slaughtered by a mob."

Rukia tried to say something about how the killer of her father-in-law and, less directly, of her husband, had now gotten what he deserved, but she found that she couldn't speak after the intake of breath intended to produce the invective. Her mind had suddenly detoured into imagining what cries and chants Fadhil might have heard from Sunni counterparts of the Mahdi before *he* was killed. She was, in truth, wearying of the retributiveness with which she'd stiffened Allison's spine a year ago. The entire country, if one could any longer—or yet—call it that, was like the cell-phone video: a kaleidoscope of chaos. She feared that the American vision of possibility would never extend beyond the Green Zone, where she could not go on living forever.

Seeing her distress, Hitchens attempted to divert her from the screen to which he'd just pointed her. He thought he would tell her some of the encouraging things he and his son had seen in the north. "Your husband's mother is a Kurd, no?"

"Yes," said Rukia, not taking her eyes from the TV.

Saddam uttered his last words before the floor disappeared beneath his feet: *Down with the traitors, the Americans, the spies and the Persians!*

Rukia looked toward her daughter, whose attention had been drawn by the triumphal shouting. She then turned to Hitchens and said, "I have been offered a visa to America."

37

JANUARY 2–6, 2007

The National Cathedral; Washington, D.C.; January 2, 10:50 a.m.

As the choir sang and the mourners awaited the coffin, Jimmy Carter, down in front, directed his wife Rosalynn's attention to the West Rose window. Did she remember the two of them being there for its dedication, in 1977, with Queen Elizabeth? Rosalynn, glad to be distracted from Nancy Reagan on her other side, nodded.

Carter himself felt psychologically sandwiched between the arriving corpse and the storied ghost of Ronald Reagan. He pondered the catafalque, that black slab ready to receive Jerry, whom he'd expelled from the White House; he wondered whether Clinton and Bush Sr. were also thinking about how long it would be before they lay atop it.

Donald Rumsfeld, at some remove from the current and heaviest hitters here, watched Condi Rice lean forward to chat with Nancy Reagan in the seat directly in front of her. The two women were all smiles and looked almost ready to high-five each other. Rumsfeld knew from all the services he'd attended here that the cathedral could hold thirty-seven hundred people, nearly a full brigade. And yet, vast as this morning's congregation might appear, it didn't seem large enough to overpower anything, even if it were armed and multiplied by five.

He recognized the strains of *Fanfare for the Common Man*, and soon enough the president was escorting Betty Ford—shrunken, frail, and grimacing—down through the nave. The tipsy, intermittently antic woman that Rumsfeld could recall executing her old Martha Graham moves, in bare feet on the Cabinet table, was unrecognizable.

George W. Bush worried about the long trudge she had to make. He kept the pace slow and steady, looking up at the flags of the states, counting them off. When he saw the clusters of Boy Scouts acting as ushers, the tender streak that widened inside all Bush males with the passage of time caused his throat to constrict. Jerry might, he thought, be the last normal guy to have occupied the White House—including Dad, who was too far up the ladder of *noblesse oblige* to qualify. Think about it: underneath his hair shirt, Carter was a nasty prick; Reagan had been an unknowable spook; and Clinton was lucky some girl's father hadn't blown his head off with a shotgun. Maybe Jerry was the *only* normal guy to have occupied the place.

Bush delivered Betty to the front row and then crossed the aisle to sit beside Laura and listen to his father, the first of the big eulogists. Kissinger and Tom Brokaw, who seemed more an emcee than a mourner, soon followed; and then it was his turn. Looking down from the pulpit at Giuliani, he remembered giving the "middle hour of our grief" speech on this spot, three days after 9/11. By comparison, today's remarks felt as quick and easy as some Arbor Day proclamation he had to recite. He extolled Jerry for civil rights—sticking up for that black UM football player long ago—and, after that, raced through the congressional career, a fast paragraph for what had taken up most of the life. Then it was on through "our long national nightmare" and the gentle rousing from it that Jerry had supplied.

The whole thing had the instructive brevity of those "bicentennial minutes" that had been all over TV in Jerry's time:

> *He was criticized for signing the Helsinki accords, yet history has shown that document helped bring down the Soviet Union, as courageous men and women behind the Iron Curtain used it to demand their God-given liberties.*

Condi's shop must have put this in. He could see Nancy giving him an *oh-brother* look.

I will always cherish the memory of the last time I saw him this past year in California.

Actually, Jerry hadn't seemed such a "common man" or normal guy out in Rancho Mirage. All the corporate boards and honoraria had fixed him up just fine. In fact, Bush could do *without* the memory of sitting across from him in air-cooled desert luxe, a crystal bowl of fruit between them, all the ex-president's little lecture points about Iraq starting to annoy him like the kiwi seeds between his teeth.

. . . and we ask for God's blessings on Gerald Ford and his family.

Done. He was glad the rules of church decorum kept there from being any applause to measure. As it was, the prayers and readings and music that followed added up to a pretty long and solemn affair for such a Rotarian corpse. The organ went laughably overboard during the recessional; as he piloted Betty back up the aisle, it was erupting in these silent-movie-theater crashes, like something out of *Phantom of the Opera.*

*

A little chapel near the altar had been turned into a holding room for the most prominent mourners, so that they wouldn't have to shake hands with too much of the throng filing out onto the cathedral steps. As he shuffled into the small space, Denny Hastert, the hulking House speaker, once again congratulated Nancy Pelosi, who would be taking his job the day after tomorrow. He also patted the shoulder of an Eagle Scout and told him what a fine job he and all the other boys had done this morning.

The Clintons avoided the Carters, their dislike of the older couple going back to 1980, when the sitting president had set Castro's discarded and crime-prone Marielitos down on the landscape of Arkansas, costing Bill his reelection as governor and forcing him, for a whole two years, into a Nixonian "wilderness," where Hillary screwed his courage to the sticking point.

Right now Bill was taking an opportunity to size up Hillary's most likely presidential opponent next year. He watched Giuliani and the ex-mayor's third wife work the chapel as if it were a private dining room at Peter Luger.

Barbara Bush, who'd found the service a lot less sad than Kenny Lay's, gave Nancy Reagan's brittle little frame a hug, figuring that with Laura standing next to both of them her predecessor would refrain from saying anything too catty.

"It all seems so long ago," the elder Mrs. Bush observed.

"It?" asked Nancy.

"Jerry's era."

"It seems like six months ago," responded Nancy, who still almost daily recalled the Reagans' losing duel with the Fords in '76: the blare of all those competing plastic horns at the Kansas City convention; the ERA types wearing ELECT BETTY'S HUSBAND buttons. Like Barbara, the newest presidential widow had always gotten a magic-carpet ride from the press. When the Ford kids acted up, they were "refreshingly normal teenagers"; when her own did, they were freaks.

"This is an awfully long day for poor Betty," observed Barbara Bush. "She seems as fragile as Pat did the last time we all saw *her*. And now she's got to go all the way back to Grand Rapids for the burial."

Nancy thought: *Try doing California.*

"Well, she's got those handsome sons to lean on," said the current First Lady.

"There's one good thing about this job," her mother-in-law declared. "Once you've got the library, you don't have to buy a plot! George and I will soon enough be baking under the soil down at College Station."

Nancy's thoughts, as always, went to Ronnie. She wondered how cold the ground in Simi Valley was today. "You confused me for a moment when you mentioned Grand Rapids," she told Bar. "Isn't his library someplace else?" The idea that he even got one still irritated her.

"The burial is in Grand Rapids," Laura Bush pacifically explained. "They've got a little museum there. The library is in Ann Arbor." She took care to appear as if she were correcting her mother-in-law and not Nancy Reagan.

"Whatever," said Barbara Bush.

"I see Dick Cheney," said Mrs. Reagan, looking off to the side of the room, "but not Don Rumsfeld."

Laura laughed.

Brent Scowcroft and Condi Rice chatted beside some poinsettias that were still in good shape a week after Christmas. "Where's Hadley?" Scowcroft asked.

"Minding the store," Condi answered.

"Gates seems to have left."

"Already gone back to the Pentagon. He's got a general to hire." Today would bring Petraeus the official offer to replace Casey.

Scowcroft, grave and fatherly, looked at the young woman who'd worked for him when he was Bush Sr.'s NSA. "Are you really *for* what's in the works, Condi?"

"I think it's the only way."

"The best way out is *out*."

Scowcroft saw her glancing around, as if expecting the president to come back into the cathedral and catch her talking to this graybeard non grata. Things would never be the same between him and the younger Bush after that five-year-old op-ed opposing an Iraq invasion. He now gently told Condi, "Maybe I should say hi to Henry," adding in a whisper: "He looks pretty awful, doesn't he?"

A few feet away, George H. W. Bush discussed the open secret of the surge with Dick Cheney. "Well, I hope this does it. I have my doubts, but I don't make them known to him. No help in that."

"There's one area in which you could be very helpful," Cheney responded.

"Happy to be, however I can."

"Tell the president to think about pardoning Scooter." Libby's trial in the Valerie Plame matter was scheduled to begin two weeks from today. "This is going to end badly for him, and we've got an obligation."

Bush looked as if he had no idea who "we"—or what the obligation—might be.

Cheney excused himself. He was hosting Kissinger and Bob Dole, another honorary pallbearer, for lunch at the vice-presidential residence.

The former secretary of state and majority leader were already in a limousine for the very short ride to the Naval Observatory. Their car soon passed the familiar lone anti-Vatican protester, whose placard today read: CATHOLIC SEMINARIES TEACH MOLESTATION. Kissinger again wondered about the strange purity of this man, and whether such implacability, the opposite of his own life's adaptive slalom, was heroism or madness.

Dole had lately taken to holding a cell phone instead of a pencil in the hand of his damaged arm. The phone now rang, and after a few seconds of listening to the person on the other end, he said, "Thanks, but I'll pass."

"Who was that?" Kissinger asked.

"Larry King's people. They want me to come on tonight to talk about Ford."

"Why not?"

Dole gave one of his grunts, sardonic and humble all at once. "My busy schedule?" He paused, and as usual a more serious answer followed the quip. "Don't feel right about it. I always worry I cost Ford the election in '76."

Kissinger, amazed by such tender guilt, asked: "You mean the hatchet-man business?" Dole had zealously performed the running-mate role Nixon had perfected when on the ballot with Ike.

"Yeah, sort of."

"You don't think it was Jerry's pardoning of our friend?"

Dole shrugged.

"Victory," Kissinger intoned, "was achieved in the long run. Carter got in and then made Reagan inevitable."

"Which makes me as big a screw-up as Carter. Well, if defeat means victory, I'm glad I was able to do my part."

"Victory is a fungible thing," mused Kissinger. "Or so I believe."

"Yeah. I've noticed."

After writing in '05 that success in Iraq was essential, Kissinger had six weeks ago pronounced it impossible.

"The Old Man understood that too," said Kissinger. "About victory."

It always seemed to come back to Richard Nixon. "What do you think the Old Man would be saying about Bush Jr.?" asked Dole.

"That he believes things too strongly," Kissinger replied, without hesitation. "He may change his mind and go on to believe something else, but he believes what he says when he's saying it. In his way, he may be the sincerest man I've ever met."

Dole harrumphed.

"Which is to say," Kissinger concluded, "that he's a disaster."

———

January 6, 5:05 p.m.; 2001 N. Clarendon Boulevard, Arlington

Ross parked his rental car outside Allie's apartment. The trunk and backseat were packed with his own last things from Wilson Boulevard, where these last several months the indulgent landlord had allowed them to stay in a basement storage bin.

He'd flown up only this morning and would drive southwest all night. It was another carful of belongings, parked just ahead of him with Pennsylvania plates, that he would now help carry up to Allie's place: all the possessions Patricia O'Connor deemed necessary for a three-month stay, while she and her old friend Anne Macmurray took care of her granddaughter.

Holley appeared quite unflummoxed by the commotion taking over the apartment. She smiled with recognition as Ross came inside with the first box. The baby's hair, he noticed, was taking on her mother's reddish tinge. Allie, with whom he'd earlier stolen an hour inside the bedroom, was set to leave on Tuesday. At the moment she was still out running errands, which allowed him a brief conversation with Mrs. O'Connor.

"I don't approve, or understand," she said. "About her going."

"But she's coming back," Ross replied. Ever since she told him about requesting the Iraq detail, he had taken Allie at her word, had silently pledged to do things her way for this last stretch, even to the point of agreeing not to stay in New Orleans for the time she'd be away.

Before he could inform Mrs. O'Connor of this, she expressed disbelief that he would be starting back for Louisiana tonight.

"It'll actually be a longer drive than that. I'm going back to Texas for a few months. I'll be living in my mother's house."

"Is she unwell? Does she need you?"

"No, I just need my old bedroom; a place to stay. I'm going to help put together a tiny organization for John Edwards out there, something that will be in place if he catches fire in the Iowa caucuses."

"You're going looking for Democrats in Lubbock? I'm glad my daughter is marrying an optimist. And I'm glad you came to your senses about Bush. Allison seems to have taken leave of hers on that score." Mrs. O'Connor paused. "I'm sorry. I keep saying 'married.' I don't know that that's in your plans—it's just my shorthand for your being together. And Texas *is* only temporary, right?"

"For sure. New Orleans is my home now."

"I'm glad things are working out as they are, though I don't understand why the two of you have to go even further apart in order to complete coming back together."

Ross thought: It's got to work its own way. *I'm not quite there yet, but I'm getting there.*

Allie's mother continued: "I'm sure this little girl doesn't get it, either, do you, honey?" She went across the room to pick up Holley.

"I wanted to tell you," said Ross, "how grateful I am you came to New Orleans in March. I'm not sure we'd be where we are today if you hadn't told me to take action."

Before Mrs. O'Connor could respond, Allie phoned from the lobby and told Ross to come down. They'd made plans to have a bite to eat before he got on the road. Mrs. O'Connor handed him Holley for a moment. "Honey, say goodbye to your daddy."

Ross and Allie drove the short stretch to Arlington's Silver Diner, which had a *Happy Days* décor and old-fashioned rock-n-roll on little jukeboxes at each booth. Ross punched the buttons for "Oh, Boy!" after ordering a plate of fish tacos. Allie leaned forward and brushed the hair off his forehead—a tender gesture unencumbered by arch-ness or irony or any fear that executing it amounted to giving some-thing away. The expression on her face seemed nearly peaceful.

"Do *not* visit Buddy's grave when you're back in Lubbock," she told him. "I would consider that morbid, sweetheart."

"More so than *digging* graves for the unidentified dead?"

"I don't disapprove of the good works," she assured him. "It's only the whiff of martyrdom that worries me. I just think you should give a brief rest to saving the drowned city. It'll give me a cheerier person to come home to."

"Give things a bit of a rest. Right." In the face of her high spirits, he could risk some pot-kettle teasing over her having sought a last detail to Iraq.

"I get it," she conceded. "But after this trip I'm giving it a *permanent* rest. You, on the other hand, have my permission to make urban reclamation your life's work if you want, once your daughter and I return to you."

"I can be 'supportive,' as they say, for three months. And I'll go easy on the beer in Texas, since I know you want me to retain my hot home-repairing, grave-digging physique."

"Good," she replied. "And if you really want to be supportive, here's a way for you to put your money where your kissable mouth is." She withdrew a folder labeled RUKIA HASANI from her shoulder bag and set it on the table. "Do you think you could find her a place to live?"

"In New Orleans?"

"No, in Texas. There are refugee communities, Little Baghdads, starting to establish themselves there. She has a visa to come over as the widow of a translator."

"Is that routine?"

"It's semi-irregular. But ten days ago I asked the president of the United States if she could have one."

"What did he say?"

Allie did her Bush imitation, jutting out her jaw and bobbing her head. "'Okay. Sounds good.' It's for Rukia and the baby, as well as the aunt, if she wants to come. She won't."

"Why Texas?"

"Why Vermont? Why Idaho? It makes as much sense as anyplace else. She's *heard* of it, at least, and she e-mailed me that she likes the way it looks in pictures. Her English, by the way, is quite good."

"Tyler didn't even work for the Scotts."

"Who are they?"

"A New Orleans family. Katrina refugees."

"Ask around. She'll need a job and a place to live. She'll have some money from the U.S., and whatever can be squeezed out of Titan Corporation. Fadhil's contractor."

"Okay."

The fish tacos and Allie's sandwich arrived.

"Are you going over on a military transport?" Ross asked.

"Partly. Three flights. To Dubai; to Kabul; to Baghdad."

Afghanistan too? Had some other scheme been folded into this?

Allie explained: "Rice, my new best friend, wants me, while I'm at it, to work on some amendments to the SOFA—status-of-forces agreement—that we've already got with Karzai's government. So I'll be in Kabul for about a day and a half. Staying at the embassy. They've told Dr. Asefi I'm coming, and he says he has a surprise for me. Some little piece of public diplomacy."

Ross fought off a wave of suspicion. He was remembering their day at the Archives with the handsome, gentle doctor-painter.

"Whatever it is," said Allie, "I'll probably accomplish more than Karen Hughes does that day. Do you know who's her latest ambassador-of-good-will appointment? *Michelle Kwan.*" She held out her arms in a figure-skater's pose.

"Am I still on thin ice?" asked Ross.

She took a bite of her sandwich. "I love you, Ross. Does that thicken the ground beneath your feet?"

It was the first time she had said it.

38

JANUARY 10–13, 2007

January 10, 8:50 p.m.; The White House

Upstairs in the Residence, Bush flexed his right hand, grasping a baseball once autographed by Don Larsen. He had last pulled it from his collection for a good-luck squeeze on October 30, 2001, before heading to Yankee Stadium to deliver the ceremonial first pitch for Game 3 of the World Series. He hadn't been looking for Larsen's perfect game that night—just one perfect throw in a city that had long hated him; then briefly loved him out of patriotic obligation; and would in short order, he knew, go back to hating him again. "If you bounce it, they'll boo," Derek Jeter had told him in the locker room. He wasn't, after all, Roosevelt, required only to lob the pitch a few feet from his hidden wheelchair into someone's mitt. He was a more than physically fit former team owner who would be throwing the full distance from the mound to the plate. He could embarrass himself, or he could earn a short extra inning of popularity a dozen miles north of the pulverized, still-smoldering towers.

And he'd thrown a strike.

Tonight, once more, he needed to get the game into extra innings; needed to earn himself the chance of leaving here, twenty-four months from now, having eked out a win. He'd shuffled the lineup with Gates and Petraeus, and this evening they were even giving the field a new look: they had him making the speech from the library instead of the Oval. A desperate touch, maybe. But if the shoe fits . . .

He took himself downstairs.

The new strategy I outline tonight will change America's course in Iraq and help us succeed in the fight against terror.

But before he outlined it he had to review everything that had happened since the Golden Mosque, eleven months of infuriating bullshit that he somehow had to own and end all at once.

The situation in Iraq is unacceptable to the American people, and it is unacceptable to me.

It was hard to say whether this was an apology or not. He himself couldn't tell. Five brigades were going to Baghdad, but

Victory will not look like the ones our fathers and grandfathers achieved. There will be no surrender ceremony on the deck of a battleship . . . A democratic Iraq will not be perfect, but it will be a country that fights terrorists instead of harboring them.

This was, he realized, the closest thing to an answer that he could give Lee Hamilton.

———

January 12, 5:35 a.m.; U.S. Embassy Complex; Kabul

Allie exited her hooch, wearing only running clothes, hoping she didn't freeze during the quick dash from the trailer to the gym. The spots of grass-covered ground felt as hard as whatever had been paved over. The cold did at least make the air of the Afghan capital smell better, less unmistakably fecal than what she recalled from two springs back. The embassy was now a sizable campus; its giant orange chancellery had opened since her last visit. And yet, Kabul's overall security was considerably worse than it had been in 2005. As far as Allie could tell, officials of the Karzai government mostly came to the U.S. compound for their meetings with the Americans, who didn't care to be around when bombs were pitched into the less-well-protected Afghan ministries throughout the city.

She turned on the treadmill and took it up to 7.5 miles per hour. Soon she was hearing George W. Bush's voice, and she raised her head to meet his televised gaze.

If we increase our support at this crucial moment, and help the Iraqis break the current cycle of violence, we can hasten the day our troops begin coming home.

Her red hair, once more getting to be a ponytail, swung vigorously. No one could say she'd failed to get her figure back since the birth of the baby, whom she ached to think about. It *pleased* her to feel the ache, this evidence she wasn't damaged—or even odd—in some fundamental way.

Everyone around her, back home and here, might wonder why she had agreed to—even sought—this last detail. They couldn't *say* anything, not with so many military mothers deployed over here and in Iraq, but that didn't stop them from thinking it.

This was, nonetheless, one thing she herself had thought *through*. She knew she didn't need to worry that absence would fray the bond between herself and her daughter. It had been forged unbreakably in the Superdome, when she had murmured constantly to the speck of Holley that was floating and expanding inside her. She remained almost weirdly secure in the connection. It was perfected and permanent. It traveled; it steadied and stilled what was febrile within herself. And it was her realization of it that allowed her to embrace Ross: she could afford to give herself, through her daughter, to him, without being afraid that her old terror of stasis would recur or that she would soon light out in another direction. She saw her life changing from a business of gestures to a matter of actual choices. She was no longer the cat who will enter a room only after spotting the way out of it. She now came in as soon as she found where she wanted to sit.

The ambassador's top aide had presented a heavy schedule for her only full day in and around Kabul. She began working through it immediately after breakfast. The first item was a meeting here at the embassy, about the SOFA, with a junior Afghan minister. She listened patiently while the young man displayed a wounded sense of sovereignty; he raised questions as to whether some provisions of the agreement were truly "reciprocal." His point was all at once reasonable and absurd: with no possibility of Afghan troops ever serving in the U.S., how could any opportunity for reciprocation arise? The chief, one-sided purpose of the agreement was to keep misbehaving American soldiers from being tried in local Afghan courts, whose idea of justice still made room for the occasional honor killing. To maintain such crucial protection, Allie let herself agree that some items on a schedule of taxes—from which U.S. troops were typically exempt—might instead be viewed as fees for services and therefore renderable unto Karzai.

At lunchtime she did a favor for Condi Rice, joining three State employees on a visit to a French-run archaeological site forty-five minutes outside the capital—an early contribution toward the rapprochement that might take place in April, if Sarkozy, now officially a candidate for the French presidency, succeeded at the polls. Jammed into a small car with the others, and followed by Aussie security in a black SUV, Allie felt herself in good spirits along the bumpy road from Kabul to Paghman. She may have been briefly disconcerted by the visible proliferation of burqas—definitely more than last time—but a bit farther on she could only marvel at the sight of men in long robes gathering branches for firewood as they might have done at the time of Christ.

The narrowness of the road left no room for the State car to pass an even smaller vehicle just ahead—a tiny putt-putt out of a French movie. When it came to a sudden halt with what sounded like a blown tire, Allie joked, "I'll bet it's hard to get Triple A out here"—a remark she regretted as soon as she saw the senior State officer in the front seat go white. He turned quickly to his left and then his right. Behind them, the Australians jumped out of their SUV, brandishing automatic weapons.

An ambush?

No. A flat tire, in fact.

False alarm or not, the mood inside the car plunged. Its occupants became stiff and nervous and remained so throughout their French hosts' guided tour of the dig. The Americans' reserve seemed to belong to the worst days of the Axis of Weasel.

The late-afternoon item on Allie's itinerary proved more congenial. With only one of the State people and a single lightly armed Aussie, she arrived at the National Gallery, back in Kabul, around four o'clock. The building seemed to belong to a once-prosperous personage losing his struggle with the upkeep. The paintings, often buckled and bubbled within their frames, needed cleaning. Many were mislabeled, often charmingly: one bowl of flowers was said to be, in the English translation beneath the Farsi, a "stay life."

A rectangular table, set with the usual tea and almonds, awaited their arrival. Mr. Masoudi, an Afghan culture official, sat at its head. He clasped Allie's hand just before Mrs. Morris, who'd come over from the embassy, greeted her with a hug. Dr. Asefi then entered the room, carrying a large album. He was followed by an Afghan man in his early twenties and an American woman only a little older than that.

After an apologetic cough, the physician-painter welcomed Allie and introduced her as "Holley's mama" to the younger Afghan man, who was training as an art conservationist; the American woman, thanks to a grant from the NEAH, had become his teacher.

"Mr. Ross Weatherall started us toward this little accomplishment about eight months ago," Dr. Asefi told the whole group. "He put us in touch with the people who led us to Miss Brockaway." He made a little bow to the restorer and her expertise.

Mrs. Morris, who had previewed the album Dr. Asefi carried, now opened the book and slowly turned its first plastic-protected pages. The contents, twenty drawings and watercolors, would soon, she told everyone, be on exhibit, first at the embassy and then here in the gallery.

The first watercolor startled Allie: the goatherd she'd been shown, in pieces, at the Archives last May. The man looked like the leathery wood-gatherer she'd seen today on the road to Paghman; the same enormous eyes. She made a silent lay judgment that the painting was moderately skilled, its proportions neither fully realistic nor display- ing any of what she supposed would be called expressionism. The thing was heartfelt, done from life, not by tracing or even by studying a photo.

"If you look closely," Dr. Asefi told those regarding the picture, "you will see that our friend is a little 'cracked.'" He pointed to a web of striations, like the hairline fractures in a porcelain glaze.

"Those lines show where the paper was once brutally torn," Mrs. Morris explained. "But thanks to Hakim and Christine the damage is scarcely visible now."

Allie softly enthused as Mrs. Morris turned the album's pages. The next few pictures, a watercolor miscellany of human forms and faces, were no more distinguished than the goatherd, but they moved her all the same. She could hear herself back in May: *The quality of the art seems less important than the principle of the thing.* What had been condemned and rent now looked up at her, fixed and redeemed. A gal- lery attendant came to take a photo of the group, the act itself a small, defiant gesture that made everyone feel good.

Dr. Asefi asked if he might have Miss O'Connor to himself for a moment. He took her to the office he still maintained in the gallery, the place where he had camouflaged the human images in the oil paintings during the time of the Taliban, and he handed her a small framed drawing of a father, mother, and child. It had been torn and mended. "For you and Mr. Weatherall. Without whom . . . as they say."

"Oh, I couldn't."

"Please. As you know, we have so many, and there is no place to put them all." He laughed, and coughed. "Please accept, with my personal gratitude."

Allie took the picture and thanked him, and at that moment, for several seconds—the second time it had happened since she entered the building—the lights went out. Dr. Asefi took one of her hands in both of his and smiled. "Go put the electric on in Baghdad. We will manage here."

———

January 12, 10:00 a.m.; 2712 Twenty-first Street, Lubbock, TX

On Thursday morning Ross awoke in his old room. In most ways it was unchanged from the middle of Jimmy Carter's presidency. A Lubbock High pennant remained tacked to a wall, along with a big Bush for Congress yard sign. A few toys that had belonged to Darryl's now-grown children had found their way in over the years, but Ross was able to move through the space like a sort of hologram inside a museum of his younger self. The house's current guest room, what had once been Darryl's, was devoid of its former occupant's things, their absence suggesting that the older brother had been fully embarked the moment he left home, whereas Ross would always be an iffy proposition, his departure reversible after even a quarter century.

He tried imagining an Edwards poster where the ancient Bush sign now hung.

Though it was past ten o'clock, his mother had left the breakfast table set. The effects of his long drive from Virginia were proving lengthier than a bout of jet lag. Allie had checked in via e-mail from Kabul, and he would time a response to be waiting for her in Baghdad. Mrs. O'Connor had also called, with a good report on Holley; she and Mrs. Weatherall engaged in a long sort-of mothers-in-law chat, the two women pretending to remember each other from thirty years before.

Buttering some toast, Ross took a look at the opinion pages of the *Avalanche-Journal*, whose conservative columnists predictably supported the surge, though with, Ross thought, a tonal weariness and lukewarmth they didn't quite know how to disguise.

The mail arrived. His mother came in and put a manila envelope by his plate. The letter it contained had been forwarded twice: from the

NEAH in Washington to his place in New Orleans, and from there, by his landlady, to the Lubbock address he'd given her last week. The original letter had, according to its postmark, begun its journey in Austin six months ago, on July thirteenth. The business envelope containing it, now crinkled and yellowed, displayed signs of aeration— what Ross even now recognized as the NEAH's mandated screening of snail mail for anthrax, a procedure still absurdly observed, at least intermittently, five years after the great scare.

He took the letter to his room and was spooked by the sight of some shaky handwriting beneath the letterhead ANN W. RICHARDS:

July 13, 2006

> *Dear Mr. Weatherall—*
>
> *I'm weak but still more or less compos mentis. E-mail seems beyond me now, so I'll have somebody get you this the old-fashioned way.*
>
> *Don't ask me how I know what happened, but trust me. You want to know who sabotaged that Bush Bash? Shrub's mother. I AM NOT KIDDING. If you tell that Bright character you know this, maybe he'll tell you the rest.*
>
> *Don't get old and don't get what I've got.*
> *Sincerely,*
> *Ann Richards*

He recalled Bill Bright tugging on his bottom desk drawer in Slaton—*The hell there isn't!*—and contemplated the useless, astonishing information that the governor had now imparted from the beyond.

"Mom! I'm taking your car for the afternoon!" He'd already returned the rental that got him here from D.C.

Before setting off, he thought he'd better make an unrelated call. He had the names of two women, Lubbock Democrats, from the Edwards people; if he phoned at least one of them today, he might justify the pittance he was being paid by the nascent campaign.

"Mary Hatfield," said the cheerful voice on the other end of the line.

Ross told her how he'd gotten her number—and Pamela Brink's—when inquiring about who headed the Democratic organization in Lubbock County.

"It's not a full-time job," she replied, with laughter.

Could he come see her to deliver a pitch for John Edwards? It really wasn't as early in the game as it seemed, and having heard Edwards up close in New Orleans, he'd like to make a case. He explained what he'd been doing in Louisiana for the past couple of years.

"I'm a little suspicious of the hair," Mrs. Hatfield said, meaning Edwards's. "And I'm pretty sure I'm for Hillary—I grew up in Arkansas under Orval Faubus: enough said. But please drop by. I can't do it today, though. I have to help with a half dozen feral cats they've rescued on Fourth Street."

"Oh," said Ross.

"They're kind of like Republicans—the cats. Very numerous and in need of neutering. But usually nice enough once they're fed and fixed. Try Pam and see if she's around today. She talks faster than anyone in Texas and will have a lot of good ideas."

Cheered, Ross set off for Slaton before he lost the impulse. It was one o'clock when he entered the town and stopped in the same bakery he'd gone to a year ago. He bought an extra coffee to take with him up the street to BRIGHT BUILDERS; the owner was visible through the window of the storefront. After entering, he went straight to the man's desk.

"I remember you," said Bill Bright, with no particular friendliness.

Ross sat down without being asked. He was amused by his own swagger, not really sure where it was coming from. "What's the smallest, cheapest mother-daughter house you could build in Lubbock?" he asked, unsure whether the old-fashioned real-estate term even applied to the case he had in mind.

Bright eyed him suspiciously. "If you've got the financing, you'd be surprised. I could put up something nice for just above a hundred and thirty grand. Nothing fancy, but like I say, nice." He began doodling.

"It isn't for me."

"Oh?"

"It's for an Iraqi woman. She lost a husband who translated for the Americans."

"Where is she now?"

"Baghdad. But she'll be coming over soon. Her name is Rukia Hasani."

Bright reached into his top drawer for a brochure.

"Before we get to that," Ross told him, "I'd be more interested in seeing what's in the *bottom* drawer."

The builder's reply was scornful. "You're still interested in *that*?"

"Barbara Bush," said Ross, evenly.

He was rewarded with a sudden agitation on Bright's face, beyond what he'd allowed himself to expect.

After composing his expression into a kind of aspirational deadpan, the builder responded to the name in *Jeopardy* style: "'Who was the First Lady in the early 1990s?'"

"That's all?" asked Ross.

"Why should there be more?"

"Okay, I'll take my business elsewhere." He got up from the chair.

"I'm not opening that drawer," Bright insisted, but weakly, indicating room for negotiation.

"Fine. Don't," said Ross. "Just tell me I'm right."

The builder looked down at the doodle he'd made, and after some hesitation, spoke in a voice lower than before: "She didn't want that life for George W. She wanted it for his old man, and maybe his kid brother. So she decided to throw a little monkey wrench into the congressional race. A friend of hers—I didn't know the connection at the time—came to me with three hundred dollars and told me to go offer it to W's campaign, at their little headquarters down on Broadway. I was to tell them that the money was intended for beer, lots of it, at the event they were planning to hold at Jim Granberry's house in a couple of weeks. I was also instructed to tell them to *advertise* the beer in a way that would get a big student turnout from Tech. The college kid who took the money thought it was a great idea; I think he skimmed off a hundred bucks. But even two hundred dollars could buy a lot of beer in those days."

"How did this friend of Mrs. Bush find you?"

"She was a lady whose car I used to wash. She knew I had a taste for mischief and offered me fifty bucks to go and make the 'contribution.' Hell, I even offered to work the event."

"And how did you know *her* friend was Mrs. Bush?"

"Because in short order she told me. And she took a picture of her check from 'Bar.'" He pointed to the bottom drawer. "They'd known each other as young wives in Midland almost thirty years before. They stayed friends after the Bushes moved to Houston and my lady moved to Lubbock."

Ross remained silent, just looked at him and waited for more.

"My friend was a nice older woman. High-spirited, not very cautious." He paused for a second or two. "I did more than wash her car that summer. I never met Mrs. 41, but my friend mentioned me to her. I guess the three of us *shared* a taste for mischief."

Ross quietly anticipated telling Allie that Holley Weatherall O'Connor might not exist but for the 1970s summertime indiscretion of a nice middle-aged woman in Lubbock. He picked up the brochure from Bright's desk and told him he'd be in touch.

January 13, 4:00 p.m.; The Green Zone; Baghdad

Allie had flown out of Afghanistan from Bagram Airfield this morning. After arriving in Baghdad, on her way here from the airport, she'd heard the Jumu'ah, the Friday call to prayer, and wondered which current events were finding their way into the imams' sermons today.

She'd been assigned an office down the hall from the last one she had used. In the wake of the surge announcement she could feel new pulsings of life among the Americans and their coalition partners. Rice had already returned to the Middle East, and Ryan Crocker, her choice to be the new ambassador here, had replaced Khalilzad, now on his way to the UN. But the onward-and-upward bustle appeared to be a strictly indoor phenomenon. Fewer people than ever had been out on the streets this afternoon, and a smell of burning tires rode the air. Rukia, telephoning to invite her to dinner, had explained that things were worse than ever. "I know you like fish," she added, cryptically, "but we won't have tomorrow." Allie assured her that would be fine, at which point Rukia told the story of a friend who'd found a wedding ring inside a carp she had broiled: something presumably worn by one of the five hundred tortured corpses recently pulled from the Tigris.

Allie opened an e-mail from Ross on the brand-new computer she'd been given:

> *I've decided I'm going to wait until you're home to tell you who actually paid for our first beers together 28 years ago. Mayor Granberry's back-yard turns out to have been a little Grassy Knoll.*
>
> *Tell Rukia I've found a man who's going to build her a house.*
>
> *Those are my accomplishments in the past twelve hours. How about yours?*
>
> *xox R.*

A U.S./NATO liaison officer entered the room and said hello. Allie seemed to remember once being introduced to him by Rolf, but couldn't recall whether he was connected to State or Defense. She told him what she was here for, and he gave her a knowing laugh: "Good luck. The real problem the Iraqi guys have with any SOFA is that we've just offered them congrats on their new constitution and legal system—but, whoa, don't think for a minute that you're going to use it on *us*."

"Noted."

"How long you here for?"

"Three months, roughly."

"Well, welcome back!" He breezed out as casually as he'd come in.

Allie went about organizing her desktops, real and virtual. No more calls to prayer were audible, but she could hear a faraway whistle and then a soft thud, like a tweeter and woofer engaged in a quiet hi-fi duel: a rocket being fired on the other side of the river.

She took Dr. Asefi's gift from her tote bag and undid the bubble wrap in order to attach a Post-it to the glass of the picture frame. There they were inside it: the mother, the father, and the child. She wrote:

Torn.

Repaired.

Whole.

Before slipping it into the mail for Ross, she considered the right envoi to put above her name on the post-it, and when it occurred to her, she wrote, simply, truthfully: *There.*

Epilogue

AUGUST 1–3, 2013

St. Louis Cathedral; Jackson Square, New Orleans

Father Montrose, who'd lately begun cupping his ear during dinner-table conversation, had no trouble hearing Mayor Mitch Landrieu's unexpected rendition of "Ave Maria." The already-delivered eulogies for Mrs. Boggs could not hold a candle to it, and as the priest raptly listened, Mrs. Caine, seated next to him, whispered to Ross Weatherall on her other side: "Are you old enough to remember Lynda Bird and Luci Baines?"

"Not really," replied Ross. She pointed out the two Johnson daughters several rows ahead, each wearing purple, Mrs. Boggs's favorite color.

A few minutes later, out on the cathedral steps, Ross watched the formation of a second-line parade behind the hearse. The nearby Cabildo had been flung open for a reception; inside it, Napoleon's death mask would be ready to greet the mourners. Mrs. Caine and Father Montrose, lacking the energy to march, decided to head straight there, and Ross promised to join them soon.

There had been little sadness in the cathedral, and there was even less outside, no matter that the clarinets had begun their dirge. Mrs. Boggs had led a long, kindly, and fabulous life, a miracle of shrewd soft-spokenness. But standing here in Jackson Square, one of the places he still generally avoided after long residence in New Orleans,

Ross felt a fast-moving internal wave of grief. The sun might be ablaze this afternoon, but he kept recalling the unearthly, spotlit darkness on the night of George W. Bush's long-ago speech. *Okay, Weatherman. Keep me informed—directly—of what you're seeing down here.*

Bobby Jindal, now the governor, talked to Mitch Landrieu on the church steps. The mayor's predecessor, Ray Nagin, was awaiting trial on twenty-one different corruption counts and had elected not to come to the funeral mass. As the hearse pulled away on its journey to New Roads, the plantation town where Mrs. Boggs had been born during World War I, Ross wondered whether it would take a momentary pause in front of her old Bourbon Street house, long since sold.

At least a couple of years had passed since he last walked down Pirates Alley. But he decided to do that before joining his friends in the Cabildo. He had no daughter to get home to: Holley, now seven, was up north with her grandmother for a couple of weeks. She remained the quiet, self-assured girl she'd been since birth, a fine companion in the passenger seat whenever he drove her home from ballet lessons to their shotgun house on St. Ann. He now taught two classes each term in the history department at Loyola. Being an untenured instructor (he hadn't published anything in years) didn't bother him. He was similarly half-in, half-out when it came to the Church, approaching but never quite undergoing conversion. Father Montrose, eager for him to go the distance, always promised to perform the baptism right here in the cathedral.

Two days a week, Ross still fixed up old houses, ones beset with age and poverty instead of storm damage, and even now sometimes dug graves for the indigent, though not often enough to have kept his grave-digger's muscles—a useless aspiration, he'd decided, at fifty-one.

"I haven't seen you in ages!" cried Grace, the woman who managed the Faulkner bookshop and had years earlier arranged for the NEAH to have its office space upstairs.

She pointed to the "Local" shelves, one of which still featured face-out copies of the revised WPA guidebook. "It sells steadily," she assured him.

"That's great."

"Oh, my God! I'll bet they're still here!"

Ross had no idea what she meant.

"The boxes! We put them somewhere in the back when the guy who replaced you moved on—what, five years ago? We made a couple of queries after we saw they'd been left behind. We didn't hear back, and then we never followed up." She led him into a tangled storeroom and they rummaged through the back of it.

"Yep! Five of 'em," Grace announced.

Ross recognized the three cartons containing Lyle Saxon's files from the 1930s, along with two other boxes he'd begun filling up himself.

"Any suggestions?" asked Grace.

"Would you feel comfortable consigning them to me?"

"Of course. You were the head man."

Ross told her he'd be back for them tomorrow and would make sure they got to the proper repository. On his way out he took another look at the "Local" shelves and spotted a coffee-table book devoted to the ever-more-popular World War II Museum. He averted his gaze and left the store.

———

The following afternoon, six hours out of New Orleans on I-20, the boxes in his trunk, Ross called Deborah to ask if he could drop in for dinner when he got to Dallas.

"That would be fantastic!" she replied. Archer would be home and thrilled to see him, even if Caitlyn, just graduated from UC, remained in Boulder for the summer. "David will be happy to have you here."

That was no less than the truth. Deborah's second husband was a lovely man whose arrival in her life, like a teaspoon of baking soda dropped into a glass of red water, had almost instantly eradicated her bitterness toward Ross. For the past several years she had been wanting to meet Holley ("Let's not wait until Caitlyn's wedding"), rather as Elizabeth Edwards, shortly before dying, had met Rielle Hunter's daughter.

John Edwards was one item on the long list of things Ross didn't think much about. He had been praising the candidate's potential to Mary Hatfield on Saturday, January 14, 2007, when his phone rang with the news from Baghdad. A year later, when he was back in New Orleans, Father Montrose and Mrs. Caine, respectively impassioned for Obama and Hillary during their presidential-primary duel, told him the story of the "bloody shirt"—the nasty little Edwards revelation they had witnessed at the end of Mrs. Boggs's party. Touched that they had so long withheld it, he otherwise didn't much care. Even back in '05 and '06 he understood the senator to have been one more spar atop the freshwater deluge that swept over him, something he grabbed on to without realizing that the fatal torrent lay farther on. Once it arrived, Edwards—and all of politics—floated far out of his mind forever.

"Where's your bag?" cried Deborah, waving him into the house with a big smile.

"On the backseat. I've got a hotel near SMU."

"No, no, no. Stay here. We insist."

**August 3, 12:10 p.m.; The George W. Bush Presidential
Library and Museum, Southern Methodist University**

He stared through the glass at the ornate silver samovar, a gift from Vladimir Putin. What was it that Bush used to call him? As Ross tried to remember the nickname, three girls on a school tour chattered about the contents of the next display case: a necklace, from Italy's Berlusconi, to the First Lady; a pair of hurricane lamps from the second inaugural.

He moved on to the twisted girders from the Trade Center; the posterboards for No Child Left Behind and AIDS relief in Africa; the don't-blink-or-you'll-miss-it Katrina exhibit. One photo was captioned THE NATIONAL GUARD RESCUED 87,000. No mud-caked artifacts? Not even a SCREW FALLUJAH, SAVE NEW ORLEANS T-shirt?

He slept-walked through the rest, until the sight of a pistol taken off Saddam Hussein during his capture made him feel the urgent need to get out of here. He had a half hour until his appointment with the archivist he'd spoken to on the phone; he would kill the time on a bench along the Laura Bush Promenade, the brick walk running past the main SMU library, a tribute the governor had donated in 1999 before becoming president. It was a pleasant, unremarkable stretch of campus that Ross had ambled over hundreds of times before he ever came to Washington. He now sat across from a building in which he often used to teach. *James Madison and the Arts* (1999), his own book, still rested on a shelf in the nearby library stacks, where it had been even before he irreversibly hitched his little wagon to George W. Bush's erratic star.

A guttering scholarly impulse had motivated him to bring the boxes here. It was where the records, at least the modern portion of them, ought to be; the Bush archivist would figure out wherever else Lyle Saxon's old stuff should go. Only the museum portion of the Bush complex was open on Saturdays, but Matthew Lang, the research-library archivist, had agreed to come in and take possession of the material this afternoon. At one p.m., as they shook hands in the lobby, Ross judged him to be twenty years younger than himself. He tried, with incomplete success, to make conversation about his NEAH days while they rode the elevator to the reading room.

"It's not very different during business hours," Matthew informed him, gesturing toward all the empty desks. The building had been open only a matter of months, and while the museum portion of it might already be going full tilt, no more than the tiniest fraction of the administration's documents had been processed and catalogued for researchers coming to the library. "It's going to take many years," said Matthew.

A porter, who'd been dispatched to Ross's car with keys to the trunk, soon came in with the boxes on a dolly. While being shown their contents, the archivist asked Mr. Weatherall if, on his tour of the museum, he'd seen the display devoted to the NEAH's medalists in the arts and humanities.

"I didn't explore as thoroughly as I might have," Ross confessed.

"Maybe you'd like to sit for an oral history sometime?" Matthew suggested. "That's one of the projects I'm hoping to get up and running soon."

"Uh, sure," said Ross. "But I don't think I'd have much to contribute." His desire to be back on the road to New Orleans now felt overwhelming.

"Will you excuse me?" asked Matthew, who went to answer a phone in the adjoining office. In the moments he was gone, Ross explored the still-scant collection of published books and finding aids on the shelves running past the pristine work stations.

"Mr. Weatherall," said Matthew, reentering the reading room in a state of considerable excitement, "your cell phone is going to ring in about one minute." He told Ross to feel free to take the call here; he would go to a desk at the front of the room to sit—and overhear.

"Hello?" asked Ross, once the phone rang.

"This is one hell of a surprise, Weatherman."

———

Three hours later, looking out the windows at some of Prairie Chapel's cedar trees, he thought: *This was something that she saw.* Maybe *exactly* what had been in her field of vision three days after Christmas in '06, when he'd talked to her from that coffee place on Decatur.

I need to make one more trip to Iraq.

He walked from window to window in the big living room, standing before each for several seconds, wanting to be certain that before he left here he would have had the precise view she did. He had been invited by an aide to sit down and make himself at home while he waited for the ex-president, but he was too nervous for that, and the room's totems—Afghan rugs, somebody's oil portrait of Tony Blair—interested him less than everything beyond the glass.

"Laura's in Dallas," said the familiar voice now coming up behind him. "Want one of these?"

George W. Bush handed Ross a Lone Star and poured himself

some iced tea from a pitcher on a sideboard. The two of them sat, and Bush said, "It's good to see you again."

"Thank you, sir. It's good to see you, too."

The president explained the coincidence that had allowed for his short-notice invitation. About once a month he had to call the archivist at the insistence of Harriet Miers or Freddy Ford, who ran his little Dallas office; it was usually about some FOIA request they were urging him to oppose. "They found Lang-Lang at the Library this morning, and when we made a minute of small talk he mentioned that a guy had just come over from New Orleans with some records from the NEAH. I knew it was you."

It had taken Ross a couple of hours to drive here, and he couldn't think of a thing to say.

Bush filled the silence: "I'm sorry—I'm still sorry—for your loss. How is your little girl?"

"Not so little anymore," Ross replied, automatically. "She's crazy about ballet. She goes to a charter school just outside the French Quarter." He hoped he hadn't hit the word "charter" too hard. He hadn't meant to sound sarcastic—or had he? "She's as calm as her mother was volatile."

"You're angry at me. It's okay."

"I *am* angry," said Ross. "I'm angry whenever I manage to feel anything at all. But no, I don't have a right to be angry with you. I know you were trying to keep her at home, that you'd come up with that museum job—"

"But it was my war."

"Yes, it was. And she went back to it willingly." *I'm trying to be honest—I want to make one more trip.* "She would have hated that we lost it," he added.

"Who told you we did that?" Bush's eyes narrowed, as if talking to an interviewer.

"Look at ISIL," Ross countered, halfheartedly. The terror group had just freed hundreds of prisoners from Abu Ghraib. "They say they're heading for Fallujah."

"If my successor had gotten a status-of-forces agreement—what

Allison was over there to get started—we'd have been able to keep some troops behind and save everything the surge accomplished. But the current president, the one I never criticize in public, couldn't be bothered. Check the record: you'll see that Biden said we left Iraq in good shape."

"I guess the historians—I'm not really one of them anymore—will sort it out. And maybe they'll take a second look at you, like they did with Truman. I hear that's what you're hoping for." Unable to keep an edge off his voice, Ross knew he sounded like the angry subset of bereaved families that had sometimes excoriated the president through the mails or over the phone or while standing next to him in a hospital room.

Bush wanted to pull back from all this, to be himself, not his policies. His next words came with an entirely different tone, from a very different place: "Where is she buried?"

A kind of laughing sob, loud and all-consuming, burst from Ross: "In Lubbock!" He paused to get hold of himself. "About a hundred feet from where we had our first kiss."

"Buddy Holly's grave?" asked Bush. "She told me about that."

"I was too paralyzed to do anything for about six months. Mrs. O'Connor, her mother, thought I'd probably wind up staying in Texas and decided it was okay to bury her there. But I went back to New Orleans that fall. Since my own mother died, I've never once been to Lubbock."

"I tried to call you."

"I know, sir. You sent a nice letter."

He was remembering the plane, with her body and three others, landing a few minutes before midnight at Dover, that polite, well-swept charnel house. He could remember Mrs. O'Connor's arm around him, and the sight of Rumsfeld, there unofficially, at a great remove, opaquely grieving for her, guessing wrongly that Ross and Mrs. O'Connor, whoever they might be, were connected to somebody in one of the other coffins.

"Another beer?" Bush asked him.

"I'll switch to the iced tea. I have to drive home." He had eight hours ahead of him on I-10.

"We can put you up in Waco. Or here."

"No, sir. Thank you."

Bush winked as he poured the tea. "I suppose I should apologize for having made beer drinkers out of you both."

Ross thought: *Actually, that would have been your mother's doing.* And the charm in the wink made him realize why she *would* have tried to set this man outside the false validations of politics by a small mischievous means that became available. The iPhone in Ross's pocket still carried a jpeg of Ann Richards's letter and one of Barbara Bush's check to her friend in Lubbock, what Bill Bright had finally shown him early in '08 when Rukia Hasani closed on her house—a place she'd now outgrown as Mrs. Michael McNichol, a prosperous truck dealer's wife. Rukia had two young sons and an adjunct-language-instructor's job, in Arabic Studies, at Texas Tech.

It was this American success story he chose to tell Bush rather than the secret of the Bash. To do otherwise seemed somehow wrong: Allie had died before he could tell *her* the details. And, as with so much else, what would be the point?

"Is there a lady in your life?" the president asked.

"They come and go. Mostly go."

"Still have any contact with folks from your agency?" It was clear to Ross that Bush couldn't remember the name of the Chairman he'd appointed.

"I'm sometimes in touch with a pal in the counsel's office there. He tells me Donald Trump has just leased the building; the Endowment is going to be evicted so that Trump can turn the place into a hotel. My friend's seen the plan for my former office—'enough gold-plating for one of Saddam Hussein's old bathrooms,' he says."

"Come on outside," said Bush, as if fearing the conversation might turn back to Iraq.

The beginning of a sunset was catching the cedar trees and the clusters of firewheel flowers. Amidst the porch furniture Ross was surprised to find an easel supporting a blank stretched canvas. A box of paints sat on a wrought-iron table.

"I was out here before I got my orders to talk to Lang-Lang at the library. Never really got going today."

"How long have you been doing this?" Ross asked.

"Since last summer. I'm better than you'd think. And I'm teachable. Sit down."

The chair he offered Ross faced his own straight on.

"Do you mind?" asked Bush, picking up a pencil.

"No, sir," answered Ross, not sure what else he could reasonably say.

The president sketched some lines that he soon began painting over. He was using oils, but Ross's mind went to the Afghan watercolor of the father and mother and child—the repaired picture whose arrival had preceded, by a day, the repatriation of Allie's body. It now hung, her Post-it placed under the glass of the frame, in the living room on St. Ann Street.

"How much does your little girl know about it?" Bush eventually asked, not looking away from his work.

"A lot of it," Ross answered. "About six months ago she started asking more questions—she now knows what a mortar attack is. She knew her mother 'lived in the Green Zone.' She thought it was *painted green*, but . . ."

"You don't have to," Bush said softly.

Abruptly coming to life, Ross asked: "Would you paint *them*, too? Not just me?" He took out his iPhone and brought up a picture of Allie and Holley that Emile had taken in New Orleans during their last and only Christmas together.

"Come in closer," said Bush. "Hold it up and hold it steady." He exchanged his brush for the pencil and began adding to his plan for the picture. He worked very fast, with a relaxed confidence; he soon went back to the paintbrush. Ross kept his gaze straight ahead, except for one stolen glance at the firewheels, ablaze in the lowering sun.

Bush said nothing, painted steadily for a considerable while, until without any urgency he said to Ross, "I've learned something since I started doing this." His eyes went from Ross's face to the iPhone and then to the canvas. "I've learned that shadows have color."

What he didn't tell him was that painting had let him discover a whole world of in-between. It had begun to slow him down, to stop the alternations that for so many years had enlivened him and worn him out, made him succeed and made him fail. He now lived along a continuum instead of on a whipsaw. He had started to understand that gray was as real as green, doubts as solid as certainties.

The ex-president's eyes glistened, and for a moment Ross thought he might wink again. But Bush turned his head away from Allie's unnerving digital smile and looked out past the porch. He pointed, with the brush, above and beyond the cedars, to some clouds.

"Weatherman," he said softly, "it's gonna rain."

AUTHOR'S NOTE AND ACKNOWLEDGMENTS

In narrative and dialogue, *Landfall* tries not to reconstruct actuality but to reimagine it. As I've noted in earlier novels: "I have operated along the always sliding scale of historical fiction. The text contains deviations from fact that some readers will regard as unpardonable and others will deem unworthy of notice. But this remains a work of fiction, not history."

———

I didn't realize I was writing the last volume of a trilogy until my editor, Dan Frank, encouraged me to see *Landfall* as the concluding portion of a political narrative that began with *Watergate* (2012) and extended itself through *Finale* (2015), two novels I had conceived of as discrete entities. Dan's calm and incomparable guidance on matters large and small has sustained me over ten books and across twenty-five years—a publishing era as tumultuous as our political one. This quick expression of my gratitude doesn't begin to cover my debt to him.

Within the walls of Penguin Random House, I also owe thanks to Sonny Mehta; Edward Kastenmeier; Altie Karper; Nicholas Latimer; Michiko Clark; Betsy Sallee; Vanessa Rae Haughton; and many others. A couple of blocks away, at my agent's office, I am grateful to Andrew Wylie, Kristina Moore, Jessica Calagione, and Katie Cacouris.

A residency at Yaddo during the summer of 2017 helped me to write this book; I would like to thank Elaina H. Richardson and the colony's staff.

Ed Cohen has once again been my dogged copy editor, and Thomas Giannettino my sharp-eyed proofreader.

I have depended on help from Jennifer Spurrier of the Southwest Collection at the Texas Tech University Library; Jeff Flannery at the Library of Congress; Brandon Zogg and Neelie Holm of the George W. Bush Presidential Library and Museum at Southern Methodist University in Dallas. The George Washington University Library is important to me on an almost daily basis.

The following people were generous with their time and insight during interviews: Jim Granberry, the former mayor of Lubbock, Texas; Ruth Schiermeyer, former chairwoman of the Lubbock County Republican Party; Peter D. Feaver (Duke University) and Will Inboden (Clements Center for National Security), both former members of the National Security Council staff during the George W. Bush administration; and Stephen Caputo, manager of the Hotel Monteleone in New Orleans. I appreciate their willingness to talk to a novelist—someone who eagerly absorbed and then departed at will from the facts they imparted.

I have similarly used innumerable published sources, including the memoirs of many real-life characters fictionalized in these pages. Among histories and biographies, I would offer particular thanks to this very incomplete list: Peter Baker, *Days of Fire: Bush and Cheney in the White House*; Dan Baum, *Nine Lives: Death and Life in New Orleans*; Douglas Brinkley, *The Great Deluge: Hurricane Katrina, New Orleans, and the Mississippi Gulf Coast*; Frank Bruni, *Ambling into History: The Unlikely Odyssey of George W. Bush*; Elisabeth Bumiller, *Condoleezza Rice: An American Life*; Rajiv Chandrasekaran, *Imperial Life in the Emerald City: Inside Iraq's Green Zone*; Robert Draper, *Dead Certain: The Presidency of George W. Bush*; John Heilemann and Mark Halperin, *Game Change: Obama and the Clintons, McCain and Palin, and the Race of a Lifetime*; George Packer, *The Assassins' Gate: America in Iraq*; Jan Reid, *Let the People In: The Life and Times of Ann Richards*; Emma

Sky, *The Unraveling: High Hopes and Missed Opportunities in Iraq*; Jean Edward Smith, *Bush*; Bob Woodward, *State of Denial* and *The War Within*.

I could not have done without the electronic archives and websites of *The New York Times, The Washington Post*, and the New Orleans *Times-Picayune*.

And I could not have done without the essays of my irreplaceable friend Christopher Hitchens, whose dialogue here is often informed by what he wrote.

For various tips, assistance, and encouragement I owe a debt to my neighbor and friend, James Graham Wilson, a historian at the Department of State. Thanks, as well and as always, to Lynn Freed and Patricia Hampl.

I lived in Lubbock, Texas, during the fall of 1978, when George W. Bush ran for Congress. I cherish the troop of lasting friends I made there—among them, Jim and Pamela Brink, Ann and Dick McGlynn, Lynn and Mary Hatfield.

Decades later, during the era in which this novel's main action takes place, I served in various capacities at the National Endowment for the Humanities (never actually combined, as in these pages, with the NEA). My work brought me to both New Orleans and Afghanistan, where I had the honor of presenting an award to Dr. Mohammed Yusuf Asefi for his heroic and ingenious resistance to the Taliban. The glimpses of him here, as well as his trip to America, are a fiction that I hope he will pardon. He is the bravest man I have ever met.

For thirty years my books—and happiness—have depended on Bill Bodenschatz.

August 1, 2018
Washington, D.C.

A NOTE ABOUT THE AUTHOR

THOMAS MALLON is the author of ten novels, including *Henry and Clara*, *Dewey Defeats Truman*, *Fellow Travelers*, and *Watergate*. He is a frequent contributor to *The New Yorker* and *The New York Times Book Review*, and in 2011 he received the American Academy of Arts and Letters' Harold D. Vursell Memorial Award for prose style. He has been the literary editor of *GQ* and the deputy chairman of the National Endowment for the Humanities. He lives in Washington, D.C.

A NOTE ON THE TYPE

This book was set in Janson, a typeface named for the Dutchman Anton Janson, but is actually the work of Nicholas Kis (1650–1702). The type is an excellent example of the influential and sturdy Dutch types that prevailed in England up to the time William Caslon (1692–1766) developed his own incomparable designs from them.

Composed by North Market Street Graphics,
Lancaster, Pennsylvania

Printed and bound by Berryville Graphics,
Berryville, Virginia

Designed by M. Kristen Bearse